CURIO

Also by Evangeline Denmark

Mark of Blood and Alchemy: The Prequel to Curio

CURIO

EVANGELINE DENMARK

BLINK

Dedication

For Kory. Thank you for joining my worlds.

CHAPTER

The Chemist came just before closing. Granddad shot Grey a warning look as he hurried to the front of the store. Time to make herself unnoticeable. As if that were possible.

She returned to her work, swiping a cloth over the filmy glass of a curio cabinet shoved against the back wall. A layer of grime coated the inside, but Granddad never opened it for a thorough washing out, and neither did Grey. As she rubbed the surface, she squinted to make out the shapes within. Movement flickered inside the case. She bent closer. *It must've been a shadow.*

An odd quiet stretched through Haward's Mercantile. Heat shot through the fabric of Grey's blouse and her skin prickled. The newcomer had spotted her. Surely she didn't stand out so much this close to Four Points. All manner of people walked the streets of downtown Mercury City, and more new and exotic folks stepped off the train every morning.

"Your granddaughter, Olan?" The Chemist's voice wrapped around Grey, compelling her to face the man. Late afternoon shadows cloaked his features—all but the pale green flash of his teeth. The face beneath the top hat fixed on her.

"Grey, best to get on home." Granddad moved to stand between her and the black-garbed man.

Maybe the man simply had business with Granddad. After all, Chemist Council equipment in various stages of repair lined one entire wall of the store. Some of the devices ticked, chimed, or emitted occasional puffs of smoke, though she was most anxious to be rid of the instruments that glowed green. But the stranger near the door ignored the machinery and stepped closer to Granddad.

The air zinged with currents that set Grey's teeth on edge. *Chemia*. And something more than the green magic—animosity. She stiffened, her lower spine pressing into the waist-high cabinet behind her. Grey reached back and grasped the cold metal edge with both hands. Her feet wouldn't budge.

"Go on now." Granddad glanced over his burly shoulder, the crease between his eyebrows the only mark of concern on his unlined face. "Curfew's coming."

Grey pried her fingers from the curio case and ducked into the back room. Haimon hovered like a ghost a few steps from the cutout doorway. She stifled a squeak and shifted her gaze away from Haimon's scars. "Is he here for an order—the Chemist?"

Granddad's assistant shuffled to the doorway, moved the curtain, and peered into the front of the shop. "No, not Adante."

"But Granddad's done nothing wrong. At least nothing *they* know of, right?" She searched the small room. The table and rug concealing the trapdoor were perfectly in place, though Haimon had no doubt crept up from the laboratory moments ago.

An instant too slowly, Haimon hid a wary expression. "All's well. You'd best get on home before the last boom."

Grey peeked through the door one more time. Granddad stood in his shirtsleeves and leather apron, a giant amongst the rows of shelves and tables loaded with knick-knacks, foodstuffs, appliances, and mining equipment. He didn't need protection from a sixteen-year-old girl no matter how her instincts screamed *stay*.

"Grey."

She started and twisted to face Haimon.

He tilted his steely head toward the Chemist. "Adante's nothing your granddad and I can't handle. Now go."

A blast echoed down the hills and carried through the city, rattling windows and displacing dust. End of the day shift. She had just over twenty minutes to get home before the deputies swept the streets for curfew breakers.

Grey grabbed her coat from the hook on the wall and struggled into the tight garment. As if the crimson wool didn't call enough attention to her statuesque frame, the fitted bodice emphasized the reason for the color requirement. Female. Untouchable. She fumbled the frog closures over her full chest and dashed out the back door.

Another blast sounded from the hills above Mercury City as Grey darted up the alley, slipped down a gravel path between storefronts, and emerged onto the Colfax Street walkway.

When her boots hit pavement she slowed her stride and checked her surroundings.

Two men five paces ahead on the sidewalk. A group of miners a ways behind. A draulie clanking up the middle of the street. The light from the hydraulic miner's headlamp glinted off his metal suit and the water cannon attached to one arm. Horses shied away from the draulie's heavy tread, and coach drivers and a lone motorist maneuvered out of his path.

Grey shivered as a bitter wind accompanied the next echo down from the mountains. With her arms clamped against her sides, she sped up and called in warning, "Excuse me."

The men in front of her looked around then stepped away, cramming their hands into their coat pockets. Neither met her eyes or gave any indication that her height and frame were unusual. She sighed her relief and rushed by. Outsiders. From the slums of New York maybe. Or Chicago. Crowded cities where immigrants and tenement dwellers believed the propaganda about the gleaming town in the West. Mercury City, Colorado, where property, provisions, medicine, even education for your children could be had in exchange for honest labor in a Chemist mine. They stepped off the train wanting to work and willing to keep Mercury's strange laws if it meant a chance for a different life. And that's what they got, all right.

By the time Grey reached the corner of Colfax Street and Reinbar Avenue, her breath puffed in quick clouds. She stopped and drew in a mouthful of air that burned as it reached her lungs. White steam shrouded the Foothills Quarter Station a few blocks to the north. A mass of dark figures emerged from the vapor, jostling each other in their hurry to get home. One by one they slowed until each miner became a distinct shape. And each one turned his head from side to side, checking alleys and side streets for deputies.

Grey turned south on Reinbar and walked quickly, the long hem of her coat flapping against her stocking-covered calves. Her knee pants didn't keep her legs warm, but at least they allowed for unencumbered movement. From the back she must look like a red column bobbing along the business district.

Another boom jarred her bones just as a miner passed on her right, giving her a wide berth. She snagged her pocket watch and pressed the catch. The fist-shaped cover sprang open, revealing ten minutes until curfew. She could cut five minutes off if she took the alley behind the ration dispensary, but that meant crossing the street ahead of a crowd of weary workers.

The train whistle made up her mind for her. The deputies would start their rounds only minutes after the last car pulled away from the station. She stepped off the curb, one eye on the returning miners and one on her destination across the street.

"Whoa." The miner nearest her flung his arm to the side as if he could hold back the procession. Heads jerked up and murmurs traveled through the crowd.

"I'm sorry." Grey met the marbled blue eyes set deep in a grime-covered face. Blue eyes? Nobody in Foothills Quarter had blue eyes, besides her family and her neighbor. "Whit?"

He frowned and flicked a glance the way she'd come. "Where's your granddad?"

A shout of "Oy! Let's move!" carried from the rear of the company.

"Held up at the shop," Grey muttered. "Chemist."

"So late?" Whit grimaced. With dirt lining the creases of his face, he looked much older than his eighteen years. He smoothed his expression. "Don't worry. Olan's more mountain than man. He'll be fine."

Grey nodded and darted for the other side of the street amidst the grumbling of the shift workers. As soon as she reached the sidewalk, the throng moved on, their measured steps growing faster as dusk and the threat of deputies stalked behind them.

The sound of boots followed her toward the brick-lined alley connecting Reinbar to the Pewter Street hill and the outskirts of town. She folded her arms, shrinking as much as her stature would allow.

"I'll see you home, Grey." Whit's voice rose above the clamor of curfew hour.

She turned and caught him standing in the gutter, scrubbing at his face with his sleeve. He crammed his tweed cap lower on his clump of coal-black hair. He'd only traded his school uniform for miner's clothes a few months ago, but already he'd changed. His limbs looked harder beneath his coat, and muscle thickened the slope of his neck where it met his shoulder. He straightened, and she could make out the arrow shape of his almost-filled-out chest and lean torso. An ache lodged in her chest and she shook her head. "I'll slow you down. You've seen your Stripe and passed it."

His frank gaze skimmed her. "And you're not far from it."

Her cheeks warmed. "I'm not yet seventeen, as you well know, Whitland Bryacre. If I get caught, they'll just turn me over to my parents for discipline. But you . . ."

Beneath the remaining dirt, the color drained from Whit's face. "Best we hurry, then."

He slipped by her into the alley papered with adverts and Chemist flyers. He turned to stroll backward, his smile gleaming in the swift dusk. "It's not against the law to take a shortcut."

Grey's gut twisted. She shouldn't let him do this. They weren't walking home from school, safe in their Council School uniforms. Whit was an adult now. And she was practically a walking sandwich board bearing the slogan Keep Away. But he'd offered to escort her and he wouldn't back out now. The best she could do was hurry and hope they both reached their homes before six o'clock.

"All right, but if you didn't live next door, I'd be refusing the offer." With a glance over her shoulder, Grey followed him into the alley. He shoved his hands into his pockets, and she picked her way over the uneven ground, staying a careful three paces behind.

The thrum of an engine began low and quiet, but it lodged in Grey's chest, sending ice through her veins. Whit melted into the shadows ahead, and she shrank into the space between the wall and a large rubbish bin.

The drone of the chug boat grew louder. *Deputies.*

She ducked and wedged farther into the corner, covering the beacon of her blonde hair with her arms. A protruding metal seam on the bin dug into her shoulder, but she didn't dare shift position.

Sharp wind lifted the hem of Grey's coat and bit through her stockings. The muscles in her thighs stiffened.

The quick scuffle of his shoes and a muffled wheeze gave away Whit's presence. He'd taken a spot on the other side of the rubbish bin. "Grey?" The worry in his voice coaxed a spark in her belly.

"I'm here," she answered. "You should go. I'll stay out of sight till they pass."

No answer came. Neither did the sound of his retreat. The hum of the chug boat vibrated through Grey's bones and sent spasms up her neck.

"Sounds like they're a block away," Whit whispered. "What can you see?"

She inched her head up. The slice of street behind them was clear. She eased her way toward the mouth of the alley, keeping her back to the brick wall behind her. A beam of light cut through the dusk, illuminating a group of deputies in long dusters with wisps of green vapor trailing up from their face masks. They stalked from Colfax onto Reinbar, their clotters drawn and crackling with energy. Behind the men a dark craft floated low on an emerald cloud of steam. Black pennants with the spiky Chemist Council emblem fluttered from a mast on the boxy wheelhouse, and more deputies clung to pipes and handrails sprouting from the deck, their attention fixed on something out of sight.

Relief mixed with a sick feeling. "They're tracking someone." She and Whit could get away, but some poor soul was bound for a punishment facility tonight.

"Can you see who they're after?"

Snarls and frenzied barking answered his question. The men in the street scrambled into a half circle that tightened with each cautious step. So they weren't hunting a curfew breaker but a pack of animals. Probably coywolves, hungry and desperate this time of year.

Grey crept back to her hiding spot. On the other side of the bin, Whit drew in a ragged breath. She pictured his chest rising and falling. Her pulse quickened and she squelched the image. Shortcuts weren't against the law, but her thoughts about the boy next door might be. "Fraternization between unmarried males and females," the Council called it, or "indecent contact."

Whit's face appeared around the bin, his blue eyes searching for her in the shadows. When he spied her, his shoulders dropped and he released a pent-up sigh. She straightened from her crouch, and gestured toward the section of street visible from the alley. "I think they have the pack cornered."

Whit stole a foot closer to the building's edge. He kept his knees bent and his body poised to run. His jaw clenched, erasing all traces of his easy smile. The shadow of stubble on his chin was thicker than it had been two months ago. What would it be like to slide a finger along his cheek?

She buried her dangerous curiosity as frantic yelps filled the air, underscored by the deputies' shouts. The rumble of the chug boat engine deepened. Whit's eyes snapped to hers.

"A second patrol," he whispered.

She lurched toward him. "You've got to run for it. Get home."

He stared at her, motionless.

"Go. I'll be right behind you."

Whit scanned her face again then his mouth tightened and he nodded once. "I'll watch for you."

He darted down the alley, but Grey hovered between a squat and a spring, her muscles tight. If Whit was caught out after curfew, they'd stripe him for sure. She had to give him a head start. She imagined him already safe in his home, watching from the window as she dashed to her front door, coywolves and deputies on her heels. The image gave her courage—Whit's angular face, his black hair falling in his eyes, ropey arms crossed over his chest. And a wall between him and the Council's deputies.

One. Two. Three. Four. Five. She scooted around the bin. Whit was nowhere in sight.

A shout and a growl sent cold iron through her limbs. Running footsteps, snarls, and a human cry of pain followed.

Grey took a step, but a silhouette in her periphery set her nerves skittering. One glance over her shoulder and the hope of escape evaporated. She whirled to face the threat creeping into the alley.

The coywolf wasn't huge. But his yellow eyes tracked her every move. Matted fur clung to the outline of his ribs, and saliva dripped from his mouth as he advanced. Starving and rabid.

Grey stumbled backward. Where was the patrol now? With Whit safely away, she'd welcome the sight of armed men.

More growls and yelps sounded from Reinbar Avenue along with the clipped tones of deputies fighting off the pack. The coywolf slunk toward Grey, separating her from the mouth of the alley and her only hope of safety.

She took another step backward into the shadow of the buildings. Pain sliced the back of her calf. Her flailing hand met a jagged surface, and she crashed into a stack of pallets behind the ration dispensary.

She braced a bloody palm on the brick wall and pushed to her feet. Eyes locked on the nearing teeth, she scrambled around the pallets. Warm blood seeped down her leg and glued her stockings to her skin.

The animal lunged, teeth snapping an inch from her leg. He charged again, but something hit Grey from behind.

She struggled as her body was swept into jostling motion. Her limbs bounced to the rhythm of panicked steps. *Whit.* She clenched the fabric of his shirt. The muscles in his shoulders bunched beneath her arms as he ran, carrying her.

"What are you doing? Put me down."

He spoke between gasps. "You're bleeding."

"It's not bad. Put me down, Whit, they'll take you."

"That wolf . . . will take . . . you."

Grey peered back into the alley. The coywolf gained on them. Whit faltered. She was equal to him in height and almost in weight thanks to her father's genes. Lugging her, he'd never outrun the animal. Grey thrashed against his chest, her wounded hands sliding over his sweat-slicked neck.

"Put me down, Whit. Please."

A heavy whirring sound preceded the blinding green light by a millisecond. Grey's heart seized.

"Drop me," she breathed in Whit's ear.

He halted but kept his grip on her.

It was too late. The thrum of the patrol craft drowned out her pleas for Whit to let go. He blinked in the light, mouth agape in a frozen gasp. His chest heaved beneath her. Figures in flapping dusters cut through the spotlight, marching toward Grey and Whit. Behind them in the alley, another deputy stood over the limp form of the coywolf.

"Please, Whit." Grey's voice shook.

Finally her words registered. He lowered her legs to the ground as two deputies reached them. Both men were massive. Dusters stretched over Chemia-enhanced muscles, and the masks covering their noses and mouths glowed green from potion-laced filters. One aimed a two-pronged clotter at them, and the other had a slender wooden case strapped to his arm. He flipped the lid to reveal a gauntlet writer with a green-tinted glass platen.

The first deputy's heavy-lidded eyes trained on Whit. "Name?"

Whit mumbled it and the second deputy typed it into the device.

"And you?"

"Grey Haward." She suppressed a flinch with each click of the keys as her name entered the Council device.

The deputy with the gauntlet writer looked up from the glowing platen. "Whitland Bryacre, you are guilty of breaking curfew and indecent contact. The laws of Mercury City forbid any physical contact between males and females without the permission of the Chemist Council."

Grey stifled a gasp. Though they were no longer touching, she sensed each ragged breath Whit drew. Tremors shook his hands, but he didn't try to run.

Guilty of indecent contact? Whit was trying to save her, not reproduce with her. Any potion head could see that. Rage sucked at her rib cage, but the fury morphed into a foreign sensation. Strength spread through her limbs as though cement poured through her body. She couldn't stay silent. Both deputies paused as Grey stepped in front of Whit, shielding him.

"He didn't mean to break the law. He was trying to help me. You can't take him."

The man with the clotter pointed the weapon at her. "Watch yerself, Miss Haward. Maybe you ain't reached your Stripe, but this'un here is guilty of indecent contact—"

Rock-hard resolve pushed all the way to Grey's fingertips and toes, locking her muscles in inflexible knots. "No, he isn't."

"Hush, Grey." Whit's voice broke through her defenses.

"Enough." The first deputy returned to reading Whit's sentence. "Having attained the Age of the Stripe and having put our populace at risk, you are subject to the full punishment of the Council and will be detained until its completion."

"No." The word exploded from Grey's mouth. She held out her wrists, her actions springing from the unfamiliar strength. "Take me instead."

The armed deputy shifted as she edged forward and stared into his masked face. She opened her mouth, but a strangled noise stopped the words on her tongue. Grey spun to see the deputy who'd killed the coywolf push Whit into the brick wall. In a matter of seconds, the agent bound her friend's hands and hauled him away from the wall. Whit sought her as the deputy prodded him toward the floating craft.

Grey's fingers curled in like claws. She lunged toward the deputy shoving Whit, but the man whipped his clotter from its holster. Arcs of green energy crackled between the two prongs of the weapon, and Grey froze as if the device's current already hardened her blood.

Her new bravery cracked when Whit reached the three-rung ladder thrown over the side of the craft. He looked back at her as the deputy disengaged the current binding the manacles around his wrists. Amid the green vapor curling from beneath the bow of the vessel, Whit's face hovered, a mask of pale stone and dark terror.

He wasn't her friend or the boy next door anymore. He wasn't the kid who'd spent Saturday afternoons at Granddad's shop playing cards and swapping stories with her. He was a name and an age on a Chemist Council record.

The deputy shoved Whit's shoulder, and Whit turned and put his hand on the rung. The last she saw of him was his back as he climbed over the railing and disappeared into the craft.

CHAPTER

G rey faced her front door with chin high, but her eyes
strayed in the direction of the quiet bungalow next
door—Whit's house. Mrs. Bryacre must be in hys-
terics by now. No doubt she watched the chug boat floating
in the street—a bulky black silhouette shrouded in steam—
hoping for Whit to climb out. Knowing that he wouldn't.

Another deputy—a dim, potion-headed chump—stood
beside Grey. He rapped on the door then rubbed his bandaged hand. He deserved to get rabies from that coywolf bite.
She clamped her lips to keep the thought inside. She was
underage and safe, but her family didn't have the same pro-
tections. What if they took her defiance out on her father?
Or her mother. Dread anchored her to the porch as footsteps
pounded inside the house.

Mother yanked the door open, and flickering gaslight
spilled into the night. Dark eyes flitted from Grey's face and
blood-stained hands to the deputy beside her, and then to
the black craft stationed at the end of the walkway.

"Grey—"

"What's the charge?" Father's voice boomed over the
sound of the engine. A moment later he filled the doorway,
harsh lines dragging at his face.

Grey's throat stung, but she kept her shoulders rigid.

"Curfew violation." The deputy recited the usual order for parents. "The Chemist Council holds parents responsible for the administering of discipline until a citizen achieves the Age of the Stripe. Do not show leniency to your child, for leniency will not be given to citizens upon reaching the Age of the Stripe. If the Council is made aware of leniency on the part of a parent, that parent shall be punished under the law."

As he droned on, listing suggested discipline, Grey uncurled her fingers and loosed a shaky sigh.

This deputy, part of the second patrol, hadn't witnessed her defiance. He wrapped up his speech with no mention of her challenge to the Chemist agents who took Whit. After Father vowed to punish Grey, the brute turned and stalked toward the waiting craft. When he'd boarded, the flying boat glided down the narrow street and around the corner, leaving green mist swirling in the frigid air.

Grey tugged out of her mother's grasp and whirled back to the yard. "Whit. They took Whit. I have to go tell his mother."

Halfway across the lawn, she stumbled in the dead grass and flung her hands out. Father's thick arm circled her before she hit the ground. He pulled her to her feet and held her tight against his chest until the beat of his heart thudded against her shoulder blade. The warmth of his embrace thawed her cold skin.

Grey thrashed until shudders overtook her. Father relaxed his hold, and she turned into his chest, inhaling the piney scent of healing ointment lingering on his clothes. He'd already seen one of the Chemists' victims today. Probably more than one.

His voice rumbled in her ear. "Come inside." He led her back to the house.

Mother waited on the porch. She snatched Grey's sleeve and pulled her closer, but the whole family froze as the banging of a door echoed through the silent neighborhood.

"Josephine." Mother almost moaned the name.

Mrs. Bryacre slipped into view and hurried to join Grey and her parents. The light from the Hawards' open door made pits of Josephine's dark eyes and painted bruises on her sunken cheeks.

The frantic throb in Grey's heart quieted. She stepped out of the protection of Father's arms and faced Mrs. Bryacre. "It was my fault. I should have been the one they took."

Josephine Bryacre looked like a child sitting in Granddad's wingback chair. Whit must have gotten his height—and his stubborn streak—from his father. How could the woman stand it? First her husband disappeared. Now her son.

Grey bowed her head and focused on the wet washcloth Mother had pressed to her injured hand. Her stomach heaved at the brownish-pink color of diluted blood. She held back a wince when the woven fabric of the sofa upholstery snagged her crusted stocking. She hadn't mentioned the gash on the back of her leg yet. What did it matter when the Chemists would carve Whit's back for touching her?

"This is a first offense," Father said. "Whit will be home tomorrow. With any luck the stripes will be few, and he'll heal in a week's time." His wooden chair creaked as he leaned toward Josephine. "You know we'll do everything we can."

At her father's words, Grey counted the potion bottles lined up on a low table near the entryway. Only four. One for her grandfather. One for her father. One for her mother. And one for Grey. She still had to stop herself from automatically counting to five.

She forced down the growing ache and let boldness fill the cavern it left. "Let me give Whit my ration."

Mother stiffened beside her and gripped the arm of the sofa. Father and Josephine jerked to scan her face.

Josephine broke the silence first. "It's true then. You're ration dealers?"

"Not dealers." Her father leaned back in his chair, his broad shoulders sloping.

How much of her family's secret would he reveal? Grey swallowed hard at the image of the Chemist bearing down on Granddad. Where was he now? Maybe it was too late for caution.

"We don't dilute the Chemist's potion with harmful chemicals," Father said. "And we don't accept payment."

"Stein." Mother stretched out her hand. Her next words were clipped. "The less Jo knows, the better."

Josephine's eyes lingered on the four ration bottles waiting for the morning trip to the dispensary. "I'll take the risk. For Whit. Tell me."

Father exchanged a steady look with Mother then turned to Josephine. "An extra dose of potion will help Whit heal faster. I'll reserve a portion of mine for him tomorrow."

"He can have mine." Grey scooted forward, her fingers clenched so tightly around the rag that drops of rust-tinted water landed on the faded area rug. "He can have it all. I told you what he did for me."

"Leave this to me, Grey," Father said.

"Let me help. Please! It's time I joined you and Grandda—"

"Grey, we've discussed this." Mother's fingers dug into Grey's arm. "You will obey the law—"

"Father doesn't. Neither does Granddad."

"But you'd die." Josephine's voice cut through. She leaned toward Grey, hunching her shoulders. The fabric of her crimson blouse gaped over her pronounced collarbone. "You can't give him all of your ration, honey. You'd die."

Realization flickered like a candle burning at the edge of Grey's sight. The shadows under Josephine's eyes. Her skeletal wrists. Whit wasn't strong because he took after his father or because the mine built his muscles. How long had Josephine been pouring her own ration into Whit's bottle and swallowing just enough to keep herself alive?

"We don't know that Grey can go without it like you." Mother's words, meant for Father, drew everyone's focus.

"Of course she's like her father." Granddad stood in the arch between the kitchen and living room, shrugging out of his coat. His yellow hair brushed the low ceiling.

The tight laces around Grey's heart loosened a smidge. Granddad was here. Safe.

He winked at Grey before turning to his daughter-in-law. "Look at her, Maire." His gruff tone reverberated from his barrel chest. "More than a head taller than you. As blonde as her Viking ancestors and built for war."

Grey's cheeks burned and she dropped her gaze. The arms resting in her lap were thick compared to Josephine's. A coil of streaked blonde hair had escaped her chignon and clung to the strained fabric over her chest. Next to the brunette waifs in the Foothills Quarter, she looked like a doughy giant.

"What do you mean 'like her father'?" Josephine's eyes shifted between Grey and Father.

Granddad bellowed into the cramped space. "My son and I are not dependent on Chemist potion to stay alive. Our bodies are different. We still digest food normally."

Josephine turned her attention from Granddad to Grey. "And you?"

"They've never let me go without. Underage or not, the penalty for giving away your ration is—" Her voice faded. Again her eyes found the corked bottles near the door. One. Two. Three. Four.

Only four now.

CHAPTER

G rey lay in bed and wished the tears would come
again. This—this staring at the ceiling only to picture Whit's back, only to imagine the number of
stripes they would cut into his skin—it was like stuffing her
beating heart into a thimble.

The bandaged gash on her calf itched. She wanted to tear
at the wound, make the stupid thing bleed again, make it
really hurt. Or cut matching lines up her leg. One for each
of Whit's stripes.

Foolish thought. Pain stalked as close as the nearest
patrol. No sense borrowing it early.

The same rationale behind why she took her daily potion
and kept her head down, just like everyone else. Everyone
except Father and Granddad. But they wouldn't let her help.
Father refused every time she offered to send some of her
ration to the refugees in the mountains.

And Granddad only humored her schemes of donat-
ing her potion toward his efforts to reproduce the mixture.
When he left for his lab hidden beneath the shop on Colfax,
he never took the ration she offered.

Grey flopped to her side. The springs beneath the thin
mattress creaked with every movement. She wrapped her
arms and legs around a pillow, squeezing as hard as she
could. It didn't help. Nothing blocked out Whit's face.

He hadn't touched her after she turned ten, as Mercury City law dictated. His smoky blue eyes had been wide on that birthday. His mouth a serious line as he set a bracelet made of buttons on the table and retreated before she reached for the gift. The withdrawal pricked her young heart. Why was the boy who raced her down the street and shared biscuits, marbles, and jokes suddenly afraid of her?

She and Whit hadn't understood the law at the time, but it wasn't long before her classes at the Council Girls' School covered Gregor Mendel's theory of inheritance and the science of disease according to Pasteur, Koch, and Lister. With the lesson came an explanation of the Chemist Council's regulations and dedication to monitoring the starvation trait passed down from the region's settlers. If Mercury City, Colorado, were to be an example of health, industry, and morality to other cities, then nothing could interfere with the Chemists' work.

And Grey had no intention to. Until one afternoon almost a year ago, when Whit had sauntered around the corner onto Reinbar and headed toward their usual meeting spot. The blue of his Council School uniform deepened his eyes, and a smile tugged his lips the moment he caught sight of her. Her stomach fluttered and heat trailed over her skin. By the time he reached her, she could do nothing but stare at the ground, mentally measuring the gap between them. They walked home together as they always had, but this time Grey never moved an inch into the three feet of space separating them. Her body told her what no one had ever fully explained.

And now he'd touched her.

She closed her eyes and felt his arms behind her back and beneath her knees once again. Her skin tingled with the memory of being pressed against him. Despite the blood and the panic, something deep inside her responded to Whit's touch. She deserved to be in the Council jail tonight. Not him.

Determination quieted the heat building in her veins, replacing the fury with a numb shell. Tomorrow the deputies would return Whit to his home. And she would be waiting with her ration.

The first blast woke Grey and rattled the framed sketch on her wall. End of the night shift. Her pocket watch read quarter to six. Father would be preparing to leave for his daily trip to the ration dispensary.

She untangled herself from the sheets and scrambled to dress in the cold. First came thick stockings rolled up over her calves, then oxblood knee pants tugged on beneath her nightgown. With shirtwaist and chemise laid out and ready, she yanked the gown up over her head and let it drop to the floor. But before she could retrieve her undergarment, her hand froze and her breath fled. A strange mark bloomed on her belly, spreading out in all directions from her navel like a veiny blue flower. On instinct she cupped a hand over the symbol. She hadn't been struck. Maybe the cause was internal. Some kind of poison? But she wasn't sick or in pain. With a deep breath she steeled herself for a closer inspection. The thread-like design forked into branches and twigs like winter tree limbs. She traced one line with her fingertip. What could cause such a reaction?

The sound of muffled conversation from her parents' room sent her into a flurry. She wasn't going to stay behind today. After buttoning the shirtwaist over her chemise, she double checked that the layers of material concealed the mark. Satisfied, she laced on boots.

When she stepped outside her room, Granddad was clos-ing the door to his chamber down the hall. He raised bushy eyebrows when he saw Grey.

"I'm going with you and Father to get the ration. I can't just wait here."

He strode toward her, not one floorboard creaking beneath his boots. How could such a massive man move so quietly? Nothing about Granddad made sense. He swore he'd forgotten his own age, but only crow's feet marked his smooth face. He wore his hair long, stood head and shoul-ders above everyone else, and told stories of trapping and hunting in the Rocky Mountains when Mercury was a tent city on the banks of the Rio de Sangre—one hundred and fifty years ago.

Now, as he towered over her, she caught a whiff of chem-icals and dust instead of sage and wood smoke.

"I just thought I'd—"

"I know what you're about." He waved away her response and continued. "Grey, listen to me. This is your choice to make. Steinar will save some of his ration for Whit, but the mountain folk need as much as he can give them." His fore-head creased. "Mine must go to the lab. It's time *you* decide what to do with your own ration."

For a moment the weight of her decision pressed the air from her lungs. But for Whit, who'd stayed too long, who'd come back when he should've run, who'd held her above snapping jaws, she'd take any punishment. A rush of strength spread from her torso outward, following the course of the mark. Jaw gaping, she pressed a fist to her midsection as a footfall behind her parents' door signaled Father's approach.

Granddad's pale blue eyes locked on Grey, a strange excitement turning them to glowing moons. "Not a word," he whispered.

She snapped her mouth shut.

Father, a near duplicate of Granddad with another inch of height and a straighter nose, stepped into the hall and swept Grey with a disapproving look.

She forced a shrug. "I couldn't sleep. I'm going with you to the dispensary."

He frowned. "We discussed this last night, Grey. You'll take your ration as usual today, and I'll reserve some of mine for Whit. I trust you don't mean to circumvent our decision."

Grey kept her expression neutral.

"You know the reasons." His features caved and the commanding edge dropped from his voice. "We can't lose you too."

She ignored the tightening of her throat. "I'll be careful."

"Let her come, Stein," Granddad rumbled behind Grey. "You know Hawards make poor statues."

"Don't." Father aimed a finger at Granddad. "None of your stories. You know my wishes."

"Stein." Granddad's tone made Grey's eyes prick with tears. "It's in her blood. Look at her, son."

But Father turned away to snag his anorak from a hook on the wall. He grabbed Grey's coat as well and handed it to her. Granddad followed them out the front door, fastening a heavy cloak around his neck. They stepped into a world of shriveled grass and cold-stiffened shrubs. The houses in Grey's neighborhood perched on the side of a foothill like boulders arranged in rows by giants. A bitter wind swept the street, snatching dead leaves and dragging them across the hardened dirt.

Mountains towered on the edge of the city, forming a cauldron around the westernmost quarter. The Magi mine loomed nearest to the town, but the outlines of the Chrysopeoia and the Panacea were visible on the higher slopes. The rest of the Foothills Quarter lay in the shadows, though the rising sun turned the snow on the high meadows a delicate shade of rose. Purple shadows filled the valleys above the mines and hung beneath the ridgelines where Father sought out the refugees. Grey's fancy reached for those hills, though she was never permitted to visit them.

Below the frigid wilderness, Mercury City lay like a vast wheel tilted against the foothills. The quarters stretched out like spokes from the black spire of the Chemist tower, the stronghold of the Chemist reign and the blood magic that kept them in power. Mills dotted the northern quarter and huge greenhouses clung to the far-off flatland in the east. On the southern horizon, the deputy outpost marked the town's boundary.

Grey hunched her shoulders and ducked her chin into her collar.

Before they reached the end of their walkway, the Bryacres' door opened and Josephine stepped out. She nodded to them but set out on her own, her slight figure a red smudge in the weak sunlight.

One by one the doors of the other bungalows on Grey's street opened. Neighbors stepped out and plodded toward the cross street, their faces lowered against the cold air and the glare of the rising sun. Most walked alone, but some of the women moved in silent clumps of crimson, thrown together by the same crucial errand. Another day. Another ration.

The stream of people trickled onto Pewter Street and made their halting way down the steep road. At the bottom of the hill, the brick morality hall signaled a change from the residential streets to the business center of the Foothills Quarter. The clock mounted to the hall read five after six.

Just before the horizon disappeared behind the nearby store fronts, Grey let her eyes fall on another clock tower, this one made of obsidian with a green face glowing like an eye. Others like it stabbed the skyline at regular intervals throughout the city, but Grey focused on the nearest punishment facility. Whit was there.

She clenched her arms against her midsection. The breath she gulped stalled in her throat. Half a block away, Whit's mother also walked with her arms hugged around her middle, her eyes monitoring the progress of her own feet. Without warning, Josephine stumbled and fell to one knee on the sidewalk.

"Mrs. Bryacre!" Grey broke into a jog. Father and Granddad followed. They remained a few feet behind while Grey stooped to check on the woman.

"What should I do?" She flinched at the helplessness in Father's eyes. Granddad's gloved fingers twitched, but he too kept a safe distance.

Grey supported Josephine's bony elbow as the woman struggled to stand. In the light of day her sallow skin appeared translucent. Bloodshot eyes stared from deep sockets and then rolled back into her head. Grey caught her before she hit the ground.

Father dared to step closer to study Josephine's unresponsive face. "I should have seen it last night. She's nearly starved."

Grey adjusted her hold. "I think she's been slipping most of her ration to Whit."

Granddad pointed to the morality hall clock. "She won't get her ration or Whit's if she doesn't make it to the dispensary on time." He dug in the pockets of his trousers, and Grey heard the faint jingle of coins. "We could hire a coach."

Father jammed his own hands into his pockets, but between the two of them they probably had only a few dollars, and he needed his money for train fare to the hunting

30

outpost in the mountains—the base of his mission opera-
tions. Besides, a hack wouldn't arrive in time.

Grey clamped one arm around Josephine's shoulders
and slid the other beneath her knees. She stuffed back the
memory of Whit's arms cradling her the same way as she
lifted his mother. "I can carry her."

"Can you make it to the dispensary?" Father glanced
around. "We can find another way."

Granddad grabbed Father's shoulder, his fingers digging
into the coat fabric. "Steinar." The one word stilled Grey.
"You cannot deny what your daughter is any more than you
can deny your life's work or mine."

The two of them gaped at her. Others paused in their
morning errand to stare at Grey holding a grown woman like
a sleeping child. Grey ducked her head, Granddad's strange
words and behavior further disturbing her calm. "Let's go."

They trudged down the hill in silence, pausing in front
of the morality hall for Grey to adjust Josephine's weight.
As they readied to cross the street, Father eyed the house of
instruction that provided his meager living. When his gaze
returned to Grey and the unconscious Josephine, he wore
his funeral frown.

Grey tightened her grip on her burden. Josephine would
not end up in a box at the front of the morality hall. She'd
march in tomorrow morning just like everyone else in the
quarter and listen to Father read from Mercury's codes of
conduct. And if Whit's stripes were few, he'd be sitting next
to his mother, his eyes wandering over to Grey when he
thought she wasn't looking.

Grey pushed Whit's face from her thoughts and focused
on the wheat-colored strands trailing out of her grandfather's hood as he strode before her. People moved out of his
way, scooting to the edge of the boardwalk to let her family

through. The atmosphere on Reinbar changed, growing hushed and still as faces lifted to watch the Hawards pass.

An orderly line snaked out of the dispensary door. Father joined the queue, but Granddad led Grey to a nearby bench beneath a bare sapling. She arranged Josephine's unconscious form on the seat then maneuvered herself onto the bench and rested the woman's limp head on her lap.

Granddad knelt and studied Grey's face. "I'm so proud of you. What you've done today—"

His words broke off. Murmured conversations in the line halted. Grey's nerves cinched tight as she looked around. She spotted him immediately. A Chemist. What was he doing all the way out here in the Foothills Quarter?

Her heartbeat sped as he strode in their direction. The queue of people shrank against the brick front of the dispensary. They ducked their heads and pulled their coats close, compacting their bodies into winter-garbed cocoons.

Granddad frowned. "Don't speak," he whispered, then rose to face the Chemist.

Tall and dressed in a suit made of shiny black material, the man resembled an elongated crow. His coat hung open, revealing a leather belt festooned with potion bottles and green-glowing instruments that whirred and whined. A mass of black hair spiked around his head beneath his top hat. Hints of iridescent green lurked in the nooks of his face—at the corners of his mouth, the creases of his nostrils, and the rims of his eyes. Pale foam-green irises—one magnified by a tinted monocle—swept over her grandfather then studied Grey and her slumped charge. A surge, like the crackle in the air before lightning hit, brushed over Grey's skin. She knew this gaze from the store yesterday. The Chemist's eyes alighted again on Granddad's face. "Olan, I see *you* made it home safely last night." His low voice slid into Grey's ears like warm oil. The accented words, though not directed at her, settled in her gut and smoldered.

"Adante, you're far from the tower this morning."

Grey started at her grandfather's familiarity. He stood, feet apart and shoulders relaxed, showing no deference to this powerful man who knew the secrets of both science and magic.

Adante ignored Granddad's silent challenge and turned to Grey. A smile tugged his thin lips. "I found something that interests me in the Foothills Quarter. I think you know that, Olan."

"Indeed." Granddad's gruff voice lost a little strength.

Father left the queue to stand near Grey. His fingers twitched at his sides, and he inched closer as if he could hide her.

"Steinar." Adante transferred his attention to her father. "As strapping as ever. Our potions must agree with you." He pivoted back to Grey. "And your daughter."

Father and Granddad stiffened, but when they said nothing, Adante continued.

"She's a well-built girl. And spirited, I hear."

Grey went cold. She slid her shaking hands out of view. So the deputy who'd witnessed her defiance *had* shared the incident. He must've included her actions in his official report.

Father's mouth pressed in a grim line. His fair eyebrows lifted in a subtle question.

Adante's form flickered like the shadow of leaves. He bent over Grey and his syrupy breath clouded in the cold air, coating her face in a sticky layer.

"I see no signs of punishment, Steinar. Here she is, out on a ration run the day after her offense. And carrying—is that what I saw?—another woman. There can be no doubt she takes after you. And her grandfather."

Granddad stepped closer, speaking low and rapid. "It makes no difference if she does. We haven't broken the pact. It's the Chemists who violate our agreement." He jutted his chin toward the bustling heart of Mercury City and the stronghold of the Chemist tower. "What does Jorn mean, turning an enclave into an empire? We won't stand for it."

Adante's sinuous form grew rigid. He spat out a reply. "And what can your mighty little family do about it? Unless you've found the means to grow your numbers, in which case my grandfather will be very interested to hear of your dabblings. I'm told the Bryacre boy displayed extraordinary courage. Been performing experiments of your own, Olan?"

Granddad's nostrils flared. "I am no blood magiker. Tell your grandfather he'd do well to remember his debts and the agreement between us."

A collection of stares now rested on their group, and Adante seemed to grow aware of the notice. He retreated a pace, and, with features arranged in a bored expression, gestured to Josephine's shriveled body. "And this?"

A muscle worked in Father's jaw. "Josephine Bryacre is ill. We are merely seeing that her family receives their rations."

"Of course." The Chemist smirked. "It seems her need is almost as great as her son's."

Grey balled her fists. Did Chemists bleed green blood? She'd like to find out. Adante's focus whizzed back to her, and his eyes narrowed, reading her. His face split into a smile that revealed tinted gums. He nodded to Grey and stepped backward, as if to signal an end to a conversation they hadn't had. But then he paused to address her father.

"I trust you're making progress with the mountain people. I expected you to be more convincing. How many years have you been attending them now?" He gestured to the slow-moving line winding in and out of the dispensary. "Why would they choose to die when health awaits them in Mercury City?"

Father looked like he wanted to speak but said nothing.

"It seems much requires my attention here in the Foothills Quarter." Adante swept the surroundings with a bored expression that contradicted his words, but his green eyes sparked when they landed once again on Grey.

Grey stepped out of the dispensary and gulped the air, but the sickly sweet smell of potion and the piney scent of wound salve followed her out the door. Her head swam until a mountain gust carried away the odor and left her shivering.

With the help of a female neighbor, she'd gotten the unconscious Josephine through the line. Under the gaze of two potion-head deputies, the dispensary worker had meted out the Bryacres' rations as well as the Hawards'. Now Grey and her helper returned Josephine to the bench.

Father and Granddad joined them, forming a semicircle around Josephine's still form.

"You'll be taking all your ration today, Jo." Father's whisper cut into Grey's heart.

"She'll be angry when she wakes up." Grey knelt by the bench. "I bet she intended to give it all to Whit when he comes home."

Granddad crossed thick arms over his chest. "What Whit needs is a mother strong enough to nurse him through his recovery." His eyes narrowed onto Grey.

She lifted her chin. "I'll give her all of it."

Granddad held her gaze, no doubt perceiving her intention to give Whit her entire ration. A brief smile quirked his mouth. "Good girl."

When she'd poured every drop of the purple liquid down Josephine's throat, Grey straightened to find her father and grandfather stiff, their attention focused down the street. She caught the flash of shiny black as a now familiar tall figure moved by a storefront.

"What does he want?" She almost added "with me," but didn't dare call more attention to her family of renegades. One thing was certain: Adante's absorption with her stemmed from more than Chemist obsession with law breakers. He'd scrutinized her in the store yesterday, before she and Whit violated the city codes.

Father motioned to the neighbor who'd helped Grey with Josephine. "We'll get Jo home somehow. You go with Granddad to the shop today. You'll be safe with him, and it'll keep you occupied better than waiting at home for Whit."

He handed one bottle of potion to Grey, his eyes holding hers in an unspoken warning. She clutched the ration, waiting for him to command her to swallow it. He didn't, turning instead to make arrangements to get Josephine home.

"Let's go." Granddad headed in the opposite direction on Reinbar Avenue.

She pocketed her ration and averted her eyes from Adante as they passed by his position on the other side of the street. The bottle weighted her coat pocket, bouncing against her thigh as she walked.

Granddad kept to his usual brisk gait, his movements deft. Despite his pace, he never risked even a careless brush of the sleeve. He nodded to everyone they passed. A few blocks ahead, dayshift miners gathered at the station. Grey searched for a lanky frame amongst the shorter figures. But of course, Whit wasn't there.

Her stomach growled as they crossed the street at the corner where Reinbar and Colfax formed a T. A display in the bakery window set her mouth watering, but an "Open After Ration" sign still hung in the shop door. An image of Josephine's hollow face rose amidst the heap of golden rolls and loaves. She would soon know which was worse: gnawing hunger or the misery of consuming indigestible food.

After they passed the bank, Grey steeled herself for the assault of Madam Maude's Crimsonery. Behind the glass a headless mannequin displayed a knee-length red frock. Grey rubbed her neck and looked away, but the white, limbless form remained as real and terrible to her as it had on her tenth birthday. For a month after her first trip to the crimsonery, she'd checked the mirror every day, touching her face and stretching her arms out, then peering down her blouse for any sign of stiff bumps forming on her chest. As her body changed, not all at once and not into the hard form of a dress dummy, she wondered why such a natural transformation must be labeled dangerous. The Council rhetoric on reproduction and population monitoring did little to erase the stigma she felt.

Grey made a now habitual inventory of her blossomed figure and winced. Much good the scarlet had done Whit.

The Colfax Street clock read quarter to seven when they reached Granddad's shop. As he withdrew his key ring, Grey found her favorite knick-knack in the display window—a painting of a stone figure with a raised fist and a crowd of people huddled behind it. This time instead of lingering on the imposing statue, she studied the throng of dark-haired, pale faces—so like the people in her quarter. So like Whit. If only her defiance could've kept him safe. She squeezed her own fingers into a tight ball. A hardening sensation spread from the center of her body outward, like living rock lined her muscles.

A shrill sound interrupted the process. Grey pressed a hand to her midsection as the phenomenon faded, half expecting her skin to change beneath her fingertips. But she detected no transformation on the outside. Another signal pierced the air.

The warning whistles from the factories in the south followed them into the shop and up the center aisle. Grey picked up a new item, a mantel clock carved in the form of an owl. The block shape looked nothing like a real bird, but she rolled her shoulders, shrugging off the sudden image of raking claws. Setting the curio down, she followed Granddad to the waist-high glass cabinets forming a three-sided box around the back of the room.

He moved about his store, distracted, touching certain tools as if they marked the place where he'd left off the project. Grey followed, lighting lamps and depositing her coat in the back room. When she returned, Granddad stood at the end of one counter, staring into the corner at the murky curio cabinet.

Grey stood next to him. "What is it?"

The shop door swished open and they both swiveled toward the front of the store. Haimon navigated the jumbled shelves. He paused, his iron eyes nipping between Grey and Granddad. "What's happened?"

He must've read her expression or Granddad's nervous energy.

"Grey violated curfew last night." Granddad made it sound like she'd received top marks in school rather than broken the law. "She's drawn Adante's attention." He and Haimon exchanged an unreadable look.

"They took Whit." Grey's voice came out husky.

Haimon rested an arm on one of the shelves, propping up his gaunt frame. "I'm sorry."

She scanned the parallel scars climbing his neck toward his ears and marring the colorless skin visible below the cuff of his jacket sleeve. Haimon knew plenty about a punisher's blade. "I—It should have been me." She clamped her lips. Why did she keep insisting on taking Whit's place?

Her words had a strange effect on Haimon, who bolted out of his informal pose and stepped forward, intent on Grey as though he studied a specimen through a microscope.

"A word, Haimon?" Granddad strode into the back room.

Grey busied herself with a tray of clock parts as Haimon slipped between the display cases and pulled the curtain closed behind him. She sorted tiny gears and springs, her ears trained on their conversation.

Excitement tinged Granddad's voice. "Everything is changing, Haimon. We're at a turning point."

One of the steam engine delivery trucks rumbled by on the street outside. When the noise faded, Granddad's words tumbled in an urgent torrent.

"I believe Defender blood is dominant. When Grey tried to protect her friend, she kindled the mark—I'm sure of it. If her Defender nature overcomes the condition she inherited from her mother, then Grey is the key we've hoped for."

Haimon cut in. "The key to a new potion, or—"

"The key to everything. But I won't risk breaking the treaty by bringing him back. It would mean a declaration of war—a war my son and I could not win. Yet."

"But it wouldn't be just you and Steinar anymore."

"Four Defenders against the entire Chemist Council?" Granddad's tone stretched with unease.

"I would stand with you."

"I know, my friend, but we would fall. And where would that leave our efforts on the new serum? Where would that leave the people? So many lives lost."

The creak of wood covered Haimon's reply. Grey's hands trembled and she dropped the tiny screw she'd held on to the floor. She had Defender blood? How could her grandfather belong to that long-gone race? The last of the Defender clans disappeared in the Cleanse a hundred years ago. But it appeared they hadn't. Granddad—a Defender—somehow must have escaped the purge.

"I'll be down for the first draw," Granddad said. Then came the scuffle and scrape as he concealed the entrance to the underground lab. In a moment he pushed through the curtain, his wide shoulders filling the cutout doorway. She stared as though she'd never seen him before. Her family was different, yes. Father and Granddad were anomalies in Mercury City, even rebels. But Defenders? Her textbooks called the race violent and cruel.

Granddad lowered himself onto a stool near the cash register. When Grey finally perched next to him on the other high stool, he pulled a paper-wrapped package out of a pocket inside his vest and set it on the counter between them. He unwrapped two oat cakes and a small apple.

Grey's stomach contracted but she shook her head. "I'm not hungry."

He gave her an odd smile, took one of the cakes and slid the rest, package and all, toward her. "Then hold on to it for later."

"But what if—?" She didn't finish. Only time would tell which parent she took after.

At Granddad's nod, Grey accepted the food and stored it in her coat pocket next to the full ration bottle.

With the afternoon quiet and her chores done, the ache in Grey's chest grew, threatening to squeeze out everything but Whit's actions, his punishment, his absence. She dragged herself over to watch Granddad repair one of the Council-issued

41

typewriter balls. He tested the L key he'd just replaced. The little button clicked, but no letter appeared on the pane.

"Is this part broken too?" She tapped the glass, which didn't glow like the one she'd seen last night.

"No." He leaned back. "It'll work with a bit of Chemia." He spat the last word out like a swig of sour milk.

Grey turned to the shelf behind him and reached for a miniature phonograph emitting a faint green glow. Her fingertip warmed as the luminosity touched it. "How do they—?"

"Grey!"

She yanked her hand back. Granddad's yellow brows scrunched. A frown stamped his mouth.

He nodded toward a stack of books, and his next words came out gentle. "Find a place for those, will you?"

Haimon stepped into the room and Grey whirled away to hide her flushing face. She knew better than to touch Council equipment. She hefted the pile of books and searched the crowded shelves for empty space. There, a shelf high above the case in the corner.

She set the load of books on top of the obscured glass surface she'd cleaned only yesterday. A reflection moved over the pane. Grey waved a hand over the case, but this time nothing flickered in the dull glass. The light was always tricky in the back of the store. She shrugged and skimmed her finger over the keyhole embedded at the edge. Though she helped in the shop often, she'd never seen the matching key. Bracing herself against the cabinet, she shelved the books two at a time. The lines of her mark prickled where her midsection pressed into the cabinet's metal rim.

She reached for the remaining books, her knuckles grazing the glass. Over her shoulder, she spied Granddad and Haimon staring at her.

"What is it?" Grey paused with the books lifted midway from cabinet to shelf. "Should I put these somewhere else?"

Granddad paced to her side, relieved her of the books, then took her hands in his. He turned them over, studying her palms like a fortune teller. Dust coated the fresh scabs from last night's fall into the pallets.

"What's the matter?" Grey searched his face.

Haimon appeared at her grandfather's elbow. "Olan?"

"She came home bleeding from a fall last night." Granddad let her hands drop. "When I saw her touch the cabinet, I couldn't help but wonder. Maybe it's a sign."

Haimon grimaced. "I thought you weren't ready to break your treaty with Adante."

Grey eyed the two men. "What are you talking about? What treaty with Adante?"

Granddad's voice deepened. "Grey, you know our family is different—"

"That's treason, Olan." Haimon tread closer. "Be careful what you tell her. For all we know, it's a one-way ticket for her as well."

The scientist disguised as a shop assistant reached toward the unused curio cabinet, his scarred hand hovering over the glass. "Would you really risk it?" he murmured.

Grey peered at the still surface of the case. "Risk what?"

Granddad's fingers closed around her wrist. He raised her hand once again and cradled it in his own massive paw. The light in his eyes reminded her of sunlight on the mountain lakes.

"What is it? Tell me."

He traced the scabbed-over lines in her palm, the brightness of his expression fading to a glazed look. He whispered something under his breath. Grey leaned in to hear.

"Love is magic in our veins. Love the hand of the punisher stays. Love heals what justice flays. Love defends and mercy reigns."

The words sank deep into Grey, humming with energy. Warmth flowed from Granddad's fingertips where they touched her palm. Last night's foreign courage returned, coursing through her body, stiffening her limbs, gliding like invisible armor to infuse every inch of her skin.

"What does it mean?" Grey breathed.

Granddad's ice-blue eyes snapped into focus, but it was Haimon who spoke.

"Is it worth it? You could lose her too."

"Not yet then. Not yet." Granddad backed away and checked his pocket watch, a duplicate of Grey's with a silver fist for a cover. He looked up. "Time to head home. Whit should be back by now."

It was everything Grey could do not to run to Whit's door the moment they rounded the corner onto the dirt-packed lane.

Granddad's voice anchored her. "We shouldn't risk more exposure with Adante so interested. Curfew's not far off, and you should be seen entering your own home."

"What does Adante want with me?" Yesterday's defiance made her a target, but there was more to it than that.

"Haimon was right. We must be careful." He stopped at the edge of their walkway and faced her. The shadow of Excelsior Peak leached the color from his hair and turned his skin to blue stone. "I promise I'll tell you everything if your mother and father allow."

She nodded and dragged her feet to the front door. The light in the Bryacres' window swept her questions into corners. All that mattered was seeing Whit.

"Mother? Father?" Grey shivered in the dark entryway.

When neither answered her call, she moved to the parlor and pressed her cheek to the cold glass of the window, scanning for activity next door. Within minutes, Father ducked out of the Bryacres' front door and strode over the adjoining lawns.

Grey met him at the door. One look at his drawn face and her eyes burned with tears.

"H-how bad?"

He frowned and led her to the settee. Grey perched on the edge. He dropped into the seat beside her and adjusted his position to study her face. "Tell me exactly what happened last night."

Grey blurted the story, from the shortcut to the coywolves to the deputies, but left out the boldness that had tumbled through her like a rock slide.

Father's eyes narrowed. "That's it? You're sure?"

Granddad paced in the kitchen, his arms crossed over his chest. His eyes questioned her too, but a fever light burned in their depths.

Father's expression twisted into a grief she recognized from the worst of his mountain excursions. "Grey, Josephine needs an explanation. They punished Whit as though this were his fourth or fifth offense, not his first."

A cracking sound split the quiet in the room. Granddad's fingers clenched around the wood trim of the archway. "Haven't I told you, Steinar?" He let go of the splintering timber and lunged to the center of the parlor. "Chemist greed will bleed this city dry."

Father stood, but Grey didn't hear his words. Stinging numbness whipped around her heart. "Is Whit dying?"

Both men turned to her. Father shook his head. "He should recover." Relief seared her lungs only to be replaced by icy dread.

"I have to go over there," she choked out. "I need to see him."

Father's face set in a cast of resistance but Granddad sprang toward the door. "I'll check for patrols. Wait for my go ahead."

He disappeared into the twilight and Father stared after him, brows furrowed. Grey rubbed her eyes and lifted her chin. Her voice sounded foreign in her own ears, small but hard. "They did this because of me."

He winced. "No, Grey. Your grandfather is right. The Council goes too far. Their greed has gone unchecked for too long."

"But I defied them. I don't know why. Something happened inside me." She pressed her clenched fist into her torso. "I told them Whit hadn't done anything wrong. I told them to take me instead."

"Oh, Grey." Her name creaked from behind Father's clenched teeth. He covered his forehead with his hand. "You have no idea what you did."

A knock on the back door yanked her off the sofa. Father followed as she hurried through the kitchen and the mudroom to crack open the door to the backyard.

"All's clear," Granddad whispered.

Grey looked over her shoulder. Her father stood in the kitchen, backlit, his expression lost in shadows. He gave a slight nod. She bolted into the night, still wearing her bright red coat with the full potion bottle in the pocket.

They stooped under the Bryacres' covered porch and Granddad knocked on the back door. The chill of the winter evening stung Grey's flushed cheeks, but beneath her clothes sweat glazed her skin.

When the door inched open, Granddad bowed to whisper, "It's us."

He loped away into the night as Josephine opened the door just wide enough for Grey to slip through. Hands balled into fists, Grey followed Whit's mother into the familiar kitchen and on to the small parlor in the front of the house. Her own mother sat in a drab armchair, busy rolling strips of white cloth. She looked up, brows arched.

Grey lifted her palms. "I had to come."

Josephine turned and Grey sucked in a breath. She was the same Mrs. Bryacre Grey had always known, and yet the face didn't belong to her neighbor. It was as though some feature was missing, and the shock of its absence overwhelmed.

Grey plunged her hand into her pocket and withdrew the bottle of potion. "I brought this for Whit."

Mother shot up, sending bandages rolling down her scarlet skirt and across the floor. "What are you doing?"

"This is my choice to make." Grey dropped the bottle into Josephine's hand. "Can I see him?"

Josephine curled her fingers around the potion as if she might squeeze the glass to grit. She nodded once.

Grey ignored her mother's protest and followed Josephine down the hall. After peeking into Whit's room, Josephine held the door open. "He's resting as best he can. I must speak to your mother before . . ."

Grey didn't hear the rest of the sentence. She stood at the threshold, breath snatched from her lungs.

Whit lay on his stomach, limbs draped over an iron-framed bed. His face was turned away from her, toward the wall. He was naked to the waist and strips of gauze clung to his back in rows from his shoulders to his belt. Crimson seeped in lines, too many to count, through the light bandages. Grey pressed her fist to her lips. The same gauze-covered, bleeding stripes marked Whit's upper arms as well.

Vomit surged up her throat, but she clamped her mouth shut and dragged in air through her nose. The pine scent of the healing ointment invaded her lungs and for a second her head spun, but the sharp odor at least overpowered the taste of bile on her tongue. She blew out a steadying breath. The shock lessened with each second she refused to look away.

"Whit?" Grey crossed the carpet and knelt at his side.

He startled, flinched, then moaned. His head moved, pressing into the mattress then shifting to face her. Sweat-soaked hair stuck to the blanched skin of his forehead and cheek. Against the white of his skin his eyes were the deep blue-gray of a shadowed ravine. The corner of his mouth not hidden by the swell of the mattress twitched into a half smile. "Grey."

A beast snarled in Grey's gut. She flattened a palm over her stomach where her skin tightened and itched. The mark writhed along with this new creature—this new Grey. Morality codes and Chemist law slipped away and nothing remained but her, Whit, and the pain.

48

She pressed her chest into the side of the mattress, dropped her forehead onto the sheet next to his bloody upper arm, and let her tears fall.

The fabric under Grey's cheek was wet, but her eyes were puffy and dry. She slumped to the floor and grasped Whit's hand in hers. He made a noise—a high, choking gasp in the back of his throat—but his eyes didn't open.

Fraternization.

Indecent conduct.

The Chemists could all rot.

She'd see them flayed and helpless.

She'd see them withered like Josephine. Stunted like the old miners.

She'd see . . . A hazy ring outlined her vision, cinching inward. She squeezed her eyes shut, but the pounding in her head swallowed everything else, pushing her toward unconsciousness. A sound at the door jolted her back. Grey pulled her hand from Whit's and clasped her arms around her drawn-up knees as Mother and Josephine entered.

Josephine held the ration bottle close to her chest as though someone might snatch it at any second. She glanced at Grey then hurried to her son. "Is he awake?"

Mother scrutinized Grey like she was some hybrid vegetable from the greenhouses. No doubt she searched for signs of illness.

Grey's presence here was proof. She was fine—hungry, yes—but not moaning and shaking while yesterday's dinner spewed from her body. She *must* take after Father and Granddad.

"Damnation." Josephine scrubbed at the sheet near Whit's face. A small purple stain bloomed on the bedclothes. "You need to take this, son," she pleaded.

Whit mumbled into the mattress. "Whose?"

Grey got to her knees once again and put her face close to Whit's. "It's mine."

His gaze sharpened. "No." He winced but repeated, "No."

"Look at me, Whit. I'm well. I skipped my ration this morning, and I'm right here in front of you. Not sick." Grey eyed the potion bottle in Josephine's hand. "You need this. It's my fault they did this to you. Now let me help."

He held her gaze as if willing himself to concentrate through the pain. His eyes blurred as he struggled to stay conscious.

Grey locked her arms against her sides and packed her overwhelming need to hold him and to avenge his suffering into one word. "Please."

His attention broke, lids fluttering to reveal white beneath the dark fringe of his lashes.

Josephine ducked closer, edging Grey away from the bed. "Help me, Maire. I can't get it into him like this."

Mother slipped to the other side of the bed, and Grey stood.

"Grey, go into the parlor." Mother's quiet command hung in the room.

Grey opened her mouth but words stalled on her tongue.

Mother's small hands reached over Whit's body to grasp his arm and bandaged side. He cried out at her touch.

"Go, Grey," Mother said.

Grey backed toward the door. Whit screamed and she fled.

The Bryacres' parlor shrank around Grey until she was a giant in a land of faded miniatures.

Chemist greed will bleed this city dry, Granddad had said. Bleed it dry.

Beneath her red coat, Grey's chest heaved.

The bloody lines on Whit's back filled her vision. *Bleed us dry.*

Red pressed in all around her. She dropped into a chair and closed her eyes but couldn't escape the color of blood. A trace of stone-like strength curled outward from her midsection, but dizziness won out. Grey touched her forehead to her knees.

A hand on her shoulder brought her upright.

Mother gazed down at her, worry dragging at her thin mouth.

Grey straightened in her seat and pushed the hair out of her face. "How is he?"

She set Grey's empty ration bottle on a table. "We got it down him before he went under."

Grey braced for a lecture, but her mother fixated on the potion bottle. "You've got the Haward gift, same as your father and Olan. I wouldn't have made it till noon without the potion. Have you eaten at all today?"

"No. I'm afraid to. What if it only appears that I've inherited Father's traits, but inside I have the starvation disease? What if I'm hiding both traits, like one of Mendel's pea plants?"

Mother cupped Grey's chin, her brown eyes soft. "You're not like me, Grey." She touched a hand to her faded red blouse. "You've never had this weakness."

"Then why wouldn't you let me help with Father's work or Granddad's? You let Banner."

"And it cost your brother his life," Mother snapped. Her lips crumpled and she covered her mouth. After a deep breath, she dropped her hand. "Banner made a choice just as your father and grandfather did. Just as you did today."

Grey pressed her thumbs into her eyes, stopping the tears, stopping the red haze that lingered at the edges of her vision. She thrust out her chin. "Then Father can take my potion with him to the mountains. From now on."

"We'll discuss that later. Let's get you home." She made a sweep around the parlor as if checking for deputies. "After what they did to Whit, I wouldn't be surprised if they lowered the age of your Stripe. Especially with that leech Adante sniffing about."

Grey's hollow stomach knotted. Adante had called her spirited. He knew of her insolence. People assumed the Chemist Council dictated the Age of the Stripe to coincide with a citizen reaching adulthood. She'd stood before the deputies who took Whit and all but declared her status. Adante didn't need to lower her age. Grey'd done it herself.

Mother padded toward the back of the house. "Come. There's nothing more we can do for Jo and Whit tonight."

Grey snagged the empty bottle from the table, slid it into her pocket, and followed.

She stiffened the moment she stepped into the kitchen. Ahead, Mother caught her breath and froze. Muted voices, punctuated by Father's taut tone, carried from the front of the house.

Mother edged around the benches shoved against the table and walked under the arch into the living room. Grey followed, stopping with one foot on the worn carpet and one still on the tile. Father's large shape blocked her view of whoever stood on the front porch.

The soft swish of the back door sent a cold breeze snaking over Grey's skin. She threw a glance over her shoulder and released a pent-up breath. Granddad stood just inside the mudroom, his eyes shining in the shadows.

"Get out of my way, Steinar." The voice oozed past the shield of her father's body to coil around Grey. A green glow washed the parlor, turning it into a nightmare scene. Sweat broke on Grey's forehead, and she hung as if suspended between consciousness and a surreal dream.

Adante. *Here.*

Two deputies pushed inside, grabbing her father and forcing him into the parlor. He towered over both men, but they trained clotters on him. Relief washed over his face when he spied Grey and her mother standing in the archway.

A green-edged silhouette appeared in the doorway. He flickered in and out of focus as though the air bent around him. Grey squinted, but she didn't need to see his features to know his mood. Energy pushed ahead of Adante as he stalked to where the deputies restrained her father.

"This is the Haward home, then?" His pale eyes roamed the shabby interior, lighting on Grey and her mother before moving on to the kitchen. "Olan, hiding again?"

Granddad sprung forward but stopped himself.

The Chemist's gaze flicked to Grey, and he raised his green-tinted monocle to scrutinize the length of her body. His voice slowed to a languid drip. "Not out defying authority tonight, are you, Grey?"

The empty bottle was still in the pocket of her cloak. Grey suppressed the thought and straightened her shoulders as Adante strode closer.

He stopped inches from her. The sickeningly sweet odor of potion clung to his clothes. Slippery words licked her ears. "Did you know, Grey, that once the Chemists discovered the cure for the First Disease, we never again needed the potion? All those of Regian blood were changed, perfected." With long, green-nailed fingers, he gestured to his face. "We are different now, a race above."

In a movement too quick to see, his hand came to hover over Grey's shoulder. Mother's squeak of protest fell into silence. Adante's fingers skimmed over her coat as he traced the length of her arm.

"It is our position—separate from our citizens—that affords us the wisdom to govern. Those who witnessed the degradation and disorder that birthed the First Disease vowed to create a better society. You can understand our abhorrence for those who would break the law now."

"Adante." Granddad's voice boomed from behind Grey. Did the Chemist flinch or was it a fluctuation in his power?

Adante hesitated, his fingers poised over Grey's hand where it hung at her side. He held her gaze, squinting through the Chemia-laced monocle. His glare carried words into her head.

You're no stranger to touch, are you, girl? Ah, yes. Heat. A blush. The deputies tell me the boy, Whitland, held you last night.

Grey willed her eyes to shut, but she couldn't blink. He was right. Her skin burned as each moment of contact with Whit replayed. Fingers of shame raked through her thoughts.

The boy deserved his punishment, but you . . . You deserve much more, don't you, Grey?

Bravery replaced the humiliation inside. She'd done nothing wrong. Neither had Whit. She narrowed her eyes, her rebellion unspoken but unmistakable.

A flame leapt in Adante's eyes. He spoke aloud. "There it is. You can't hide your offenses from me."

His hand darted into the pocket of her coat. The maneuver drew a gasp from everyone else, but Grey kept her rigid stance as he withdrew the bottle and presented it on his palm between their bodies.

Adante took a swift step backward and raised his voice. "Grey Haward, you were seen entering your neighbor's house after curfew. Your thoughts reveal your guilt. And this"—he held up the bottle—"confirms the purpose of your visit." He unbuttoned his top coat and stored the glass tube in the belt that held a number of other vials: many green, some purple, and a few blood red.

Grey's mouth went dry. An image of Whit's carved back flashed before her eyes. A chill snaked down her spine.

With a tilt of his head, Adante signaled the deputies. One man stepped forward, holstering his clotter. The other agent remained guarding her father. Mother whimpered.

Adante halted the deputy just before he reached Grey. "Ration dealing carries the death penalty, but I think we all realize this is a special case. Don't we, Olan?"

Grey tracked Adante's gaze as he looked past her to Granddad. Flint encased her grandfather's expression, but his eyes widened. Fear. He'd never shown it before. Her own panic surged and the defiance slipped away. Pain was coming.

"Hawards are special, Grey. Did your grandfather tell you? Of course he didn't, because that would break our little agreement." Adante lifted his hand, mimicking the action of cupping her cheek though his fingers never touched her skin. "It'd be a shame to waste blood such as yours."

"Enough." Father's voice hurtled into the spell of Adante's words. He didn't move from his position under guard, but his presence seemed to expand, pushing into the very corners of the room. Even the muscled deputy at his side inched a step to the left.

"That wasn't Grey's ration. It was mine. She simply brought the bottle back."

Adante whirled around. "You can't prove she took her ration."

A voice in Grey's head argued that neither could Adante prove, outside of Chemist mind tricks, that she'd given her ration to Whit. Not that proof mattered with the Council.

Father inched his hand up in a cautious arc toward his pocket. "May I?" He reached into his coat and withdrew a ration bottle.

Grey scrutinized his face. Had he saved his own ration knowing she'd give hers away—knowing her actions had plucked Adante's suspicion? The realization carved a pit in her stomach. Who had died, up in the mountains, because Steinar Haward brought no potion today?

Adante swooped down on the bottle, snatched it from her father, and yanked the cork. He sniffed the potion and let a drop fall into his palm. A tiny puff of purple smoke lifted from his hand.

"You saw us this morning." Father's explanation sounded prepared. "I received the ration for my family, but with Josephine Bryacre's unexpected condition, I neglected to give Grey her ration before she left with my father."

"Then why is she not ill?" Adante's voice drawled. "And why are you not ill, for that matter, if it was your potion your daughter gave to the boy?"

Granddad inserted himself into the living room, a sneer on his face. "No more games. You know the answers to these questions."

The Chemist's crow-like head cocked toward Granddad. His lips spread in a wide grin. "Indeed, I do. And I have proof that you've broken the law, Olan. You, your son, and your granddaughter."

Again Father's silhouette loomed, but his voice remained even and low. "You have proof that I've disobeyed the law. Let Grey obey the law and take her ration now. Take me to your Council. In exchange my father will keep our family's treaty with you. Your secret will remain hidden."

The smile fled Adante's face. His whole body shook as he bore down on her father, one finger aimed at his face.

"Don't!" His voice fell but rage roughened his words. "Don't threaten me, or I will make your death longer than any on record."

"If you think I'm going to let you take my daughter the way you took my son—"

Granddad's voice filled Grey's head. *Run to the shop, Grey. Haimon will help you.*

She schooled her face to hide her shock. *What are you talking about?* She tried to direct the question to Granddad but until this moment telepathy had been a Chemist tool, possible only through blood magic. She could no more speak with her mind than she could fly.

Across the small room Father glared into Adante's eyes. The Chemist stood motionless, his hands positioned as if holding an invisible ball in front of his torso.

Run. Granddad's voice swept her thoughts at the same moment he stepped in front of her.

Adante whirled and a microburst exploded in the living room. Electrified air whooshed by on either side of Granddad's body. Grey shrank inward to avoid the streams of magic. Her grandfather's broad back stiffened. The ruddy skin of his neck paled and turned gray as stone.

Mother screamed.

Now, Grey. Granddad's voice thundered in her mind.

Grey dashed to the mudroom and wrenched the door open, forcing herself not to look back.

She hurtled into the night, rounding the back of the house and vaulting the fence. Shouts sounded from the open front door. A chug boat loomed at the end of the walkway, a mechanical creature ready to spring into pursuit.

Grey shot past the floating craft. Hot, green exhaust from the turbines swished around her ankles. A deputy hollered, but she ran. She'd reached the street connecting her neighborhood to Pewter Hill when something snagged her right arm. A force tugged her backward, and she pumped her legs harder. Another yank, this one to her shoulder, nearly pulled her to the ground. Grey staggered then regained her pace. At the top of Pewter, she glanced back.

The hulking craft plunged toward her on a seething fog of green. A spotlight illuminated the knife-thin figure of Adante rising from the front of the ship like a mast. His hair blew about his face, and his hands curled before him. A white-hot force like a ball of lightning barreled into Grey's chest, squeezing out air and knocking her backward. The energy ball skimmed over her face, leaving behind sparks of green that snapped against her hair and clothes.

She gulped a breath and rolled toward the curb on her right. The gravel reopened the scrapes on her hands, and the gash on her leg throbbed. But the alley connecting Pewter to Reinbar was only a few feet from where she'd fallen.

The whirring of the ship's engines filled her ears. Hot air whipped her hair. She dragged herself to her feet and ran for the alley, shouts following. Bricks buckled from the building on her right as a ball of energy missed her and slammed into the wall. A backward glance revealed the black vessel rocketing past the mouth of the alley. It'd take them mere seconds to turn around and follow. Or they might loop around and cut her off at Reinbar.

She sprinted into the darkness of the alley. The thrum of the engines faded. Then grew louder.

It didn't matter. All she could do was run.

Grey's lungs burned. She searched for the Council craft as she ran, even as the drone of the engine filled her ears and jarred her teeth.

The spotlight caught her just before she reached Reinbar. The ship swooped over the row of shops and bore down on top of her.

Grey flung her arms over her head as the vessel's underbelly neared. Noxious exhaust choked her. Any second they'd crush her. She ducked and caught sight of a flat object just beyond the beam of the light—a ration pallet. Yesterday evening's incident here in this alley replayed in rapid detail.

Grey lunged for the pallet. Thick, green vapor clouded her vision, and the pressure beneath the craft nearly pasted her to the ground, yet she reached until her fingers closed around one of the pallet's slats. She hoisted it off the ground and heaved it up and back. A loud crunch broke the whirring pattern of the engines and shards of wood rained down on Grey, grazing her skin. She dove for the darkness outside of the shuddering ring of the spotlight.

Shouts mingled with the sputtering engines.

Grey pulled her body back into motion. She shot out of the alley onto Reinbar and careened toward the opposite sidewalk. After a near fall, she sprinted the length of the street. Colfax beckoned, quiet and empty. Behind her a booming thud filled the night. She'd brought down the craft. Yells and curses followed her as she rounded the corner onto Colfax.

Frigid February air walloped her full in the face, stinging exposed skin and penetrating all the way to her bones. She'd never make it. They'd run her down before she got to the store.

How could Haimon help her anyway?

Something flickered in the shop window ahead, making Grey squint into the darkness. The storefront next to Granddad's shimmered green. She slowed her pace, but it was too late. A form materialized on the sidewalk in a column of red and green smoke. She barreled into it, tangling with limbs not her own. With a crack she flew backward over the sidewalk and into a lamppost. The imprint of energy burned her chest.

Adante stepped out of the vapor. An empty potion bottle rolled away from his feet and into the gutter. Scraps of material from one shredded sleeve dangled about his arm, and his hair now clung to his face in matted clumps. He raised his hands in an attack stance, and she braced for the impact.

"That's enough running for tonight, don't you think?" The Chemist's voice sounded breathless despite his casual words.

Grey scrambled up, her back still pressed into the lamppost. The cold surface wouldn't give. In fact, the metal seemed to join with her spine and spread throughout her body. She gulped for breath as the hardening sensation crept beneath her skin.

"Your father will be executed for ration dealing. Your grandfather is now a permanent statue in your home, and you . . . you are ripe for an exsanguinator, Grey Haward.

Such Chemia I'll achieve with your blood." He vibrated with anticipation.

The strength in Grey's veins receded and she fought to control her voice. "I broke the law. It was my ration. Not my father's."

Adante's jade-tinted features darkened in the mix of light and shadow from the streetlamp. "I believe you." He inched closer, hands still curled in front of his narrow midsection.

Grey sidestepped the lamppost, but the ring of distant footsteps drew her up.

"But what can I do?" His voice almost soothed. "Your father has confessed."

Behind the Chemist a steel-colored head emerged from the Hawards' shop. Grey shouted to cover Haimon's approach. "Of course he confessed. To save me."

Adante stiffened and flexed his fingers. "Then Steinar is guilty of lying to authorities, a crime punishable—"

"*Not* by death." Desperation cracked Grey's voice. She swallowed the rising panic.

Adante's shoulders whipped back and his nostrils flared. His fingers angled outward, toward her, and electricity zinged in the air. "Don't tell me the law, child."

Grey refused to close her eyes. She stared at the Chemist, waiting for the blast.

But his tall frame went rigid. He toppled backward, landing like a plank of wood on the sidewalk in front of Haward's Mercantile.

Haimon stood with his glinting, metallic eyes fixed on Grey. He pocketed some sort of device that resembled a deputy's clotter. "Come. He won't be out for long."

Grey stepped over the Chemist's immobile form and ducked through the shop door Haimon held open. "How did you know?"

"Olan had me wait." Haimon hurried deeper into the store with Grey following. He stepped behind the line of display cases at the back of the room and stopped next to the unused curio cabinet. "Your grandfather believes you're special, Grey."

He stared down at the cabinet's murky surface then held his hand palm up toward her. "Give me your hand."

Grey shook off a shiver and glanced to the front door. What did it matter now if Haimon touched her? She placed her hand in his. The gaunt man flipped it over in his own scarred hand and studied her palm. He let out a sigh.

"Ah, there's a relief. Blood." He held her hand up for her to inspect.

Drops welled in the open scratches. She met Haimon's eyes.

He offered an apologetic smile. "I didn't want to have to cut you."

Haimon jerked her forward. Caught off guard, Grey stumbled against the cabinet. He pressed the heel of her hand onto the keyhole of the curio case. "Blood is the way in and the key to get out. Fist, hand, and cup. Remember."

"What?" The cool metal grew warm and slick, and a tug registered deep in her hand as if the lock sucked on her skin.

She struggled to focus on Haimon's face. What had he said to her? A door swished open somewhere nearby and yet far away. His face whipped away from hers, blurring into the shadows of the shop.

The pull of the curio case traveled up her arm. Was her blood draining or did the emptying sensation swirling through her have something to do with the Chemist attack she'd faced?

Haimon drew near, his expression distorted as though she looked at him through a peephole. His beady eyes jumped into hers. "Find him and bring him back."

What?

"Find him and bring him back, Grey."

Haimon disappeared. Grey lost all contact with her body for a moment. Sensation returned like the current of a rushing river. She tumbled down, her bones and skin lost amongst the fluid force. The pressure built in her ears and pushed at the back of her eyeballs. Rose-colored fog filled her vision.

Then, nothing.

A shape plummeted through the fog hanging over Curio City. Blaise jerked midflight, dipping into a lower airstream before regaining altitude. He shook his head and scanned the mist-shrouded horizon. He hadn't really just seen something fall out of the sky, had he?

He disengaged the fins on his boots and let his legs drop beneath him so that he hovered above the roofs of Blue Willow Heights. Pushing his goggles up to his forehead, he inspected the gables and steep pitches. Nothing unusual. No cries of alarm rang out. The quiet neighborhood in the fashionable part of town was all dark windows and orange streetlights. A few carriages bumped along the bordering streets—porcies returning from the evening's entertainment.

Blaise ascended a few feet, an eye on the approaching vehicles. Humid air coated his skin despite the constant whoosh of the canvas wings. The fog clouded his eyes, and he dragged his shirtsleeve over his face, blinking hard to clear his vision. Still nothing out of the ordinary.

He pulled the bellow cord at his side and the pack on his back hummed with building steam. The wings beat harder, and he engaged the steering fins on his boots. Angling back into a horizontal position, he readied himself for flight.

The hair on his arms and the back of his neck rose. A twang of excitement passed through his core. He paused before turning in the direction of Sir Hinderoot's home. He *had* seen an object fall into Curio. Certainty built with every second. Nothing had fallen out of the strange, fog-laden sky over Curio for one hundred years. Not since *he'd* tumbled, bleeding and terrified, into a world where one home replicated into twenty or thirty, streets and gardens sprang into existence, and people—the strangest people—went from motionless figures to walking, talking beings.

Sir Hinderoot's tune-up would have to wait. Anticipation coiled in Blaise's gut, and a tug drew him toward the falling object's trajectory. He fitted his goggles over his eyes and took off in the direction of the newest curiosity in Curio City.

Pain jerked Grey out of numbness. Her head throbbed. Rhythmic flapping broke through the darkness cradling her. The whooshing sound changed into running footsteps.

She had to get up.

She struggled to open her eyes.

Muggy heat filled her nostrils, blocking breath. Her mind swam.

The footsteps slapped nearer, jarring her head. Someone bent over her. Creaking and muted jangling seemed to come from all sides. The scents of sawdust, machine oil, and sweat blended with the sticky air. A rough hand touched her cheek.

Grey's lids fluttered just as another sound invaded—the cadence of many feet. The shape kneeling beside her jerked. Rope-like strands whipped through the darkness and a strange outline came into view. A wing? Shouts rang out and the winged being bolted away.

She strained to hear the flapping noise again, but the thud of the marching feet pounded nearer, sending reverberations through the surface beneath her. Wincing, she lifted her face then eased her upper body off the wet pavestones with her elbows. She lay in a darkened street. A layer of fog overhead gathered light from street lamps and shed a faint brown glow over her surroundings. Vague outlines of buildings lined her peripheral vision.

Grey peered at the approaching figures. They moved as one entity, their clanging steps bearing down on her. Scrambling to a sitting position only sent the shadowy street spinning. When her vision cleared, Grey scooted backward.

She searched for an escape route. At first glance, the structures on either side of her appeared to be connected shops, like the business center of the Foothills Quarter. But a closer look revealed ornate facades, groomed gardens, and decorative iron fences—a residential neighborhood. Grey wobbled to her feet and peeked over her shoulder. The rows of terraced houses stretched on into the night.

She clutched her aching head. Where was she?

The soldiers nearing her didn't belong in the drab ranks of the United States military. Long guns perched on their shoulders and stretched up into the night like a moving forest of stripped branches. The gun muzzles and metallic buttons on their chests glinted in the hazy illumination. Grey squinted. Their long coats reflected light like a tin bucket in the moonlight. Underneath bushy black hats, the men's faces gleamed as well. Metal. Their clothes, their shoes, their faces. All metal.

The group halted. One soldier—an exact replica of the man next to him and the man next to him and so on—stepped forward and bowed at the waist.

A mechanical hum accompanied the opening of his mouth, and a monotone voice spoke.

"Do you require assistance, Mistress Porcelain?"

Grey gaped.

The flat voice continued. "Are you fully animated, Miss?"

"I . . . I . . ."

The soldier next to the apparent leader broke into the same mechanical whirring. His jaw opened and he spoke in an identical voice.

"If I may, Lieutenant?"

The lieutenant's head rotated to the left. "Yes, Sergeant?

The second soldier stepped forward to join the lieutenant, but kept his round eyes locked on Grey. His unblinking gaze reminded her of the glass-eyed dolls in her grandfather's shop.

Granddad. The store. Haimon. Grey almost crumpled. She'd been in the shop. Haimon had pressed her bleeding hand to the curio cabinet. Then he'd told her to find *him* and bring him back. Find who? She glanced about the street. Pain and bursts of light accompanied the movement. More streets. More muted orange streetlamps. What was this place?

The two metal figures before her conversed in their unnatural speech. She caught the end of the sergeant's sentence.

". . . not a porcie I recognize, sir."

The lieutenant's head swiveled back to examine her. He took another step closer and his mechanized jaw released. "You are correct. And the Mad Tock left her. I've never seen anything like it."

"Indeed."

Grey turned from the shiny soldiers. She would run. The metal men were slow, and they'd never catch her. She studied her feet. Why weren't they moving? She pitched forward. The wet cobblestones rushed toward her face.

Something pulled at Grey's hand. Her head ached. She ignored the little tug and drifted back to sleep. Sometime later, a tickling sensation registered on her palm. She flinched as a smooth object pressed into her scraped flesh. Another poke and she yanked her hand away.

A gasp accompanied the swish of her eyelids. Pink. A swathe of pink like the sky at sunset hovered over her head. No. The pink thing wasn't hovering. It remained motionless as Grey focused. The smooth material above her looked soft, but the sheen of the light on the satiny fabric reminded her of the glinting metal men. She opened her mouth to cry out but only managed a cough.

"We gave you water, but you didn't animate. What manner of porcie are you?"

Grey shifted toward the voice, grateful for the cushioning support beneath her head. All the swirling pink faded into the background, and she jerked.

A woman sat studying her. Grey blinked, but the exquisite figure remained. A delicate, heart-shaped face regarded Grey. Large blue eyes fringed with long, black lashes sparkled despite the woman's grave expression. Auburn hair rose from her forehead into a mountain of jewel-studded curls and cascaded down her shoulder in perfect ringlets. But her skin. Grey had never seen anything like it. Translucent. Flawless. The woman's alabaster face belonged in a painting. Her cheekbones bore a faint rose blush, and her full lips were a shade darker than the pink canopy and bedspread. A high-collared gown of blue and gold was cut away from her bosom to create the shape of an upside down heart. Long, pink-tipped fingers wove together on the bedspread. Elbow-length sleeves revealed graceful forearms and wrists. Every inch of visible skin appeared to be made of porcelain and yet alive, supple.

A tiny frown pulled at the woman's perfect mouth. She looked confused, though no lines marred her brow. "Are you without speech? I can have more water brought up if it would help. You never cooled completely. We saw to that. We've been tending you, my maids and I. I am Fantine."

Grey cleared her throat. "Where am I?"

Fantine beamed, clasping her hands to her expertly displayed chest. "You can speak. Oh, I am so relieved. The glueman repaired the cracks on your hands and leg—such strange cracks!—but when you did not reanimate, we feared some terrible disaster had befallen you. Oh, but as to your location, you are in the house of Lord Blueboy."

As she spoke the name, her sapphire eyes widened, and her smile conveyed a dazzling blend of pride, pleasure, and secrecy. When Grey said nothing, Fantine nodded, her curls bouncing.

"I know. Speechless is right. He has taken an interest in you. Such a mystery. And you so pretty. Well, in your unusual way, of course. My lord is fascinated. Simply fascinated by your variable skin and the little brown dots on your arms." Fantine's gaze skimmed up Grey's arm to her face and then down to her body beneath the sheet. Her cheery tone faded. "And your softness."

A real frown, not the former pretty pout, crossed her features.

Grey tore her eyes from the doll-like woman and took in her surroundings. She lay in a massive bed decked in pink satin and white lace. The room beyond was as big as her whole house. On her left tall windows opened onto a small balcony. Several groups of burgundy-upholstered chairs dotted the expansive floor. At the far end of the room a massive mirror and a towering wardrobe dominated the papered wall. A low vanity cluttered with an array of beautiful bottles stood in between them. She scrutinized the jewel-toned containers. No potion bottles.

The realization provoked a physical reaction. Grey pressed her hand to her stomach as a sharp pang preceded a loud gurgle.

Fantine coughed delicately.

Grey turned to her astonishing hostess. "I'm sorry. I'm confused. Where did you say I am?"

Fantine loosed a musical laugh. "They should have checked your head twice for cracks." She arranged her features into a wise mask and spoke in a sing-song voice that reminded Grey of a nursery school teacher. "You are in Lord Blueboy's mansion—the grandest home in all of Curio City. His lordship took pity on you when the platoon brought you in. We summoned the glueman to repair you, supplied you with water, and waited for you to reanimate."

Curio City? Glueman? It made no sense. Grey rubbed the tender spot above her forehead and winced. She must've broken her head.

"Fantine?"

"Yes?"

"How long have I been asleep?"

"Ah, sleep?"

"Um." Grey searched her foggy brain. How had Fantine put it? "How long have I been inanimate?"

"Oh, let's see then. They brought you here at night. Nettie fetched me a cuppa in bed and nattered on about you while I warmed. The glueman came in the morning—yesterday—so this is your second day with us."

Two days! What had happened to her father in that time? Grey pushed against the pillows, struggling to sit. She had to get back, make Adante understand. Or was it already too late? She swallowed the rising panic.

"I have to get out of here. I can't stay." Grey peeled back the covers then yanked them to her chin. She wore nothing but a filmy gown nearly as sheer as the gauze curtains framing the tall windows. "Where are my clothes?"

"Don't be silly . . . Oh dear, what is your name?"

"Grey."

Fantine wrinkled her perfect nose. "That's not a very pretty name, is it?" She shrugged. "Don't be silly, Grey. You can't leave. We must have the glueman back to see that you're properly mended. And then we must present you to my lord and hear your miraculous tale. And *then* there will likely be a ball, and various presentations and paintings and the like. The whole house is practically suspended waiting for news. Which reminds me."

She rose and Grey gawked at her outfit. The extravagant dress with its odd neckline—a mixture of prim and indecent—hugged Fantine's waist in panels of gold-embroidered blue satin. What had first appeared to be a full skirt fell over her hips, but the front of the skirt ended in a lacy ruffle that skimmed Fantine's molded ivory thighs. The rows of fabric and lace tapered to the floor, framing the woman's elegant, bare legs. Fantine turned away, revealing a back section that reached the floor and swished behind her as she walked to a small decorative door in the wall.

As soon as Fantine opened the little panel, the tinkling sound of water made Grey squeeze her legs together. She needed a bathroom. Now.

Fantine reached inside the cabinet, fiddled with something, then withdrew a silver teacup. She smiled as she returned to Grey's bedside.

"Here we are." She placed the cup on a table at Grey's right. "Drink that up while I share the good news that you've reanimated."

Grey eyed the silver cup and bit her lip while Fantine fumbled with the curtains tied to the canopy frame at the head of the bed. Her delicate fingers closed around a braided gold rope, and she tugged on it twice.

"There, my own maid Nettie has instructions to respond to this room. She will help you dress."

Another loud rumble from Grey's stomach halted Fantine's chatter. She turned to Grey with alarm stamped on her polished features.

Grey flushed and picked at the lace ruffle on the coverlet. "I'm hungry, and I really need to use the restroom."

"Hungry? Rest room?"

Somehow Grey had expected this reaction from Fantine. She closed her eyes, blocking out the strange, gorgeous woman and the decadent room. The dull ache in her head intensified and tears rimmed her eyelids.

She had to find a way out of this place and back home.

Grey perched on the edge of the bed while wrapped in the pink satin coverlet. Though the mattress was high off the ground, her legs reached to the floor. She tapped a quick rhythm with her toe. With Fantine gone to tell the household of her recovery, now was her chance to escape. Though three things barred her way: A full bladder, an empty stomach, and the fact that the room went black whenever she tried to stand.

She gathered her strength for another attempt, but a soft knock at the door cut off her plan. Securing the blanket around her shoulders, Grey called for the visitor to enter.

A white lace cap appeared. Glassy eyes peered from beneath the mop hat, and Grey expected to hear the whirring mechanical voice as the maid entered. But this individual spoke in near-human tones. The faint hum accompanying her words sounded almost breathy.

"I'm Nettie, Miss. I'm here to dress you."

Clothed in a black maid's uniform complete with white apron and piles of white ruffles peeking from beneath the skirt, Nettie moved with a precise locomotion not quite natural but not as stiff as the metal soldiers'. Grey studied the maid's crafted face. How could a mechanical creation be so obviously alive?

Nettie tilted her head to the side. "Are you cooling, Miss? Should I fetch you some water?"

What was with all the water? Grey chewed her lip as the pressure in her lower regions intensified. She couldn't hold it any longer. "Nettie, I need to go to the bathroom."

"You wish to bathe?"

"I need to use the facilities. The bathroom. Washroom? Potty?"

Nettie's painted eyebrows rose. "You would like a plant in your room?"

Grey moaned and dug her fingers into her tangled hair. She dropped her hands when her head throbbed in response and leveled a gaze at the perplexed maid. "I leak, Nettie. I need something to, um, leak into."

Nettie's gaze plummeted to the floor. "Oh, Miss, I am so sorry, Miss. The glueman said he'd never worked on such as you. We did our best, Miss. Perhaps the leaking is only temporary and will vanish when your cracks seal completely."

A word slipped out of Grey's mouth, but under the circumstance she was glad only the curse escaped her strained body. She tried again. "Do you have a vase or a bowl? Some sort of container—not worth anything—that I could use?"

Nettie curtsied and smiled, her enameled metal cheeks squeaking slightly. She trundled out of the room and returned moments later with an elaborate flower arrangement secured in a short vase.

Grey lurched to a stand and shaded her eyes as the room turned to wobbly shadows. Gentle pressure beneath her elbow steadied her. Grey dropped her hand to peer into Nettie's glassy brown eyes. The maid's eyebrows drew together. The corners of her mouth drooped. She leaned closer, and Grey caught a whiff of something sweet and thick masked by a powdery scent that reminded her of the linen closet at home.

Nettie cocked her head and whispered, "You're not a porcie at all, are you?"

Grey shook her head.

"Then what are you, Miss?"

Grey shrugged, the pounding in her head and the weight in her bladder muddling her efforts at explanation. "Human?"

"Human," Nettie said, her shiny mouth exaggerating the syllables. She shook her head. "I don't know the word."

Grey held her breath and watched the mechanical woman. Nettie stared back with obvious curiosity and compassion. If the maid could look at her with such emotions, then how could the two of them be all that different?

Grey clutched the pale, painted arm extending from the capped sleeve of Nettie's uniform. The smooth metal was cool but not cold as she'd expected. Faint lines made a rectangle near her wrist. A panel of some sort? Nettie followed the movement, clearly feeling the pressure of Grey's hand on her arm.

"I'm going to need your help, Nettie. First, you'd better take the flowers out of the vase."

Grey's cheeks still burned as Nettie settled her back against the pillows. She waved toward the floor on the left side of the bed, where the now full vase was hidden away. "I'm sorry you had to help me with that."

Nettie tsked, the noise a cross between a clink and a sizzle. "That's all right, Miss. I've just never seen anything like it is all."

Grey's stomach rumbled, adding another layer of heat to her cheeks.

Nettie frowned at the satin coverlet she'd just tucked around Grey's midsection. "What is it now?"

"I'm hungry." More like starved. "I need to eat." A pang blazed through her belly followed by a spasm so hard it raised perspiration on her upper lip. Was it hunger or something worse? Mother's words in the Bryacres' parlor replayed: *"You're not like me, Grey."* But maybe she was. Maybe the wretched illness carried by all in the Foothills Quarter was about to overcome her in this strange place with none of her family close by. Panic tightened her throat.

"What do you need, Miss?" Nettie's softly buzzing voice washed over Grey. The woman hovered near, her strange face drawn in lines of concern.

She needed to get back home, and to do that she'd have to regain her strength. Grey glanced toward the cupboard where Fantine had retrieved the cup of water. "The porcies need water, right, Nettie? It allows them to function?"

"Yes, Miss. They've got to have water for their jitter pumps to operate."

Jitter pumps? Grey pushed the phrase aside for later consideration. "But you're not a porcie. How do you operate?"

"I'm a tock." Nettie made a circling gesture over her torso. "I've got clockwork inside. Wind me up and tick tock, tick tock."

Grey scrutinized the maid's form before she remembered her manners. "I'm sorry if I'm being impolite."

Nettie's laugh was equal parts whir and jingle, but then her face grew serious. She peered around the room as though checking for eavesdroppers. Grey stiffened when the maid perched on the edge of the elaborate bed and swiveled, exposing the neat back of her uniform. With one hand she lifted the lacy cap on her head to reveal a coil of brown hair. Nettie's delicate fingers, with their almost imperceptible hinges and screws, dug through the bun, lifting it away from her neck to reveal a tiny, protruding key.

"I'm lucky," she said, still angled away from Grey. "I can reach mine easily. And the key stays in place. Most tocks need help with winding, and many have detachable keys which can be lost or taken." Her voice caught on the last word.

"Who would take your key, Nettie?"

The tock pivoted back with an arranged smile on her smooth face. "Oh, no one here, Miss. We're quite safe inside the mansion." Her smooth palm covered Grey's knuckles where she clenched the coverlet. "Now you know my secret, as I know yours."

Grey swallowed past a lump in her throat. "I need to try to eat, but because of certain circumstances, well, eating might not go so well. It might be, um, messy."

Nettie straightened her shoulders. "I'll help, Miss." A frown snagged her pretty features. "Only you must keep this eating and leaking business a secret. I'm afraid it isn't beautiful at all."

Grey's mouth worked as she struggled to form a reply. Nothing appropriate came to mind.

Soon the maid continued. "Don't worry, I won't tell them. It'll be easier if they think you're some kind of unique porcie. You're pretty enough to pass for one of them. And when I'm done fixing you up, you'll be Beauty's Best all right. Now, what is it you run on? I can fetch oil from the tock quarters downstairs if you've grown stiff."

After a long-winded explanation of food and where it came from that drew more than one horrified exclamation from Nettie, Grey remembered the oat cake and apple in her coat pocket.

"Where are my clothes? I had food in one of the pockets."

The maid clicked her disapproval. "Your clothes were dirty. And not beautiful at all, I might add."

Grey rolled her eyes. "And that's all that matters, is it?"

Nettie nodded without a hint of amusement. "Of course it is. But I remember the items in your pocket. We saved them in case they were of value."

She bent and slid out a drawer in the elegant table by the bed. The apple rolled into sight at once, and Grey snatched it, biting into the wrinkled surface with barely a thought to potions. When she'd gnawed the shriveled fruit down to the core, she accepted the mangled oat cake Nettie held out and devoured every crumb.

They both jumped at a knock on the door. Fantine's voice called, "Is our guest fully animated yet?"

"Just a moment, Mistress Fantine." Nettie burst into action, brushing crumbs off the bedspread and tossing the apple core back into the drawer. Then the maid straightened into a rigid pose for a moment before darting around the footboard to hide the soiled vase beneath the bed.

Nettie moved toward the door but stopped and rotated back to face Grey. She wore an intense expression. "I won't tell them about you. I promise."

Grey started to answer, but Fantine's impatient call stopped her. A moment later the stunning porcie glided into the room, the cutaway skirt of her gown swishing behind her like a curtained backdrop for her legs. An adorable frown puckered her mouth.

"You are not even out of bed. I thought Nettie'd be arranging your hair by now." She swooped to a white lacquered wardrobe with stenciled pink roses and threw the paneled doors wide. The piece looked like it belonged in Granddad's shop. Grey glanced about the room. Was she somehow still inside Haward's Mercantile, or had she slipped into a different world?

The porcelain woman was busy rummaging through the cabinet when Grey doubled over. Pain gripped her stomach, and she clenched her teeth to keep from moaning. Nettie rushed to the bedside, her movements near silent. The maid's hand pressed into Grey's back, the metallic weight both foreign and comforting.

Grey forced herself to breathe and shifted back into a sitting position. Fantine's voice carried from within the wardrobe. She rambled about clothing, the back of her own elaborate dress spilling from the wardrobe as if the large cabinet vomited blue and gold satin.

Another wave of pain assaulted Grey. So this was it. She did carry the starvation trait. Soon Nettie's promise to keep her secret wouldn't matter. The truth would be all too evident. Grey pressed her lips between her teeth, her nostrils flaring with the effort to breathe through the spasm.

Nettie produced a white scrap of cloth and dabbed at Grey's forehead. The maid's voice whirred at a pitch almost inaudible, but Grey caught the occasional phrase. "Leaking again. Poor dear."

The sharp twinge eased. Despite the pain, the food she'd eaten stayed down. Grey fidgeted with the smooth texture of her satin coverlet as her father's stories of the deaths he'd witnessed returned. She imagined herself writhing on the bed, her body spewing her stomach contents. Another spasm twisted her abdomen as Fantine turned, but the redheaded beauty focused on the dresses draped over one arm. She glided about the room, hanging one exquisite costume after another on any available curtain rod or doorknob.

"Benedict is all but steaming with anticipation, my dear Grey. It was all I could do to keep him from coming here directly."

Fantine paused, her fingers hovering over a length of lavender fabric. Grey studied the other woman's expression in an attempt to distract herself from the ache in her belly.

Fantine's rosebud lips frowned, and her jeweled blue eyes faded, but then she rushed to arrange the shimmering dress over the carved footboard. Her gaze lifted to Grey and her face regained its sparkle.

Grey schooled her own features, and Nettie disguised her ministrations by arranging Grey's hair, pulling it this way and that as though pondering hairstyles.

Fantine bent to inspect the beading on the gown. "I convinced him that bringing you into the ballroom this evening after the day's governing duties are concluded would be such a grand and beautiful juxtaposition to your rather ugly arrival."

Nettie gave an embarrassed cough.

"Oh, not that it was your fault, dear." Fantine stretched a hand toward Grey. "It must've been awful, whatever happened to you. We're all eager for the tale. But first we must decorate you, mustn't we?"

She pushed away from the footboard to pace between the piles of finery. Grey took the opportunity to assess her condition. Her stomach ached but the pain had dulled. The apple and cake weren't fighting to leave her system, not yet anyway, and her forehead had stopped sweating. Maybe Granddad was right and the Defender blood she inherited from Father was strong enough to ward off the starving condition. Maybe.

Grey examined her limbs as Nettie helped her to the side of the bed. Where had this Defender condition come from? Of the immigrants from the Old Country, only her family and the Chemists were free of the affliction. Even the outsiders who flocked to Mercury for work, or to escape outbreaks, exchanged one form of suffering or another for a lifetime of potion dependence.

As Nettie and Fantine conversed, Grey positioned her hands around an imaginary ball in front of her torso as she'd seen Adante do. She closed her eyes and focused. Nothing. She certainly possessed no discernable magic.

Nettie's whisper broke through her concentration. "Are you well, Miss?"

The maid stood before her holding a cloth, two bottles, and a brush, ready to transform Grey into something the porcies found beautiful. She obeyed Nettie's gentle command to stand in the center of a thick circular rug before a gilded mirror so large it took up three-quarters of the wall space.

For a moment, Grey searched for signs of illness in her familiar reflection. She was pale, but some color remained in her cheeks. At least Fantine and Nettie had kept her well-hydrated. The other two women appeared in the mirror, standing on either side of her. Grey's eyes widened.

Nettie's head came only to Grey's shoulder. Even with her neat appearance and well-painted face, the tock faded, growing plain and shrunken in contrast to Fantine's splendor. The porcie stood an inch or two taller than Grey. Without her beaded high heels, Fantine would match Grey in height. Though by no means flawless, Grey's skin was smooth like Fantine's. Her hair bright and plentiful, unlike Nettie's twig-colored bun beneath her cap. Grey did indeed look more like a porcie than a tock.

She continued to gape at the mirror as Nettie and Fantine set to work. The tock brought a chair and prodded Grey to sit before applying her brush in efficient strokes. Fantine moved in and out of the mirror's boundaries, pausing to hold dresses close to Grey's face and debate their suitability with Nettie.

After what felt like hours, Grey's backside was stiff and her hair unrecognizable. She rubbed at her palm as Nettie pinned the last curl into a cluster on the back of her head.

"That's the hair all done." Nettie bustled over to the vanity, depositing the tools she'd used for Grey's elaborate hairstyle and retrieving a circular tray that she loaded with small pots, tubes, brushes, and applicators.

Grey sighed and dug her thumbnail into the pad of her left hand. She winced and flipped her hand over. A drop of blood welled from one of her scratches. Closer inspection revealed a thin, milky film covering each shallow cut. Glue.

A quick gasp on her right made Grey jump. She looked up to see Fantine hovering near and clenched her hand, but a moment too late. The porcie snatched her wrist. Grey stiffened at the woman's touch. But instead of the cold, glassy pressure she'd expected, Fantine's fingers were satiny smooth and warm. She pried Grey's fist open, examining the smear of blood.

Fantine dropped to her knees, still gripping Grey's wrist. Her glittering eyes hardened. "Such a beautiful color."

Grey went cold. She shrank from the porcie's nearness.

Fantine raised Grey's hand closer to her own face. "Such strange cracks." She pressed the tip of one butterfly-soft finger to the bleeding scrape on Grey's palm. "How does your jitter pump turn the water red?"

"I, um, I don't know." Grey suppressed a shudder as the porcie dropped her injured hand and lifted her own blood-smeared finger up for examination.

Fantine's eyes narrowed onto the red tip of her finger. "So pretty," she murmured. Her mouth opened. Fantine's finger hovered over her rosy lips for a second, and then darted, quick as a hummingbird, into her mouth.

Grey froze as the porcie's eyes closed then opened and focused on Grey's face. Nettie stood in Grey's peripheral vision, suspended in her task, her face stamped with horror.

But the porcie rose from her kneeling position, smoothing her bodice and setting her skirts right before starting for the wardrobe. "I think we'd best add gloves to tonight's ensemble, Nettie."

Grey gulped a breath of air and lowered her gaze to her palm. The decadent room and the two strange creatures within it faded, and Grey stood once again before the unused curio cabinet in her grandfather's darkened shop. Haimon held her wrist much like Fantine had, showing Grey her own blood as though it were the answer to some question he knew and she didn't. Then he'd pressed her hand to the lock and everything changed.

The pink room crystallized in Grey's vision once again. Fantine and Nettie continued with their project of dressing Grey as though nothing had happened. But Grey replayed Haimon's actions and heard his urgent command. "Blood is the way in and the key out. Find him. Find him and bring him back."

Find who? She glanced at Fantine and caught the shimmer of the woman's eyes like the sparkle of light on sequins. *Would* these creatures help her, even if they could?

ettie's hand snagged Grey's arm, tugging it loose from the clenched position Grey had adopted as she followed Fantine down a long, opulent gallery. She shot Nettie a "help me" look, but the tock nodded toward Fantine's rigid back, arranged her own mechanical body into a similar posture, and with a glare indicated Grey should do the same.

Sweat slicked Grey's palms, but she sucked in her stomach, left uncovered by the gray satin bodice of her gown, and took another wobbly step over the thick rug. Once Fantine discovered the delicate blue whorls circling Grey's belly button, she declared them "Beauty's Best" and redesigned a gown to display the "decoration."

The porcie had winked as she arranged the gray silk in a simple wrap style ending just beneath Grey's ribcage. "The perfect color for you, am I right?"

She couldn't deny the metallic shade suited her skin tone far better than Mercury's required crimson, but it took all her patience to submit to the beauty routine when somewhere her father faced death and her grandfather might already be lost.

Beneath the close-fitting skirt, Grey's knees locked. She forced herself to take a breath. Fantine's head jerked at the ragged sound, and Grey froze, her high heel sinking in the heavy pile of the carpet. She teetered, her ankle dipping toward the floor. Nettie shoved herself beneath Grey's arm and arrested her fall. Something white darted to Grey's cheeks, dabbed, and disappeared.

"No leaking," Nettie whispered, pocketing the cloth.

"May we proceed?" Fantine's musical voice carried an edge.

"My heel caught on the carpet."

Fantine smirked. "Good thing you didn't fall. You can't afford any more cracks, can you, my dear?" She lifted one long leg and twisted her foot, admiring her own beaded blue satin heel. She placed it carefully back on the floor and her hand glided up to cover her throat. "One risk worth taking, am I right?"

Grey didn't offer her thoughts on the subject of outlandish footwear. She busied herself with lifting her skirt and disengaging her shoe from the thickly woven burgundy rug. When they moved on, she resumed her role as the exotic porcie rescued from misfortune on the streets of Curio City.

Grey held her head up, ignoring the brush of the dress against her thighs and the tickle of air over skin she'd never exposed before. She'd do whatever it took to get back home. And if meeting this ridiculous Lord Blueboy got her a step closer to helping her father, then she'd smile for the pretty little thing and play the part until she figured out how to escape.

Fantine led them into another gallery, even finer than the one they'd left. Lush portraits of landscapes brimming with flowers and fruit trees almost hid the cream-and-gold papered walls. One painting in the corner behind a small circular table caught Grey's eye. She frowned at the squat vase and flowers in the picture. Hadn't Nettie brought an exact replica to her room? The maid's eyes surveyed the painting as well.

Nettie whisked over to the corner, reached up and plunged her hands into the artwork. Grey muffled a gasp as the painted scene rippled around the maid's hands. Nettie pulled the vase and flowers from the portrait, but even as she placed the arrangement in the center of the elegant table, a reproduction appeared in the picture.

The tock met Grey's gaze, opened her mouth and then snapped it shut. Her brown eyes held the sparkle of their shared secret. Grey clamped her own lips and swiveled back to her porcie hostess. An explanation of the miraculous painting would have to wait.

Fantine walked to a waist-high railing that opened the upper portion of the house to a view of the grand foyer below. Grey followed, sliding her hand along the smooth surface of the wood rail just as Fantine did. But the porcelain woman's fingers clenched the handrail despite her casual movements. Once again, her white hand darted to her high collar, tugging the fabric as if ensuring it covered her neck.

Below them, a fountain dominated the entrance hall. Instead of elegant marble statues like those surrounding the Chemist tower, a gleaming apparatus crowned this water feature. A metallic version of a giant inverted snail shell funneled water up from a shallow pool and into a graceful arc that curved back over the sculpture. A sizzle whispered amidst the tumble of the rushing water, and steam rose from the wide basin. The humid air pasted Grey's curls to her neck.

She tore her gaze from the spectacle in time to see Fantine halt a good six feet from the wide staircase connecting the gallery to the foyer. Grey tottered toward the flight of stairs, her heels clicking on the polished wood floor.

Fantine stopped her. "No, no, dear. Only tocks and lower porcies use the stairs."

Grey glanced around the room for Nettie. The maid had disappeared, but Grey hadn't seen her take the stairs. A tock in a plain suit now stood by a panel in the far wall.

Fantine waved a delicate hand in Grey's direction. "We'll take the lift. Over here."

The tock shifted the panel in the wall aside to reveal a tall metal gate, which he opened as Fantine approached. Tendrils of steam seeped from the floor around the base of the cage.

Fantine relied on the tock for assistance as she stepped inside the enclosure, but Grey declined when the servant offered his hand. Dodging a ribbon of steam, she tested the elevator floor with one foot and then the other. The surface beneath her felt solid enough. She ducked all the way in and trailed her fingers over the padded blue satin interior walls.

"Lovely, aren't they?" Fantine rested against the decadent inner panel as the tock closed the gate. "Benedict—Lord Blueboy—loves blue, as you might imagine. The north wing is mine to decorate, but most of the house, as you'll see, reflects his tastes." She smoothed the shiny sapphire fabric of her gown and winked at Grey. "As do I."

Grey looked away from the lurid spark in Fantine's eye and folded her arms over her naked midsection. When the porcie woman pressed a button, the elevator lurched into action. Grey whimpered as the motion rearranged her internal organs.

"Now don't be nervous, dear. Benedict is proud and exacting, yes, but he's taken an interest in you. He feels sorry for you." Fantine handed Grey a pair of long white gloves. "Wear these and none of your cracks will be visible. You've no reason to be ashamed."

Cover the scratches on her hands but leave her mark visible to everyone? Grey pulled the gloves on and almost wished for her stiff school uniform with its line of buttons from throat to waist.

The ride down was a chugging, jerky experience. Fantine braced herself in the corner with each shoulder pressed into the soft elevator lining. She clenched the handrail affixed to the wall.

Grey grasped the bar for balance but otherwise stood tall. Her limbs were weak and her head light, but she wasn't afraid of breaking like Fantine. Not here in this bizarre land of extravagant beauty or at home under the grip of the Chemists. What more could they take from her? The rock-like sensation flickered behind her belly button, and Grey dropped her hand from the railing.

The elevator jolted to a stop, but Grey kept her footing in the center of the padded cage, standing with head high and shoulders back as though she owned the mansion. Fantine stepped away from the wall, her eyes narrow and gleaming. The outer panel slid away and another tock opened the metal gate, but before Grey could move, Fantine snagged her arm, detaining her in the lavish cell. "You're a bit careless with yourself, aren't you, Miss Grey? I know there are some in our city who find risk-taking admirable, even attractive." Her voice hardened. "I assure you Lord Blueboy is not one of them. He scorns the Valor Society." The porcie's gaze whisked over Grey. "If you're here to make some kind of point, to flout the Designer with your recklessness, Benedict will see you punished."

Valor Society? Recklessness? All this because she hadn't clung to the rail on their ride down? Grey lowered her lids in case her boldness showed in her eyes. "I did not intend to flout anything, I assure you."

Her hostess ignored the protest and advanced. "You do not want to anger Benedict. Don't think that he won't send a porcie to Lower. He's done it before." She shuddered and a bit of her delicate persona returned. "All those exposed pipes and machines. The mindless tocks. You'd be cracked in half before the day was out."

Grey's chin tilted up, but she bit back her response. Whatever Fantine meant by "Lower," it didn't sound like a place that would get her closer to home. And until she knew more about Curio City and its inhabitants, she couldn't afford to reveal too much about who and what she really was.

Fantine seemed satisfied her scolding had put Grey in her place. The porcie's exquisite face softened, and she reached a hand out to rest on Grey's own gloved fingers. "As fragile as you are, my dear, due to your curious condition, it's a favor of the Designer that Benedict's soldiers found you. Whatever rough sorts you were mixed up with surely can't offer anything as magnificent as this."

She led the way out of the elevator and made a sweeping motion with one hand.

Grey had only glimpsed a third of the grand foyer from the gallery above. To her right lay the front of the house, with the shell fountain as the focal point to the entryway. Beyond it double doors stretched toward the ceiling, both framed by towering windows. Outside, dreary light revealed a courtyard with tall brick walls and outbuildings that obscured anything beyond. Topiaries and trimmed hedges guarded the front of the manor.

Fantine led Grey into the cavernous rear portion of the entrance hall, their heels clacking over the white marble floor. Like the gallery above, the walls were lined with breathtaking works of art, all depicting landscapes, flowers, or buildings of fascinating design. A grove of jeweled trees grew out of a recessed portion in the floor. Brown glass branches soared upward, and cut emerald leaves filtered light from a bank of windows on the far wall.

A tock moved amongst the trees. He wore black trousers and a white shirt and slipped between the glossy trunks with a zipping sound. He disappeared only to reappear in seconds on the outer edge of the glittering grove. In one hand he held a white cloth. More cleaning rags hung from his belt. He raised a feather duster to one of the trunks, and Grey stifled an exclamation. The duster was attached to his arm like a hand.

Without giving Grey a moment to recover her wits, the tock began to stretch. The zipping sound accompanied the elongating of his body as his limbs extended, changing him from an average figure to a pulled-taffy version of a man. He skimmed the edge of the outer tree, dusting and polishing the very top branches. As they drew closer, Grey studied the tock's metallic skin visible beneath the cuff of his now short pant leg. The smooth scale-like surface of his legs reminded her of snake skin.

"Come, Grey. We mustn't keep Benedict waiting." Fantine motioned for her to follow, but more masterpieces awaited.

Lavish tapestries, sculptures of animals, some glassy-smooth and others rough and multifaceted, and intricate contraptions part machine, part artwork decorated the foyer. A network of light fixtures illuminated each work of art. Grey lingered at each new discovery, but Fantine strutted toward an imposing door of dark, paneled wood.

Her hostess stopped, one hand hovering above the door handle, and glanced over her shoulder. "I'll just pop in and make sure the assembly members have gone and Benedict is ready to entertain us."

The porcie woman turned and then staggered backward as the door opened from within. A tock dressed in an impeccable suit complete with waistcoat and shiny black shoes emerged from the room.

Fantine's hands flew out for balance before she regained her composure. "Crack you, Drakon, you little imbecile. I might've fallen."

Grey expected the slight man to bow and beg forgiveness as Nettie would've done, but the tock held his rigid posture. He spoke in a flat voice. "I meant no harm, Mistress Fantine. His lordship asked me to waylay you."

"I beg your pardon?" Fantine straightened her shoulders, thrusting her chest out.

Drakon didn't back down but held his neutral expression. He looked neither old nor young but had generic features, as though he were made to represent any man.

Fantine reached to open the door, but Drakon rested a hand on the brass frame of the handle. "I'm sorry, Mistress Fantine. Lord Blueboy wishes Miss Grey to appear alone. He asked me to convey his greetings to you and to, ah . . ." The tock's monotone voice faded. His eyes slid from Fantine's face to a spot of empty air above her shoulder, but he plunged ahead with his instructions. "He bade me tell you to proceed to evening sip. He will escort Miss Grey tonight."

With that, Drakon slipped away. Fantine didn't storm through the door, but stood still, her shoulders drooping with every passing second. Finally she turned, her expression arranged in a lovely mask. She held up one hand, her polished nails tapping the door, and offered a polite smile.

"His lordship will see you now."

Fantine swished away, her sensuous skirt swaying behind her.

Grey faced the door. Her hands were clammy against her bare stomach. When had she covered herself again?

She glanced around the entry hall. All was silent—even the tock who'd cleaned the trees was gone. A door closed, most likely Fantine slipping into one of the many rooms. Grey was alone. And the man waiting for her held all the power in this city.

Whit's face, twisted in pain, flared before her eyes. Her father's face with his wide blue eyes and square chin followed. She couldn't think of his face without seeing her grandfather's as well. But the face that followed—she hadn't allowed herself to dwell on it for months. Grey's knees buckled. She clenched the door handle and forced herself upright. Banner's face, wide and strong like her father's but with her mother's dark, serious eyes. Banner. Why did her brother come to mind now when she needed strength, not the horrible void his memory opened?

Grey let her hands drop to her sides. She wasn't the little girl Banner tried to protect. And she wasn't the one recovering from a striping or detained in a punishment facility, even if she deserved the blame. No. She was here, in this mysterious place, with a job to do. She positioned both hands against the door and shoved.

A large room, richly appointed in dark brown and pale blue, opened before her. No lights burned in the wall sconces, but a wavering yellow glow spilled from a burnished brass lamp onto a broad desk in the corner of the room.

Ten wingback chairs formed a circle in the center of the chamber. Grey crept toward them, craning her neck to see if Lord Blueboy waited in one like a stern uncle in a story. She pressed her hands against her thighs to keep from wrapping her middle in a protective hug.

Movement flickered behind a pair of glass doors that opened to a veranda. Heavy air, dripping with the scent of green things, seeped into the room, reminding her of the greenhouses where Chemist scientists bred their twisted plants.

She edged around the high-backed chairs, lost in the shadows of the room for a moment as the furniture blocked the light from the french doors.

As she emerged the skin on her arm prickled. A silhouette appeared in the doorway, dark against the backdrop of the veranda. A man stood with his shoulder resting on the door frame, his long legs crossed at the ankles.

Grey blinked, struggling to take in the porcie before her. Where was the stuffy aristocrat she'd expected? This man with his startling blue eyes, languid half smile, and tailored indigo shirtwaist looked nothing like a pampered monarch. In fact he looked nothing like any man she'd ever seen before. She was staring just as she'd stared at Fantine. Could one ever grow accustomed to such beauty?

He offered a mock bow. "Miss Grey, I'm relieved to see you animated."

His cool voice cut through the humid atmosphere invading the room. She nodded at the porcie, distracted by the way his skin crinkled at the edge of his smile then smoothed back into porcelain perfection.

Her voice betrayed her nerves. "Lord Blueboy?"

He inclined his head in a charming show of deference. "As my guest, I insist you call me Benedict, Miss Grey." His smile changed to a wicked smirk. "It will make Fantine fairly drip with jealousy."

Grey started to object but caught herself. He was teasing, of course. She took a steadying breath. "Benedict, please call me Grey."

A spark of interest flashed in his eyes when she spoke her name, but he cloaked the expression and gestured toward the terrace. "Will you join me for a chat before evening sip?"

When he didn't move from his casual position in the doorway, Grey stiffened and prepared to slip by him, taking up as little space as possible. He smiled and lowered his long, coal-colored lashes as she neared. An image of Adante's face flashed, but she shook off the memory. Just because Blueboy possessed power didn't mean he was cruel like the Chemists. She relaxed and stepped over the threshold onto the stone patio outside.

A strange sensation drew her up. Warm pressure tingled at the small of her back. Eyes wide and mouth open, Grey turned to look into Benedict's handsome face. He was touching her.

She schooled her face as he guided her through the door, his fingers smooth and strong against her bare back.

Grey's heels clicked as she strode to the center of the veranda and out of Benedict's reach. He followed, standing so close she could've touched him with a flick of her finger.

When she lifted her gaze, she caught him searching the periphery of the walled courtyard outside his towering estate. His eyes whisked back to her face and he took a step back.

The sigh of relief died in her throat as he began circling her, eyes traveling up and down her body. When he stopped in front of her and held out his hand, Grey merely gawked at the pale palm.

"May I?"

Grey raised an eyebrow. "May you what?"

He shook his head as if dismissing something not worth his time then snatched her hand with his own. He stripped her glove off and let it fall to the ground. Smooth fingers skimmed the flesh of her arm, and patches of prickling heat bloomed wherever he touched.

Grey's voice shook. "What are you doing?" She drew in a steadying breath and followed the progress of his fingers. Should she pull away or was this an accepted Curio custom?

He paused to study the scratches on her palm, then captured her left hand and removed her glove to perform the same inspection.

Still cradling her hand in his, he met her eyes. "These cracks are accidental, not inflicted. Why don't you have any lines?"

Trapped in Lord Blueboy's gaze, Grey forced herself to respond. "Lines? What do you mean?"

His eyes tightened. Molded lips quirked downward. "No games necessary between us, my dear. I know you're from outside Curio City."

The breath in Grey's lungs froze. She couldn't form an answer. Benedict's face flashed with triumph. His gaze lowered to her exposed midsection, and she clenched her hands to keep from covering her mark.

"Is it because of this?" He bent for a closer look. Grey sucked in her breath as he brought his face near her torso. "Does this symbol make you invulnerable to the others?" One long finger reached to trace the blue web circling her navel, but Grey shrank back.

"W-what others?"

He straightened, lips pressed in an irritated line. "The cracks. The ugly cracks. He has them"—Benedict skimmed his own arm from wrist to neck—"everywhere."

Grey gulped a breath. "Who? Who has them?"

"The gray one. The man who comes every few arbor cycles for a report on the city."

Her heart jolted. Was this man the one she needed to find? She opened her mouth to question Benedict, but the porcie's next words crushed her hopes.

"His hair and eyes are the color of iron. Such a drab, gray creature. And those lines—everywhere!"

"Haimon? Haimon has been here?"

Blueboy turned away as if bored with the conversation. "I don't know his name. Or where he comes from," he said over his shoulder. He walked toward the edge of the veranda.

Grey took in her surroundings. Behind her the mansion loomed in reddish brick and black iron. The secluded veranda where they stood formed a circular platform against the side of the house. Narrow steps led into a side yard hedged by tapered trees. Beyond the uniform line of trees a high wall ran out of Grey's view toward the front and back of the property.

Only a gradual dimming of light like a winter afternoon hinted at the time of day. A layer of fog hung high overhead, blocking anything beyond the near environs.

Lord Blueboy halted at the carved stone trellis edging the veranda and splayed one hand over the flat surface. Grey shivered and willed away the returning sensation of his fingers on her skin, like marble sheathed in silk. The porcie settled into a pose of casual elegance. From the longish dark hair that whisked over his ears and neck to the neat proportions of shoulders, back, and waist, Benedict carried himself with a Chemist's assurance. The similarity had her searching for others. Were the porcies capable of magic?

After a moment, he turned to face her. Leaning against the ledge, he stretched his hands along the railing on either side of him. Metal glinted from beneath the line of his shirt where it pulled away from his chest. A chain of some sort? She shifted her gaze from the smooth gleam of the porcie's collarbone to his face.

Benedict quirked a half smile as if pleased by her scrutiny. "Are you the new overseer of the city? Another *gray* caretaker? I confess I much prefer you already."

Grey shook her head. "I don't know anything about Haimon's business here. I need to . . ." She held back the words. Perhaps there were things Lord Blueboy shouldn't know.

Benedict's gaze sharpened. "He didn't send you here?"

"Well, he did, in a manner of speaking."

"Why? What does he seek?" Benedict's hands clenched on the balustrade for a moment, but then he relaxed his long fingers and resumed his casual pose. "What does he want? Is our beautiful city not to his satisfaction?"

Grey took a step forward. "I told you, I don't know anything about that. I-I came here in a hurry. There wasn't much time for explanation."

"I see. And what of the Mad Tock?"

"Who?"

He leaned toward her. "The Mad Tock was spotted the night my soldiers found you. They saw him leave you in the street."

The footsteps. The wings. The scent of machine oil mixed with something warm and spicy flooded her memory. "I thought there was someone, but I didn't see—"

"Then the Mad Tock didn't bring you here?"

"No, I . . . I was alone when I came to Curio."

"And how are you to return?"

She swallowed past an itch in her throat and lifted her chin. "I will return when my job is done."

A scowl darkened Benedict's perfect features, but he pushed away from the railing and donned a smile. "Then we'll have to make your stay as pleasant as possible." He sauntered toward Grey, hand extended.

Clearly laws were different in Curio. Still Grey cringed from the contact. Benedict's smile remained in place even as her hesitation lengthened. He inclined his head toward the house. The murmur of voices and the familiar clatter of tableware filtered through the open door behind her.

"It's time for evening sip." Benedict offered his elbow. "If you'll allow me to escort you?"

She ignored the goose bumps that rose on her skin and slid her arm through the porcie's.

He covered her hand with his and led her through the room with the circle of chairs and out into the museum-like hall. His arm beneath her hand was firm, and the cool fingers that rested on hers drew tiny circles of frost on her skin.

What would it be like to live without laws preventing touch? The memory of Whit's arms holding her brought warmth to her cheeks. She shifted her scrutiny from a sculpture of a winged horse to the man beside her.

Benedict's attention centered on a doorway ahead that led off of the gallery. The double doors were flung open, and tocks in black-and-white uniforms bustled in and out.

Grey stumbled, dangling on Benedict's arm a second before righting herself.

The porcie's head swiveled in her direction. Something was wrong. His movements were stiff and jerky.

Grey shivered as Benedict's dazzling smile twitched into place.

"I do apologize, Miss Grey. I'm afraid we lingered on the veranda a bit too long."

Grey stared at him. They'd stopped walking and he seemed . . . frozen.

His head jerked to face forward and he called out, "Della, here."

A tiny tock woman who'd just slipped out from the open doorway changed her course and scurried over to stand before Lord Blueboy.

"Yes, my lord?"

He glanced down at her, something like boredom in his eyes. "I've cooled."

"Shall I fetch a cup, my lord?"

"I've no wish to draw attention."

The tock, Della, bobbed her head. "Of course not, my lord." She fumbled with the buttons on the cuff of her white sleeve, exposing a panel in the metallic skin of her wrist. She winced as she pressed it and the metal slid open a notch. Clear liquid bubbled from the slit. She raised the leaking arm to Benedict's mouth.

Grey's stomach rolled. She turned, catching the maid's widened eyes before the grandeur of the foyer swam out of focus. She saw Whit, blood seeping from endless cuts. A scream built in her chest, but if she opened her mouth her meager meal would rise.

"Miss?" The whisper thrummed low in Grey's ears.

Filling her lungs, Grey straightened, her hand still tucked in the crook of Benedict's stiff arm. A faint hiss sounded deep within the porcie's chest.

Della was buttoning her sleeve, her dull eyes fixed on Grey. "Are you well, Miss?" She paused in her task. "Fully animated?"

Grey jerked her head in a nod.

"Very well, then." The maid adjusted her sleeve and scuttled away.

Benedict shuddered, sending a tremble through Grey's arm. The fingers over hers grew warm, and the porcie took a step forward and another. He didn't move his head to look at her, but his arms and legs moved with the fluidity she'd observed on the veranda. Grey staggered along until she managed to match his stride in her unfamiliar heels.

What had just happened? What kind of . . . ? Benedict had drunk from Della like some storybook vampire. Grey set her jaw and tried to bring some rationality to the ghastly display. It wasn't blood. It was likely water. And since tocks ran on clockwork, not water, Della probably carried the reserve for just such an occasion. But it had hurt the little maid.

She'd seen pain in the tock's eyes. Grey's skin crawled under the porcie's heated fingers.

Benedict paused before moving into the doorway. A tock in an embellished uniform stood just within the entrance. Beyond him stretched an expansive room with a gleaming floor reflecting strings of light like glowing pearls thrown over the surface of a glassy lake. The liveried tock nodded to Benedict then turned toward the interior of the room.

His mechanized call reminded Grey of the metal soldiers. "Lord Blueboy and his honored guest."

Benedict ushered her through the double doors into the cavernous room. Above them, huge chandeliers spread tentacle-like arms dripping crystals. Half a dozen miniature fountains tinkled and shimmered on small, high tables arranged throughout the room. Goblets circled the water features and lined the edges of the room on narrow buffet boards festooned with shimmering gauze.

Grey's eyes widened as she took in the porcies milling about the sparkling room. Exquisite faces peered from under elaborately styled hair. The women wore shades of gold, silver, and white, the light so dazzling on their shining clothes that it almost hurt to look at them. But she couldn't look away. Many of the men wore lighter shades as well, their pale grays and muted tans mixing with the elegant black suits of others.

A spot of color caught Grey's attention as Fantine emerged from a glittering cluster of ladies, her blue gown a focal point amongst the pale splendor.

She rushed over, a long-stemmed glass nestled in one of her tapered white hands and a frown dragging her pink lips.

"There you are." She attached herself to Benedict's other arm but shot him a cool look. "You've not changed for sip."

Benedict moved amongst the groups of porcies, smiling and nodding. Grey caught the low words he flung at Fantine. "I don't care much for your themed evening sips, my dear."

He led Grey and Fantine to one of the raised tables in the center of the room. A tiny fountain bubbled in the center, and Grey kept her eyes on the feature. But she didn't miss the pout in Fantine's next words.

"All is not lost. You are wearing blue, of course. We shall still stand out as Beauty's Best among our fair guests."

Benedict shifted as though observing the milling porcies, but Grey heard him mutter, "Oh, thank the Designer. Our evening will not be ruined because I've forgotten to change."

Following Fantine's example, Grey snagged a glass from the table, dipped it into the fountain, and drank. Water. It felt good going down but refused to settle in her stomach. The oat cake and apple were a distant memory. She'd need something more than water, and soon. Grey gripped the edge of the tabletop as the periphery of the room quivered.

The porcies gathered in clusters or walked between fountains, dipping their glasses in and sipping as they conversed. But jewel eyes darted in Grey's direction, or fixed on her person in bold stares almost punishable back home in Mercury.

"They find you fascinating." Fantine leaned over the table, the bodice of her dress straining at her bosom. Grey's hand moved to her own chest, but she stopped short of yanking the neckline of her gown higher.

Fantine edged around the table until she stood by Grey. The porcie rested her delicate hand on Grey's shoulder and inclined the tower of burnished red curls toward Grey's own piled-up hair.

"They've never seen anything like you and are eager to hear your tale."

A group of females floated by, their movements slow and graceful. Grey stared at the display of elegant attire and exposed skin. The light twinkled off satin, gems, and teeth.

She leaned into Fantine and murmured, "You're all so beautiful. How—"

"Of course we are. We were designed to be beautiful, were we not? It's our duty to make our creator proud, to be the most beautiful that we can be. Beauty's Best."

"And the tocks?"

Fantine offered a delicate snort. "As long as they function properly, they please the Designer, don't you think? But that doesn't mean they shouldn't try to look as pleasing as they can. Why, Nettie is almost presentable, isn't she? The poor dear does try."

Fantine rambled on, but Grey's attention followed the striking figure of Benedict as he moved throughout the room. He'd left their table after a quick sip from the fountain and now slid from group to group. The men bowed and the women gave him looks that made Grey blush. The heat on her cheeks increased as Benedict sought her gaze. All the porcies clustered around him followed suit, smiling at her as he spoke.

Grey flinched as the white fingers on her shoulder tightened. Fantine watched Benedict's progress as well, and the lovely porcie's eyes glittered like shards of crystal.

Turning away from Benedict's probing stare, Grey launched into what she hoped would be a welcome topic. "How long have you and Lord Blueboy been, er, that is to say . . . how long have you cared for one another?"

Fantine's brows nipped together and she scrutinized Grey. "I've been Benedict's mistress for five arbor cycles now. Do you not remember the ball welcoming me to his estate? Even the most remote villages received a detailed account."

She leaned in, her smooth face inches from Grey's. "Where *are* you from? Beyond the countryside? Surely not the Glass Forest."

Lord Blueboy's raised voice cut off Grey's response.

"Welcome, my friends. Fantine and I are honored by the beauty you bring to our home. Surely the Designer is pleased by your efforts."

He'd moved to a stage at the back of the large room. Behind him chairs and instruments waited for musicians. The porcies gathered in a semicircle around the platform while tocks whisked into the room, silently removing the tables and fountains.

Following Fantine's lead, Grey drifted toward the assembled porcies. Benedict's eyes followed her. He wore a small smile that told a story of closeness and familiarity, a story she didn't know. The porcies smirked.

"I know you're all anxious to meet our lovely guest." Benedict held out his hand. "Grey, would you join me please."

Her feet refused to move. Glints of light bombarded her, like dozens of lamps lit at once. Benedict smiled and beckoned.

Grey glanced down and didn't recognize her own body. Who was this woman wrapped in the thinnest layer of silver silk? Her cheeks flamed as though she stood naked in a morality service.

A jab to her back jolted her out of the horrible daydream.

"Go up there," Fantine whispered. "Benedict is waiting for you."

After one uneasy step in her towering heels, Grey regained command of her limbs and moved through the crowd. The porcies smiled and nodded. Smooth figures in elaborate clothing pressed close, and warm fingers touched her arms and back. Grey forced herself not to recoil. The heat of the crush made her head ache. She almost thanked Benedict when he met her at the stairs and took her hand as she climbed the two steps.

He led her to the center and rested one hand on her lower back as they faced the sparkling circle. Grey tightened the muscles in her stomach, arching her back away from Benedict's satiny fingertips. He ignored the subtle movement and loosed his most charming smile on the assembly.

"Grey joins us from one of the southernmost settlements, near the borders of the Glass Forest."

She forced a nod of agreement to accompany Benedict's lie.

He turned toward her, his smile softening. "Her unusual yet enchanting condition kept her prisoner in her home for all our time here in Curio."

His hand slid up to grip her elbow as he faced the porcies again and raised his voice. "She feared that we would reject her for her uncommon design, but as for me, I have never seen such amazing craftsmanship."

Lord Blueboy took a step back and motioned toward Grey as though showcasing a rare piece at an auction. "I declare her Beauty's Best and commend her bravery as she walks among us."

A murmur spread through the gathering, punctuated by low words and a few harsh notes.

"Now, now, no politics tonight, my friends." Benedict silenced the growing unease with a tone that carried both friendly reproof and unmistakable command. "I speak of courage as an ideal—a quiet and strong condition of the mind—not the foolhardy whims you've heard whispered in the streets. Grey is cautious and mindful, as we all strive to be. I hope you'll welcome her as Fantine and I have and appreciate the new beauty she brings to our city."

An odd sound, low and ringing, spread from the back of the room, growing louder with each second. Grey searched the crowd, their stunning faces almost blinding in the white light. After a moment she noticed the movement of their hands. Each porcie rubbed his or her palms together in slow circles. Applause?

Benedict gave her the slightest of nods and tilted his dark head toward the crowd.

Was she expected to speak? Apparently not. After an almost smooth curtsy, she allowed Benedict to lead her from the stage.

Musicians filed into the row of chairs, each dressed in black clothing.

"Their music is their beauty tonight." Benedict's whisper came on a warm puff of steam that settled on her ear and neck like dew.

A thrill zinged through her veins, raising goose bumps, weakening her knees, and troubling her heart. When a many-layered hum swelled from the stage, she welcomed the distraction from Blueboy's nearness. The perfect note filled the room and throbbed within Grey's chest before the instruments broke out of the unified sound, each somehow distinct yet perfectly blended. Percussion and brass paraded while strings and wind built monuments of resonance. Grey held her breath. She could listen to this forever if her heart could bear the sweetness. She strained forward, aching to join the sound.

Smooth fingers glided over her upper arm and she whirled, stunned by the grace of her own movement. Benedict captured her hand, extending her arm into a perfect line. His other hand circled around her back and rested near her shoulder blade.

And they were moving. No, they were floating. The music hollowed Grey then filled her. Benedict's blue eyes magnetized hers. Around and around the room she drifted, twirling away from him only to be anchored back into the frame of his body. Light glinted off the other porcie couples, an ever-shifting pattern in Grey's peripheral vision. She couldn't blink. It was all so beautiful.

A spot of black flickered before her eyes. She almost stumbled. A cottony cloud filled her brain, muffling her thoughts. Deep within her, hunger stretched like a yawning chasm. No, not now. She breathed in the delicious music.

A clatter sounded from elsewhere in the house. The noise jarred her fuzzy brain, repeating over and over as if demanding her attention.

Benedict's gaze tore away from her.

Grey wobbled, her head spinning as a moan slipped from her lips.

Dancing couples broke apart. Someone far away shrieked.

Grey was sliding into a dark place. Diving into blackness. The hungry chasm opened wide to swallow her.

A dusty, faintly sweet scent filled Grey's nostrils.

Her stomach growled and she came fully awake. Darkness washed the bedclothes of their rosy color. She shivered as a breeze skimmed the sticky layer of sweat on her skin.

A rustle.

She bolted upright.

The figure in her room froze halfway between her bed and the tall, open windows, his face turned toward the freedom of the outdoors.

"Who are you?" Grey squinted at the strange silhouette. A bulky shape protruded from his shoulders and covered his back to his waist. What appeared to be a headdress composed of long feather-like coils sprang from the back of his head, sticking up at angles and cascading over his shoulders. His metallic attributes glimmered even in the dark. He was bigger than any of the tocks she'd seen. And misshapen.

Grey struggled to rise, hampered by the constricting dress twisted around her legs. Her heartbeat raced. "I said, 'Who are you?'"

She strained to hear his voice. When the mechanized whir of tock speech followed, it crushed a vague hope growing in her chest.

"I left you something." His head swiveled ever so slightly over his shoulder but the gloom distorted the lower portion of his face. Or did he wear a mask?

She glanced around her room. A quick tread vibrated through the bed beneath her and into her bones.

He was gone. A whooshing noise faded into the night air outside Grey's window.

Blaise dashed onto the veranda, bounded to the railing, and jumped. The moment of falling sent thrills chasing through his body. Or maybe the buzz in his veins had more to do with the girl he'd just left.

He punched the lift button on his steam pack, and the wings spread out on either side of him, leveling his fall into a downward glide. Shadowed ground neared and the sounds of the disturbed household carried closer. He yanked on the bellow cord. Once. Twice. Three times. The cinderite pellets in the chamber should still be warm. He hadn't lingered in Blueboy's mansion. Even though he'd wanted to.

A shout rang from the corner of the great house. Mechanical. One of the serving tocks, which meant he'd been spotted.

He pumped the cord again. The whoosh of air and steam filled his ears just as his foot touched ground. He ran straight for the high back wall, taking flight just in time. Accompanied by the faint, high-pitched squeal of steam as it coursed through the tubing and activated the pistons in the joints of his wings, Blaise sailed over the wall and flew over the city, leaving Lord Blueboy's mansion behind.

Light and color burst in the streets outside Blueboy's high walls. The homes, galleries, and halls of the town center bustled with the highest class of porcie, parading their splendor for each other to see. None of them looked up as Blaise careened over the streets.

Once he'd gained altitude, he rubbed his heels together, disengaging the clamps that fastened the fins on each boot. The canvas stabilizers expanded, and the buffeting wind around his legs calmed into a smooth stream.

Blaise fled the glare of Curio City's nightlife, cutting south through the ever-present layer of fog toward the factory district on the edge of the Shelf. He pulled his goggles from their perch above his forehead, fitted them over his eyes, and settled into steady flight. His mechanized wings beat a slow rhythm powered by the constant flow of warm air from his steam pack.

A smile tugged the corner of his mouth. He'd like to see Benedict's perfect face now. The little porcie king probably leaked all over himself at the intrusion. The maid he'd startled had screamed like her key'd been stolen.

But what had happened to *her*—the girl in the north wing? His stomach flipped and heat burned his cheeks despite the rush of air. Was she ill? Was she a prisoner?

The face he glimpsed in the street two nights ago flashed in his memory: eyes closed, lips parted. Lips like his. Skin like his. A second sighting confirmed it. His brain bulged with the reality of *her*. A still body on the bed. All that hair spilling out onto the pillow. Her voice, lower than the porcie and tock females, thinned by concern but not yet weak with starvation. She wouldn't suffer like he had. He'd made sure of that.

He changed his course to the southeast. The hollow pit in his stomach was only a memory, and the bread and cheese in his pockets would soon banish the current small pang. He left thoughts of starvation in the vapor behind him and scanned the familiar horizon for the hulking shape of the warehouse.

A small green light burned in the far upper corner of the darkened building. Blaise frowned and increased his speed. Callis's signal pulled him forward. He was needed at home.

He came in fast, only twisting the gauge to ease off the steam when the factory's roof appeared below him. His boots thudded onto the flat rooftop and he ran a few steps, scrabbling to a halt six feet from the stall-like structure providing access to the building below. He pushed his goggles to the top of his head and unfastened the grid covering his mouth.

Callis stood by the doorway, a sliver of faint light from the stairwell below glinting off his metal hand.

"Did you find her?"

"Yes." Blaise jabbed the lift button and his wings retracted. "She's safe for now. The light?"

Callis reached to open the door he'd left ajar. "A child. Porcie. His leg is shattered. The boy's keepers are merchants. One of their shop tocks brought them here."

Blaise ducked into the building, pausing to fumble with the straps of his pack. Callis stepped behind him and gripped the bulky apparatus, waiting for Blaise to shuck out of his harness.

"What do you make of them, the keepers?"

Steam sighed from the cooling pack as Callis set it in a corner of the stairwell. Or was it Callis who sighed? Blaise turned to meet the mismatched eyes.

Callis shrugged, his shirt and jacket masking the whir of his mechanized left arm. "The man is curious. The woman is hysterical."

Blaise trudged down the first staircase, pulling his arms close to his body as the tight space closed in on him. Callis's light step followed him.

"And the child?" Blaise shot the question over his shoulder as they descended.

"Finally cooling, thank the Designer."

The woman's wails tore at Blaise's ears before he reached the door to his workroom. He stepped into the office-turned-surgery and took a deep breath. The lights were off, but Blaise maneuvered around the huge center table and avoided the cluttered shelves lining the room. He kicked a rolling stool out of his way and stepped into the cavernous open space of the warehouse floor.

The porcie couple huddled on chairs near the entrance of the abandoned furniture factory. A small form rested on a bench beside them. Strange clinking sounds accompanied the woman's weeping.

Blaise strode across the room, ignoring their gasps, and knelt by the child. The ghost of a grimace marred the boy's face, but his expression settled into a blank stare as Blaise touched his cold, smooth hand.

"You're him?" The merchant's words tapped at Blaise as he cautiously shifted the child's form.

"You can repair our little Finnegan?"

The tinkling sound increased, drawing Blaise's focus. The woman fingered something in her lap. Her sobs choked into gurgles, and she lifted one hand to point at Callis.

"Will Finnegan be like him? Oh, George, I don't want Finnegan to be like him!" She collapsed against her husband, her hands returning to rummage through the mound of chinking pieces in her lap. In the dim light, the scraps looked flesh-toned.

Blaise gave Callis a nod and watched his friend's retreating back. He moved slowly, perhaps giving the porcie couple time to prepare. Blaise took a breath as Callis reached the knob on the wall and began to twist it. Orange light quivered in the sconces on the walls, creeping nearer and nearer until the illumination reached Blaise. He turned back to the couple; their perfectly molded features stretched in shock.

The man recovered his voice first. "You're no glueman. Who . . . What are you?"

Blaise straightened his back, allowing the porcies to take in his height, build, and his foreign features.

"I'm the one who can fix your child. If you'll let me." He curled his lip at the shards of Finnegan's leg gathered like hairpins in the woman's lap. "That rubble is useless now, but I can make him better." He twisted to the right as Callis came up beside him. "I think Callis here will tell you that being half porcie and half tock isn't half bad."

The woman's shriek drowned out Blaise's chuckle.

Blaise found a strip of red cloth and used it to tie his hair back. Then he rummaged through the tools on the narrow counter against the wall, keeping his back to the slab in the center of the room. His thoughts followed Callis on his errand. Would his friend go down to Cog Valley for parts? He should have told him to go straight to Old Reese in the northern stacks. The junk dealer owed Blaise for cleaning a clogged gear in his chest last week. He half turned, a whim to dart out of the factory and into the night pulling him from the workroom. No, Callis was faster. The modified porcie would bring back exactly what they needed to do the job in half the time Blaise took for similar missions.

Once he'd assembled a selection of bolts, screws, and fittings, Blaise retrieved several lengths of thin copper tubing from where they hung on the workshop wall. He estimated rather than turning around to measure.

A rumble in his stomach put a halt to his preparations. He dug in his pocket and yanked out the crumbling roll he'd stolen from a painting in Blueboy's servant quarters. A sharp scent mixed with the faint, sweet odor of machine oil ever present in his workshop. He closed his eyes and bit into the bread. If he ignored the smell that told him he was eating paint, the food tasted like nothing. He chewed and swallowed, appeasing the gnawing in his gut. Would *she* get past the smell and manage to down whatever food she retrieved from a painting? At least now she knew where to get sustenance.

He closed his eyes and concentrated on the startled expression she'd worn when she caught him sneaking out of her room. Who was this girl? Why had she come?

The scrape of the heavy warehouse door jarred him back to the present. He tensed and slid his hand toward a bulky wrench. The hum of machinery muffled by clothing set him at ease. Callis.

Blaise snagged a stained canvas apron from a hook on the wall and threw it over his head, not bothering to tie the strings. He turned in time to see Callis step through the workroom door, arms loaded with parcels.

"Are you ready?" Callis deposited his burden and unwrapped the first package. "I went to Harbinger's and Old Reese's, then I looked in on the Wind-Up. Seree had closed up already, but she said she'd come in the morning and help us talk to the boy's keepers."

Callis's gaze passed over Blaise and settled on the small body arranged on the metal table. Blaise looked at the child too, forcing his eyes not to see a dead body but a statue. He took a deep breath and moved over to the patient.

"He'll have to hide from now on," Blaise said. A wave of energy passed through his veins, hinting at another possible solution, but he ignored it.

Callis joined him at the edge of the table. "Smaller gears are quieter, and once the steam is going well, the workings will be near silent." He laid his metal hand on the white forehead. "And the children don't care so much."

Blaise pressed his knuckles onto the cold steel table. "And what if his keepers don't return tomorrow?"

Callis stepped away and retrieved his own heavy apron. "Then we'll find him new keepers who aren't so uppity. Seree will help."

Knots bunched in Blaise's shoulders. He snaked a hand under the thick cords of his hair and rubbed the tight spots in his neck. "Our modifieds are getting too numerous to hide, except in Cog Valley. I hate sending the little ones there."

"So we stop hiding." Callis's challenge, disguised in casual tones, triggered a familiar argument.

They moved around each other, Callis cutting away the porcie boy's trouser leg and Blaise readying the handheld grinder. When Callis plunged into schemes for cutting off the water supply to Curio City's wealthy neighborhoods, Blaise flipped a switch and the grinder whizzed into action. Callis flinched and backed away from the inanimate child.

The buzz prevented further conversation and cut off all distraction. Focusing on the jagged line where Finnegan's leg had broken off, Blaise blocked out his friend's talk of revolution, the doubt that always surfaced when he repaired a porcie, and the image of a girl, stretched out in sleep.

He left the workroom dark except for the slow light of coming day. Callis retired to sip. The repaired porcie child lay frozen on the slab. What would he think of his new limb when they reanimated him?

Blaise climbed the stairs built for slender tocks. His shoulder grazed the wall, and he rolled and flexed the muscles in his back, fighting the need to stretch out his arms. Maybe he could risk a flight into the country later today. A blip of excitement accompanied the thought of wide green fields slipping beneath him. The roads to the outlying villages were seldom used and the animals stood motionless, forever waiting to be wound or reanimated. Maybe he'd start up a flock of sheep just to watch the country porcies fuss over the damage to their gardens.

As he reached the third story, morning light filtered through the dirty windows of the spacious attic room. Day seeped into Curio City as though someone turned a dial, increasing the gray light by increments.

Blaise strode over creaking floorboards, his boots sending dust and wood fibers up into the air in little puffs. He checked the signal light—Callis had turned it off—before moving to the next window and on down the line of small glass squares that illuminated his living quarters. When he reached the last window, he stopped.

Blueboy's mansion wasn't visible from the factory, not even from his attic. That was a good thing, of course. But how much longer could he stay hidden from the ruling porcie? How much longer could he repair the tocks and porcies who came to him, talk revolution with Callis at the Wind-Up, and dodge the tin battalions patrolling the city?

Blaise turned from the view of the waking city. The mattress in the corner called to him. Fatigue weighted his eyelids and wrapped his muscles. He crossed the floor, kicking his boots off somewhere near a support beam and scraping his knuckles on the low ceiling as he pulled off his shirt. He let it fall then yanked the scrap of fabric out of his hair, freeing the long coils so they fell down his back. The thin copper wires woven through his locks skimmed his bare skin, coaxing a memory. He halted the recollection before it formed and dove for his makeshift bed.

Once on his back, Blaise squeezed his eyes shut, picturing the operation he and Callis had just performed. He tried to focus on segments—the new metal leg they'd constructed, the copper tubes running up to the porcie boy's jitter pump—but the still, white face leapt into his mind's eye. He shuddered at the memory of cold, hard skin.

The porcelains were fine when they were warm and animated. He could forget their strange makeup, and the fact that beneath their smooth skin lay brittle clay. He could pretend he was like them. He'd almost succeeded with Seree, until the night she'd grown cold in his arms. A wave of revulsion burned through him.

With eyes squeezed shut he fumbled around on the bed until he located a threadbare cushion. He pressed the pillow over his eyes then wrapped both arms over it, clamping it to his face.

Sleep. Time for sleep.

The warmth of the morning stole through the windows and the cracks in the floor to soak into his skin. He relaxed his arms, letting them fall beside his head. *Her* face swam into his thoughts. Eyes wide. Mouth open in shock. In the darkened bedroom she'd looked pale, but in his vision he saw color rise in her smooth cheeks. Her lips looked soft. All of her looked soft. His mind glided over the form he'd seen lying on the bed, chest rising and falling, still animated even in sleep. The delicate pattern on her stomach flared in his memory, and he slid his hand to his own midsection, where blue whorls marked him.

He tried to hold on to the warmth, but in his dreams his own skin grew hard and cold as a frozen porcie's. An unseen force battered him, forcing him to take refuge in a stone-like state. Then the cracking began. No, not cracks. Someone sliced lines into his skin. One after another. Thousands of cuts into cold flesh.

Blaise woke to Callis's muffled voice. White light glowed around the edges of the windows, and the attic smelled of warm timber. He rolled out of bed and cocked his head toward the argument going on below him. Seree's clear tones interrupted another panicked male voice.

Little Finnegan's family had returned.

Blaise tossed his loose shirt over his head and bent to snatch his boots as he headed for the door.

He found everyone assembled in the workroom, an angry circle around the slab in the middle of the room. One glance revealed Finnegan still cold and motionless. Callis nodded but Blaise's eyes sought Seree.

Outside of her establishment, the dark-haired porcie rejected the laws of beauty and wore what she pleased. Today she adopted an errand boy style, with slim tan pants tucked into tall boots, a vest over a close-fitting shirt, and a tweed cap. A canteen strapped to her hip further flaunted the ridiculous porcie notions that held sleekness of form over practicality. If they all carried their own water, the disturbing "tock-sipping" craze never would have taken hold in the upper classes.

Seree flashed Blaise a smile, her amber eyes lingering on his face before she returned her attention to the blustering porcie, Finnegan's male keeper.

"What will we tell our neighbors? Our customers?" The man looked from Seree to Blaise, avoiding Callis's mismatched eyes. "Our establishment is respectable. None of the riffraff that muck about down here near the Shelf."

Seree crossed her arms over her chest. "And what's wrong with the kind that clink about down here?"

The keeper winced, either at Seree's coarse language or the thought of wandering riffraff.

Callis took a step toward the agitated man but halted when the porcie shrank away. Callis's voice, unaffected by his accident and subsequent repair, filled the workroom with the modulated tones of a high society porcelain. "We believe Finnegan's repair will be near undetectable to the unsuspecting eye. Of course we haven't woken him to test the new leg, but the copper tubing will allow steam to reach his limb much as it did before. True, there are hinges in the knee, but if you keep those well-oiled—"

"I don't want to hear any more about his clockwork." The man's white hands rose and fluttered toward his head as though he wanted to cover his ears.

Blaise's jaw clenched. He leaned toward the child's keeper and widened his eyes. "Then you're a fool. How long do you think your silly gluemen will be able to repair the children? Soon they'll be nothing but cracks and dust. You've got to accept another solution!"

The keeper's features contorted. "I can't bring Finnegan back to Penelope *like this*. I can't risk our clientele discovering we're harboring a *modified*."

Callis's shoulders straightened but the mended porcie said nothing.

Seree moved to stand by Finnegan's head. She brushed the blond curls away from his pale forehead then pinned the child's keeper with her glittering eyes. "We'll see that Finnegan is cared for. You and your worthless lot can say he's gone to live with other keepers in the country. And in exchange for the three of us not sending *you* home with a few new cracks, you'll keep your mouth shut about what Blaise and Callis do here."

She placed her hands on the table on either side of Finnegan's head, keeping her sharp gaze on the porcie man. "There are more of us than you think, and if you ever breathe a word about Blaise to the authorities, you'll meet with an *accident* far worse than Finnegan's."

Blaise half expected the porcie keeper to run from Seree's snarling threat, but the man met her challenge with a calm, almost relieved expression.

"Very well then, Madam, we have an understanding." He smoothed the front of his green morning coat, and without another word whirled and marched out of the workroom.

Blaise dipped his gaze to the still form on the table then eyed his companions. "We've another modified on our hands to find a home for, and two more less-than-friendly porcies who know of our existence."

Callis stared at his clockwork hand, flexing the fingers almost as though he were unaware of the action. When he spoke, his voice was soft. "You regret saving another?"

"Of course not."

Seree rolled her eyes and set about examining Finnegan's clothing. No doubt she'd have him outfitted in comfort before the afternoon was out.

Callis moved to stand near Blaise. "We've no choice, my friend. They must either accept the modifications or we must force them to accept." He gestured to Finnegan. "It won't be long before all the children are this way. And no matter what the upper class thinks, they cannot avoid accidents forever. But we must act before we are betrayed and banished. We cannot lead a revolution from Lower."

Blaise turned away and raised his hands, clasping them behind his head.

"I know you hate this subject, but we must face the truth."

Blaise dropped his arms to his sides. He did hate talk of revolution, but not for any reason Callis might guess. He wasn't reluctant or afraid to face Blueboy's well-ordered tin army. Quite the opposite. It was the need that frightened him. He longed for confrontation. He longed to march straight into the porcie assembly and declare himself as . . . what? As protector? As other? As martyr?

It was rash and stupid, but he fought the urge to rise up, to instigate revolution, and to bear the punishment for such rebellion.

A high-pitched whine registered in Blaise's ears. Behind him, Callis and Seree had begun the reanimation process. He waited a moment more before turning.

Seree removed a tube from Finnegan's mouth. Callis stood with his porcie ear inclined to the new mechanical leg. He raised his right eyebrow, but the metal ridge above his left eye didn't follow suit.

"The steam is moving nicely." Callis touched the hammered copper toes. "He's warming."

Seree positioned herself at the boy's head. Blaise stepped back. His presence was alarming to fully conscious porcies, let alone reanimating children. The boy jerked, his limbs responding slowly to the steam. His lashes fluttered.

A piercing scream filled the workroom. Blaise's jaw locked.

"Shh." Seree cupped the porcelain cheek. "Shh, Finn, my boy. It's all right."

The scream faded to a wheezy whimper. "Penny. Where's Penny? I want my Penny."

Callis shared a look with Blaise. The modified frowned.

Seree smoothed the hair from the boy's forehead. "Penny isn't here now. My name is Seree."

Finnegan twitched and looked about. "But where did Penny go?"

Blaise fled the room. He burst onto the factory floor and strode toward the door without a thought to where he was going. This morning's dream dimmed the daylight streaming through the large windows in the front of the spacious room. He stopped and pressed a hand to his stomach.

An ache began at his navel, not hunger but a yearning for a battle he was meant to fight. The sensation crept under his skin, a hardening, as though liquid stone flowed just beneath the surface. Fully conscious, he recognized it. The Defender state, a physical reaction meant to strengthen him to battle a Chemist. He was far removed from the Defender justice system, yet his body was preparing for such a fight.

CHAPTER

11

Whit slid one hand into his sleeve and stopped, frozen. His shirt dangled from his arm, trailing the floor of his room. It wasn't the pain. After a week, the cuts over his back and upper arms were closing. The lines itched and stung, but he was healing. Grey had seen to that. So had his mother.

He clenched his fist. The tight new skin forming over the stripes on his arm puckered and pulled. The angry red lines paled then darkened once again.

Too long. He'd stared at the scars too long. He was transported back to that room, that table. The scent of copper filled his nostrils till his eyes stung. His arms hugged the table, bound beneath at the wrists. Shackles locked his ankles in place. In the corner of his eye he saw again the black and green shape of a Chemist. The man held an instrument Whit could not focus on. Only the glint of sharp metal penetrated his brain. In the background a machine hummed, the sound blending with the rush of blood in his eardrums. He bit down hard on his lower lip to keep back the scream clawing at his throat.

The pain of his teeth grinding his lip brought him back. He was in his room. He swiped at his bloody lip, and the red on his fingers reassured him. He'd seen none of it in the

Chemist lab even before he'd passed out. Only when they brought him home and his mother removed the dressings had he seen his stripes.

He blew out quick breaths and focused on his shirt. No more bandages. No more gaping cuts. The freshly laundered but worn cloth glided over his healing skin.

He stared down at the gap between the edges of the gray flannel. His chest and abdomen looked the same as they had a week ago. Familiar ridges and planes.

The horror of the Chemist facility receded, and he rushed to do up his buttons. The train wouldn't wait.

In the kitchen he found his mother, coat on, gulping down tea. She looked up, dark circles ringing her eyes.

"I'll go today, Mother."

"No, you won't." She set the cup down.

He wanted to shake her. Instead he rested a hand on the countertop and spoke with careful nonchalance. "Let me get today's ration. I heard Mrs. Haward tell you I should get out of the house. I'm strong enough."

"Whit, I'm not sure you're ready."

He hated the tremble in her voice. Without answering her, he snagged the potion bottles from a shelf by the door and grabbed his coat from the rack.

"I'll be back," he threw over his shoulder as he banged out of the front door.

Grey's mother was at the end of the Haward's front walk-way when Whit emerged. She met his gaze and nodded. He fixed his eyes on the ground. In one night, Maire Haward had gone from a household of four to living alone. Well, not alone. Olan Haward remained a statue, frozen in the family's home as some cruel reminder of the Chemists' complete power. How did she walk by her ossified father-in-law every day? How could she stand to be in the same room with his stone body?

As he fell into place among the mindless stream of people fetching their morning ration, Whit lifted his eyes to the mountains. Today would be different. The cold air pricked the exposed marks on his neck. His feet quickened. Mrs. Haward startled when he overtook her but she said nothing. By the time he reached Pewter Street and began the descent into the center of the Foothills Quarter, he was jogging. His breath clouded before him.

Murmurs rose from the citizens shuffling on their morning errand. Whit gave them a wide berth but retained his pace. He didn't know how long it would take to pick up his ration, return home, fool his mother into believing he'd taken all of his, then make it to the station in time for the hunting train.

Between the arrest and what little Grey had hinted at over the years, Whit put together what Grey's father had actually been doing with his ration each day. But would there be someone waiting at the outpost for Steinar Haward? Maybe they'd given up when he hadn't come for days.

Whit was one of the first in the ration line. His skin burned, and he struggled to slow his breathing and calm the heaving of his chest. At the sight of the deputies standing sentry on either side of the ration counter, he squared his shoulders.

The woman behind the protective glass—Lara was her name—looked surprised to see him. She tapped a B into her typing ball, but her hands paused over the keys that stuck up from the green orb like porcupine quills. "How is your mother, Whitland?"

The deputy on Whit's right eyed him lazily then resumed a bored posture.

"She's well, ma'am. Thought I'd let her rest this morning."

Lara's fingers flicked over the device, then she dropped her voice to a whisper. "And you?"

"I'm well, ma'am," Whit said through his teeth.

The deputy shifted toward them. "Enough chitchat." He glared at Lara. "Do your job."

She scuttled away to fetch rations for Whit and his mother.

Where was the other dispensary worker? What was her name? Nothing came to mind but an image of yet another middle-aged woman in fading red clothes. He didn't dare ask Lara when she returned with two small bottles and slid them into the indentation under the glass.

A weight settled in Whit's gut as he plucked the bottles from the compartment. It wouldn't be enough.

Stowing both bottles in his pocket, he spun and headed for the door. The scars on his back seared as though flames licked his skin. He took a breath and shook his head when he reached the street. It was just his imagination. A deputy's stare couldn't burn you.

Back at home, he had Mother to deal with, but lying to her was easier than he expected. He fished one bottle out and handed it to her. She took it and narrowed her eyes.

"Where's yours?"

He wrapped his fingers around the second bottle in his pocket so that all liquid was obscured, then pulled it out. "Already took it."

She glanced at the ration in his hand then returned to scanning his face. A smile lifted the corners of her mouth. "There's color in your cheeks." She came closer and reached up to brush spikes of hair out of his eyes. "It's good to see you like this. Are you sure it wasn't too much, fetching the ration?"

"Not at all." He stowed the full bottle back in his pocket. "In fact, I think I'll head into town. It's time I took my name off the recuperating list at the station."

She snatched his wrist. "Whit, you're not mended enough to return to the mines. Take a few more days. Heaven knows there are plenty of workers, and we can get by on my wages a bit longer."

"Can't you see I want it behind me?" Whit snapped. He reined in his tone when she flinched. "I need to work, not just so we can eat. I need . . ." How could he put it into words? He needed the crushing fatigue of a day's work to replace the terror of his dreams with blessed oblivion.

She clutched his arm a moment longer but the tension in her face smoothed. "I understand." She let go of him and turned toward the kitchen. "I'll have to check your back when you get home. We need to keep applying the salve a little longer."

Whit swallowed past the sudden dryness in his throat and made his escape. Pulling his collar up against the February wind, he made for Reinbar but turned onto Colfax rather than continue on to the Foothills Quarter station. The shops on the thoroughfare began to open as he strode toward the hulking brick buildings of downtown. His steps slowed as he passed Haward's Mercantile. A tacked-up board barred the doorway, and a sign printed in ornate letters read "Closed by order of the Chemist Council."

Whit pressed his face to the glass, cupping his hands around his eyes to block the glare of the morning sun. The mercantile looked like the pictures of the Galveston hurricane damage. Lamps, knickknacks, and furniture—Olan's precious antiques—lay broken and scattered on the floor next to piles of gadgets and Chemist contrivances. No signs of life met Whit's scrutiny. He dropped his hands to his sides and turned. In the corner of his eye, a figure moved. His heartbeat jumped into his throat and sweat coated his palms. Instinct told him to keep his eyes on the sidewalk ahead of him, but his gaze slid across the street inch by inch.

A dark silhouette edged in green leaned against a street clock across the way from Haward's Mercantile. The black top hat shaded his features and made his head look disproportionate to his slim-shouldered body, but Whit didn't need to see the face to know the Chemist studied him. His throat went dry and his mind blurred. Was it true they read thoughts? He couldn't tear his focus away from the thin figure framed by the shop door. The Chemist reached inside his coat and drew something out. His outline flickered, and Whit stared at empty space.

He threw a last glance at the Haward's store before returning to his errand. Had he drawn the Chemist's attention, or did the man simply watch Olan Haward's closed shop?

And where was Grey? Her absence gnawed at his insides. Her mother said she was safe, but the way she said it offered no reassurance. More was going on with the Hawards than Maire admitted. The ration missions Steinar ran to the mountain outposts were just one of their many secrets. Whit meant to uncover them all.

The Four Points station lay to the west of the Chemist tower in the heart of Mercury City. A shadow of the black spire fell over the sandstone building and all who moved along Boyle Street, hurrying to their destinations in the orderly fashion of Mercury residents. Carriages, motor cars and delivery trucks, and men on horseback navigated the road. A gleaming black steamer chugged past, its driver muffled in a thick coat, scarf, and goggles. As the boxy vehicle turned onto Lavoisier and disappeared into traffic, a strange excitement raced through Whit. But the station clock in the center of the courtyard showed ten till seven. He had no time for dreams of speed.

A familiar queue of citizens filed through the huge doors of the station beneath a sweeping arch gilded with copper. A green patina covered the scrollwork as though the city's entrance were marked by Chemist magic. Whit hunched his shoulders as he passed beneath the arch and into the station.

The cavernous interior shone with brass fixtures and flecked marble. A newly arrived family, the mother not yet wearing red garments, gawked at a golden statue in the center of the lobby. Whit bypassed them and headed for the farthest platform, located in a small building adjacent to the main station.

Compared to the opulence of the grand atrium, the hunting train hub looked dingy. Maps of the four quarters, the mines, and train routes covered the walls. A stuffed elk head with a branching rack hung on one wall. Photographs surrounded the trophy, showing hunters with their kills, black blood staining the snow around fur-covered bodies. Others were taken in summer with leafy aspens and rocky riverbanks in the background. Dark-eyed faces stared at the camera. A few smiles appeared among the displays of fish and game.

Under the watchful eyes of deputies, citizens wrapped in long coats and fur-lined parkas waited to register their names in exchange for hunting rifles. Whit took his place in line and read the plaque on the wall listing regulations for borrowing a weapon. His stomach sank at the last item. *Should a hunter not return his registered weapon by curfew, his family can expect no ration on the following day.* How could anyone exchange the lives of their family for a weapon and a fugitive's existence? But it happened. People cracked. Men took their chances in the wilderness. Sometimes they just went to work and never came home.

The queue inched forward. A figure in scarlet stepped away from the counter and made her way to the gate, a rifle balanced on her shoulder. Would his mother hunt if her job at the factory ended? He pictured her frail figure hunkered behind a deer stand, shivering and waiting for prey.

One after another, the hunters stepped through the turnstile, weapons secured against their bodies and heads lowered to avoid attracting attention. Whit reached the concrete bordering the ticket window. Moisture coated his palms. He shoved his hands into his pockets, his fingers closing around the full ration bottle. As if prompted by his action, his stomach pitched. He grit his teeth until the pain passed then risked a glance at the nearest deputy. The man eyed him, no doubt guessing at his age. How could Whit explain his trip to the outpost? Reaching the Age of the Stripe didn't mean they'd let him have a gun. Quite the opposite in fact. It took years of "good behavior" to earn the privilege of hunting.

The man in front of him moved aside. Whit forced his eyes ahead and stepped up to the counter.

The uniformed ticket agent gave him the once-over and frowned. "Name?"

Sweat beaded on Whit's upper lip. "Whitland Bryacre."

The agent entered his information then checked the green platen beneath his typewriter ball. He rubbed his fingers over his stubbled chin and eyed Whit over a pair of spectacles.

This would never work. The clerk was about to ask him why he wanted a ticket to the hunting outpost. Whit had no answer for him. He forced his fingers to uncurl from the ration bottle and let his hands drop to sides. Nothing to hide. He had nothing to hide.

The ticket agent leaned over the counter and dropped his voice. "Ice fishing?"

Whit opened his mouth, snapped it shut, and jerked his chin down once.

The man nodded to the poles and tackle boxes lined up against the back wall. "Your family will be right pleased if you bring home dinner tonight, eh, son?"

Whit bobbed his head. He handed the man his money, accepted the fishing equipment, and bolted out of the ticket office. The deputies on the platform ignored him, and he found a seat in one of the cars marked Men. Around him conversations about herds and weather buzzed. He eased his shoulders back against the seat and winced.

"What they get you for?" A man with red whiskers and a wide-brimmed hat jerked his chin in greeting. "First stripe? What'd a city boy like you get caught doing? You steal something?"

Whit dug his fingers into his knees, biting back the "none of your concern" that sprang to his lips. This man was older, though he guessed only by about ten years. Still the codes required Whit to show respect. He kept his voice even. "I didn't steal."

The man shifted a pack off his lap and leaned across the aisle. He had broad shoulders and probably stood above average height. "S'alright, kid, I won't tell no one."

The train jolted, and Whit looked out the window, pretending to be absorbed by their departure from the station. The hunter seemed to take the hint. No more loud questions pelted him as clouds of steam billowed past the window, obscuring the streets and buildings of downtown.

The hunting train cut through town toward the northwest, following a different route than Whit saw on his way to the mines. The houses and storefronts thinned and the train climbed into the canyon. Rock walls angled above, casting shadows over the track, which cut deep into the narrow ravine. The motion of trees and stone-littered hills sliding by played with his mind. His vision blurred and the ache in his empty belly grew. He turned from the window and focused on the fishing pole balanced between his knees.

The big man opposite him nodded at Whit's rented equipment. "Been ice fishing before?"

Whit stifled a sigh. "No, sir."

"I'll get you in with some fellas that go out on the lake all winter." He craned his neck, inspecting the other passengers. "There's Ed over there. The others must be in another car." He tapped the rifle lying at his feet with the toe of his boot. "I'm better with this. Like to have some power in my hands, ya reckon?"

Whit nodded as though he too knew the power of a gun in his hands. The thought zinged through him. He flexed his fingers, watching a scene play out in his head. The deputies would never see him coming. He yanked his thoughts back to the present and fought a wave of heady exhilaration.

"Don't worry, I'll see you settled," the hunter was saying. "Name's Burge, by the way."

Burge's murky eyes narrowed on Whit. "Judging by how you're sitting, it ain't been that long since your striping. You're a tough kid—"

He leaned in farther, an unspoken question tugging his eyebrow.

Whit gave in. "Whit. My name is Whit."

Burge's quiet tone caught Whit off guard. "I shouldn't call you a kid, Whit. Anyone who goes up hunting, or fishing, right after a striping is a man, no doubt about it."

The greenish brown eyes held his for a moment. Whit pressed his lips in a line and nodded.

Cold air bit Whit's face as he stepped down from the passenger car. The outpost lay before him, a mining town built and abandoned in the course of ten years. The men filed into the narrow space between two boarded-up structures and spilled out onto a boardwalk that lined the main street. The snow had been swept away from the sagging planks and piled in filthy heaps every few yards. Farther up, the women congregated in the middle of the dirt road, where the thin sunlight skirted the shadows of the weathered buildings.

Ahead, Burge was scanning the crowd. He had a pack slung over one shoulder and his gun balanced on the other. Whit ducked behind a man in a parka.

What should he do now? He gripped his pole and tackle box, conscious of the bottle in his coat pocket. Sweat broke out over his skin. The wind froze it, setting his teeth chattering.

What was he doing up here? He had no plan. No names. No contact to meet. His stomach clenched, offering a reminder of his mission and his weakness.

Groups of three and four broke away from the crowd to plan their day, while others trudged out of town toward the forested hills nearby. Whit hovered by one of the larger clusters as the men discussed a strategy for tracking an elk herd.

Movement registered on the edge of his vision. A small figure darted behind a building on the opposite side of the street. Whit stepped away from the hunters and into the street, searching for the waif.

Burge no longer glanced around but seemed intent on his own path out of town. He hiked up the steep main street, clambering through snow drifts and over fallen rubble. Whit squinted to follow Burge's disappearing figure as he neared the edge of town. The trudging silhouette shifted, and Burge lowered the pack from his shoulder to his hand. Without breaking stride, he dropped his supplies into an alley between two sagging wooden shops and continued on, following the line of the ice-locked river hugging the sides of the pass.

Why had the man dropped his provisions?

Whit shuffled after Burge, keeping his face toward the river but scanning the street and side buildings for deputies and scurrying shadows. The Chemist agents lingered close to the train as though they didn't care to deal with the ice and ruin. Still, there was no mistaking their presence. He'd counted twenty masked figures in their black dusters lurking about as he'd tried to disappear amongst the men.

The cold wet of snow seeped through his trouser legs as he slogged up the hill, trying to step in the tracks Burge left behind. The wind lashed his face and the marks on his back, neck, and shoulders throbbed with the combination of cold and movement.

When he reached the last two buildings, he slowed. The snow muffled the sound of his footsteps, but his pole and tackle clattered together as he walked. He stowed the equipment on the nearest doorstep. Keeping a shoulder to the wall, he moved at a pace he hoped wouldn't attract attention. He stopped at the edge of the alley, sliding his eyes to the patch of ground where Burge dropped his pack. It wasn't there.

Whit ducked into the alley in time to see a flicker of movement at the other end. He followed, rounding the back corner just as a foot disappeared into one of the doors in a row of similar two-story structures stacked up against each other across the street.

He waited. The back street was quiet. On his left, it curved out of view. A few structures clung to the side of the mountain, decreasing in size farther up the steep slope. To his right the attached buildings continued. Broken windows, peeling paint, and a few collapsed entryways suggested long disuse.

Heart thudding, Whit picked his way after the narrow imprints in the snow. The Chemists knew of the exiles surviving in camps, caves, and the old mining towns. Part of Grey's father's assigned job was to talk with them, teach them the morality codes, and convince them to return to civilization. Before Steinar Haward's arrest, his large figure tramping about these streets must've drawn little attention from the deputies. But Whit didn't belong.

He paused at the base of the sagging steps leading to the door and checked over his shoulder. It had to be a refugee he was following. Why else would Burge have dumped his sack in that alley? Whit almost laughed. The man he'd avoided led him straight to the object of his search. With one more scan of his surroundings, he leapt up the stairs and jerked the door open, slipping inside and closing it behind him.

He blinked in the gloom. A stale smell tinged with mold invaded his nose. His eyes watered and he screwed up his face, fighting the sneeze. All was still around him. A massive desk stood in the center of a large foyer. Behind it a staircase curved upward. Dark carpet with an indistinguishable pattern covered the floor, the flight of steps, and the room visible through a double doorway on his right.

A door on the left, set behind a counter, disappeared into the back portion of the ground level. It probably led to the back door. He started for it but stopped when the room went fuzzy. A wave of hunger slammed into him followed by a sharp pain deep in his gut. He shook it off. He hadn't taken his ration today, and he hadn't eaten since yesterday, but a day without wouldn't kill him.

Disjointed memories floated in his brain. Grey's face, blotchy and wet. Agony. Potion poured down his throat. His mother had explained it all. Grey had gone without her ration. He could too.

A light tread jerked his attention to the second story. The refugee had gone upstairs? That didn't make sense. He took a sluggish step toward the staircase and steadied himself against the wooden counter. His head swam and his gut felt hollow. The potion bottle dragged at his coat pocket, thudding against his hip.

The creak of old wood snapped him out of the haze, and he stumbled to the bottom of the staircase. Gripping the banister, Whit heaved his legs up the first step. Then the second. And the third.

He paused, head down, eyes trained on the shadowy design of the carpet. How long had he slumped here, one arm slung over the railing? He pulled himself up and dragged his body one more step. The landing came into view.

"Stop." The voice was high but strong.

The dark figure at the top of the stairs wouldn't come into focus. Whit stared at the upper portion of the body, trying to make out the odd shape. His focus narrowed on a tiny, sharp point. An arrow.

"I said stop." She inched forward.

Whit forced words past uncooperative lips. "I know Steinar." He reached in his pocket and pulled out the ration bottle. A twang juddered through the silence of the inn.

CHAPTER

Grey slipped into the east gallery, her bare feet silent on the plush rug that covered most of Fantine's domain. At least if she dropped one of the cherries cupped in her hands, it'd leave no discernible stain on the wine-colored carpet. If only the fruit tasted as good as it looked. The most she could hope for from these morsels was that they'd fill her stomach.

The note her mysterious visitor left in her room almost a week ago explained how to focus on an object in a painting, then reach in and grab hold of it. But how the system worked remained a mystery. "The food doesn't taste good," the writer warned in careless script, "but it will keep you from starving." There'd been no signature, no further instructions, no hint as to who her unexpected friend was or why he bothered to help her. But when Nettie told her of the maid who'd bumped into the Mad Tock in a back hallway, Grey had her answer. She'd had two run-ins with Curio's masked renegade, but no one needed to know.

On tiptoes, Grey continued toward the door to her bedroom. She'd left it ajar when she sneaked out. Only tocks stirred this early, and they went about their business regardless of strange doings on the part of porcies or their guests. Nettie tried to help with Grey's surreptitious meals, but the sweet maid was just as likely to bring her a raw fish or a lump of candle wax as a slice of bread. So Grey conducted her own hunt and gather missions in the early morning hours when Fantine and Lord Blueboy retired.

She'd almost reached her room when a draft brushed the hem of her nightgown. She froze, her skin prickling. Silence permeated the gloom of the gallery, but she wasn't alone.

Grey shifted to peek at Fantine's door across the hallway. It was closed. Beside it, Lord Blueboy leaned against the cream-and-white papered wall, his mussed dark hair a contrast to the pale background. He held a mug to his lips, but his gaze tracked her.

Grey glanced from the cherries in her hands down to her nightgown and robe. Neither flimsy garment provided a pocket. She straightened her shoulders and tilted her chin.

"Good morning, Benedict." The words came out more timid than she'd intended.

He pushed away from the wall and ambled toward her. His movements were odd. Not stiff as though he'd cooled, but slow, almost lazy. He set the mug on an accent table and moved to stand before her. The line of his blue dressing gown revealed a molded chest and a metallic chain disappearing into the deep V of the rich material.

Blue eyes, almost black in the dim light, slid from Grey's face to the fruit in her hands.

"What's this?"

"Ch-cherries." Grey winced at her stutter then flung her eyes open to meet his gaze. Who cared if this man thought her dependence on food unattractive? Just because the porcies would find digestion revolting didn't mean she should be ashamed of it. Besides, Benedict knew she was different.

"I know what they are." His full lips twisted in a smirk. "I'm merely curious as to why you find it necessary to swipe them from the drawing room painting in the wee hours of the morning."

Warmth spread up Grey's neck, but she forced a casual tone. "I found myself in need of a snack."

His black brows furrowed. "A snack?"

Grey dialed up her blasé tone. "Yes, I'm going to eat them."

"Eat?"

"Oh, for mercy's sake!" Grey popped a cherry into her mouth, yanking the stem out so it remained between her thumb and forefinger. She chewed carefully, enjoying the shock on Blueboy's face. Cherries were supposed to have pits, but either the artist hadn't known that or wasn't thinking about it during the painting's creation, for this fruit had none. She swallowed, her throat constricting under the porcie's scrutiny.

"Do it again," Benedict demanded. "No wait. Allow me." He brushed her fingers away from the cherries in her palm and selected one himself. The cherry's skin gleamed dark against his pale fingers as he lifted it toward her mouth.

She blushed but let her jaw fall. She'd started this, after all. Best to satisfy the insistent ruler's curiosity, or he'd pester her with questions. Instead of dropping it into her mouth, he paused, holding the cherry a breath away from her lips. Heat crawled through her veins. When had he closed the gap between them? She shut her eyes, willing away the panic of breaking Mercury City law. Willing him to release her from the magnetism he wielded.

Something soft brushed against her lower lip. Grey stiffened and peeked from beneath her lashes. Benedict traced her lips with the silky surface of the cherry. She shivered. It was just the porcies' way. They were all like this. So physical. They didn't know—*he* didn't know—how it made her insides scream.

He tucked the cherry behind her teeth and Grey closed her mouth. The tug of the stem on her lower lip left behind a faint throbbing. Under Lord Blueboy's scrutiny she chewed and swallowed. His gaze traveled from her lips, down her neck to a spot just below her collarbone.

"What an incredible design you have." He breathed the words as if caught in a spell. A moment later he stepped back, putting a couple of feet between them.

Grey's cheeks burned and her breath shook. Benedict still watched her, lids at half-mast as though he was bored. An urge to run gripped her. She pictured the cherries rolling on the floor, her nightgown floating behind her as she bolted for the door to the outer gallery. Would Benedict laugh or summon the serving tocks to restrain her?

She took a step backward, one hand out to feel the surface of her bedroom door. Her fingers found the doorknob.

Benedict straightened the front of his robe. A crystalline object attached to the chain about his neck slid into view but disappeared as he smoothed his clothing. He turned toward the door at the end of the long gallery and didn't glance at her when he spoke.

"Fantine wishes to attend a performance today. You may accompany her if you are sufficiently animated."

Grey's pulse sped. Outside the estate? She was going out into the city?

Benedict's figure disappeared into the room beyond. Grey stared after him. Despite his bold ways, he wasn't unkind. He touched her because he was curious, and to him it was natural to satisfy that curiosity. No Council laws prevented it here. The porcies could never conceive of the world she came from. Grey ducked her head and wrapped her arms around her middle as if she stood in a ration line. He didn't mean to make her feel trapped and examined like an animal in a laboratory. He didn't mean to make her blush and want to hide. Grey peeked in the direction he'd gone, rubbing her arms where goose bumps rose.

She escaped to the safety of her room, tugging the door closed with a little more force than necessary. Today she would get out. See this city where Haimon banished her. Maybe she'd find a connection between her grandfather's assistant and this world within the cabinet.

Excitement replaced the clammy residue of her encounter with Benedict. Grey placed the remaining cherries on her nightstand and made herself comfortable on the bed. How long would she have to wait for Fantine to rise?

"Do the porcies rest, Nettie? I know they don't sleep like I do, but Fantine must be doing something in her chamber all morning."

"They allow themselves to cool for a bit, Miss." Nettie set a tray on Grey's lap and nipped to the other side of the bed to stow an empty vase for later use.

Grey studied the contents of the tray. A cup of warm water, a bunch of daisies, and an onion. Good thing she'd nabbed those cherries. It all tasted like paint anyway, but she just couldn't bring herself to bite into an onion like it was an apple.

Nettie slid the gauzy curtains back to reveal daylight and the little balcony just outside. The tock who visited her—the Mad Tock—had jumped from that balcony. He'd almost crashed, Nettie had told her, then the soldiers claimed he flew over the wall. She needed to find out more about this Mad Tock. Whoever had sent him knew she was human and needed food. What else did her mysterious benefactor know?

"It makes them less fragile," Nettie was saying.

Grey tuned back into the conversation.

"They hate to cool, but shortly after the Grand Animation they found it was necessary to quiet their jitter pumps and allow their bodies to rest. When they're warm, they're more flexible, but if they keep their pumps going too long they grow warped and distorted. On the other hand, if they remain inanimate and cold too long, they grow brittle. A balance of heating and cooling keeps them strong, more resistant to cracks."

Sipping the warm water in her cup, Grey imagined the liquid traveling to some sort of internal engine in her chest that heated it to steam then pumped it throughout her body. She didn't quite understand the process, but it sounded similar to the way her heart circulated blood.

Nettie paused, one of her delicate metallic hands poised over the door to the wardrobe. A distant expression clouded her face. "Many of them can't afford more cracks."

"How long ago was the Grand Animation?"

Nettie lurched then returned her attention to the contents of the wardrobe. "A hundred arbor cycles ago."

Grey pushed her tray off her lap and swung her legs to the floor. "Arbor cycles?"

Nettie cocked the painted line that was her eyebrow. "The changes in the trees."

Of course. But how—? "Nettie, where does the water come from?"

The tock faced the wardrobe but her back stiffened. It took a moment for her to answer but when she did, she spoke in a chipper voice.

"It comes from Lower, of course." She whirled and held up a short red dress.

Grey shook her head. "Not red."

Nettie scrutinized the garment then made a negative gesture and tucked it back into the closet. Grey stood and joined her in time to utter an appreciative "ooh" when the tock slid aside a long gown of deep blue. It had a high collar and a pattern of shimmery fans imprinted in the satin fabric. A slit would allow ease of movement but would also expose the length of Grey's left leg.

Grey touched the smooth material. Surely the slit could be sewn up. "It's beautiful."

Nettie pressed her lips together. "It's blue."

A pair of cerulean eyes set deep in a smudged face blinked out of Grey's memory. Her voice came out husky. "I like blue."

"Mistress Fantine may object. Wearing blue is her right."

Grey cleared her throat but couldn't quite banish Whit's face. "So no one else in Curio City is allowed to wear blue?"

Nettie tossed her a saucy smile. "Oh, they do. They just don't wear it around Fantine." She held the dress up against Grey and cocked her head. "It does suit you, and since you are going out today, it's appropriate to wear blue to signify you're under Lord Blueboy's protection."

Grey's hand dropped from the dress. *Under Lord Blueboy's protection.* The phrase crawled over her like an insect. The porcies would think she *belonged* to Lord Blueboy. Would they think he visited her bedroom the way he visited Fantine's? Did Nettie think that?

"Nettie, I—"

The maid swiveled from the wardrobe. "Yes, Miss?"

Grey's cheeks flushed and she couldn't find the words to explain. Benedict's actions this morning would raise no eyebrows among Curio's citizens, but the heat of his nearness remained like a film on her skin.

Nettie waited for her to continue.

"Never mind," Grey pushed her hair away from her face. No point in making a fuss over a passing moment with the city's ruler. She nodded toward the dress. "If you're sure Fantine won't mind . . ."

"I'll let a few words slip when I go to dress her, so she'll be prepared."

When Fantine exited her boudoir sometime later, she presented a warm smile to Grey, who waited in the gallery. The porcie wore a dark blue velvet bodice with the high collar and cutaway neckline she favored. A large sapphire dangled from the lace-edged band at the base of her throat. The stone twinkled with the same hue as Fantine's eyes. Her bodice dipped in a corsetted V shape over her slender midsection. Below it she wore a pair of loose, short pants in burgundy satin that reached her mid thigh. What appeared to be stockings made of bright blue strings encased Fantine's legs, giving the impression of spider webs clinging to her milky skin.

Grey stammered a "good morning" and followed her host to the elevator in the next room, then through the entry hall and out the grand front doors. She'd seen some of the estate grounds earlier. They'd had a midday sip in the garden a few days after Grey's head quit throbbing. But as Drakon now led the way to the stables, Grey fought an urge to bolt past the dignified butler and run to the outbuilding that housed their means of escape.

If only Fantine could walk faster. When Drakon stopped to discuss the arrival of the Curio assembly members with a stable tock, Grey edged around him and through the wide doorway. The building accommodated a number of velvet-coated horses, an elegant cream-colored horseless carriage, and other contrivances ranging from a chariot to an enormous pair of metal legs attached to a large basket with seats.

Drakon slipped around Grey, his nose in the air as he led the way past the legs, which shifted slightly as though adjusting weight.

Fantine let out a little squeal and peered at the odd contraption. "Whatever are those, Drakon?"

The tock butler ticked his annoyance. "Sir Weatherton's new conveyance, madam. He insists on tinkering, as you know. The dreadful thing sways awfully. He'll fall to a smash, you can bet on it."

Fantine put a hand to her collar. "And after what happened to Lady Weatherton?" Her voice lowered. "Some might call it brave."

Drakon's eyes zipped to his mistress's face. "Quite so."

"Does Lord Blueboy know of this . . . this dreadful mechanism?"

"I've made him aware." Drakon offered a slight bow more concurrence than deference. The butler might hold little esteem for the mistress of the estate, but one thing they did agree on was that beauty was the highest measure of worth. Though a new form of thought skirted the edges of Curio society. At private sips Benedict told stories that shocked Fantine and forced Grey to suppress a giggle. Porcies scaling tall buildings, *riding* horses instead of being drawn in coaches, taking risks. Such actions were suitable for tocks and porcies of the lowest stature, but not for the upper class.

Grey glanced to the smooth cement beneath her feet. What would it be like to fear a minor fall? To walk, like Fantine, slowly and carefully, mindful of every threat. She started. Images from Mercury City collided with one another. Walking home from school with three precise feet between Whit and her. Gauging the location of every male in a public place. Hugging her arms around her middle to keep her full-framed body compact. She knew what it meant to walk in fear. Even now, she stood two feet from Drakon, her arms pressed against her sides to avoid brushing the tock butler who helped Fantine navigate the portable steps to the carriage.

She shook off the weight of her life back home as Drakon held out his gloved hand to her. Here in Curio she was free, not only from the Chemists' codes, but also from the porcies' limitations. She could spring into the open coach like an acrobat if she wanted. Bounce along in the seat next to their tock driver. Or better yet, gallop astride one of the glossy horses who puffed steam out of their mouths in steady streams like boiling teakettles. What was stopping her?

Fantine leaned over, one hand clamped over her throat and the other motioning for Grey. "Come on. Let's go."

The porcie's expression doused Grey's daydreams. For all her caution and well-executed beauty, Fantine strained like a child in uniform.

Grey accepted Drakon's assistance and joined Fantine on the cushioned seat. As the tock driver prodded the glistening horses forward, she reached for Fantine's hand. The porcie's smooth fingers squeezed Gray's as the wrought iron gates swung open to allow them passage onto a wide street beyond.

A line of soldiers, all alike in their tin uniforms, blocked the traffic so Lord Blueboy's carriage received the right of way. The driver guided the horses in a smooth turn to the left and they were off, gliding down a tree-lined road beneath the pearlescent haze of low-lying clouds.

Fantine pointed to the mansions they passed and rattled off the names of the inhabitants as well as their latest fashion achievements or the artists and musicians they sponsored.

Most of the homes were set behind tall fences like Lord Blueboy's, but graceful colonnades, towers, and gables soared above the barriers. Strange spheres gleamed in the filtered midday light. Mercury City boasted nothing so grand.

A few vehicles traveled the road with them, open carriages like theirs and coaches straight from storybooks. One well-dressed porcie sat in a stylish two-wheeled cart pulled by a metal horse with large gears for flanks and an articulated neck that creaked as the horse raised and lowered its head.

They left the seclusion of the residential area and merged into the traffic on a main street. Boxy horseless carriages in candy colors chugged between the horse-drawn conveyances, steam curling from rear pipes. An omnibus trundled by on slow-moving treads. Tock faces, visible through the windows, stared straight ahead as though their keys had yet to be wound. Some had smooth cheeks and painted faces like Nettie and others looked like a mishmash of gears and parts. The bus crept away down the street edged by quaint shops and sipping establishments.

A door on a white townhome opened and a porcelain woman stepped out, leading a girl with long brown ringlets.

Grey pointed. "What a beautiful mother and daughter."

Fantine frowned. "Mother?"

"Over there." Grey swiveled in her seat and gestured to the walkway behind them. A closer look at the woman and child revealed no similarities other than perfect porcelain skin and gem-like eyes. "Didn't you see them—the little girl with brown hair and—?"

"I saw." Fantine's voice brought Grey back around. The porcie's features hardened.

Questions built on the tip of Grey's tongue but she bit them back. She was supposed to be from the country, not a different world.

They continued deeper into Curio City. The buildings were larger and closer together, but none of them soared to reach the sky like the tower in the center of Mercury. Rosy brick, white lattice, arches, and stones in varying hues combined in captivating patterns and façades.

A few structures, all elevated and cylindrical, stood out in the cityscape. One looked like a massive metal tulip. Another had scalloped edges, giving it the appearance of a giant's crown. Grey pointed to yet another dome-shaped construction rising into view as they neared the busy heart of the city.

"Are those water towers, Fantine?"

The woman beside her glanced at the golden sphere looming above a sprawling building taking up a block of the city square. "Water towers? Is that what they're called in the country? We call it a purification locus, or hydro hub."

"They're so pretty."

Fantine wrinkled her nose. "On the outside, of course. But inside"—she shuddered—"all that filthy water. Ugh! I hate to even think of it." Lowering her hands to her lap, she adjusted the jewel-encrusted clips securing her stockings. Condescension colored her next words. "You're right, I suppose, we were clever to make the hubs as pleasing to the eye as they are necessary for the plumbing."

Their carriage pulled into a line of vehicles navigating the streets that formed a square around a patchwork park. Though crowded and busy, order prevailed on the wide walkways and in the transportation lanes. Porcies ambled well-tended paths and shrub-lined sidewalks, their clothes a twinkling rainbow against the backdrop of manicured grass and elegant buildings. The tocks moved faster, skirting the porcelain pedestrians and darting in and out of doorways.

The carriage stopped in front of the largest building in the square, set back from the street by a wide courtyard and portico. Only one story high, the building stretched from one end of the block to the other. A shimmering white façade, rounded edges, and decorative carving gave the appearance of a galleria made of sugar. A banner hanging from the roof depicted costumed porcies on a stage. Above it, the golden hydro hub seemed to float, its support structure hidden by the galleria's glistening architecture.

Porcies streamed from the sidewalk down a carpeted walkway toward double doors visible between the columns of the portico. When the tock driver—dressed in the distinctive uniform of Lord Blueboy's household—hopped down and zipped to the carriage door, the other porcies halted.

Fantine alighted first, clinging to the driver's hand but with head held high. Smiles and warm murmurs greeted her. One or two porcies moved forward to welcome her. Grey accepted the coachman's help and joined Fantine on the carpet. She recognized a few of the faces—high society porcies who'd attended functions at the estate.

As the group drifted toward the entrance, the carriage whisked away, replaced by an enclosed coach pulled by—Grey blinked—a small elephant the color of bark. Grey lingered, her eyes wide to take in the spectacle around her.

Humid air pressed close, gluing her dress to her skin and carrying a heavy floral scent. She zeroed in on the source. One corner of the courtyard harbored a flower garden. With Fantine occupied, Grey wandered toward the blooming plot. Real flowers, not arrangements pulled from paintings. She dipped down to a blue rose, inhaling a scent both familiar and yet too musky to resemble any she'd encountered before. If only she could find a real fruit tree, maybe—

A loud boom cracked overhead. Grey jolted. Her heartbeat skipped and sped.

The porcies looked about, their features twisted in confusion.

Grey stepped out of the garden and walked toward the crowd that hid Fantine. A creaking, grinding sound echoed through the air. Many of the porcies covered their ears then dropped their hands to exclaim to one another. They craned their necks, mouths drawn in worried lines.

Another sound pierced the rising murmurs. Or was it many sounds? Grey winced as the high-pitched wail rose to an ear-splitting decibel. Though constant, the tone quivered, underscored by a throaty wheeze. She covered her ears, but the screech only grew. Before her, porcies stood in the square, mouths open. Screaming.

At the other end of the galleria the porcelain woman and child Grey'd seen earlier stood immobile on the sidewalk, their eyes lifted above the molded ridge of the opera house roof. A dark sheet of liquid descended, burying them with wave after wave. The flood kept coming, rolling over the galleria's roof and down into the courtyard like a muddy waterfall.

The shrieking continued, like a hundred tea kettles boiling over. Grey forced her legs to move.

"Fantine! Fantine!" Her voice drowned in the chaos. The water kept coming; thick as oil, it poured from the rooftop into the street, swallowing the performance-goers, snagging carriages and the animals pulling them and lifting them on the advancing tide.

The wall of water crept closer. Grey stood, petrified. All around her the porcies ran. Across the street a man in a gray suit jumped away from the floodwater and fell, crashing into a bench. His mouth opened, but his shriek was lost among the others. He lurched up, clutching the jagged edge of his shoulder where his arm no longer connected.

The sludge swirled over the carpet Grey stood on a moment ago and slid toward the corner of the courtyard. She needed an escape. The retaining wall enclosing the garden swept up into an arc, rising to meet a decorative pillar at the farthest crook of the courtyard. She bunched her dress in her fist and ran toward the highest point.

Behind her, the water surged, spilling into the courtyard. The screams were ahead of her now as the porcies at the intersection watched the flood advance. Grey's boots splashed in ankle-deep water. She leaped to the top of the stone barrier on her left and ran along the narrow surface elevated above the courtyard.

The black water licked the stones at the base of the partition. She eyed the path in front of her, conscious of each footfall in her sprint toward the corner column. The wall swept into an incline, rising toward the arch in the corner. Grey faltered. Her caution cost her speed and momentum.

Water slapped against the wall beneath her. She scrambled another step, but the slope was too steep. She teetered, arms out for balance. Her boot slid on the next step. She willed her muscles to fight the pull of gravity, willed her feet to follow the curve of the arch.

Something yanked her from behind, compressing her ribcage. She braced for the tug of the water. But it wasn't a wave that took her. She hung, suspended above the surface of the water as it swelled over the retaining wall. Her legs dangled, her toes skimming the dark river of sludge for a moment before leaving the water, and the ground, behind.

She couldn't breathe. Something clamped her midsection, holding her body like a child toting a limp cat. Wind whipped her hair and skimmed the goose bumps on her arms. Desperate for air, she scrabbled against the restraints at her waist.

"Stop moving." The words buzzed from just above her.

Grey froze, her arms hanging limp below her. She twisted her head and squeaked.

Someone. Someone with great, beating wings, held her fast. They flew over the black tide rushing into the square below. Grey searched for Fantine's bright red hair, but everywhere she looked another wave obliterated any hope of spotting her. The indistinct screaming lessened, replaced by a chorus of names being called, the yowls of animals, and the slap of water against building sides.

The flight lasted only a few moments, but the view of destruction seemed endless. Her rescuer made for a row of attached buildings on the opposite side of the square from the galleria. The slanted roof grew closer. Grey tensed, preparing for a drop. Her arms and legs still swung like ropes beneath her despite her attempts to straighten. The tiles loomed larger.

They swept up and over the apex of the roof, skimming down over the back portion of the building. The pressure against her back shifted, spreading down her hips. A pair of legs wearing odd boots descended behind her, stretching out to steady her own limbs. The arms securing her torso tugged her upright. Together they tilted into a vertical position. The compression on her midsection lessened as her shoulders eased back to rest against a bumpy surface.

She jumped at the voice in her ear. "Brace yourself."

CHAPTER

13

Grey stretched her toes toward the tiles below, anxious to feel something solid beneath her feet. Her rescuer's leg, pressed flush against hers, bent at the knee, forcing hers into the same position. When her boot connected with the surface, she scrabbled and pitched forward. The roof whizzed up to meet her outstretched hands and she slammed down hard.

"Oof." A metallic exclamation mixed with Grey's own groan. Weight pinned her to the slope, and the scent of sawdust and machine oil filled her nostrils.

The pressure lifted as the tock rolled off her, but the air was slow to fill her lungs. She lay with her cheek pressed against the smooth tile and struggled to pull in shallow breaths. From the corner of her eye, she caught one large wing folding in on itself.

Footsteps clattered on the roof, breaking through the ringing in Grey's ears. She rolled onto her back and planted her feet on the slant beneath her. The colorless sky played scenes of screaming porcies and rolling water. Knees bent, Grey braced herself until the trembling stopped.

When she could move her head without an accompaniment of stars, she searched for the flying tock. He perched on the far edge of the connected buildings, peering down to the side street below. The tips of the folded wings jutted above his shoulders. Thick ropes of dark hair fell between them, glinting as though threaded with strands of metal. He turned, revealing the profile Grey had expected. Her visitor.

Unbending from his squat, he scaled the roof with a practiced tread, stopping at the apex to survey the square.

Grey sat up. The bruises and scrapes on her body performed an involuntary roll call, but at least she could breathe. She clambered to her feet, waiting to get her balance before she crept after the tock who'd saved her once again.

He must've heard her movement. He whipped a gloved hand behind him in a gesture that clearly meant stay back.

The sight of his arm brought Grey up short. Black stains seeped up the fabric of his sleeve from wrist to elbow. The heavy material of his boots bore signs of the foul water that burst out of nowhere into the center of Curio City. Grey wrapped her arms around her middle, wincing at the tenderness of her ribs and the wet residue on her clothes.

"What happened?" Her demand made him jerk. "Where did all that water come from?"

He turned and took a few steps away from the peak of the roof, leaving plenty of distance between them. A pair of goggles pushed the hair away from his brow, and his eyes scrutinized her from above a grid-like mask covering the lower portion of his face. She faltered and nearly lost her balance. He looked like a deputy. Grey's muscles tensed as she gestured toward the city square.

"You're the Mad Tock, aren't you? Did you cause the flood? They're dying down there."

He tossed his head, a quick, restrained gesture but unusual for a tock. His voice, however, still carried the familiar mechanized whir of tock speech. "They're not dying. The water will damage them but not kill them."

He crossed his arms over his chest, and the exposed skin at the base of his neck drew Grey's attention. Smooth skin, not tock metal. Was he a porcie?

She moved closer, examining him. He was tall, even for a porcie, and broad-shouldered. The skin she glimpsed wasn't the cream color of a porcie's complexion, but golden brown. He wore brown pants tucked into the tall boots with—were those fins on his heels? The straps holding his flying contraption to his back crisscrossed over his shirt, secured by buckles.

"I saw the water cover a mother and child. I saw a man's arm shatter. I—"

"A keeper. You saw a keeper and a child," he said. "They don't procreate." He flung his arms wide. "And what were you doing out there anyway? You had to pick today of all days to leave Blueboy's mansion? *You* could've drowned."

"I . . ." How did he know so much about her? She thought back to the note he'd delivered. Without it, she might've starved. "Who *are* you?"

He made a jerky bow, buckles and straps jangling. "I'm the Mad Tock, as you said. I'm the bogey man. The Big Owl. A flying nightmare. And I have things to do."

He tugged a handle attached to a cord threaded through the straps at his side. A soft whooshing sound followed. With his thumb he jabbed a button over his shoulder and the wings spread out on either side of him.

"Wait." Grey picked her way across the roof as fast as she dared, keeping her focus on the tiles beneath her feet. "Just wait a min—" She lifted her gaze to the tock, now only a few feet away, and sucked in a quick breath.

The eyes looking down at her were near black with just the slightest hint of deep brown at the edge. The skin around them crinkled as he inched away from her. The scent that had lingered in her memory since she arrived in Curio invaded her senses once again. Beneath the rich tones of oil and wood, the faintest tinge of sweat remained.

"You're human."

For a moment he studied her with those liquid eyes. One word slipped through the mask. "Yes."

He reached up and yanked on a strap, detaching the mechanism that covered his mouth and nose. The grid dangled to the side of his head, revealing the lower portion of his face. His bronze skin tone and full lower lip caught her eye first. He had a straight nose with a subtle dent at the end that was echoed in his chin. If they were back in Mercury she'd guess he was just out of school. Maybe working in the mines like Whit, though the breadth of his shoulders would better suit him to laying railroad ties.

"What's your name?"

He rolled his eyes and shifted his attention to the apparatus he wore. Between pulls to the cord at his side, he said, "Blaise," adding a surname in warmly accented tones.

"How did you get here?"

He was already fastening the mouth grid back on. The answer came in the simulated tock tone. "You don't understand. I have to *go. Now.*"

He trotted to the back edge of the roof and studied the skyline.

"Wait. How am I supposed to get down?"

Grey crept to the eave and risked a glance down. She jerked backward. The alley running behind the adjoined buildings was several stories beneath them. A dark rivulet cut through the gravel. The water oozed, leaving black sediment wherever it touched.

Blaise turned, the tip of his wing brushing Grey's shoulder. "I can set you down somewhere safe, and then I have to find my friends."

Grey stabbed a finger at her chest. "*I* have to find Fantine. She was at the galleria when—"

He muttered a distorted curse. "The worst of the flood is over. We can fly over once and look for her."

Grey straightened her spine and glowered at him. "You can set me down, and I'll wade through that muck and find her."

"Suit yourself."

They squared off on the rim of the roof. Grey fumed. She'd found another human in Curio, and he wouldn't even stick around long enough to explain his existence there. Worse yet, he was some kind of revolutionary.

He motioned her closer. "Come here."

The heat of her anger altered to a warmth that swirled in her core and burned her cheeks.

He jerked the cord at his side again. "Would you come on? I can't risk my cinderite cooling."

Grey pressed her lips together and stalked over to him. He took one step back from the edge of the roof and grasped her by the shoulders. His gloved hands cupped her upper arms as he positioned her in front of him, facing the opposite way.

Years under the crimson laws told her to shrink from his touch, yet she stood firm. He stepped close, bringing his body up against hers. A firm chest pressed against her back, hips aligned with hers, and muscular legs framed her own. Her breathing grew shallow as strong arms encircled her waist, pressing into her ribcage. She flinched.

"All right?" His voice buzzed in her ear.

"My ribs are sore."

"Oh." He loosened his hold and spread his fingers over her torso, moving them in gentle exploration.

For a moment her breath fled and a haze muffled all but his touch. When he pressed a bruise, a whimper escaped her lips. Blaise stopped his prodding and hung his head above her shoulder, his mask hovering by her cheek.

His replicated tock voice hummed in her ear. "I've never carried a human before. I'll try to adjust. I'm sorry I hurt you."

Her knees went soft, but she forced her mind back to the situation. He hadn't denied her accusation; he was involved in whatever caused the flood. Blaise's chivalry toward her made his disregard for Curio's citizens all the worse.

She focused on the vista of Curio City spread out before her. Word would be reaching the more distant neighborhoods. The porcies and tocks were probably desperate to hear news of their loved ones.

"If I may?" Blaise moved his hands beneath her arms and lifted her up and back. "Stand on top of my boots. When I take off, wrap your feet behind my legs. That should help take the pressure off your middle. I'm going to put one arm here and one here."

He reached across her body and secured one hand on her hip. The other arm he tucked gingerly under her bosom. Her face flamed. She held herself rigid and conjured Whit's face, but a pair of liquid brown eyes broke into the vision.

Behind her, Blaise twisted, checking his contraption. "Are you ready?"

"Yes."

He slid his feet to the edge of the roof. Her hands darted back, finding holds among the straps at his hips. She held tight as he tilted forward. For a split second, they fell. Grey's stomach jolted and her veins flooded with exhilaration. They jerked midair as the wings arrested their plummet. Blaise's grip loosened for a moment, then his hands clamped onto her hip and side. Swinging her legs back, she hooked her feet behind his calves just above the fins attached to his boots.

They flew around the side of the buildings where they'd landed and over the city square. The wind plucked Grey's exclamation from her lips. Below them porcies, tocks, and various forms of animals waded through the knee-high water. They were covered in muck, but the water no longer surged. Above the galleria, the golden hydro hub teetered. Water dripped from a gaping hole in its side. One jagged shard of metal hung from the opening, dangling like a giant chip of paint.

Grey wrinkled her nose at the smell of rust, rotten eggs, and some chemical she couldn't name.

"Do you see her?" His voice carried over the wind and the shushing sound of his wings.

She searched the scene below for Fantine. Her lungs tightened. Despite what Blaise had said, porcies crumpled in heaps on benches and walls, some moving and some still. The residue covering them didn't hide the jagged edges of broken and missing limbs. Fantine was nowhere to be seen.

Grey blinked stinging eyes. "Set me down. I'll look for her."

Blaise headed for a raised dais in the center of the park. Grey disentangled her legs from his and braced herself. This time she didn't trip when they landed.

He let go of her and she swung around to face him. Words stuck in her throat. He'd saved her, been gentle with her, and yet all around her porcies and tocks suffered. Wails and frantic conversation filled her ears.

He took a step forward. On level ground he was a head taller than Grey. He looked down at her a moment, a question scrunching the corners of his eyes. Then he yanked his goggles down, hiding all of his face from view.

He said something that sounded like "I'll find you." Then he ran to the edge of the dais, his feet leaving the concrete just before he would have plunged into the murky water.

Apprehension tugged Blaise into frantic flight and warred with the urge to track a certain blonde head through the chaos below. But if Callis and Seree were here—he glanced at the smashed hub—if they were involved, then he needed to find them now. He heard no calls of "Mad Tock, Mad Tock!" But it wouldn't be long before he took the blame.

Why hadn't they told him of their plan? Callis had hinted at such a demonstration, but when it came down to it, he'd left Blaise in the dark.

He'd happily crack their heads together.

Blaise flew toward what remained of the purification locus. The closer he got the more he fought the urge to vomit. The pipes inside were visible, the incoming water still poured into the bottom of the basin, slowly refilling the sabotaged hub. An elaborate structure of girders and beams supported the sphere. In the center stood a large concrete cylinder containing pipes running up from Lower and back down again. He searched for a figure or two shimmying down the metal supports but saw none. The street at the base of the hub was submerged.

The brackish water below him showed no signs of life. A cold arrow shot through his heart. He pictured the worst: Callis and Seree blown to bits by whatever explosive they used to strike the hydro hub. Maybe they kept this plan from him knowing it was a suicide mission.

He flew lower, peering in windows. Most of the porcie upper class had likely been attending the play. Their tock staffs probably hid on the top floors, terrified of the polluted water invading the elegant homes and shops of downtown.

No sign of his mended friend or Seree. Blaise flew to the intersection and on down the next street. He doubled around, zipping back and forth over buildings. He bore to the south. Where else would they go but to the outskirts of town?

There. Two figures hobbled down a row of cheap boutiques. As he watched, a cloak slipped from the taller of the two. Dirt crusted Callis's blond hair. The modified porcie moved slowly.

Blaise hovered above them, dropping to the street just as Callis turned his head. He pushed his goggles up to his forehead and rushed toward his friends.

Muck smeared the porcelain half of Callis's face. The modified's jewel eye darted about in its socket. His mechanical eye rolled out of synchronization but slowed as recognition overtook his features.

"Blaise, what are you doing here?"

Relief, sharp in his chest, made his voice harsh. "What have you done?"

The other cloaked figure turned. Seree held a handkerchief over the lower half of her face. Frenzy danced in her amber eyes.

He spread his arms. "What have you two done? You might've been smashed to bits."

She lowered the scrap of material, and Blaise smothered an oath.

Delicate brown lines etched Seree's face. The sludge from the hydro hub had stained the fine cracks invisible until now. He'd seen it before when he'd visited Lower, and in the slums of Cog Valley. And he'd cleaned out enough corroded gears and springs to know the tocks weren't safe from the untreated water either.

She smiled, dark lines spidering across her cheeks, but her voice sank. "Don't look at me like that, Mad Tock. Don't *you* look at me that way."

He schooled his face. "You're as beautiful as ever, Madam Seree."

She chuckled softly.

Beside her Callis emitted strange grinding sounds. He'd raised his mechanical arm to cover his roving eye. Greenish-brown buildup covered the outer sheaths of his tock limb. No doubt it crept through the inner workings as well.

"I suppose you're congratulating yourselves." Blaise hooked a thumb toward the center of the city. "They'll all look like you two now. That was the goal?"

Seree's disfigured face hardened. "The goal was for them to know how it feels to have filthy water running through their jitter pumps. Maybe now they won't dismiss our pleas for more hydro hubs and access to purified water."

Blaise crossed his arms. "You couldn't have told me?"

"You'd have argued, old boy." Callis quirked a smile.

"Of course I would have." He flung his arm toward the disaster. "There were children, innocent people—"

"They're not innocent." Seree pounded her palm with her fist.

Blaise tore his grid away, fixing Seree with a glare. "Grey was there. She could've drowned, you know. I told you she's like me. That much water could've *killed* her."

She took a step back from him. "I never thought of that. Blaise, I'm sorry. Did she . . . Did she . . . Is she well?"

He lowered his voice, aware of a few merchants poking their heads out of their shops. "She's fine. I picked her up just before the flood reached her."

"You met Blueboy's new prize then? You spoke to her?" Callis was shaking his head to one side. A trickle of dirty water ran out of the hammered copper ear Blaise had designed for his first patient.

"Yes."

The porcie and the modified exchanged glances.

Seree cracked a smile. "Maybe now you can woo her properly instead of tailing her like the great spectacle you are."

"Not likely! She thinks I blew up the hydro hub and maimed her friends."

A little crowd that included a few shabbily dressed porcies and gearish tocks had assembled up the street and were whispering amongst themselves. Blaise put his hand on Callis's shoulder and turned him toward the factory, motioning for Seree to come along. "Never mind the other human. Let's get you both cleaned up."

Callis's mechanized eye bounced in Blaise's direction. "Did you find out where she came from?"

"No."

"Why she's here?"

"No."

The modified porcie returned his attention to his malfunctioning parts, and the three made their way toward the factory district.

Blaise tried to watch his surroundings in case he needed to take flight, but the moments he'd spent on the rooftop with Grey replayed. The memory slowed and deepened. He felt her in his arms again, the curve of her body against his. Even when she'd stiffened as he situated her for their second flight, her limbs were pliable, her skin so soft compared to the porcelains. Curio's humid air clung to him, recalling the sensation of Grey stretched against him. He tingled from head to toe, his Defender mark pulsing with exhilaration. Forcing his thoughts from that sweet, almost painful path took immeasurable effort. He filled his brain with questions to keep the longing at bay.

Had the Chemists sent her here? What crime earned her imprisonment in Curio City? Did she have any knowledge of the key he sought?

The closer they got to their factory hideout, the more a certain balcony, back at Blueboy's mansion, called to Blaise. He had to find a way to visit Grey again. No, not just a visit. She belonged with him, the only two humans in a world of porcelain and tick-tock people. Even if it meant having to steal her away from Blueboy, he'd bring her home with him to the abandoned warehouse.

CHAPTER
14

Whit's cheek stung. A thud corresponded with the pain. He tried to make sense of the noise, but his attention narrowed to the slice on his cheek as his skin folded open. The sensation flipped his gut inside out. Warm liquid trailed down his jaw. Cuts and blood. Cuts and blood. Screaming. The darkness took it all.

He awoke to the sensation of something pressed against his lips.

"Come on, Ration Boy, drink up."

The voice snapped like an electric shock, but the way it teased over "Ration Boy" made him want to hear it again. Whit opened his eyes.

A mass of dark hair hung above him, filling his vision. Orange light picked out individual strands, turning them to distinct black lines. Whispered conversation and the scent of soap-masked urine invaded his awareness. He moved a hand to clutch his stomach as pain gnawed deep within.

The hair whisked away, replaced by a face with light brown eyes, a wide mouth, and sharp nose and chin. "He's awake," she hollered without taking her eyes off him.

"Holy Chemist elbows, man, I thought you were a doe or a baby deer or something, collapsing like that when my arrow scratched you. Then I saw your stripes and the potion, and I said to myself, 'Marina, you gotta think before you shoot.'"

Whit blinked. Before he raised his eyelids she was talking again. Her voice stopped just short of scratchy.

"Niko fixed you up. It's too bad about your pretty face." She leaned closer, touching the skin beneath the cut on his cheek with her fingertips. "Don't worry, though. When this heals, you're gonna look wicked, man. Wicked." She said the word like it tasted good.

He shrank away from her fingers, but he was flat on his back with nowhere to go.

Her eyes sparkled at his movement, and a smile took over her face. "Don't worry, Ration Boy. Nobody here gonna turn you in to the deputies."

Whit searched his narrow field of vision. "Where is 'here'?"

Marina followed his gaze. She looked back at him and shrugged. "This is our hospital."

"Hospital?"

"It's where sick people go in cities that don't have Chemists."

"I know what a hospital is." Whit heard the bite in his tone, but couldn't take it back now. His stomach roiled, and he clamped down on his lips to keep the vomit down.

She jerked and lifted the bottle she held. "Oh, you need to take this. It's not the potion you brought. This stuff's already been processed. Sorry, but it's not gonna help much."

Marina bent closer, sliding one hand behind his head to lift him toward the bottle she held. A mixture of shock, humiliation, and misery nearly dragged yesterday's food out of his stomach.

"Come on, open up." Marina pressed the bottle to his lips.

Whit swallowed the watery mixture and let his head sink down. He compressed his mouth again and breathed through his nose, nostrils flaring. He squeezed his eyes shut and opened them again to find the sharp-featured face still hovering above him. She stowed the bottle and dropped her chin into her hand.

"What'd you do to get all those stripes? You can't be much older than me. Niko said he thought it was your first. He said, 'That was no warning stripe.' Niko got striped a lot before he left."

"I helped a friend," Whit said through clenched teeth. He raised his hand to prod at the throbbing line on his cheek. His fingers touched knots of coarse thread.

"Niko had to stitch you up. We can't always get ointment up here. They'll have to come out in a couple days."

Tremendous. Just what he needed, another scar to call attention.

As the burning in his stomach faded to an ache, he raised himself on his elbows. He lay on one of two narrow beds in what had once been an inn room. The faded floorboards sagged and creaked with every movement. Draped material blocked the only window, and a lantern on a stool emitted light that barely reached the corners.

Across the room, a slight man with a mustache studied his pocket watch as he pressed his fingers to the other patient's wrist. All Whit could make out of the person in the bed was mussed hair at the back of the head and a frame that suggested a man's height.

"That's Niko," Marina said, nodding toward the dark-haired man. "He helps when people get sick. Steinar used to help too."

The way her voice lowered when she said *Steinar* brought Whit's mission crashing down on him. He sat up and swung his legs to the floor, his knees almost brushing Marina's trousers. Not a stitch of red was visible in her clothes, which were clearly assembled for warmth and necessity. "Listen,

Marina, Steinar was arrested for ration dealing. I came up here to see if I could help."

She tilted back in the chair positioned at the side of the bed. "But you're not like him. You need the potion." Her eyes darted to the pocket of her oversized coat where Whit suspected she'd hidden the ration bottle. When they returned to his face, they were hard and narrowed. "So are you looking to deal? We can trade meat—deer, elk, rabbit—"

He held a hand up to stop her. "No, I'm not aiming to be a ration dealer. I want to help like Steinar. No payment required."

Whit cleared his throat and pushed back the lurking weight of the Hawards' sacrifice.

Marina's expression lost its wary edge. She held a hand out to him. When Whit simply studied her grimy palm, she whisked it back to her knee. "Sorry, City Boy, I forget how tight you all are down the mountain."

"My name is Whit."

Her wide mouth slid into a quick grin. "All right then. If you want to help, I'll show you how you can. You up for it?"

He stood. The room whirled around his head for a moment, but settled. He pressed a hand to his empty gut.

Marina's quick eyes followed the action. She stood as well, and Whit found himself looking down. The top of her head barely reached his shoulder.

She tilted her face up to look at him. "I think we better get some food into you first. You ought to be able to keep it down, but I gotta tell you, it's not gonna be pretty when it comes out. But a little bit is better than none."

It was then he noticed the hollows in Marina's cheeks. Under her baggy coat, her frame was tiny. A glance over at Niko revealed bony wrists protruding from the sleeves of his shirt. Whit felt the difference in his own physique. He knew now. How had he ever missed the truth? The years his mother had poured most of her own ration into his bottle showed in his height and the thickness of his limbs. As he followed Marina out of the room, shame threatened to swallow him. He couldn't meet Niko's eyes and averted his gaze from the miserable form in the bed.

The nausea rose again, but Whit stuffed it down. He had no room to complain.

Marina led him down a hallway with the same musty carpet he'd glimpsed below. A few open doors revealed old beds and still bodies. When they got to the staircase, his guide stopped.

"Sorry I shot you, Ration Boy. It was only supposed to be a warning."

An arrow remained lodged in the wall at the bottom of the staircase. His coat lay on the step where he'd passed out. He studied the girl at his side. "You were guarding them, weren't you? That's why you ran upstairs and not out the back."

She nodded, her wavy hair bouncing, and started down the stairs.

What if he'd been a deputy? Marina would be on her way to one of their facilities now. His mouth hardened into a line as he watched her small figure sprint down the stairs. An image of a deputy dragging Marina off burst over him. He'd attack the potion head, tear his mask off, and beat his face in.

"You coming?" Marina motioned to him from the bottom step.

Whit thumped down and Marina led him back around the desk in the foyer and through the door he'd spotted earlier. A short hallway opened into a large kitchen with a cook stove and a center table. A smaller table in the corner showed signs of a recent meal.

The door clattered and Whit froze, his gaze flying to Marina. She popped over to hold the door open as a gray-haired woman stepped through carrying a wide, metal bucket packed with pinkish snow and—were those chunks of raw meat? Whit took a steadying breath.

Marina jerked her chin to the woman. "This is Betty. She's cooking tonight. Betty, this is Whit. He knows—knew—Steinar."

Betty's eyes whipped to Whit's face. "What happened?"

"He was arrested."

She accepted the news without question, but her eyes shimmered with unshed tears. She turned away and moved to one of the large basins against the wall.

Marina waved a hand at the wooden table on the other side of the kitchen. "Go sit. I'll find you something to eat."

Whit obeyed and watched her shrug out of her coat. He was right. She had a small build, but it curved in just the right places. She hopped up on a chair and stood, stretching to reach something in a tall cabinet. Whit admired the view until Betty gave a forced cough.

When Marina arranged the food she'd gathered in front of him, his face heated. He couldn't refuse her offer, his stomach was cramping so hard he had to bite his tongue to keep from moaning. But the oat cake and dried meat should go to one of the refugees, not to him.

He raised an eyebrow at Marina as she slid into a seat across the table from him. "Will you share my meal?"

She grinned, and he found he couldn't look away from that wide mouth. It softened the sharp points in her face. He was still looking at her lips when she answered.

"I've already had mine. But you're gonna be hurtin' if you don't get something down. Go slow, okay?"

Whit broke a piece off the stale oat cake, stuffed it into his mouth, and chewed. He wanted to gulp it whole despite its resemblance to a rock, but how would his stomach react to the food with only watered-down potion to process it?

Marina folded her chapped hands on the tabletop. "So what's your story? Why are you up here?"

A hunk of the cake lodged in his throat. Whit swallowed and lowered his gaze. "I owe a debt to Steinar."

"He helped you out too?"

"Something like that."

She seemed to sense his discomfort. Silence, broken only by Betty's preparations, filled the kitchen. Whit looked up to find Marina's tea-colored eyes on him. Next to the light brown of her irises, her lashes looked like soot. Questions tumbled out before he could stop them.

"So what's *your* story? How did you come to live here?"

She tossed her dark head. "My ancestors traded with the Apache and Comanche before the *diablos verdes* came to this land. When the green ones bought the land from Spain, my people were told not to deal with them, but we kept up our trade with the tribes. In fact, mi familia traveled from Sante Fe de Nuevo México as far as Pueblo for generations, but Papá decided to settle here. Everything was fine until Mamá became pregnant with my brother Tonio, and the influenza came. A man came to town selling cures, but he wasn't one of the green devils our traditions warned of. Papá believed his lies. We all survived but"—she gestured to her thin frame—"like this, you know? Papá got caught buying more potion a few months after. My brother Maverick and I were four and Tonio was a baby."

She fell quiet, and Whit studied the contrast of her black hair against her creamy brown skin. When she met his gaze, he returned his attention to his lunch.

"And what of your mother?" he asked after a mouthful of dried meat.

"She died last winter. Infection."

Whit's stomach soured. He forced the meat down his throat but couldn't go on with the meal.

Marina's chair scraped away from the table. "I got rounds to make, and I gotta get Burge's pack back by the time he comes down off the mountain. You coming?"

Whit nodded and got to his feet, gesturing toward his unfinished meal. "I'm obliged for the food."

She stood nearer than Grey ever had, her face angled up to his and her hands on those curvy little hips. "You earned it, Ration Boy. We take care of our own up here."

Despite the ache in his gut and the weight lodged near his heart, a smile spread on Whit's face. He winced as the sliced skin on his cheek pulled, but he didn't mind the pain. He followed Marina back to the lobby, where they snagged his coat, and she hoisted the bag of supplies Burge had smuggled. She promptly set it down again and rubbed her pointy chin as she regarded Whit.

"You look too City." She dashed into the room with the double doors and returned, arms loaded.

Standing in front of him once again, she mashed a hat with earflaps down on his head then went up on tiptoe to loop a knitted scarf around his neck. The edge of one tooth pressed into her lower lip as she wound the scarf around him. Whit couldn't look away from that little indentation. The more he looked, the warmer he got. He hooked a finger in the heavy yarn and tugged it away from his throat.

"You gotta let me breathe, woman," he muttered before Marina sank back on her heels.

She looked him up and down. "That's better. You won't draw notice."

171

After checking the street for deputies, Whit and Marina slipped out of the inn door. She hurried uphill toward the curve in the road, darting from shadow to shadow like a fox. He jogged behind, avoiding ice in the shade and slush puddles where the midday sun had melted the snow.

As they neared the bend, Marina pointed to a tall wooden structure built into the side of the mountain. Peeling paint over the door labeled the building the Rio de Sangre Mill. "This is where we dilute any potion we can get. I already sent over the bottles Burge brought. Now I gotta pick up my stock and make deliveries."

Whit checked behind them as Marina dashed toward the dilapidated mill. The Chemists had to be aware something was going on up here. If the refugees didn't find some access to potion, they'd all be dead within days. But the knot of deputies back at the train hadn't looked too interested in patrolling. Maybe a few miserable outcasts and their suppliers weren't worth the Council's time.

He ducked into the building, blinking in the dimmed light.

A hand came out of nowhere and clamped his shoulder. Whit stifled a cry as fingers squeezed his damaged skin. The owner's voice barked behind Whit.

"What are you bringing the city boy here for, Marina?"

"Let him go, Mav. He's a ration runner, not a dealer."

All movement stopped in the room as Whit turned to face a boy who matched him in height but not in breadth. Eyes a shade darker than Marina's sharpened on him. "How do you know he's trustworthy?"

"Same way I know you're not a potion head, Maverick. I just know." Marina stood at Whit's side, glaring at the other boy.

"It could be a trap. Wouldn't be the first time Chemists lured refugees with rations."

Marina crossed her arms in her oversized coat. "Steinar sent him."

The brown-eyed boy, Marina's twin brother, stepped closer. The cords of his neck stood out, tension vibrating from his body like a plucked string. "Is that true? Steinar sent you?"

Whit reached up to unwind his scarf. "More or less. I owe him."

"Maverick, you're wasting time." Marina jerked her head in Whit's direction. "He's gotta get back to the train, and I got my deliveries to make."

Her brother slouched off and positioned himself near a window, watching the quiet street.

Marina tugged on Whit's sleeve. "Come on. I'll introduce you."

She pulled him to face the mill that processed potion instead of ore.

Against one wall a set of stamp mills stood idle, their cams and axles rusted. Activity focused around a giant cauldron big enough for a person to climb in. A man stirred the contents of the vat and a woman used a funnel to fill bottles with the mixture. A wooden contraption made up of troughs, pulleys, and conveyor belts took up the center of the room, around which a handful of raggedly dressed exiles moved, switching out bottles and containers and packing the full ones into crates, boxes, and bags.

A fire burned in a makeshift pit at the end of the room, the only source of heat with the stamp mill's boilers out of operation. The back door swung open and a skinny boy trekked in, carrying a bucket of snow. He dumped it into a pot hanging over the fire. Clods of snow fell from his gloved hands and sizzled as they met the flames.

"Everybody, this is Whit. He's replacing Steinar."

The boy near the fire looked up at the sound of Marina's voice. He had her mouth and chin and her hollow cheeks. He tossed her a wave before heading back outside.

"That's my brother Tonio. He helps in here and makes deliveries too."

Marina set the bag Burge left in the alley on the warped wooden surface of a table and pulled items out—soap, canned food, articles of clothing, and a faintly glowing typewriter sleeve like some of the deputies wore. Whit moved to peer over her shoulder, but she slid the gadget behind one of the loaded crates. A woman came over and stuffed a couple wrapped packages into the bag then began sorting the supplies. She didn't retrieve the hidden device.

With the newly loaded bag over her shoulder and a carton of bottles packed in dirty cloth in her arms, Marina led the way back to the door. Maverick remained at his post, scowling at Whit as they walked by.

Outside, long shadows crept over the street. Whit stiffened. "What time is it?"

Marina eyed the sun as it dipped toward the mountains looming over the outpost. "I'd say near three thirty. You'd better get back to the train." She tossed a smile over her shoulder at him. "Or are you staying up here tonight?"

A rush of heat slid beneath Whit's skin, but he shook his head no. "If I don't get the fishing equipment I rented back to the station today, it'll be on my record."

"No potion for your family tomorrow. How many?"

Whit monitored the progress of his boots through the snow, but his mother's skeletal face rose up. "Only mother and me now."

"Better get ya back to her then."

Her words could've sounded condescending. After all, she was an orphan. But he detected only sympathy in her comment. They trudged toward the alley where Whit had spotted Marina earlier.

"I can carry the ration if you want, or take the bag."

Marina glanced around then relinquished the crate of potion bottles. "Thanks. I'll keep a lookout. You can hand it back after I hide Burge's bag."

"Couldn't I just give it to him? I met him on the train."

She shook her head. "Best not to draw eyes. Burge is . . . too loud. That man is loco. He's gonna get caught one of these days, and then we're done in. He's our best supplier."

Marina stopped at the end of the alley and signaled for Whit to flatten himself against the side of the building. "You never know when the deputies might be taking a little walk away from the station. I think they mostly take this post to shirk patrol, but all it takes is one potion-packed nut job to land us all in Chemist spit."

Despite the cold mountain air, sweat broke out on Whit's palms and forehead as he imagined a juiced-up deputy with extra potion running through his veins lurking at the other side of the alley.

Marina peeked around the corner then pressed her back against the brick wall, rolling her head to face him. "I'm gonna run in, drop the pack, and run out. Then we'll watch, and if all's clear, you can go. Just walk right by the bag as if you don't see it. You got it?"

She held his gaze for a moment, her small face framed by the black waves of her hair. Then she vanished before he could say, "Don't go. It's too risky."

He set the crate of rations down and scooted to take her place at the mouth of the alley. She dashed to the other end, dropped the bag in the shadow of one of the buildings, and ran back. Whit caught her when she reached him and pulled her back around the corner. In the moment he stood with his back against the wall and Marina tucked into his chest, a swirl of images raced through his brain. Carrying Grey. Her panicked face so close to his. The floating chug boat. The facility. His stripes. Marina's face when he'd opened his eyes. Marina's lips.

She pulled back, and he reined in a vision involving her lips and his. It couldn't be worth the pain of another striping. She kept her torso pressed against him as she peeped around the corner. The warmth of her body against his made his pulse pound.

"It's Burge."

Whit forced himself to slip around her and peered over the top of her head. At the other end of the alley, Burge hoisted the bag over his shoulder and stalked on down the street.

Marina slid back behind the safety of the building. "Give him a minute to get down the hill before you follow." She caught the look on his face. "What's the matter?"

"I can't come back until Sunday. I have to go back to the mines."

Her mouth dipped at the corners, but she jerked her chin down once. "That's all right. We make do. Burge'll be up again, and Maverick and I can make a trip to the South Quarter dealers."

Whit's heart hammered. "How often do you have to go there, to the South Quarter?"

She hunched her shoulders. "Couple times a month. Depends on how much ration we get from our suppliers and who's sick and how bad, you know?"

"Why doesn't Maverick go alone to buy from the dealers?"

Her eyes slid to a point on the brick wall left of Whit's head. "Maverick gets in trouble when I'm not around." Her voice lowered. "And the dealers like me."

The words lodged deep in his gut like her arrow had stuck in the wall. He wanted to pound any degenerate dealer who'd ever so much as looked at Marina. He clenched his hands at his sides to keep from shaking a pledge from her. "Don't go there. Just promise me you won't go there. Someone else can go."

She gave him a look he couldn't read. Her voice was gentle. "Time to go home, Ration Boy."

She offered a smile before hoisting the crate of remixed ration and hiking up the street. He watched till she ducked behind a loose board propped in a doorway then he stomped down the alley toward the main street.

Why was he angry? True, he had a million reasons to be angry. But why did the rage push everything out now, even the pain of his stripes and the spasms in his stomach? The visions swirled in his head. Shaking Marina till she promised to stay safe. Kissing Marina until neither of them could breathe. Beating deputies. Beating ration dealers. He put his hands to his ears as though he could block out the thoughts and discovered the hat she'd given him. He yanked it off and pulled at the scarf.

Below him the hunters gathered in groups on the street, holding weapons, buckets, and strings of fish or rabbits. On the platform, visible over the storefronts, several deputies worked with two men to winch a deer carcass into an open-air car at the back of the train.

Whit tucked his hat and scarf in the doorway of the store where he'd deposited his tackle. With his fishing equipment in hand, he started toward the spot where the men congregated. A commotion halted his progress.

A swarm of deputies closed around one man. A flash of cropped red hair appeared in the sea of black. Burge.

Whit's feet moved forward.

One of the agents grabbed the bag Burge held and dumped the contents onto the snow at his feet. Pinkish liquid oozed through the paper-wrapped packages.

"I butchered a rabbit I caught," Burge shouted. He held up a string of small dead creatures. "See, here's the rest."

The deputy who'd dumped the bag pointed to the meat the refugees had traded for potion. Whit couldn't hear what the man said, but two figures in black dusters dragged Burge out of the street and toward the train. Whit craned his neck, but he couldn't see where they'd taken him.

"Hey, you," a voice called from the deputy pack. "Yeah, you, kid, you were with Burgeous Clint. I saw you."

Whit met the gaze of the deputy who'd accused him. Above the glowing mask covering the man's face, hard eyes targeted him.

"I—"

"What's your name?" The agent advanced, flanked by two others.

"Whitland Bryacre."

One of the deputies yanked back his sleeve to reveal a gauntlet writer and whisked his fingers over it. He didn't look up when he issued his command. "Search him."

Whit's heart pounded, but he stood still as the two agents approached. His jaw clenched when one grasped his shoulder. As they investigated his clothes and fishing equipment, the deputy with the arm device spoke.

"Whitland Bryacre, eighteen, Age of the Stripe. Breaking curfew and illicit contact. You adding ration dealing to this list?"

"No, sir." Whit worked to steady his face as a hand dipped into his coat pocket. The bottle. Marina still had his potion bottle.

The other agents stepped back. One of them held his tackle.

"He's clean, Wade."

The deputy took a step closer. "What are you doing at the outpost?

With a nod toward the tackle, Whit said, "Fishing."

"Didn't catch much, did you?"

All three of them sniggered.

"You a friend of Burgeous Clint?"

Whit swallowed past the knot in his throat. "No, sir. Met him on the train just this morning."

The deputy with the gauntlet writer jerked his head and the other two agents peeled away. His eyes trapped Whit's as if reading a confession there. A wisp of green, potion-laced vapor escaped his mouthpiece and evaporated in the winter air. Whit held his posture, feet apart, arms at his sides, and shoulders loose. Hopefully this potion head saw nothing but a submissive, *innocent* citizen.

"You can go."

Whit hid a sigh of relief, retrieved his equipment, and shuffled toward the train, head bent. He risked a glance. No sign of Burge. As he placed a foot on the first step into the train car, the air drained from his lungs.

Marina had his potion bottle. She'd saved him from another striping. But there'd be no ration for him in the morning.

The tin soldiers stationed inside the front doors followed Grey with their flat eyes. She lingered by the steaming fountain long enough to imagine dashing by the metal men, but the door they guarded was locked. So was the gate outside. For three days the platoon had only allowed assembly members in and out of Blueboy's estate.

She made a show of studying the arrangement of goblets and cups on a nearby trolley, but her eyes made trips to the various doors and hallways leading off the main gallery. The ballroom, formal entertaining room, and library offered no access outside. Every veranda and terrace had been closed off, and Drakon patrolled, checking and rechecking locks.

Grey pretended to decide against a sip from the fountain and moseyed toward the back of the great house. She wandered to a small door set in the rounded corner. It must contain a stairway to the tower and maybe a door to the outside, but the handle wouldn't budge. A frisson of panic clenched her lungs, but she shook it off. She just had to wait out the porcies' alarm and safety measures. Benedict was still on alert after the explosion in the city center. And Fantine hid in her room, haunted by the hydro hub flood even though she'd escaped injury by dashing into the galleria when disaster hit.

Raised voices carried from behind the double doors of the assembly room. Grey ducked into the copse of jeweled trees and strained to pick up any tidbit of news, but the conversation quieted. With her back to a smooth trunk, she slid to the ground and drew her knees up. Her shimmering green dress blended with the glittering leaves all around her, concealing her from passersby.

A muffled swish signaled the opening of the chamber door. Grey tilted her head as Drakon's voice carried to her hideout.

"Right this way, please. I'll show you out."

"I hope his lordship isn't angry," a female tone pleaded.

Drakon murmured his response and the group moved past the jeweled forest. Grey crawled between two large trees near the front of the sculpture and peered out.

The tock butler's stiff back was visible between the bodies of two porcelains, a man and a woman, who followed him toward the fountain in the entryway. The man patted the woman's arm.

"I'm sure Lord Blueboy understood our predicament, Penelope dear. We did the right thing in coming forward. Especially under present circumstances."

The three stopped at the fountain, and Drakon slid a palm toward the bubbling shell. "May I offer you refreshment before you leave?"

Grey scooted back to the oval beneath the canopy of emerald leaves. What information had this couple shared? They showed no signs of damage, so it probably wasn't about the flood, yet whatever they'd said had caused an uproar among the assembly.

The jingle of Drakon's key ring and the whoosh of the heavy front door drifted from the front of the house. Grey settled in to wait and listen. She closed her eyes and held in a breath as a dark-eyed face floated before her. The tree trunk at her back became his firm torso aligned with hers, filling her with the reality of him. Another human in Curio.

Find him and bring him back.

It had to be Blaise. He belonged in her world even if he was a renegade and a mutineer. All those cracked and shattered porcies, and she couldn't stop thinking about a flying boy and wishing he'd spent more time with his mask off.

She banished that liquid gaze and full lower lip and opened her eyes, occupying her vision with ruby primroses, amethyst lilac blooms, and colored glass tree trunks. The Mad Tock would be caught. Benedict would see to that. Then she had a job to do. But how would they get out of this world within a cabinet? And what could it change? Father was probably dead.

She drew her knees up once again, folded her arms over them, and dropped her head.

Sometime later, footsteps sounded close by, jerking her head to attention. Blueboy entered the bower, his gaze over his shoulder as if he watched for followers. Grey tensed. She had no time to duck out.

He turned and his startling blue eyes widened.

"Grey, what are you doing here?"

She tilted her head back against the trunk as he stepped closer. One of his dark brows arched.

"Your face is leaking. My dear, are you well?"

Grey rubbed at the tears on her cheeks before Benedict did something crazy like lick them off. He held a hand out, and she accepted his help, scrambling to her feet with a wince. Tingling spread through her foot.

"You're not well. What is it?" He retained her hand in his and bent his dark head.

"It's nothing. My foot's—" She stopped, searching for an explanation. "My foot is stiff."

"Oh." His lashes lowered as he swept her body with his gaze. "Do you need warming?"

"No, no. I'm perfectly warm. I just need to stretch." She tried her weight on both feet, wiggling her toes in the soft slippers Nettie had paired with her dress.

Benedict dropped her hand and straightened. "You haven't answered my question. What are you doing in the emerald arbor?"

"I like it in here. It's beautiful," Grey said. When he didn't reply, she stammered on. "With Fantine, um, resting, I've been exploring on my own and—"

"Listening in on assembly meetings?"

Grey's cheeks flamed. Benedict brought a finger up to trace her cheekbone.

"This heat, where does it come from?"

Grey opened her mouth but no explanation came out.

He moved his hand to the pulse in her neck. "You never cool. Tell me how I can be the same, and I will forgive the secret you've kept from me."

"W-what secret?"

His mouth hitched into a smirk. "Did you think I wouldn't find out? Nothing happens in Curio City that I'm not aware of. Now"—his thumb glided beneath her jaw—"tell me how I can be soft but strong like you, never cooling, unbreakable."

"I am breakable." Grey bit her tongue.

Ice glinted in his eyes before he hid the expression behind hooded lids. His fingers tightened at her throat. "I would never break you, Grey."

Grey tried to swallow past his choke hold. He loosed his grip, stepping away and back into the role of charming host.

"Again, please tell me what makes you always warm, and I'll overlook your offense of withholding information."

Grey slid a hand to her bruising neck. What did Benedict suspect her of? "Blood, I suppose." She held her wrist out, tapping the veins with one finger. "You have hot water running through your system and I have blood, but it's more complicated—"

He drew close again and snatched her hand. The languid façade was gone as he examined the blue lines beneath her skin. He brushed a hand over her navel, and she shivered despite the gown covering her skin.

"Is this the source, the mark on your stomach?"

Grey frowned. Her mark did resemble a trellis of curling veins. But what did that have to do with her blood? Her stomach fluttered. No, not a flutter. The sensation flickered from her mark, spreading out like a shell growing beneath her skin. The same reaction she'd had the night Whit was taken.

She looked down and recoiled. Benedict's hand skimmed her thigh, his white fingers gathering her skirt inch by inch. Cool air whisked over her ankles and shins.

She jerked away. "What are you doing?"

He watched the fabric of her dress slip down to cover her ankles. "I want to see all the blue lines. Do you have other marks? Show me."

Grey crossed her arms to hide her trembling. "No, I won't."

His eyes widened, the whites gleaming a faint green in the tinted light of the arbor.

"I'm not a sculpture or a painting." Grey inched away. Her back bumped into the tree trunk. Benedict's lip curved as he noted her predicament.

New strength, that hardening from within, surged from her mark. "I'm not a doll to be dressed or undressed . . . or locked up."

His face was inches from hers now, and a strange smile lifted his mouth. "Ah, but don't we lock away our most precious belongings?"

"I don't belong to you, Benedict."

The smile vanished. His hand closed around her upper arm, and Grey let out a yelp as he yanked her across the bower to an opening between the trees. The strength she'd felt vanished. She winced at the vise pressure of his fingers.

Silent, he dragged her to the elevator and tossed her in. Grey crashed into the wall and huddled there as Benedict wrenched the metal gate closed. Her lungs refused to fill, and the words she pushed out sounded thin and small. "What are you doing?"

He pinned her to the wall. Steam hummed deep in his chest, and his eyes burned into hers. "If you ever speak to me like that again, I will have you banished to Lower. You are a guest in my house. A guest who's already betrayed me once."

The elevator rocketed upward then ground to a stop. Steam rose from the threshold as the doors skated open. Benedict sprang from the lift, towing Grey and rushing past a surprised tock who jumped out of their way. He hauled her across the wide landing toward the north wing. A maid scuttled behind a screen that hid the servants' stairway, and Grey couldn't catch her eye to communicate her panic.

The soft click of the door signaled the beginning of Benedict's next harangue. His voice was low and edged with poison.

"Had you come to me and told me of your association with the Mad Tock, I would have been lenient. As it is, my curiosity is the only thing keeping you from the Dulaig's cages or the crushing pits of Lower."

Someone had seen her with Blaise.

Benedict burst through the door leading to the gallery and pulled Grey over the thick carpet. She tripped and he dragged her back to her feet, his hard fingers digging into her flesh. She cried out.

He threw her against the door of her room. Her skull cracked against the panel and spikes of light consumed her vision. She scrambled for the handle, nails gouging into the wood. Her fingertips met Benedict's marble-smooth skin as his hand curled around the doorknob. One stone-like forearm crushed her shoulders and collarbone, trapping her against the door.

"As for what I *will* look at and *will* touch, I require no permission. Your body hides as many secrets as your tongue. Secrets I want. And you'll give them up, Grey. By the Designer, you will give them up."

She couldn't move. Couldn't breathe. The hard planes of his torso pinned her. The hum in his chest built to a buzz that traveled through her.

A cloud of heat smothered Grey, but cold rage spread beneath her skin. She stretched her neck out, her mouth inches from his. "Touch me, and I'll break you."

"We shall see who breaks." Steam seeped from behind his clenched white teeth and stung her face and eyes.

A surge of power traveled from Grey's gut as waves of strength radiated from her mark. She pushed him with all her might, but it wasn't enough. She wrestled a block of marble.

The knob rattled under his hand, and the door at Grey's back gave way. With a growl, Benedict shoved her backward. A faint sound brought him up short. He looked away from Grey and over his shoulder.

Fantine's voice shook. "Benedict? What's going on?"

His hands left her body and Grey dragged in a breath. Over his shoulder she spied Fantine in a lacy dressing gown, her fingers shielding her throat.

Benedict strode across the rug toward Fantine, who clutched her doorframe as though unable to keep herself standing. Grey slammed her own door and fumbled with the handle until reason sliced through her panic. It locked from the outside. She scrambled to the nightstand and hauled it to block the door. Next she wedged a chair beneath the handle. When nothing movable remained for her to pile at the entry to her room, Grey sat on her bed.

Shivers wracked her body, and she scrubbed at the wetness on her cheeks. Where was that surge of strength now? She covered the spot on her stomach where the mark bloomed. Cold permeated her skin, wrapping icy fingers around her heart. She grabbed a pillow and hugged it to her.

Breathe. Just breathe.

The doorknob rattled and Grey leapt from the bed. A crack appeared at the doorframe, but after a shove Benedict relented. His voice cut through her bedchamber.

"I hope you understand, Grey, that with my city in danger, I don't have the luxury of time. If you know of the Mad Tock's plans, I suggest you confess the knowledge now. As for the mystery of your own workings, my soft one, I will uncover every enigma."

The sneer in his last words reached inside her, squashing her newly discovered source of strength. The door snapped shut, but his voice penetrated the wood.

"One more thing. I'll be ordering the servants to remove every painting within these walls."

Blaise slouched lower in his chair, an eye on the door leading to the Wind-Up's common area. Two tock women slipped in and moved to an alcove in the dim back room, settling to the right of him. One, a smooth-surfaced girl in a maid's uniform, turned her back to the other, partially unbuttoned her blouse, and slipped it down over her shoulders. The smaller tock's fingers zipped down the maid's back until she reached the key in the middle. Blaise looked away. Winding required trust, making it an intimate gesture. What would it be like to expose yourself and put your life in the hands of another? Not once, but daily.

An old guilt rose to constrict Blaise's lungs, but his eyes returned to the key between the tock woman's shoulders. The metal was plain, the design functional. It was not the key he sought.

Across the table Callis shifted, a question lifting the fine line of his remaining eyebrow. Blaise shook his head and let Callis continue murmuring treason in the back of Seree's establishment.

"We've made them lift their foolish heads." The modified addressed his congregation of a liveried footman, a gearish tock with cogs rotating in his cheeks, and two porcies in cheap suits.

"We've made it harder to get pure water is what we've done. Or what *you've* done, Callis." The porcie's amethyst eyes glinted in the low light. One finger tapped the tabletop in time with his complaints. "More restrictions, more paperwork, more money. How does that help those of us trying to run a business? How can we prove ourselves brave if we're forced to cower for the battalions and our clientele?"

Callis lifted his porcelain hand toward the door. His mechanical arm rested motionless in his lap. "Seree is making do."

"Her prices have jumped," the other porcie grumbled.

Callis turned the full force of his half-porcelain, half-tock gaze on the slender man. "Don't you dare wheeze on Seree."

The door opened and Blaise lifted his mouthpiece, but at the sight of Seree he dropped it again, letting it hang to one side of his face. A buzz of tock speech punctuated by the clink of porcie sipping glasses carried into the quiet back room. The two tock women darted out to join the gaming in the common area.

Seree approached their table with a tray in her hand. Tonight she wore the expected garb of a female tavern owner. Her low-cut dress further revealed the damage done by the untreated water. Brown fissures crawled down her once milk-white neck, over her collarbones, and across her chest.

The porcies at the table nodded and the gearish tock cranked an arm up in salute. Callis kept track of every move Seree made as she circled the table.

Blaise refused the glass of pure water she tried to set in front of him. He nodded toward the door. "Give it to one of them."

She returned the glass to the tray and leaned in. "The soldiers were here earlier today. They're looking for the Mad Tock." She caught his eyes with her topaz ones. "Be careful. Promise me?"

He quirked his mouth into a casual smile. "Madam Seree, you know I always am."

"Don't tease now, Blaise. If they send you to Lower, you'll starve."

"You and Callis wouldn't let that happen."

She glanced to Callis, whose eyes were on her despite the continued conversation around him. "And if we're imprisoned? Or worse?"

She touched his cheek and Blaise let his lids lower. He shouldn't let her caress him. No matter how his body responded to her touch, his heart never followed. He opened his eyes and hardened his features.

"I promise I'll be careful. Perhaps you should say the same to Callis." He let the cool smile return. "And to yourself."

She withdrew her hand, a flicker of something rash in her eyes. She should be locked up for her own good. Maybe he'd find her a quiet farm in the country and a handsome shepherd with nothing better to do than keep her warm. But she'd find her way back to trouble like a porcie child found sharp edges.

Continuing around the table, Seree delivered drinks with the grace of an upper-class lady. Callis smiled at her when she slid his mug of steaming water on the table in front of him. At least the accident that shattered half his friend's body left his mouth intact.

When Seree returned to her customers in the front, Callis leaned in, wrapping his hands around his mug. "Sirs, I understand your concerns. We anticipated this crackdown before we triggered Gagnon's device." He nodded to the tock with the exposed gears. "That's why the next step of our plan is to divert the water supply from Ames Weatherton's estate to Cog Valley. Think of it . . . all the water coursing through that property, pouring into our own hub."

"You're building your own purification locus?" The purple-eyed porcie jerked his lapels twice in quick succession. "How? How can you keep such a thing hidden?"

Callis pointed to his inventor friend. "Gagnon here has been working on it in his factory."

The rugged tock spoke, his voice rough and grating. "There are advantages to working at the mouth of Lower. Even the soldiers avoid it."

Talk at the table took on an excited edge, but Blaise returned to Seree's warning. They searched for him. They had from the beginning, when Blueboy's power structure was nothing more than a collection of empty-headed individuals paying homage to the most handsome among them. Even then the citizens of Curio City whispered of one who was different. When Blaise became the Mad Tock, his actions drew more attention even as his disguise provided anonymity. Hadn't the hundred years he'd spent locked away in this enchanted prison been leading to this? Rebellion. Revelation. Then what? They could kill him if they knew how.

And Grey. Every nerve came to attention at the thought of her. What had she told Blueboy of their meeting? Probably everything. His hands clenched into fists. How he'd like to smash that porcie's pretty face to pieces.

"Are you with us?"

Blaise came out of his musing to find every face directed at him. So it was time for swearing allegiance. He put his hand flat on the table and leaned in.

"I'm with you. Let's take them down."

Blaise and Callis's footsteps echoed along the cramped streets of the Shelf. A darkness blacker than the city night spread across the horizon beyond the factory district—the only sign of the sharp descent into Cog Valley. The porcies and most of the tocks hated Cog Valley by day. By night even the soldiers avoided it, relying on a few crooked tocks to keep the denizens of Lower where they belonged.

"You were quiet tonight," Callis said.

Blaise inspected the shadows ahead. "You had them in hand."

Callis shoved his hands in his pockets. "New recruits are always a gamble, but I think the two porcies are with us, even if they're just enamored with all the valor talk."

They fell silent as they walked. Who had started the whispers of revolution now raging through porcie parlors and sipping establishments? Blaise turned over the possibilities. Sir Hinderoot had been seen riding his black steamer horse around town, attracting attention from other bored upper-class porcies. Ratiki, the wealthy tock with a hand in all of Curio's new buildings, had publicly disagreed with an assembly member. Even Ames Weatherton, whose estate was slated for a strike, had a fondness for shatter-defying contraptions.

Callis interrupted his thoughts with a few calm words.

"It's Grey, isn't it? You've been more . . . surly since she arrived."

"Surly?"

The mended porcie fixed him with a direct stare. "You haven't said what her coming means. Do you know?"

"No."

"She's stayed longer than the man does."

Blaise shuddered. "Don't talk to me of him."

A smile tugged the corner of Callis's mouth. "She's Beauty's Best compared to that mangled creature."

Blaise's palms went slick and his mouth dry. Beauty's Best didn't begin to describe Grey. And she hated him.

Noise carried from a few streets over, and he snapped back into focus. Callis cocked his head, his expression tense.

"A street game, do you think?" Blaise said.

Callis shook his head. "Too late for that."

They rounded a corner, the ground gradually sloping to carry them farther into the maze of large factories clinging to the edge of the Shelf.

"Too bad I left the pack at home. I could've flown ahead."

"Mind your disguise, just in case," Callis said.

Blaise lowered his goggles, the colored lenses giving his surroundings a bronze tinge. The mouth grid he fastened on did nothing to block the metallic tang in the humid air.

They made their way through the outline of streets bordering the massive textile plants on the edge of town. The still carts of the cable tower dangled high above as they crossed the square of concrete beneath and neared their own quarter.

Two short streets lay between them and home. They turned on the first and Callis held up his hand.

"Footsteps. Tock."

Blaise picked out the tread of many boots. His stomach dropped. He looked to Callis. "Soldiers."

Callis nodded, his porcelain lips tipped downward.

They crept fifty or so feet to the next corner. This road ran parallel to the factory that stood directly in front of their abandoned warehouse home. Blaise trotted over the sidewalk to a stretch of grass at the base of the building. Callis followed and the two inched their way to the corner. The noise increased. Tock soldiers never seemed to feel the need to be stealthy.

Blaise craned his head around the corner. His heart turned to rock in his chest. A line of Blueboy's soldiers marched in the front door of the factory. A twin line marched out. The metal men tramping out carried equipment from his lab, armloads of clothing, a few prototypes of mechanical limbs he and Callis had designed. The stone in his chest pressed into his ribcage as a soldier emerged with his steam pack.

Blaise cursed and Callis sucked in a breath as the tock trooper lugged the flying contraption to the commanding officer. Before he could stop himself, Blaise charged around the corner, feet pounding toward the man holding his pack. Arms jerked him back, and Callis spoke in his ear.

"We can't fight the whole platoon."

The stone gripping his heart spread, growing like a layer of ice beneath his skin. He let his Defender state take hold and fill his veins with liquid strength. When he shook Callis off and barreled forward he felt nothing but impenetrable power.

The soldier and his commanding officer looked up, faces frozen in their usual blank expressions. Blaise crashed into the tock holding his pack. A crunching sound reached his ears as he met the solid wall of metal, but he didn't stop. The steam pack clattered to the street a few feet from where Blaise now struggled under the grip of both soldiers.

Out of the corner of his eye, he spied a commotion at the door of the factory as soldiers stopped to gawk. Callis burst onto the scene, swinging a plank of wood with his porcelain arm. The numbness covering Blaise broke for a moment, and pain, deep and grinding, registered in his shoulder. He turned from his friend and the granite strength inside him surged.

With both arms locked in the grip of the two soldiers, Blaise brought his boot up and aimed a sideways kick at the commanding officer. The man staggered backward, losing his hold on Blaise's shoulder.

Callis's shout mingled with the whir of platoon voices. Blaise used his free arm to grab the metal shoulder of the man still restraining him. He thrust his other hand forward, breaking the tock's grip and hooking him beneath the arm. A second later, the tin soldier sailed through the air to clatter into his commanding officer. Both went down.

Blaise snagged the pack from the ground and slid it on as he ran to the knot of soldiers around Callis. The modified porcie swung the hefty plank in wide arcs, keeping the ring of soldiers at bay. Barely.

He couldn't get to Callis. Not through a circle of soldiers growing every second. Blaise turned on his heels and ran, speeding past the two soldiers he'd knocked down.

A jab of pain in his left shoulder cut through his concentration, but he ignored it and ran on. Pulling the cord to the bellows with his right hand, he reached up to release the wings with his left.

"Ahh." He bit down on the cry of pain and made his arm obey. The wings extended. The puff of the bellows over the smoldering cinderite in the chamber carried to his ears despite the noise behind him.

Blaise looked up and his heart sank. The street wasn't long enough and the cinderite couldn't possibly heat fast enough for him to get airborne. The black pellets were probably all but cold. Still he ran, pumping the bellows until the muscles in his arm burned. The wall of the neighboring factory rose up, immovable, final. But the pistons were moving. The wings flapped.

The street beneath Blaise's feet fell away and he skimmed the side of the factory, the hastily fastened harness dragging him straight up into the dark haze of the Curio sky. Without the support of chest belts, the strap at his shoulder dug into his muscles like wicked fingers.

He doubled back and swooped down between the buildings. Callis held his ground, but the soldiers were gaining, pressing in on his friend from all sides.

"Callis."

The modified's head whipped up. Now to see if the repairs Blaise made to Callis's arm worked. Callis lifted both arms as Blaise neared. After a moment, the soldiers raised their hands as well. They grabbed at him with fingers like metal traps. They tore his clothes but couldn't pull him out of the air. His hands connected with Callis and he pulled. A howl escaped Blaise's lips as pain seared his shoulder. Callis's weight strained the injured joint, hauling him downward. Blaise kept his grip as Callis kicked out with his rebuilt leg, bashing heads and toppling soldiers. The ring of tin men below shifted and swayed under the assault.

And they were away, climbing into the sky. A few musket balls followed their escape, but sailed wide of their flight path.

Blaise flew, Callis dangling beneath him, to the very edge of the Shelf. The muted lights of Cog Valley below spun in dizzying patterns as pain muffled all other thought. He grit his teeth and struggled to reach a factory rooftop. A spasm burned from his left shoulder down to his hand. His fingers jerked and went slack. Callis slid but grasped his right arm with both hands. With one last push, Blaise glided over the flat surface of the roof. Callis dropped and Blaise tumbled down a few feet away. He rolled, clutching his shoulder.

Callis scrambled to his side. "You're damaged."

Blaise tugged the loose collar of his shirt down to examine his left shoulder. The skin bloomed blue and purple. Callis bent his head, studying the bruise.

"Surface only?" the porcie asked.

Blaise shook his head. "No, something inside. Not a break but maybe torn tissue." He tested his fingers, wrist, and elbow and winced at the movement. At least he still had some use of his arm.

Callis lowered himself to sit on the rooftop. "Do you need repairs?"

Blaise cringed inwardly but kept his face impassive. "I don't know, but we've got to get off this rooftop. They'll come looking."

"You can't carry me with your arm like that." Callis pointed to a door set inside a low, sloping structure much like the one on their rooftop. "I can get down and disappear in the streets. You head back to Seree's and see what can be done about your arm."

The Defender state that had protected Blaise as he fought slipped away, dropping beneath his skin like clothes shed from the outside of his body. Pain closed in along with the certainty that no porcie or tock could fix his arm if the damage was severe. He pressed his lips tight and nodded to Callis.

"We'll meet up at Seree's then," Callis said.

The modified got to his feet and disappeared through the door and down into the factory below. In a few moments, Blaise was airborne again. Keeping an eye on the darkened streets below, he wove through the layer of mist in the direction of the Wind-Up.

The sight of a black coach blocking the Wind-Up's entrance sent apprehension zinging through him. From the air it looked like a slab of flat slate. Mechanical horses stood motionless as soldiers milled about the courtyard. Blueboy's men never frequented Seree's place.

Blaise's chest tightened. He struggled for a deep breath in the choking fog.

A knot of soldiers emerged from the door, moving strangely. They all turned inward with their arms interlinking, creating a swarming huddle. Porcelain skin flashed in the middle of the cluster.

Seree.

They held her fast. A dozen soldiers moved as one to drag the porcelain woman into the waiting prison coach.

"Miss Grey?"

Grey jolted awake and grabbed a pillow, yanking it over her torso like a shield. Pointed shadow fingers stretched across the floor, inching toward her bed.

Another knock made her jump. "Miss Grey, it's Nettie. Let me in."

She loosened her grip on the pillow. "Are you alone, Nettie?"

"Yes, Miss. I have your vase."

The maid would never call attention to such personal needs with a porcie present. Grey slid off the bed and picked her way through the furnishings she'd piled against the door. She removed the chair wedged beneath the handle and cracked the door enough to see Nettie's face. The maid's shiny mouth drooped and her brown glass eyes held concern. Light from the gallery beyond spilled through the sliver of an opening, but no one lurked behind Nettie.

Grey kicked a chest full of gloves and stockings out of the way and opened the door wider. Nettie bent to retrieve the vase she'd placed on the floor and entered, a silver tray balanced in her other hand.

On cue, Grey's stomach rumbled. "Oh, Nettie, you're the best."

Nettie's expression changed from concern to confusion. "Indeed I am not Beauty's Best, Miss."

Grey's heart squeezed. She took the vase from Nettie's hand, placed it on a chair, then clutched the tock's metal fingers. "You are beautiful, Nettie, and so kind to bring me food."

"It's not my doing." She set the tray down on the vanity and twisted a dial on the wall to fill the room with amber light. "Lord Blueboy sent me with this."

A silver bowl held a pile of blood-red cherries. Next to the fruit lay a folded sheet of paper and a goblet of water. Grey retreated to sit on the edge of the bed, her appetite squashed.

"What happened, if I might ask?" Nettie trundled closer. "My mistress is distraught. She refuses to allow me to dress her and won't leave her room. It's not just the flood that upsets her."

"Did Fantine say anything about an incident earlier today?"

Nettie's thin metal lips pressed in a line. For a moment, Grey thought she wouldn't speak, but the maid lowered herself to a chair and twisted her hands in her lap.

"She knows Lord Blueboy finds you beautiful. She thinks you're to be his next mistress, and she'll be sent away."

Grey dug her fingernails into the pink satin bedspread. "You can tell Fantine that in no world, this one or any other, will I *ever* be Benedict's mistress."

Nettie's eyes widened. "Oh, Miss Grey, you mustn't speak like that. If anyone hears—if Lord Blueboy hears—you'll be banished to Lower straight off."

Grey scooted to the center of the bed and folded her legs, resting her elbows on her knees. "What is this Lower I keep hearing about?"

Nettie shuddered. "It's the subterranean level of the city. We get our water from the lake down there. The pipe system goes all the way down. They say it's dark and cold, but the worst is the manner of tocks and porcies that live beneath. There are tocks as big as carriages working on the pipelines, and there are porcies so maimed they can't do anything but beg. And it's crawling with modifieds."

"Modifieds?"

"Porcies that have lost limbs and have mechanical replacements."

Grey winced at the memory of the smashed porcies. "Wouldn't an artificial limb be better than no limb at all?"

Nettie paused, her features caught in contemplation. "Well, that's what I would choose. But I'm a tock. I'm not built for beauty."

"Who gives the broken porcies their mechanical limbs?"

Nettie leaned forward in her chair. The faint whir of her internal clockwork drifted to Grey. The maid's tone was hushed. "Some say they go to Cog Valley. Some say there's a rogue glueman doing it. And others say it's the Mad Tock."

Grey sucked in a quick breath. "What do you know about the Mad Tock?"

Nettie tucked her arms protectively around her midsection. "He kidnaps folks. A long time ago it was just tocks he stole. That's why he has extra parts and can fix the porcies. I've heard he's so good at it that you can't even tell the limb is mechanical—if it's hidden by clothes, of course. They say some porcies even seek him out. Can you imagine? They say he's strange, more hideous than the gearish tocks and, well, mad."

Nettie's words settled into Grey, chilling her heart. Despite the handsome face at odds with the maid's description, the rest of her account sounded accurate.

"They've been hunting him since the hydro hub explosion. Talk in the servants' quarters is they've made raids tonight."

Grey's head whipped up. "Did they catch him?"

Nettie shifted to the edge of her chair as if to rise. "No, they caught another rebel though. That's what I heard." She stood and nodded toward the tray she'd brought. "So Lord Blueboy knows about your, er, needs?"

Grey jerked her chin once.

Nettie wrung her hands a moment then took a step closer. "It's best not to anger him. Look at Mistress Fantine. He takes good care of her, doesn't he? She has everything she could ever ask for, and he's gentle with her now. He'll provide for her when she leaves. You'll see. All will be Beauty's Best."

Grey's eyes stung as she looked at her friend. "No, it won't, Nettie, because I'll never belong to Benedict."

Nettie backed toward the door, skirting the clutter with precise steps. "Then I am sorry, Miss. I truly am." She slid a hand into her apron pocket and produced a brass key.

Grey sprang off the bed. "No. Please don't."

The maid dropped her gaze. "I'm sorry." She slipped through the door, and the key grated in the lock.

Bracing one foot on the wall, Grey yanked the door handle with all her strength. The wood creaked but the lock held fast. She raised a fist to pound on the door but stopped. The only one close enough to hear was Fantine, and the porcelain woman likely hated her now.

She turned, pressing her back to the door. She was locked in, but at least Benedict was out there. She'd do everything in her power to keep him locked out, but the spoiled ruler wouldn't put up with this game for long. The bowl of cherries caught her eye. A cruel joke?

Grey crossed the room and swiped the folded paper from the tray. Inside she found a note written in an ornamental hand. After a few seconds, she made out the words.

My Tender Beauty,

Consider the cherries a gesture of repentance. My behavior today was inelegant. Take the evening to rest and tomorrow we shall talk again. I assure you I will be satisfied, but I hope for a shared experience of beauty rather than forced cooperation on your part.

Until tomorrow,

Benedict

The paper fluttered in Grey's hands. Her body shook, but underneath her skin a layer of strength spread. She scanned the room, contemplating each candlestick, vase, and chair leg. She needed a weapon.

Blaise flew far enough back from the last marching soldier to remain hidden. He followed the coach to Harrowstone, the prison built into a cliff face on the western edge of town. The carriage passed beneath an arch set in the tall, rectangular structure protruding from the rock. A portcullis lowered, blocking his pursuit of Seree and her captors. The remaining members of the mechanical platoon positioned themselves as sentries before the gate.

They were expecting an attack from the Mad Tock. Deep inside a voice urged him to strike, fly straight into the metal men and send them toppling like so many lined-up blocks in a tock tavern game. But his shoulder burned, the weight of the steam pack pulled like a load of bricks on his injured joint. And what if Callis were walking into a trap at this very moment?

He swore under his breath, took a final look at the prison—red brick against gray rock—and launched into the air. An aerial search of the Wind-Up revealed soldiers posted at the front and rear entrances and no sign of Callis. Blaise gave the tavern a wide berth and circled back to the Shelf. Maybe Callis had already been to the Wind-Up, spotted the soldiers, and slipped away unnoticed.

Blaise headed deep into the factory district, avoiding his home in case an ambush waited. A sliver lodged in his chest when he glimpsed the familiar roof from three streets away. The lab. His loft. They'd ransacked the place, taken everything he'd collected over the years. Well, everything in the factory anyway.

Before he was aware of his intentions, Blaise found himself nearing the steep footpath leading down into Cog Valley. A form stole from shadow to shadow on the empty trail. He flew lower and recognized a blond head.

"Callis."

His friend jumped and flattened himself against the rock wall on his right. But by the time Blaise set down, Callis was jogging toward him.

"The Wind-Up. There were guards when I got there." Callis stopped, worry twisting his mishmash features. "I waited under the awning of Clayman's, but when you didn't come—"

"Seree," Blaise couldn't hold it in any longer. "They took Seree. I got there just as an entire platoon dragged her out."

Callis muffled an oath. "To Lower?" He craned his neck, searching the darkened path. "But I didn't see—"

"I followed them. Callis, they took her to Harrowstone."

His friend collapsed against the rock wall. "They'll break her. Bit by bit, they'll crack her in pieces."

Blaise gulped past a stone in his throat. "We can fix whatever they break." They were hollow words and he knew it. Seree would be in agony until she cooled. If they allowed her to cool. There was no telling how she'd come out of

Curio's prison. The damage might be beyond their skill. And without their lab . . .

"A trade." Callis pushed away from the cliff face and staggered toward Blaise. "We'll offer a trade. Seree for one of their own."

"Who?" Blaise ran through the list of upper-class porcies. Who was valuable enough to trade for Seree's freedom?

"Blueboy's new prize." A sneer spread on Callis's face. A wild gleam lit his jeweled eye.

"What?" But Blaise knew before the word left his mouth. Grey. Callis wanted him to kidnap Grey. His heart tripped and a surge of anticipation simmered deep in his gut.

Callis's smirk spread into a grimace. "Ah, yes. You see the beauty of it now, don't you? He's paraded her by all the nobles just like he does with his protégés. She's his new masterpiece. His new obsession. She's the perfect bargaining chip."

Blaise struggled against the urge to take to the air now, fly back to Blueboy's estate, and steal Grey away, but not just for the purposes of Callis's plan. Questions pelted his mind, and with her under his guard she'd have no choice but to answer. His pulse raced at the thought of flying through the night with her pressed against him.

A lash of pain in his socket brought him up short. "My arm. I can't snatch her from her bedroom and carry her across the city with my arm like this."

Callis frowned. "How long will repairs take?"

Blaise eyed his shoulder as if the answer might be written on his tattered shirt. "I have no idea."

"Then she'll have to come willingly."

"I told you she hates me."

Callis shrugged. "Then lie. Tell her you weren't involved—"

"I wasn't."

"Tell her you want to show her something. Tell her you'll explain everything. Use that strange charm that makes Seree's jitter pump purr."

The modified's last words came out with a bitter edge, and Blaise shifted his gaze to his boots.

"Just get her," Callis said. "Bring her to Gagnon's."

Blaise didn't stay to listen to any more ranting. Turning, he marched back up the path, yanking on his bellow cord. "I'll bring her."

When he took to the air, the strain of the harness on his shoulder made his eyes water. Banishing the pain, he flew straight across the city, high enough to avoid notice but without any other regard to stealth. This errand had to be quick. He needed to be long gone with Grey by the time morning arrived.

What was that sound?

Grey uncurled from her spot on the rose-upholstered sofa she'd dragged to her makeshift fortress against the bedroom door. Her fingers tightened on the parasol she'd unearthed from the wardrobe.

Benedict had promised she had until the morning, and only the faint light of gas lamps shimmered through the frothy curtains at her window and into her darkened room.

A creak and a jangle reached her stronghold.

She threw off the sheet she'd tugged over from the bed and bolted to her feet. The knee-length bloomers with their frilly cuffs felt gloriously unrestricting after days spent in gowns. With a simple blouse, low-slung belt, and sturdy boots, the outfit provided necessary ease of movement. She clutched her collar closed and, with eyes shut, went over her plan.

Hide in here as long as she could.

Fight Benedict off. Possibly take the parasol to his handsome face.

Escape the first chance she got.

Her eyes popped open as a thud drew her attention to the window. Through the curtains, a bulky form straightened out of a crouch. The silhouette was unmistakable. Grey's stomach tightened. She slid a hand over the whorled design around her navel. Beneath her shirt, the lines of her mark warmed as though traced by invisible fingers.

Grey took a shallow breath before the glass door burst open, the lock snapping after one quick blow. Blaise ducked down, his folded wings and the top of his head skimming just beneath the edge of the casement.

Grey stepped forward. "What are you doing here?"

He shoved his goggles to his forehead and detached his mouth grid. He wore a pained expression beneath his gear. Grey's heart pinched despite her better instincts. After a glance at the barrier she'd erected, his concerned eyes sought her.

"I told you I'd find you." Weariness threaded the voice she'd been waiting to hear.

Her heart softened, but she checked the warmth spreading through her and straightened her shoulders. "What happened to you? The raids?"

He examined a long slash in his sleeve. "You heard about the attack?"

"I heard they caught a rebel."

His head jerked up, fire flashing in his near-black eyes. "They caught Seree."

"One of your co-conspirators?"

"Seree believes all of Curio's citizens deserve pure water. As do I."

"That's what this was about, then?" Grey clenched the hand still covering her throbbing mark. "You bombed the hydro hub to make a statement?"

"I didn't bomb it." He ground the words out. "But I stand with my friends, and I suggest you reserve your judgment until you've seen a little more of Curio than this posh palace."

Grey balled her fists at her sides. The room's jumbled contents pressed in on her peripheral vision. She'd seen enough of her luxurious prison.

Blaise jerked his chin toward her barricade. "What happened to you?"

She folded her arms over her bosom. "Let's just say I found it necessary to protect myself."

He strode across the room to stand before her. Dark head bent, his gentle eyes studied her face. "Blueboy?"

Grey nodded.

"Did he hurt you?"

All the panic and determination of the last few hours swelled to a bubble in her chest. Blaise's presence sent a current through the ball of emotion. Grey dropped her arms and took a ragged breath. "No. I won't let him touch me." She raised her chin, locking eyes with the Mad Tock.

To her surprise, Blaise took a step backward. His gaze traveled to the bed then whizzed to his boots. "They're not like us. Their only concern is keeping sufficiently warm and pliable. There's no disease, no pregnancy, no one looking over their shoulders."

"Like in Mercury?"

His brow creased.

"When did you come here, Blaise? Nettie, the maid, made it sound like you'd always been here, but that would make you over a hundred years old. You had to have come through the cabinet, like me. Who are you, really?"

He shook his head, the long threads of his hair brushing his shoulders. "I—that was so long ago."

"Why are you the only human in this place?"

"I'm not the only human anymore." Focus returned to her features. "Come with me, Grey."

The pattern on Grey's torso flared. She put a few feet between her and the tall boy standing by the bed.

"Are you asking me to join your militia?"

"I'm not asking you to join anything. Just let me show you Curio. When I'm done, you can always come back here." His voice flattened on the last word, and he gestured toward the obstructed door.

Maybe it was his confusion a moment ago, the way his forehead crumpled in concentration. Maybe it was the torn clothing and his loyalty to his friends. Maybe it was her sheer dread of the morning and Blueboy's steam-driven touch. A fence folded in Grey's heart. She set the parasol down and moved to stand next to him, her thigh brushing the end of the bed.

"All right. I'll come."

Liquid eyes locked with hers. He fumbled with a strap on his chest and tilted his head toward the window. "Let's go."

She followed him onto the tiny stone veranda. Heavy Curio fog blanketed the side yard and estate. She and Blaise stood on an island surveying a wispy sea. He turned to her, his wings extending behind him like an angel preparing for flight. As he brought his left arm across his body, a wince gripped his features, but he quickly covered it. He held the strap on his chest open.

"This will help hold you when we fly."

She took a step closer and started to turn her back to meet his chest, but a hand on her arm drew her short.

She looked up over her shoulder. His face hovered an inch from hers, his full lower lip a mere breath from her cheek. In the shadows she couldn't read his expression.

"In the raid, I met with one of Blueboy's metal soldiers."

Grey pivoted. The closeness of their bodies invaded her senses. Her thoughts slowed until a realization surfaced. "You're hurt."

A small smile quirked at the corner of his lips. "I'm afraid you'll have to hold on."

Heat flooded the space between them. Grey searched the depths of his eyes. Like Whit, he was part boy, part man—pain and burden mixed with vigor and passion for life. Old eyes in a young man's face. A silent plea creased the skin at the edge of his black-fringed lids. Grey stepped into his arms. His chest stiffened, but he tucked the strap around her body, securing it beneath his arm. Did he tremble from the pain? Grey bit her lip. Her pulse raced.

"Can I help?" she whispered, her lips brushing a canvas strap.

He moved his hand to the small of her back and guided her closer. Grey gasped at the same time he jolted. Her mark flared hot and pulled at her belly, like the swirls tried to leave her skin and hook into Blaise's. He froze in the act of securing another strap and sucked in a breath. The hard planes of his stomach inched away from hers for a moment, and he turned his head away as if steeling himself. Grey's cheeks burned, and she held herself still despite the lava flowing beneath her skin.

With a deep breath, Blaise faced her once again and finished fastening the strap at her waist, locking them together in his harness. Grey slipped her arms around his broad back, her hands gliding over hard muscles. Again he went rigid.

Her mark danced between them, tugging her skin toward his. Could he feel it, or was he just unaccustomed to human touch? Not that she'd ever experienced anything like this before. Maybe this was why contact was illegal back home.

He cleared his throat. Grey watched the cords in his neck move. She couldn't see his eyes from her position.

"When we're in the air, lock your legs around me. The straps are tight, but you could slip out and I don't trust my arm to hold you."

She nodded against his chest and wove her hands underneath the steam pack, finding a grip among the belts of his harness.

"Ready?"

"Yes."

His hand moved at her side, tugging the bellow cord out and away from their tangled bodies. After a few moments a whir sounded from the joints in the wings. They began to flap on their own.

"Takes a little longer to lift off when I don't run or jump off something to gain momentum," Blaise said.

The humid air and his warm, spicy scent made her head swim. When their feet left the ground, she clutched Blaise to anchor herself as dizziness pushed in from all sides. His good arm tightened around her.

They ascended in a vertical line, the huge wings beating the air. A cool breeze skimmed the low-lying fog. For a moment they hovered, the draft playing over exposed skin and tangling her blonde hair with his dark coils. The clouds hid the city below. The rise and fall of their breathing matched, and with her ear resting on Blaise's chest, the beat of his heart echoed through her.

She wasn't alone in Curio anymore.

Blaise tilted his upper body, and she hooked her legs around his waist just before gravity dragged her feet toward the earth. He groaned low in his throat.

"Your shoulder?"

He gave a low laugh and they glided forward, gaining speed.

"Just hang on," he said.

With Grey clinging to him, Blaise struggled to keep his attention on picking out the route to Gagnon's in the fog. She shifted, her legs tightening around his hips. The movement sent sparks skittering through his veins. She must be getting tired, but when she spoke, it wasn't to complain. Her low voice underscored the rush of wind around them.

"You don't remember how you got here?"

Blaise moistened his lips. His mouth grid hung to the side, allowing for unencumbered speech. "I remember. I just haven't thought about it in a long time."

That wasn't true. His own arrival in Curio had hurtled into his thoughts the moment he glimpsed Grey's form falling through the fog. Since that night, memories leaked in at the strangest times.

Her head twisted into his chest, her breath warming the base of his throat. "I was sent to find someone. I think it's you."

"Why?"

"I don't know precisely why. I broke the law and they came for me, even though I'm underage. Adante wanted my blood. My grandfather"—her voice caught—"he told me to run to his store. When I got there, Haimon, his shop assistant, told me to 'Find him and bring him back.' That's all there was time for."

Blaise stiffened. Back. Back to that bleak place. A muted ache invaded his heart. "Why?" he said again.

"I told you I don't know. I—"

"No, why do you think I'm the one you're supposed to bring back?"

The whistle of air around them filled half a minute, then her breath tickled his collarbone.

"Well, who else could it be?"

Blaise didn't have an answer.

He navigated by the cable line. Once the Shelf fell away underneath them, the labyrinth of Cog Valley stretched to the great basin that emptied into Lower. Clusters of light in the dark expanse marked the tock boxing arenas. A brownish glow hung over the mouth, a combination of dim light from the workers' lanterns and fumes leaking up from the underground lake.

Gagnon's line of hangars formed a semicircle around the eastern edge of the mouth. Blaise made for the first structure, where a green light beamed into the night. Callis must've altered one of the fixtures to act as their signal. Grey grunted and swung her left hip higher against his torso, sliding her right foot down his leg in a stretch. Blaise fought for control of his breathing. This flight needed to end. Soon.

They set down in a dirt yard tainted by the weak light spilling from a window. Grey's feet met the ground, but she slumped against him.

"My legs are asleep."

He unfastened the straps binding them together, and she wobbled a step backward. The absence of her body left him cold and hungry.

As she stamped her feet, Blaise surveyed the nearest section of the huge lot. Wagons with equipment and hulking devices that resembled hunched, inanimate mining tocks lined up behind the open door of one hangar. The building with the signal light was small compared to the others. Bits of mismatched metal clung to the side of it like scales.

He walked toward the door, but it opened before he'd taken three steps. Callis emerged, followed by Gagnon and another gearish tock. Out of the corner of his eye, he saw Grey straighten. She edged closer to him.

"Here he is." Callis spread his hands. "Well done, Blaise."

The mended porcie shifted to peer around Blaise at Grey. She stepped out from behind him, her back stiff.

"Callis, may I present Miss Grey." Blaise turned to Grey and opened his mouth to introduce his friend, but whirring motion halted his words. In a matter of seconds, the tock Blaise didn't recognize stood behind Grey, his crude hands clamped on her arms.

She gave a startled cry and looked to Blaise. Her blue eyes widened. For an instant, Curio blurred out and only he and Grey stood there facing each other. Two humans alone among strange creatures. Stages of betrayal played over her features. Shock. Denial. Hurt.

The moment passed, and Grey thrashed against her captor. Blaise whipped around to face Callis.

"What are you doing? Tell him to let her go."

Confusion stamped Callis's melded features. "This was our plan, was it not?"

Grey paused in her struggle, and Blaise felt her glare penetrate his thick hair and bore into his skull.

"I-I didn't mean for it to be like this," he said.

The tock, who surely had boxing experience, hoisted Grey off her feet. She writhed, her blonde hair whipping about her head and lips spewing abuse, mostly at Blaise.

He flung a hand toward the boxer. "No. We can't do this. The plan has changed." But the tock disregarded him and hauled Grey into the metal building, Gagnon following with a nod aimed at Callis.

Ignoring the twinge in his shoulder, Blaise grabbed his friend and gave him a rough shake. "Grey came with me willingly. Blueboy's obsession with her has grown dangerous. You should have seen it—she was barricaded in her room, keeping him out! We can't give her back to him. He'll take her apart in the name of Beauty."

Callis broke away from Blaise's grip. "And what are they doing to Seree *right now*? Tell me that." He paused, and when he spoke again it was with a measure of calm. "I'm sorry Blueboy turned against her, but it doesn't change my mission."

"How can you say that? You're not a monster, Callis. You never were, even in Lower."

The ping of rising steam against metal sounded from the porcie's chest. "What would you suggest, Blaise? We have to get Seree back."

"I know." Blaise slid a hand into the woven hair at the base of his neck. The wires bit into his palm, but the pain helped him focus.

"Let me talk to her. At least let me explain she isn't our prisoner."

"Indeed, she is."

Granite lined Blaise's chest. He took a step toward Callis, using the five inches he had on the modified to tower over him. "You will treat Grey with the same kindness you would show a broken porcie child. We are not the brutal beasts who run this city."

"Not yet," Callis said. He swung around and strode toward the door.

Blaise followed, his thoughts racing ahead to Grey. He had to keep her out of Blueboy's grasp and somehow get

Seree back. And after that? If Grey truly was sent to bring him home . . . No, he wasn't free yet to travel back to the human world, not even in speculation.

Grey bumped about her new prison cell, her eyes slow to adjust to the darkness. Her hands and shins detected a table and chair in the center. The walls were empty and square save for an alcove by the door.

She slumped into the chair. Blaise had tricked her. From the sound of it, kidnapping her had been the plan all along.

Tears formed in her eyes, but she smacked them away. He was a lunatic. Of course he was a lunatic. A hundred years in this place, how could he not be? But when he spoke of his friends and their cause, well, maybe it was the low timbre of his voice that made him sound so rational.

Grey stared around the empty room. Would she be trapped here with hard creatures and one insane human boy for a hundred years? What about her father, her mother, Granddad? Whit?

Stars blinked in her eyes and she scrubbed them. Her palms came away wet.

Another circuit around the room helped to even out her breathing. She found the chair again and sat, placed her arms on the desk, and lowered her head. Weariness crept through her limbs. At least the threat of Blueboy's examination was lifted for the time being. Her lids lowered.

When the door opened, Grey jumped and wiped the corner of her mouth.

Blaise stood in the doorway, outlined by the light behind him.

Grey got to her feet. Then she threw the chair at him. It crashed to the floor a couple feet from where he stood.

He stared down at it then back at her. "I'm sorry."

"You let them lock me up."

He stepped in and closed the door behind him, blocking the light source. Grey disobeyed the pulling of her mark and moved away from him, putting the table between them.

He stood for a moment as if uncertain. She couldn't read his expression in the dark.

"You're just going to give me back to Lord Blueboy?"

"No, I mean, that was the plan, but that was before—"

"Before you knew his intentions for me?"

He shuffled to the table and set a bundle on top of it. His right hand found the base of his neck and rubbed. He'd cleaned up and changed. He wore what she guessed was a borrowed vest, buttoned up over bare skin. Even in the dark, the contour of muscle was unmistakable. After a moment he turned and headed for the door.

Grey opened her mouth to say something to keep him from leaving, but he bent to retrieve the chair. Placing it back in the center of the room, he motioned for her to sit. Then he lifted himself up to the table, his long legs dangling. He was barefoot.

Somehow the sight of his toes eased the clench in Grey's lungs. She moved to the chair and lowered herself, crossing her arms over her chest.

"Well, what's the plan now?"

His eyes found hers, whites gleaming in the dark. "I won't let Blueboy hurt you, Grey. But I have to get Seree back. She's . . . one of us."

"A renegade?"

"A liberator. A water warrior." He barked a laugh, then his tone grew serious again. "You've only seen the mansion and the center of the city. They go through pure water as though it belongs only to them, while the rest of Curio suffers depravation and the effects of tainted water."

"All right, I'd gathered as much. And you and this Seree, and the tocks out there, are trying to do something about it?"

"Yes." He shifted on the table, his hands smoothing his trousers as if he couldn't stay still. "I have to. My nature forces me into the middle of Callis's cause. He thinks my involvement is due to his leadership skills, or"—Blaise rolled his eyes—"whatever's left of his porcie charm." His voice lowered. "But it's not that. I can't stand by and watch others suffer."

Grey loosened her pose, leaning forward to rest her elbows on her knees. "I don't understand. They feel pain like we do, feel . . . other things . . . like we do, even the tocks. They're metal and yet they feel. They're alive. How?"

"It was the Chemist who sent me here, I think. He cast a spell on the cabinet to keep me in and keep me alive."

"Why?"

His tone flattened. "I can only assume it was because he hated me more than any other Defender alive."

"You're a Defender?" Grey scooted forward in her seat. "Until a few days ago I thought the Chemists killed them all."

"Not all." Blaise lifted the edge of his vest, exposing the skin at his belt line. A pattern circling his navel glowed with blue-white light.

Grey gasped. She slipped off her seat and stood before him. With one finger she rucked the fabric of her shirt up. Her own mark gleamed with the same hue. Blaise reached a hand out then stopped, his fingers hovering over the pattern on her skin. He met her eyes, a question in his. Grey nodded and held her stance, her skin quivering when his finger brushed it. He traced a line curling away from her navel.

"A Defender's mark," he whispered into the darkness.

The emblem tingled beneath his touch. Grey expected the whorls to spin and dance. She lowered her shirt and took a steadying breath. Blaise dropped his hand as though he'd been caught playing with a potion bottle.

"It just appeared one morning after I . . ." She flattened her palm over her mark. Whit's face as he'd looked climbing into the chug boat flared through her mind.

"After you sacrificed for someone else?" Blaise nodded. "That's what kindles the Defender state. Didn't they explain when they gave you the wellspring water?"

"Water? What water? No one explained anything. Granddad said I was different, *we* were different, that's all."

"Wait." Blaise held up one long finger. "In the air, you said your grandfather sent you to his store. Olan? Olan Havardsson is your grandfather? Then you're a Defender by blood."

"You knew my granddad?" The conversation Grey'd overheard in the store came back. "I don't understand how he and my father escaped the Cleanse. The Council knows they're different. Adante knew I was different."

"Steinar." Blaise's voice sliced through her musing. "You're Steinar's daughter?"

"Yes."

He jumped off the table. Grey's mark flamed as they stood facing each other. Blaise's chest heaved, and his fists curled at his sides. Before she collected her wits, he spun around and marched for the door.

"Wait. You knew my father and grandfather. Tell me—"

"Yes, I knew them." He stopped, his hand on the door-knob. His voice ground like a rough gear. "Steinar Haward is the reason I'm here."

Blaise clicked the lock despite Grey's pleas. The flimsy door between them begged for his fist. But he needed her on the other side. Steinar's daughter. His old friend's face wouldn't come into focus. Ah, but Grey's face. Grey's face burned at him through the wood that separated them. Blue eyes and those apple cheeks that made her look both innocent and strong, like she fought lions all day then came home to bake pies.

She had to go and be Steinar's daughter. Blaise turned from the door before the temptation to tear it down got the better of him. He headed out to the main room of Gagnon's house.

His host sat on a stiff chair. The boxing tock, whom he'd learned was named Rusher, had gone, but Callis sat in a sagging armchair.

When the half porcie started to speak, Blaise cut him off. "Gagnon, let's see this hydro hub you're working on."

Gagnon's metal slit of a mouth spread into a grin. "Oh, it's not just the hub I've been working on." He jerked his brassy head toward the hallway. "The prisoner secure?"

Blaise nodded once, ignoring Callis's jewel and metal gaze. Grey's presence, her existence, and what it meant to him wasn't something he cared to share with his friend. Not yet.

Gagnon ratcheted out of his seat and retrieved a set of keys from a hook on the wall. Blaise's fingers itched to curl around the dangling keys, but he followed the tock out the door with Callis bringing up the rear. The green light no longer shone in the window, and only the ruddy glow from the nearby mouth lit the machine yard.

They followed the wide, dirt-packed road connecting the huge bays housing the equipment Gagnon rented out. Blaise's shoulder throbbed with every step, and his mind flipped between images of Grey and long-ago events. By the time they reached the second-to-last hangar, his fingernails cut into his palms. He all but ran through the door Gagnon held open.

Pitch-black greeted him, and an imprint of Grey's Defender mark seared his vision until Gagnon flipped a switch, flooding the cavernous space with light.

Blaise drew up, his eyes wide. A bulbous shape as big as a building occupied the center of the room. Like Gagnon's house, patchwork metal comprised its shell. Out of the bottom, segmented pipes extended, stretching out along the floor like great arms. One of the pipes almost reached the group by the doorway. Blaise peered inside, picturing water rushing down from the orb. Gagnon's invention wasn't as elegant as the upper class porcie's water system, but the long appendages could provide water to many neighborhoods at once.

Callis strode forward and trailed his metallic hand up the pipe. "This is a marvel, Gagnon."

The tock smiled his stripped-down grin. "It's not much to look at. The porcies'll hate the thing. But here in Cog Valley, it'll get the job done. Wait till you see it in operation."

"I can't wait to see the assembly blow their pumps." Blaise moved closer to the contraption.

Gagnon creaked. Blaise studied him a moment before the sound translated to laughter.

"That's not all. Come with me."

They trooped to the last warehouse. Blaise prepared himself for darkness and Grey's form rose like a beacon in his mind, but the flash of her face rattled him nonetheless. He shook his head as Gagnon raised the lights.

Another pieced-together machine took up most of the space in the huge hangar, but Blaise couldn't make sense of the long shape. He studied the snubbed end nearest them. Were those windows high above the nose-like tip meant for navigation? The cylindrical body extended back like a tubular-shaped fish. Halfway between the front and rear, two huge pipes attached to the hammered metal exterior. The three-blade spinner inside the tubes clued him in. He turned to Gagnon.

"It flies?"

Gagnon croaked again. "Thought you owned the sky did you, Mad Tock?"

Callis laughed as well. "Brilliant, Gagnon, brilliant. Let's get a good look at this masterpiece."

After they'd circled the flying machine, boarded it via the open stern, and walked around the interior—which resembled the enclosed deck of a ship—they exited and took up positions near the wind chambers.

"You've never tested it?" Callis asked.

Gagnon wagged his head back and forth. "No. There's no hiding her once she's up. Was waiting for the right moment."

Callis tapped on the hull, his metal fingers clanging against the metal exoskeleton. "Now is the time to reveal your contraption."

"I nicknamed it the Clang," Gagnon said.

"Why?" Blaise asked.

Gagnon's bead-like eyes traveled over the machine. "Well, she clangs a bit when we start her up."

"Definitely no hiding her then," Blaise said.

"We don't need to." Callis's gem eye sparkled. "This is perfect. We'll send the Clang to the Weatherton estate."

Blaise squinted at the contraption. "How can this floating bucket reroute Weatherton's hub?"

"It can't. We must access the pipes to his locus from the tunnels beneath. But the Clang can demolish the hub—and make a lot of noise doing it. It'll draw more than one platoon. If we're lucky, the soldiers stationed at Harrowstone will respond."

"Seree."

Callis shot Blaise a conciliatory glance. "We'll try a diversion first. Like you said, I'm not a monster."

A cord around Blaise's heart loosened. He nodded. "When do we stage our attack?"

"Tomorrow."

Gagnon's head twisted toward Callis. "We have to haul up enough cinderite to fuel the engines. And we need time to plan."

The modified thumped his metallic hand with his porcelain fist. "Seree can't wait."

Gagnon rested his jagged fingers on Callis's mechanical shoulder. "I know. But we've no chance of rescuing her if the Clang goes down before the Toppers even recognize the threat."

Callis's eyes tracked with intense precision as they darted between Blaise and Gagnon. "I won't wait longer than a day."

Grey heard the footsteps in her dreams. She jerked. The left side of her body ached from contact with the hard floor, but at least the bundle of clothing Blaise had brought cushioned her head. She opened her eyes at the knock on the door. Dim light filtered from the crack beneath the wood panel.

Morning. Would she be traded for Seree today? Maybe Blaise wanted her gone after learning who her father was.

She pushed away from the floor, shook out her wadded pillow, and slipped her arms into the dark blue coat. The sleeves brushed her knuckles, and the length covered her from her shoulders to her calves. She pulled it close and stood in the middle of the room.

The lock clicked, and Blaise walked in, holding two cups. A splotchy indigo bruise covered the top of his bare shoulder and disappeared beneath the vest he still wore.

"Your arm!" Grey jerked toward him and grabbed the mugs.

He chuckled as she set them on the table. "I think I can manage breakfast." Without goggles, dangling mask, or steam pack, he looked achingly human. But his face froze in a blank mold when he noticed her scrutiny.

Grey's stomach dropped. "They're sending me back?"

He shook his head. "No. Callis has a new plan, but it'll take a day to prepare." He gestured to the cups. "I want to show you something after you eat."

She studied his controlled expression. Obviously he didn't feel the pull between them. He hated her now for whatever her father had done. And why wouldn't he? He was stuck here. But she was stuck here too. And the sight of him: The dark, tangled hair. The full curve of his lower lip. The tan skin that gave beneath her fingertips, so unlike porcie flesh.

"Don't hate me." The words came out before she could stop them.

His restrained expression wavered. He looked away.

"I don't hate you, Grey. When you've been around as long as I have, you learn to control your emotions. Especially anger. It holds off the stone."

She inched closer to him, one hand propped on the table for support.

"The stone?"

His eyes rested just to the right of her face. "You don't know anything about Defenders, do you?"

"The history books say they carried the First Disease even though they were immune to it. The Chemists think it all started with them."

"Wrong. The First Disease was a plague, taking some lives but sparing others like any pestilence. It was the Regians—ancient alchemists—who used the event to seek power beyond their grasp, and in doing so set in motion the starvation and the struggle between Defenders and Chemists." The near-black eyes lost a bit of their frost. "I'll show you what it means to be a Defender. That's why I want to take you out today."

Grey's breath swelled. "Out?"

His mouth quirked up. "Yes, out. Now eat. I have to see Callis before we leave."

When he left, Grey listened for the lock. When she didn't hear a click, she released a pent-up breath and sat down. One of the cups held water and the other a thick crust of bread, a hunk of cheese, and a mound of berries.

She brought the bread to her mouth and bit. It tasted like paint but she swallowed it down. Even after more than a week without potion, she expected instant pain when the food hit her stomach. Not only did she not suffer, according to Blaise everything she knew about the starvation trait was wrong.

A Defender by blood. She'd heard the truth in Granddad's store, but why had her family never explained? She'd grown up believing Father and Granddad's freedom from the potion was a fluke. After all, her family came from the Old Country like most others in the Foothills Quarter, who all traced the starvation trait back generations.

In Council School, she'd been taught that the people later known as Defenders brought the starvation illness to her ancestors, who only survived because of Chemist intervention. The condition passed from parents to children, and while the Chemists struggled to keep the community alive, the outsiders among them remained strong and immune.

In a harsh bid for justice, the Chemists subjugated the outsiders, turning them into scapegoats for a weak populace and giving them the mocking title of Defender. Any citizen accused of a crime could make arrangements for a Defender to receive his punishment. When it came time for the Defender to pay, he faced a Chemist in a gruesome showdown meant to keep Defenders and citizens in their place. On it went until the rebellion and Defender Cleanse.

There was nothing about strange marks that appeared after a self-sacrificing deed. Nothing about the hardening sensation that spread through her body.

And where did her family fit in? Day after day, her father helped the mountain people, and her grandfather searched for an alternative potion. But when she'd tried to help Whit, both Father and Granddad lost everything.

She pushed the scraps of food away. It was wrong. Wrong that her father paid the price for *her* crime. Wrong that her brother had been taken because he shared his potion with the sick. Wrong that Whit had been striped. It was all her fault.

The surge of power started at her navel, spreading outward like living rock. Grey pushed away from the table and lifted her hands, experiencing the sensation through new eyes. Did this mean she was hardening? Turning to stone like Granddad? She jabbed at the back of her hand with a fingernail. A white splotch accompanied the prick. But the granite-like shell was on the inside. What if it spread to the outside?

She pinched a chunk of her wrist. Did it hurt as much as it should? She snagged a lock of her hair and pulled. Her scalp stung. Tears rimmed her eyes. Maybe the head was last to go?

"What are you doing?"

Grey turned toward the voice, and Blaise came into focus. A weight shoved down on her, constricting her air. He stepped closer, and she lifted her hands.

"What's the matter, Grey?" His voice carried through the fog.

She trembled, the growing shell under her skin threatening to lock her lungs. "Am I turning to stone? My grandfather . . . he spoke into my head and then he turned into a statue, right there in the parlor. Am I like him?"

Warm fingers closed around hers, guiding her hand down to hang in his. She dropped her other arm to her side and stood, shaking, before Blaise. He rubbed his thumb over the back of her hand.

"Do you feel that?"

She nodded. The heat of his touch melted the rock lining and soaked into her skin, sending warmth curling around her bones.

"It takes hundreds of years and countless battles to turn a Defender to stone. Olan Havardsson, your grandfather, is one of the oldest of our kind. Olan defended in the Old Country, he defended the colony when they came to the new land, and he defended the Mercury settlement. I remember him. Big as a bear."

The tears escaped and ran down Grey's cheeks, and her voice shook. "He was protecting me. They came to get me and there was a fight. I didn't understand. I didn't know protecting me would make him a statue."

"It wasn't your fault. And unfortunately, turning to stone is the natural end for a Defender." Blaise kept her hand trapped in his. "But it takes a long, long time. You're not going to ossify anytime soon." He ducked his head, his dark eyes searching her face. "Understand?"

She swallowed and avoided the deep brown irises probing hers. "It should have been me. My father, my grandfather, my brother, even Whit—all of them paid for crimes not their own."

Blaise shrugged, not unkindly. "That's how the Defender system works."

"It isn't right."

He let go of her hand and headed for the door. "You want to see true injustice, come with me."

Blaise led her through a cluttered house to the yard where they'd landed the night before. Hazy daylight wrapped the metal buildings and tall iron fence in a dull woolen blanket.

The tocks whirring about the complex paused in their work to turn flat eyes on them.

"No disguise today?" Grey eyed Blaise's brown duster over the pants and vest he'd been wearing earlier. "What about me? Won't somebody spot us and report to the soldiers?"

"Not here."

They'd reached the gate, and he unwound a thick chain before swinging it open. He turned to Grey, lids lowered and a firmness about his mouth that told her something unpleasant awaited. He motioned toward the opening.

The instinct to run flared, but Blaise trusted her enough to show her whatever waited beyond the gate. Minutes before, he'd held her hand and talked her out of panic so heavy she thought she'd suffocate. If she bolted, she'd be lost in minutes. And then there was the delicious dancing of the mark on her stomach. It linked her to him somehow, and part of her hated to sever that link.

Grey brushed by Blaise and through the gate. He followed, securing the chain behind him. A dirt road led away from Gagnon's yard. To Grey's right, a forest of scrap metal and junk stretched into the distance. To her left, the fence bordering the machine yard followed the course of the road, breaking off beneath a high cable line that disappeared into a cavern in the ground.

Blaise set off and Grey matched his stride. The muscles in her legs tingled at the chance to stretch and move after the confines of Blueboy's estate. The long coat swirled about her calves, blocking out the chill that hung over Cog Valley.

"Where are we going?"

He didn't answer.

After a few minutes of trudging, the fence gave way. Carts moved along the cable above their heads, disappearing into a low-lying cloud that hung over the black cliff face.

Blaise followed her gaze. "That's called the Shelf. The factory district is up there. All the materials from Lower are sent there for handling."

Grey turned to the huge crater gaping feet from where they stood. The carts disappeared into it, and brownish vapor floated up in wisps and reeking curls.

"And this is Lower, I assume? How do you get down there?"

He pointed to the edge of the basin near the machine yard. A steep road slanted down from the complex. Wagons pulled by clockwork mules lumbered into the pit, tocks clinging to their sides.

Grey crept closer, craning to see over the side of the hole. "Nettie said there was a lake down there."

Blaise snatched her arm and held tight. "There's a lake, the pipe system, cinderite warrens, mines, and other things that don't even have names. Creatures that glide through the burrows, snatching tocks and triggering cave-ins."

A grinding shriek drifted from far beneath, and Grey stepped back. She lifted her chin. "Are we going down?"

Blaise's face cracked into a smile, revealing a row of white teeth. "No, brave one. We're not going down today." He jerked his head toward the towers of debris. "We're going for a walk in Cog Valley."

She hid her sigh of relief and trailed after Blaise. Openings between the rubbish stacks dotted the line of the road. He paused by one then moved to another then another, rubbing his chin.

"Did you forget which one it is?" Grey asked.

"No." He propped a hand on a wall of interlocking junk and gave a mirthless half smile. "I was just trying to decide which one to choose. Why don't you pick one?"

"But I don't know where we're going."

"We're going inside." He pushed away from the stack and plunged his hands into the pockets of his duster. "It doesn't really matter which entry we choose. In Cog Valley, all paths lead to misery."

At his words and demeanor, a fierce protectiveness surged inside. She wanted to wrap him in a tight hug, but instead she faced the nearest gap. "All right. Show me."

They slipped through the entry only to meet another wall of junk. Paths led away from where they stood. Grey tossed Blaise a glance. "Right or left?"

He raised an eyebrow, his dark eyes tossing the question back to her. After a moment of deliberation, she took the trail on the left.

Blaise deferred to her when they reached the next corner and the next and the next. Deeper and deeper they walked into the labyrinth of building materials, cast-off furniture, and mechanical parts.

Blaise snagged her coat and directed her attention to the base of one pile. When she gave him a puzzled look he bent and lifted a coarse cloth off a stack of paintings. The first painting depicted flowers, the second an empty urn, but the third had a cluster of grapes, a loaf of bread, and a goblet. Blaise grabbed all three, sharing the food with her.

"How did you find out about the paintings?"

He swallowed and handed her the rest of the bread. "I nearly starved before I saw a porcie child playing with a painting on his family's wall. He'd reach up and scratch the canvas. His fingers came away with tufts of grass."

"How?"

He frowned and leaned against a carriage missing its wheels. "This prison supports life. I believe it was designed to keep me alive." He looked up at the pillars surrounding them. "The rest . . . sometimes I think the rest was an accident."

Grey set the grapes and bread on an overturned pot and moved closer.

"Who sent you here, Blaise?"

"The Chemists." He stared at one of the stacks, the frozen mask back on his face. "And your father."

"But why would my father banish you here? He's a good man. He was." Grey's voice broke.

"I don't know." He took a deep breath, as if drawing in strength. "My father and I returned to Mercury to find everything changed. In the years we'd been away, the Chemists had grown stronger. They had created warriors of their own, men seething with green power. We sought out Olan Havardsson, the man who'd given my father the wellspring water and the power to fight for his people. Olan explained that the water he'd brought from the Old Country was running out, and the party of Defenders sent to fetch more had vanished. The Chemists were no longer content with Olan's offering or with the Defender justice system. Their blood greed grew like gold fever, and they had begun to mine from weaker veins."

Blaise swallowed and took a moment before he went on. "The Defenders were on the verge of a treaty, offering their own blood to satisfy the Chemists' requirements in exchange for protection of those bound to the potion and an end to further blood experimentation. My father's loyalty lay with his people, so Olan urged us to return to the Jicarilla lands. We were preparing to leave when they came, Adante and his guard. They hurled their bottled blood magic through our windows and smoke filled the cabin." He pressed a hand to the center of his chest, his face a grimace of remembered pain. "We were forced outside. I saw Steinar then, standing in the trees. My father and I fought, but against the new potion-breathers, even mighty Chief Tazo could not stand.

232

They dragged him away and bound and blindfolded me. Adante and Steinar, men I'd known since boyhood, took me to a place that reeked of blood and potion. They removed my blindfold a moment before cutting my hand. I remember a glass case, my blood dripping into the lock and somehow pulling me inside. Then I was here."

"But Father would never help—" She couldn't finish the sentence. Because he had. Pieces of Blaise's broken story dashed through her mind, shredding everything she'd thought she knew. No, there had to be more to it.

Blaise stalked away toward the next bend and she followed. "I heard my grandfather talking about the treaty between Chemists and Defenders. He said he wouldn't risk breaking it. Lives depended on it."

He whirled on her, his duster whipping in a circle around his legs. "Life is always the price. I would've paid it. Instead I'm here, suspended in time with a collection of lunatic toys. We should've fought the Chemists rather than making deals, believing they would temper their obsession."

"And if you'd lost?"

With lids lowered, he blew out a defeated breath. "A generation. Saint Gerodi have mercy." Brown eyes opened to meet hers. "Yes, an entire generation would've died without Defender blood to sustain them, but with them the potion dependence would've ended. Yet those lives were a price we could not pay. Rather surrender every drop of our own blood." He moved as if to cup her cheek. "Well, almost every drop."

He dropped his hand, turned, and strode deeper into the shadows of the stacks, shoulders slumped under a weight just beginning to press on Grey. Defenders were not the monsters of the Council textbooks, nor were they subjugated whipping boys. Their existence, their function in the society she knew, was a thing of terrible beauty. The mark on Grey's belly whispered a call that traveled through her blood and took root in her heart. She hurried after the warrior with the copper-threaded hair.

They walked in silence until a rhythmic squeak carried from somewhere ahead. After a few more turns, they emerged onto a wider path.

A strange shape approached from the other end of the road. As they got closer, Grey made out a rough wheelbarrow-like contraption piled with wares. At first she thought the porcie behind the cart was sitting, but when Blaise stopped to sift through the merchandise, Grey saw that the man was missing both legs below the knees. He sat in a wheeled chair attached to the wagon and propelled both by cranking levers at his sides.

The peddler looked at her, confusion in his gem eyes. Brown cracks mapped his face, shifting when he opened his mouth to speak. Blaise forestalled the porcie's questions with one of his own. "Would the lady fancy a new hat?" He held up a wide-brimmed black hat with a gray ribbon trimming the rounded top and a plume of silky material jutting up like spray from a fountain.

It wasn't red. It wasn't Beauty's Best. And Grey loved it. She grinned and nodded her approval.

"How much?" he asked the peddler.

"Five pieces or whatever you've got to trade."

Blaise pulled a handful of coins out of a pocket in his duster and dropped them in the porcie's gloved palm. The merchant thanked him and rolled off, leaving squeaks in his wake.

Blaise drew near to position the hat on Grey's head. The scents of sawdust and machine oil carried off him, wrapping

Grey in a sweet-smelling haze. She leaned in and admired the line of his strong jaw as he concentrated, tilting the hat brim this way and that.

The pull between them surged. She twisted her fingers together to keep from reaching out to him. It was either close the gap or distract herself. "What happened to him?"

"Some sort of accident." Blaise stepped back and studied her.

"Like a flood?"

Dark eyes held hers and a deliberate tone marked his words. "Or a carriage crash or a fall."

"Why isn't he like your friend?"

"When I found Callis, he was missing half his body. His jitter pump system was broken, and there was no way he'd ever reanimate without help. I experimented until I brought him back." He moved on down the aisle between the debris, tossing another comment over his shoulder. "But most porcies would rather stay cold than look like Callis."

How ridiculous. Grey sighed and followed Blaise's towering figure. A handful of twists and turns brought them to a street bustling with dilapidated tocks and porcies. A little girl with a cracked face and tangled hair tugged on Blaise's coat.

"Buy some cinderite?"

He squatted down. "Let's see what you have."

With one arm she held a small bucket full of black pellets up for his inspection. She concealed her other hand in the folds of her dirty skirt.

"I'll take the lot," Blaise said. He dug for more coins in his pocket.

The little girl set the bucket down and held out her left hand for the money. When a coin slid off the pile she snatched for it, revealing a right hand missing most of the fingers.

At least five more children stopped them, selling cinder-ite, sludge-like water, and various gears, clothing, and parts. Blaise sent them all off with piles of coins.

A boy in a miner's cap darted behind a stack when he saw Grey watching him. Jeweled green eyes in a cracked face peeped around the heap at her. "Why are there so many children here?"

Blaise turned away from the market stall of a tock who had black corrosion covering every visible limb. "No one ages here. The children are wild and reckless. If they're lucky, a porcie couple will keep them, take care of them, try to prevent them from breaking. But most of them end up here after one too many accidents."

"Why do their parents—"

"Keepers."

"Why do their keepers not, er, keep them?"

Blaise lowered his voice, his gaze moving about the widened portion of the maze that passed for a village. "The porcies believe the Designer made them to be beautiful. If you're not beautiful, you run the risk of angering the Designer. He might de-animate you permanently. So the ugly ones hide away here."

A porcie woman in a padded dress tottered by, patting herself as if checking for missing pieces. She flinched and stepped around a jagged stack of machine parts.

Grey's throat tightened. "And it just gets worse down here, doesn't it? They're all so damaged."

"It doesn't have to be this way." Blaise tugged her arm, and they walked on. "I can fix them. They can learn how to fix themselves. They'd live and function. But it wouldn't be beautiful, at least not according to their standards."

"But Callis is *much* better off than these people." Grey turned to watch the shuffling figure of the porcie woman.

"And Callis isn't afraid. Not of the Designer. Not of breaking. And that absence of fear has made him something of a visionary." He gave a low chuckle.

"Is Callis part of the Valor Society?"

Blaise plunged his hands into his pockets and shifted to smile at her. "You've heard the talk, then?"

"You and Callis are behind it?"

"Actually, no. We didn't start the movement." Blaise surveyed the long corridor before them, but his face bore the stamp of faraway thought. "Somewhere in Curio, there's another porcie or tock who's lost everything and no longer fears breaking a few rules."

Grey stopped walking and closed her eyes, but the image of Whit's striped back remained clear as the night she'd knelt by his bed. She looked up to find Blaise studying her and thrust her chin in a defiant angle. "Better to live without fear than follow rules that will bring you down anyway."

A smile hitched his full mouth. "Look who's talking revolution now."

"That's why you brought me here." Grey motioned to the jungle of junk. Shadows stretched from the stacks towering over their heads, swallowing paths and dousing the place in hopelessness.

Blaise stepped closer. "Tell me what you're feeling now."

Her Defender mark leapt into a warm dance at his nearness. "Um . . ."

He jerked his head in the direction of the little community they'd passed through. "What did seeing them do to you?"

She dropped her gaze to the top button of his vest. Beneath it smooth, caramel-colored skin outlined the planes and dips of muscle. The brim of her hat blocked his handsome face, but his presence stirred her concentration. "It made me angry, and it made me want to help." A surge of strength pulsed from just behind her mark, and her eyes found his again.

He offered a slow smile. "There's the Defender I thought I'd find in here. It's in your blood, Grey. In our blood."

A strange power rushed between them. In her mind they were flying again, the wind buffeting their bodies together. She opened her mouth to speak, but Blaise let out a soft, frustrated groan. The pull of the mark won out. Space melted between them, and his arms wrapped around her. When her hat got in his way, he yanked it off, holding it against her back as he crushed her closer.

His lips touched hers and moved away, grazing her jawline as if asking permission to explore further. A little moan, just an exhalation of breath, escaped Grey's open mouth. Blaise responded with a kiss too hungry to be gentle. Fierce need ignited deep in her belly and spread outward. She threaded her fingers through the locks at his neck and pulled his head down to hers. The fine wire woven through his hair bit into her hands, but her fingers burrowed deeper as electricity pulsed at her navel. He slid a hand beneath her coat to the hem of her shirt and skimmed her waistline, his thumb brushing the Defender imprint on her skin. Grey gasped against Blaise's lips. He broke the kiss and backed away, questions and apologies widening his eyes.

With no words to give him, she dropped her gaze and traced the indentations on her palms.

"We have to find our way out," Blaise said after a moment. "Not that wandering around with you the whole night isn't appealing, but there are plans to discuss at Gagnon's."

Grey nodded, though she ached to be back in his arms. If his mark burned the way hers did, how could he ignore the connection? She curled her hands into fists. When he stepped close again she almost lifted her mouth to him, but he settled the hat back onto her head, tucking strands of hair away from her face as he did.

"Beauty's Best," he whispered and caught her hand. He seared her palm with his lips then laced his fingers between hers.

They moved through the spreading shadows toward the next bend in the labyrinth.

Blaise studied Grey as she bent over the table in Gagnon's sitting room. Callis stood next to her, pointing out Curio's landmarks on a map. The modified porcie had accepted that she'd joined their cause and taken her into his confidence. She glanced up during a political digression and caught Blaise staring at her. Pink stained her cheeks. He fought the pull deep inside. His fingers itched to touch her hair, her cheeks, her throat. His arms ached to hold her. Even his blood called out for her. If Callis weren't there . . . He turned away, blocking the images scorching his thoughts.

All his talk of justice and compassion had found its target in Grey's heart, but she'd call him a liar before they were done. She'd pull away, and he'd be trapped forever in this prison, hated by the only other human in his world. Or worse, remain in Curio without her.

A hand tugged on his arm. When he turned and caught her eyes, the memory of an immense blue dome flashed. The sky outside this prison. He let himself absorb the soft aqua so different from the hard gem eyes of the porcies. But Grey was tugging him toward the table. Her arm slipped around his waist and he stiffened. The more contact they had now, the deeper the betrayal when she discovered the truth about him.

"Callis says I can choose which mission I want to be a part of."

Blaise forced his eyes away from the girl at his side and down to the map he knew as well as his own Defender mark. She pointed to the Weatherton estate, perched on top of the Shelf to the east of the factory district.

"The airship is going to explode the hydro hub. Gagnon's diggers have been tunneling up from Lower." She traced a line up the cliff face beneath the industrial baron's home. "By the time we hit the hub, the water will be drained into underground pipes and heading for Gagnon's new purification locus."

She looked up at him. "No flood. If everything goes according to plan, no one will get damaged."

Blaise crossed his arms. "You're forgetting the airship strike is a diversionary tactic *meant* to draw the soldiers guarding Harrowstone." He jabbed his finger at the prison located to the west of the factories, opposite the Weatherton estate.

On the other side of the table, Callis shifted his weight. Blaise directed his next words at the modified. "Who's to say the Clang can even take a musket hit, let alone cannon fire?"

"The mission to save Seree will be no safer." Callis waved his porcelain hand over the map. "Blueboy's estate is nearby. Word will reach him fast and more troops will be ordered to defend Harrowstone."

"Where will you go tomorrow?" Grey asked.

With her gaze on him, he strained to form words into an answer. "I will go where my abilities are most needed," he managed.

A battle waged on Grey's face. After a moment she angled her chin out. "The strike on Weatherton is all for show. The real work is already being done underground. You should help Callis."

The mended porcie slammed his metal fist on the table. "I don't need his help."

"What?"

Callis's jewel eye glittered and the mechanical eyeball—still glitchy after the flood—vibrated in its socket. He rounded the table, and Blaise squared his feet for a hit. Maybe the tainted water had reached the modified's mind. The rebuilt face thrust into his.

"Let me be the one to rescue Seree," Callis said through clenched teeth. "Give her gaze a chance to land on me for once. You don't love her. You never did."

Callis held Blaise's eyes a moment then turned and stomped out of Gagnon's house. Heat climbed up Blaise's neck.

When Grey spoke her voice was even, careful. "What did he mean by that?"

"Exactly what he said, I imagine."

"You and Seree are . . . ?"

"Not anymore. Not for a while now. He's right. I didn't love her."

Blaise leaned on the table as if studying the map. A rigid hush fell over the room. If only he could dash out after Callis. Maybe root him out in the hangar and make jokes about the Clang until his friend loosened up . . . A hand covered his. Grey stood at his elbow.

"You must have been very lonely all these years, stuck in here."

He forced a bravado he didn't feel. "Oh, Curio City is quite charming once you learn to blend in."

She hesitated at his retort. The hand that had begun to move to his forearm stopped when he added another jab.

"At least the women are beautiful." He hated each word as it left his lips.

"B-but you don't belong here." She fell silent, her fingers trembling against his skin. Minutes passed before she spoke. "Blaise, do you have any idea how we can get out?"

He could say no. Her hand moved again, gliding up his arm, fingertips skimming the bruise on his shoulder.

His secrets could remain hidden, and they could stay in Curio. So what if the food was paint? He'd have Grey to hide with. Grey to explore with. Grey to kiss until she moaned.

"We have to go back," she said. Her forehead grazed his upper arm. "The Council has my father. He may already be dead."

The reality of that world, Grey's world, roiled in his gut. He straightened and turned to her. "Your father is a Defender. It's in his nature to take punishment for others. He would want you to be free. Stay here with me, Grey."

Her mouth quivered. "I can't. If there's a way I can get back to my family, I need to find it. Will you help me?"

He didn't look away as she searched his face. He could say no. "Yes."

She sucked in a breath and stepped closer. "Then you do know how to get out?"

"There's a keyhole set in a tree trunk deep in the glass forest. I think it might be the exit."

Grey's brows rose and a smile played over her tender lips.

"But it doesn't work the same as the lock on the curio cabinet." He swallowed and forced the next words out. "You need an actual key."

The smile vanished, but the blue eyes held his. "Will you take me there after the mission?"

He nodded.

When she stepped closer and lifted her face to his, he knew the gesture for the invitation it was. Her hands rested lightly on his waist despite the tow of their Defender marks.

He longed to drag her to him and make use of the table so conveniently placed behind her back. But he kept a sliver of space between their bodies as he leaned down.

She'd lost the boldness of their encounter in Cog Valley, but he coaxed her lips to follow his. Though the moment her fingers curled at his hip bones, he broke away.

He couldn't meet her eyes, but when she made a noise—a mixture of surprise and desire—he rested his forehead against hers.

"We're not porcies with pumps for hearts and delusions for souls," he whispered. Then he kissed her forehead and walked out the door into the night.

19

Whit closed his hand around the money in his pocket, the last of the stash he kept in an old coffee can on his bedroom shelf. Another spasm gripped his gut, but he walked on down Colfax.

A figure appeared in his path, just steps away from the Haward's store. Winter sun shimmered on the Chemist's suit, and his dark hair jutted in spikes like a midnight mountain range.

Whit scrambled to replace the day's mission with thoughts that wouldn't land him in a facility. Maybe he could pass by unnoticed, just another miner on the way to work. Except he walked against the stream of men heading to Reinbar Station.

He buried the realization and conjured a picture of the draulie he worked alongside, inventing a glitch in Kauffman's hydraulic suit that required a quick errand downtown. He focused on the grinding sound of a faulty gear as the Chemist held up his hand.

The man had a smooth voice, like liquid pouring into a glass. "You're the boy that got striped for Grey Haward, aren't you?"

His fabricated errand evaporated. Sweat beaded on his upper lip.

The Chemist lifted the corner of his mouth. "Friendship with the Hawards is dangerous business."

Whit studied the sidewalk, his boots, the brick wall of a nearby shop. Anything to banish his striping and the Chemist's probing green eyes.

"Do you know who I am?" he asked.

Whit shook his head.

A note of irritation edged the Chemist's slick tone. "I'm Adante, the one who ossified Olan Haward and ended his son's defiance."

And Grey? What happened to her? Whit's head came up as an image of her kneeling by his bed popped into his thoughts.

The flash of green-tinted teeth sent ice down Whit's spine, but the Chemist arranged his features into a cool mask. He raised a bottle-green monocle to one eye and leaned an inch closer.

A dull ache spread from a point on Whit's forehead back over his skull and deep into his brain. He tried not to think about the last time he'd seen Grey, but her worried face flickered in and out of focus as if someone picked at a thread in the tapestry of his thoughts. He couldn't get control of his own mind.

In a flash of green light, Adante's features replaced the memory. Pale eyes, one of them grotesquely magnified, held Whit's, and he could only stare, his mind blank and wandering.

"I suspect we'll be seeing each other again, Whitland Bryacre." The Chemist stepped to the side and motioned for Whit to continue. "Be sure to watch yourself when you go to the outpost. The mountain folk can be treacherous."

Whit filled his thoughts with a frozen lake, snow, and silver-scaled fish. He struggled to hold the image as he lurched down the walkway, but the day's task broke through and his spine went rigid. He didn't dare stop, though he threw a glance back toward Haward's. Adante stood just outside the shop, watching him walk toward downtown Mercury.

Station Four, South Quarter—the end of the line for the Mercury North-South passenger train. Whit waited till the last woman in faded red clothes stepped down onto the platform before he followed. The ladies moved in clusters—easily spotted and avoided—through an open-air waiting area with weathered metal benches and a high, narrow strip of roof. Though out of the way, this station crawled with deputies stationed at the edge of the city. In the distance, the lookout tower jabbed into the horizon, surrounded by the long, low barracks and training grounds. He didn't have a good excuse for any deputy who stopped him, but the flurry of activity around the water tower and gantry as the fireman set about refilling the engine's tank drew the attention of a knot of men in dusters and masks.

Cramming his hat low and tucking his chin into his collar against a shredding wind, Whit left the station behind and ducked between delivery trucks crowding a wide thoroughfare. A wall of factories lined the street, and the women filed through the doors as a piercing whistle signaled the start of the shift. Across town, his mother likely slipped through a similar entrance, intent on reaching her station at the mill before her supervisor reprimanded her for dawdling. He trailed a group moving up an alley between rows of warehouses. A few shot him wary glances, but no one asked his business. When the last two people headed for one of the doors, Whit continued toward the alley opening.

A cramp bit into his gut, and he had to stop and blow out quick puffs of air until it subsided. Would he ever get used to this? Like Marina had. Like his mother had. He pushed on, another step and another. For three days now, he'd watched his mother pour most of her potion into a glass for him before he trudged off to the mine. He'd even considered going back to the hunting outpost to retrieve his bottle, but the thought of showing up empty-handed made him feel like a schoolboy in short pants. No more. He wasn't leaving the South Quarter without a ration bottle.

Whit emerged from the alley between the factories onto another wide dirt street boasting shabby businesses and shops. Tiny square homes and squat buildings with dingy windows dotted the flat ground beyond the business district, with the lookout tower the only grim relief in the monotony. He'd expected crowded neighborhoods constantly patrolled by deputy chug boats. But he saw no one for the first two blocks he trekked.

A wrought iron fence enclosed the winter-brown lawn of a morality hall. A few ragged children played on the dead grass, watched by three young women wrapped in layer upon threadbare layer of crimson. The girls looked only a few years older than Grey or Marina.

Whit started to move away, searching porches and bare side yards for someone who looked like a ration dealer. A figure, a boy, emerged from a doorway facing the morality hall. He staggered across the street, let himself into the gate, and edged into the shadow of the building. He stood no taller than the women, but at closer range his face showed age beyond the fifteen years Whit had guessed. The women exchanged glances, then one ambled toward the young man. He listed in her direction, one toe dragging as though he couldn't raise his leg to complete a step.

The boy and woman stopped a dangerous two feet from each other, protected by the meager shadow of a barren tree. The woman glanced toward the tower then around the deserted street. Her gaze rested on Whit but moved on. The two other women stepped closer to the children, turning their backs to the conversation across the gravel plot.

Whit's breath caught when the woman reached into the pocket of her coat and pulled out a potion bottle. The young man thrust a wad of money at her, snatched the ration, and stumbled away.

Stomach heaving, Whit turned from the scene.

Of course. Of course it would be the mothers. He breathed through his nose, lips clamped. No deputies swarmed onto the scene, but Whit suffered a vision of the black-garbed agents dragging his own mother away. He bent and heaved without relief.

When his pulse slowed, he crept back the way he'd come. A stripe on his lower back stung. If he focused on it, the line of pain blocked out what he'd just seen.

On his left, tan buildings three stories high lined the block. Tenements? Two men exited the door of the farthest one and stood arguing on the stoop. Whit crossed the street and continued up the walkway, passing a five-and-dime store and ducking under the canopy jutting away from a boarded-up building.

He stopped in the shade, eyes fuzzy from the bright sun.

Fingers closed on his arm and yanked him to an open door. The figure ahead of him was dark-haired, but once inside the building Whit's vision blurred in the lamplight.

"What the codes, Ration Boy?" A high-pitched voice rang in his ears. "You got a death wish or something?"

"Yeah, he does," a lower voice growled.

248

Whit's sight adjusted and a weight in his chest lifted as a pair of tawny eyes sparkled at him. Marina wore trousers beneath a dark brown frock coat, and her hair was tucked under a bowler hat, giving her pointed chin an even sharper angle.

Maverick prodded him in the rib, and Whit dragged his gaze from the boy's sister.

"You following us?" Maverick shoved closer. "You some kind of deputy recruit?"

Whit splayed his hands. "No, man. I'm here because I left my potion bottle—"

"With me," Marina finished.

"Right." Whit's gaze darted between their faces. "Did you hear about Burge?"

Maverick nodded and Marina's lips pinched together.

"That's why we're here—"

"Shh." Maverick made a small lunge toward his sister.

She rolled her eyes at him. "Whit's here scrounging on the South Edge because of me."

"I'm not in a facility because of you." Whit nodded at her raised-eyebrow stare. "Up at the outpost, they searched me and didn't find anything because you had my bottle."

"Holy Chemist knees, Whit. You are the luckiest potion head I ever met."

"I've got stripes that say otherwise." Despite his serious words, Marina's vernacular dragged a smile onto his face.

Movement behind a door across the lobby killed the smile. He stiffened. "So what's going on here?"

The twins were silent.

Whit stared them down, and Marina worried her lower lip with one tooth. His train of thought derailed for a moment, but he pulled his concentration back to the tiled lobby with its grime-covered chairs and dusty curtains.

"Well, with Burge out, we gotta find a way to get potion for the camp," Marina said.

A man's head appeared around the door leading off of the lobby. "Who is he?"

Marina whipped around. "A friend. He's a friend, Miller."

"Well, get your friend out of here." The head disappeared back into the room.

"Let's go." Marina snagged Whit's sleeve.

Maverick blocked the door. "It's safer if I go with him."

She clutched Whit's arm a second longer then dropped her hand. Whit scowled at Maverick's back as the boy reached for the door. "I'll see you on Saturday—if I get a bottle, that is," he said over his shoulder to Marina.

"Oh, Mav'll get you a bottle. Just be careful, you hear?" She smiled and zipped away to the back room.

"So what's with the mysterious meeting?" Whit caught up to Maverick as he strode away from the building.

The boy pivoted, eyes flashing. "What's with the meeting? I met you four days ago, City Boy." He held up four fingers to emphasize his point. "I don't trust you."

"I can see that. But your sister does."

"Marina's a potion head." Maverick turned and started walking. "I wish she'd given your bottle back that day you came up. Then you'd be in a facility instead of messing about with me."

Red haze burst into Whit's vision. He shoved the lanky kid square in the back.

Maverick rounded on him, fists raised.

Whit planted his feet. His voice was ice. "You have no idea what you're talking about."

"Oh, I don't? You think one striping is worse than starving every day of your life?" Maverick mimicked his sister's voice. "Oh, poor Whit. His back looks like train tracks. Oh, he's so brave."

Whit hurled a fist toward Maverick, but the kid side-stepped and landed a punch on his jaw. Pain splintered from the contact point, sending spikes of light through Whit's vision. The blow reopened the gash on his cheek. He dove to the right, crashing into Maverick and staggering toward the ground. He came up with his arm locked around the kid's skinny neck.

It was Maverick's scrawniness that penetrated the fog. Boney fingers clawed at Whit's arm. He relaxed his hold. A kick to his shin sent him stumbling back. He held his hands up.

"All right. I don't want to fight, man. I'm sorry I hit you."

"You didn't." Maverick spat into the street.

"Whatever." Whit gulped in air. His stripes burned, and the fear of getting caught by deputies mixed with the rush of the brawl.

"Look." Whit took a step closer, hands still raised to signal peace. "I'll prove myself to you. You don't trust me? Fine. I'll show you I won't bring harm to you or the refugees."

Maverick's stance lost a measure of defiance. "Why? Why have you appointed yourself our new savior?"

"Because Steinar's daughter saved me. He's gone because of me."

The other boy's face twitched, but he didn't press further. "Okay. Make me believe you, then." He turned his back to Whit and sauntered off. "We'll see what the dealers make of you."

Back to the dealers. Marina said they liked her. Relief mixed with aversion. Of course the mothers dealing ration had a soft spot for her. But his stomach turned at the thought of endangering the young women, even though they needed the money.

He caught up and walked shoulder to shoulder with Maverick. "Hey, I don't want to do this at the morality hall."

Maverick barked a laugh. "I'm not taking you to the mamas, City Boy. We're going to Cagey's."

Minutes later, Whit studied a boardinghouse with crumbling masonry from behind a rubbish heap.

"If there's a raid or we get separated, make your way to the alley behind the cannery on Sand Street. Marina and I have a delivery truck hidden halfway up."

A spark of respect for his companion flared. It'd take equal measures of ingenuity and guts to obtain a truck and drive it around Mercury in full view of deputies and Chemists alike. He'd take the risk, though. In a heartbeat.

Maverick did another scan of the street. A rickety wagon sat by the curb and an orange cat scurried down an alley. Half a block up, two old men sat outside a storefront, smoking pipes. No one went into the building they watched and no one came out. Maverick strolled from behind the crates of refuse and Whit followed. Just before they reached the door, Maverick halted, one hand raised.

"Don't take any of Cagey's mix. We only use it on the hospital cases. You're here for a bottle. That's it."

Whit jerked his chin. "What's in the ration?"

"You don't want to know. You got money, right?"

Whit nodded.

Maverick swung the door open and they stepped onto a sagging wood floor.

The stench of vomit closed in. Whit's eyes watered and he backed toward the door.

Maverick said something, but Whit gagged and reeled. *He stumbled into the washroom at home. He'd been dreaming. He was confused. His mother lay on the floor, unconscious. Spots of yellow puke sprayed the walls, the commode, the floor.*

Trails of pain along his back brought him back to the present. Maverick shook his shoulder.

"Suck it up, City Boy."

Whit trained his eyes on the carpeted stairs. A flight led down to a basement level and another up to the floors above. A long hallway ahead of them ended in a glass door at the opposite end of the building.

"You ready?" Maverick's face popped into Whit's field of vision. A hint of concern made his eyes mirror Marina's.

"Yes, yes." Whit shook off the memory and followed Maverick below ground.

Doors on either side of the hall were marked with 1A, 1B, 2A, 2B. They stopped before a door on the right with nothing but a 3 hanging above the peephole. Maverick rapped a pattern on the wood.

When the door swung open, the sickly sweet smell of potion mingled with the odor of vomit in the hallway. Whit wiped his nose.

A man in shirtsleeves with a hooked nose and small, round glasses scrutinized them. "Who've you brought to see me, Maverick?"

The man's tone twisted a hole in Whit's chest. He crossed his arms and found himself summoning counterfeit thoughts as though he faced Adante again.

Maverick offered a polite smile. "Cagey, this is Whit. He needs a bottle."

Cagey smiled. The skin over his jaw shifted, dragging at the stripes on his neck. "Do come in then." With a scarred hand, he motioned them into a space more cramped than a newly blasted drift deep in the mine. Light from a gas lamp flickered over dark shapes in the far corners. Whit peered into the shadows then looked away as one of the forms moved.

A stove sat against the wall on the right. Equipment, bottles, clear containers of a liquid he didn't recognize, and stacks of boxes, both empty and packed, crowded the floor space.

Maverick walked to a sagging couch and slung himself down, but Whit toed the dingy line of the Oriental rug covering the floor. If he stepped onto it, he'd lose something. He pictured his soul oozing out of him like a snaking line of smoke.

Cagey shuffled closer. Thin, greasy hair hung to the man's shoulders, failing to hide the raised lines on his neck. "This your first time, kid?"

Maverick answered for him. "He just needs a bottle. He lost his. No potion."

"Ah." Cagey whipped his head in Maverick's direction. "And what about you and your sister? Where is little Marina today?"

Maverick glared for a second and then offered an answer that didn't exactly fit the dealer's questions. "The camp's all good right now."

"That so?" Cagey moved to the stove, turning sideways to slip between the walls of stuff.

Maverick rose, bouncing on the balls of his feet. The look he shot Whit was some kind of hint.

Whit took a step toward the kitchen. "Look, I have money—"

Maverick let out a small groan.

"All I need is a bottle."

The other boy joined Whit. "I brought him here because I know you've got plenty of extra supplies. And you're a good guy, Cagey. Marina and I know that."

The slim man disappeared behind a stack of crates. When he returned he lifted a potion bottle up toward the dim lantern. The light picked up the slosh of liquid in the dark green glass.

Maverick skimmed low words out. "Just a bottle, Cagey."

A gruesome smile split the dealer's face. "Oh, the bottle is his. After he takes the potion."

Beside Whit, Maverick tensed.

"Sure thing." Whit fished in his pocket. "Hand it over, and I'll take it later."

Cagey chuckled. His eyes cut from Whit's face to Maverick's. "I don't think you're aware of my new business motto, Maverick. Leave no customer unsatisfied. I'd never dream of allowing a client to walk out my door without sampling the product first."

At the word *door*, Maverick threw a look at the entryway behind them.

"I don't think so." The dealer's quiet words froze the boy to the spot. Whit had the impression the man must know plenty to get Maverick and Marina locked away, or worse.

"I'll do it." Whit's pulse pounded in his ears. His hand clenched as if the doorknob was already in his grasp.

Maverick sucked in a breath, but stayed quiet.

Cagey strolled the few feet between them and held the bottle up to Whit. Dark eyes leapt into his as though they could ferret out secrets.

Whit grasped the bottle and tilted it to his lips. Potion, sweeter than the Chemists' but with a tang of an unknown chemical, trickled down his throat.

It was done.

He thrust the cash at Cagey.

The dealer didn't bother to count it. He tucked the bills into his pocket and gave Whit a faint smile.

Whit smiled back. Tension flowed out of him. It was over. He had a bottle for tomorrow's ration run and for next Saturday's trip to the outpost. Maverick frowned next to him, but Whit nodded to Cagey and strode toward the door.

A woman emerged from a doorway Whit hadn't noticed. The color of her hair reminded him of oranges in carts outside the grocer's. Maverick's hand intercepted Whit's as he reached to touch the strands. Whit shook his head. Why had he done that?

The woman's dry voice interrupted. "Cagey, we've got potion packers coming up the walk now."

Whit sucked on the tip of his tongue. It tasted syrupy sweet.

"Let's go." Maverick yanked him toward the door.

The dealer pulled the door open, his eyes on Whit.

"Until next time, Whit."

After a quick salute, Whit followed Maverick through the door. Light in the stairwell tugged his attention. He moved in the direction they'd come from, but Maverick swore and dragged him backward.

"Didn't you hear her? There'll be deputies coming down those stairs any second. Stupid potion heads. As if they don't get enough."

Whit rolled his heavy eyes in the direction of the stairwell. Boots sounded on the landing above.

"This way." Maverick ran toward the other end of the building.

Whit trailed a finger along the wall as he walked. The potion bottle was safe in his pocket. Safe where no one could take it away.

His shoes sank into the carpet with every footfall. He stopped and leaned against a door, studying the ground that floated up toward him.

A boy his own age ducked into view. Sweat blistered on the brown skin of the kid's forehead. Was he yelling or whispering? His hands made ovals in the air.

Whit followed. His footsteps sounded like the heavy tread of boots.

20

Grey stood on the perimeter of the hangar, gaping as the roof lifted up into the colorless sky, folded at the apex and slid down the outside of the building. The final clatter jarred her bones. A gigantic balloon attached to the pile of scrap metal referred to as "the Clang" swelled upward as if it wanted to escape the charged atmosphere of the hangar and take to the open air.

Inside the body of the airship, another pop sounded as the tocks powered the contraption. Long before daylight, they'd loaded barrels of water and wheelbarrows of cinderite into the hold. Now Gagnon shuffled around, monitoring every aspect of the airship's launch.

Blaise ducked out the back of the airship. The stray hairs not weighed down by his heavy coils stood on end. He ran a hand back from his forehead, smoothing the flyaways. The link of the Defender marks snapped between them even at a distance, and he looked up, dark eyes fixing on her. She had to look away to keep from hurling herself into his arms. This connection could get inconvenient, not to mention confusing. How could she sort out her true feelings when the draw to be near Blaise ran through her blood?

While tocks carried bins of round metal balls on board, Grey checked her disguise. Nearly everything she and Blaise purchased in Cog Valley the day before served as part of her costume. The gloves, goggles, and long scarf would protect her from the wind on the airship and help her blend in with the rest of the crew. The boots Callis had unearthed were covered in an intricate design of clockwork, mimicking a gearish tock's appearance to a careless eye. With the long coat and her hair piled beneath her hat, she looked very little like Blueboy's fancied-up prize.

Her gaze darted up as her mark surged. Blaise walked toward her, carrying one of the metal orbs. He wore a dingy white shirt with dark, pinstriped pants tucked into his navigation boots. A pair of goggles hung from his neck.

"What's that?" Grey pointed to the ball.

He tossed it up a few inches and caught it. "One of Gagnon's devices. This is what Callis and Seree used to take out the hydro hub. We'll be using them today on Weatherton's locus."

"And you're just throwing them around?"

He grinned and silky heat slithered through Grey's joints. "It takes a hard impact to make them explode."

"Don't bounce it off your head then."

He chuckled then looked her up and down.

She smoothed a hand down the front of her coat. "Will this do?"

He moved so near she could feel the airship's electricity zinging from his skin to hers. "As long as no one gets too close."

When he stepped away, Grey hauled in a breath and reined in her galloping thoughts. Blaise sauntered over to the wall, reaching with his good arm to snag his steam pack. His shirt gaped at his chest and the goggles slid across his tan skin. The edge of one lens slipped beneath the fabric. Grey zeroed in on the movement. In the back of her mind a similar scene replayed. She blinked.

"Blueboy."

"What?" Blaise straightened, wincing as he shrugged into his harness.

Grey hurried over and reached under his injured left arm for the chest strap. As she fastened it, she whispered, "Blueboy has the key. I'm sure of it."

"What are you talking about?"

"The lock in the glass forest." She met his eyes then returned her attention to the strap. "It's in the glass forest, so it's made of glass, right?"

He stiffened. "Yes."

"Blueboy wears a chain around his neck with something attached. I thought it was a crystal, but I bet it's the key. Haimon comes to see him periodically to check on the city. I bet he's checking to see if Benedict is still in power and still has the key."

"Who is Haimon?"

"He works in my grandfather's store. He's got hair and eyes the color of iron." Grey made slashing motions up her arm. "Scars all over him."

Blaise's voice dropped to a rumble. "I've seen him. Something about him repels me. No, not what you're thinking. I could care less what the man looks like. Something prevents me from approaching him, as though a force holds me back. It's the same when I fly too high into the fog. I reach a point where I can push no farther. I'm not sure if this Haimon can see me, for though he appears alert and watchful, he's never responded to my signals."

"That makes sense. Benedict asked me what Haimon was looking for. He must've been looking for you. I bet when Haimon couldn't find you he gave Blueboy—the most visible porcie in all of Curio—the key." Grey tucked the belt tight into its clasp then let her hand rest on Blaise's chest. "I can get it."

He frowned, dark brows drawn together.

"I can get the key from Blueboy."

"No." Blaise grabbed her hand, crushing it in his grasp. "No. Don't you understand what he wants?"

"Knowledge."

Disgust twisted Blaise's expression. He dropped her hand. "That's one way to put it."

Grey shook off his suggestion. "You don't understand. He's just like Adante. His true fascination is with himself and what he can do. He thinks my inner workings hold secrets that will make him stronger."

"Grey, he thinks you're Beauty's Best, just like he thought Fantine was."

"Which will allow me to get close enough to steal the key." She held up a hand to ward off Blaise's objection. "Benedict prefers elegance and refinement. If I seem willing to answer questions over a private sip, he will seize the opportunity. He might even trade a certain trinket in exchange for information."

"And if you're wrong?" Blaise thrust his face close to hers, eyes flashing and mouth hard. "How do you plan to escape before Benedict takes what he wants?"

Grey pulled away and hugged her arms around her middle. "They're breakable. I'll go for his face or his fingers."

He yanked his harness with his good arm. "Breakable, yes. But they're hard. Could you break a dish with your bare hands back home?"

She jutted her chin out. "Defenders are strong. It's time I tap into that power."

"We're meant to battle Chemists, Grey. Our strength counterbalances theirs." He pegged her with a glare. "Benedict is strong. Do you really believe you can fight off a moving statue?"

"Do you really believe I'll let anything stand in the way of getting home? He has the key. I'm sure of it."

"We'll storm his estate after today's strike."

"The strike is the perfect diversion. Callis said it will draw Benedict's guards away from the estate. If worse comes to worst at the prison, we can follow Callis's original plan. I'll give myself up in trade for Seree. They'll take me right to Benedict."

Blaise leaned in, ice in his tone. "This is foolish, Grey."

His words rattled around in the hollow space in her gut, clattering against the resolve hardening deep within. She stared fiercely into his obsidian eyes. "Don't you have a hydro hub to demolish?"

He turned and stalked toward the Clang. For the second time in less than a day, he left her swollen with the glut of unfinished business between them.

The Clang lived up to its name as it vibrated up and out of the hangar. Standing on the open rear deck, Blaise found Grey's upturned face among the small army of tocks assembled below. She gave him a short wave.

This was all wrong. They should be on this branch of the mission together. She was insane to think she could go up against Blueboy alone. Blaise shook his head one last time. If she saw the gesture, she ignored it.

If only Callis would see reason, but Blaise's last-minute pleas to join the modified's team met with hostility. He could leave the airship once they were over Cog Valley and tail the rescue party, but Gagnon needed him to scout. Limited visibility from the bow of the ship to the ground put the airship in danger from a ground assault.

A cheer went up as the hull cleared the hangar walls. The cords attaching the ship to the balloon above creaked with the weight of the apparatus. A conveyer pulley whirred on Blaise's right, dragging a belt up under a large metal dome where another pulley brought it back down again. Arcs of electricity built between the dome and half a dozen metal receptors attached to jars. Wires led from the jars down beneath the floor grid to a tank of contaminated water straight from the underground lake. Two glass tubes jutted from the vat up through the floor again, heading to openings in the Clang's roof. One fed gas into the massive envelope above them.

Blaise studied the mechanism. Any disruption and the contrivance would fail, sending the ship plummeting to the ground. Up on the quarterdeck, Gagnon maneuvered a wheel and the Clang rattled over the machine yard and out above Cog Valley.

Blaise readied his steam pack and leapt off the deck. Air currents caught him, pushing him back into the Clang's wake. He engaged the fins on his boots and circled the ship, giving the hull a wide berth to avoid the stream of displaced air. The cobbled-together bits of metal gleamed in the diffused morning light. Outside of the ship, the power mechanism wasn't nearly as loud. The clink of metal against metal set his teeth on edge at close range but lessened when he put distance between himself and the behemoth.

The maze of Cog Valley stretched beneath them to the base of the Shelf. A few tocks and exiled porcies stopped their work and pointed at Gagnon's contraption. They posed no threat, but once the Clang cleared the Shelf and floated over the factory district, word would spread of the flying metal ship.

After a fruitless jaunt in the direction of the wide dirt road leading out of the valley toward Harrowstone prison, Blaise flew back to the airship. He aimed for the open stern, but a current pushed him back. The force of the wind strained the framework of his wings. On his second attempt, he flew above the airstream until the top of the stern opening was only feet away. Folding his wings, he dove for the exposed deck at the rear of the ship.

A tock buzzed in surprise as Blaise crashed onto the floor grid. The man's metal-planed face hovered over Blaise.

"Are you fully animated, sir?"

Blaise got to his feet and brushed off his pants. "I'm not a porcie, but yes, I'm sufficiently animated."

"You're the one they call the Mad Tock."

Blaise gave a little bow. "I am, but as you can see I'm not a tock either."

"What are you, sir?"

Blaise suppressed a smile. "I'm afraid no one really knows."

The smooth-faced tock considered this for a moment, one corroded hand resting on the handle of his shovel. He shrugged, and his line of a mouth spread into a smile. "I'm called Myver. I'm in charge of the cinderite."

The tock pushed his shovel into a half-full bin of pellets, kicked a lever to open the firebox, and deposited his load within.

"Is that all there is?" Blaise nodded toward the cinderite.

"It takes a lot to fuel the engine and get the balloon filled," Myver said. "Now that we're in the air, we won't need to burn as much, so Captain Gagnon tells me."

"How secure are the boilers?" The tanks he'd seen lashed to the outside of the Clang rattled with the airship's flight.

Before Myver could answer, a jolt shook the airship, and Gagnon's raspy voice called from the bow. "Ascending the Shelf. Give 'er more cinderite, Myver. Blaise, take a look at the factories."

Blaise pulled his bellow cord to reheat the cinderite in his steam pack, then he walked to the edge of the stern and stepped off. Once he was clear of the air current, he pressed the button at his shoulder to release his wings. Nothing happened.

He jabbed it again and again. Wind whipped at his clothes as he plummeted toward the junk stacks of Cog Valley. He reached behind him with his good arm, yanking the wings out. A click sounded, and the wings whooshed into their full spread. Blaise sucked in his chest and stomach as he skimmed over a tall pile.

Pulse thudding against his ear drums, he made a wide turn and flew toward the black face of the cliff and up, gaining speed on the slow-moving airship. He passed her and shot up toward the top of the Shelf. In the distance on his left, the gondolas moved up and down the cable line, a sign that work in the factory district went on as usual.

Blaise cleared the edge of the Shelf. Below, the short, narrow streets between the factories bustled with working tocks. A few porcie overseers, dressed in suits, walked between offices or rode in carriages. Glimpses of red and white among the throng sent alarm skittering through his veins. He retreated to a higher altitude. Soldiers patrolled the district, probably stationed there after the raid on his warehouse. Clearly Blueboy was on high alert. He probably suspected the Mad Tock of stealing his prized masterpiece right out of her bedroom.

He circled back, dipping below the Shelf and heading straight for the Clang's bow. Gagnon and his first mate, a tall tock with thick bolts on either side of his head, opened hatches on the side of the airship's snubbed nose.

"Soldiers," Blaise called through cupped hands. "Lots of them."

He gestured to his right. Hopefully Gagnon understood that he needed to cut through the corner of the factory district, exposing the Clang for as little time as possible. They didn't want to raise the alert until they'd reached the Weatherton estate.

The Clang banked to the right, her sides rattling with the motion. Blaise escorted the airship as she climbed, eyeing the edge of the Shelf as it drifted into view. Immediately, he noticed the hull was too low. Pipes protruded from a factory roof ahead, jutting into the sky like tock fingers ready to grab the ship.

Blaise signaled to Gagnon to bring the ship higher. Myver likely stoked the firebox at double time as the Clang climbed higher an inch at a time. One eye on the smokestacks and one eye on the ship, Blaise motioned for Gagnon to steer toward him.

The ship continued to turn. The bow cleared the first pipe. And the second. Blaise checked the streets below. This far corner of the factory district was quieter, but a few redcoats marched at the next intersection.

The Clang ascended. Her bow cleared the third conduit. Blaise held his breath. Just a little higher and they were safe.

A resounding scrape echoed from the stern of the airship. Blaise whizzed to the side of the ship. The great boilers weighed the stern down. The keel dragged over the pipes, sending a grating noise out over the factories like fanfare.

He turned in time to see tocks and soldiers freeze in place like pieces on a game board. Commotion followed. Voices carried even to Blaise's position high above. He whipped back to the bow, motioning frantically.

"We've been spotted," he shouted when the first mate opened the hatch.

"Figured as much," the tock answered.

"Let's see some speed." Blaise looped back to the stern. A jab to his lift button met with a grinding sound. A mechanical hitch? After a heart-pounding moment, his wings lowered and he shot back into the open stern, landing in a pile of cinderite on the floor. He rolled away from the heat of the firebox. Myver shoveled with efficient speed. The pile of cinderite had dwindled to a mound since he was last aboard.

After a nod to the busy tock, Blaise rushed around the mechanism in the center of the ship, passing more working tocks as he loped for the quarterdeck. The first mate hung over a railing, shouting orders to the tocks below. Blaise thundered up the stairs and came to a halt by the great wheel.

Gagnon dragged the wheel to starboard, his bead-like eyes fixed on the airspace visible out of the windows.

"We've lost the element of surprise, I'm afraid."

Gagnon didn't take his eyes off his course. "We were always meant to draw attention."

"Where are the arms? Maybe I can take some soldiers out before they have a chance to drop us from the sky."

"Melc, get this man a gun."

The first mate opened a long metal box stowed on the deck. Inside an array of tock-designed weapons waited. Melc chose a strange metal sleeve with long cylinders running the length of it, as well as a small shooter with a clear barrel and a pouch attached to a belt.

Blaise took the pouch first and found long bullets inside. Wincing, he buckled the belt to his waist and slid his right arm into the metal sleeve. When his left arm refused to cooperate, Melc helped him fasten the gauntlet straps.

"The ammunition is for this." He pointed to slots on the sheath covering Blaise's forearm. "You reload here."

The first mate held the small glass-tubed gun up. "This'll disrupt a tock's mechanisms." He cracked a smile. "So be careful where you aim it."

Blaise tucked the shooter into one of the straps on his harness. He nodded to Melc and turned as the first mate bellowed to the crew.

"To arms. Weapons at the ready."

Blaise quickly made his way to the stern, checking that he had the space he needed before pressing the button to extend his wings. The mechanism responded with only a slight grating sound. He folded them in again and shuffled to the edge of the opening. Head and shoulders slanted into the airstream, he prepared to dive.

A blast rocked the airship. The grid beneath Blaise's feet tilted, leaving nothing below him but empty air.

The ring of metallic footsteps reached their hiding space first. Grey shot Callis a look, and the modified porcie nodded. The line of his mouth hardened.

The figure of a running soldier appeared between the spokes of the carriage they crouched behind. The tin man approached the guards positioned before the portcullis. Bits of speech carried across the street as the soldier waved his arms.

"Great ship . . . floating in the air . . . gearish tocks . . . attack!"

Four of the six identical soldiers split away from their formation and ran for a long stone building flanking the prison. In a matter of minutes, redcoats poured from the barracks. They fell into line, forming two rectangles of about forty soldiers. At a signal from one of the soldiers in the first row, they moved as one, trotting down the street in the direction of the factory district.

"Excellent." Grey smiled at Callis and squeezed the long black cane she'd brought from Gagnon's house. "We can take the two they left behind."

Callis lifted his porcelain hand in a halting gesture. "Wait. It's not just the guards. There's the portcullis to lift."

"So we need someone on the inside. Maybe if we hold a guard hostage—"

"We need Artor."

"Who?"

The ground vibrated, sending tremors through Grey's tightened muscles.

"Here he comes now. He was waiting in the valley for a signal from one of our tocks."

The carriage they hunkered behind jerked forward. The horses stamped their feet, steam jetting from their nostrils and ears. Grey planted her cane to keep her balance as the street shook.

Callis pointed down the road that led out of town and branched off into Cog Valley. A huge corroded head appeared, followed by a thick, square body. Massive limbs swayed with each step.

"Artor is a digger by day and a star in the tock boxing rings by night," Callis said. He caught Grey's eye. "Blueboy had Artor's brother dismantled after a cave-in caused a delay in his sapphire shipment."

"Halt!" one of the guards cried. When Artor barreled on, both soldiers dropped to one knee and aimed their muskets at the approaching tock. Sparks and smoke sprayed into the air as they fired. Pings sounded from Artor's frame, but the tock lumbered on.

"Now," Callis said into Grey's ear.

He darted around the back of the carriage, staying low and moving with porcelain grace. Grey followed, eyes on the soldiers reloading their guns. Callis slipped to a position a few feet behind the first distracted soldier. Grey moved behind the second just as they'd planned. The next shot was their cue.

Eyes on the small key protruding between the metallic tails of the tock's coat, Grey rushed forward, dropping behind the man as he retrieved ammunition from a bag at his waist. Her fingers brushed the key, but the soldier whirled. She raised the cane, intercepting the barrel of his musket as it whizzed through the air. The impact knocked her back and she landed hard on the dirt road.

The soldier scrambled to his feet, leveling his musket at her.

"Callis!" Grey pushed up to stand.

In the corner of her vision, the other soldier crumpled to the ground. Callis stepped over him, heading for the redcoat who had his gun trained on Grey. From above them, Artor thundered to a halt.

In a blink, the tin soldier clutched his musket to his shoulder and ran for the city. Grey started to follow.

"Wait," Callis shouted after her. "Let him go."

Grey drew up and looked over her shoulder. "But he'll alert more troops."

"Our mission is to get in and get out." Callis tilted his head toward the prison.

Grey spun around and ran back to where Callis and Artor studied the portcullis.

"What do you think?" Callis angled his gaze up at the massive tock.

Artor grunted and slid thick fingers beneath the grille. The mechanism creaked. As Artor hoisted the lattice, pops and the sound of splintering wood rang out from above their heads. The grid buckled in the middle, and Artor folded the metal and wood in on itself, creating space for Callis and Grey to duck under.

Callis stopped to face the tock from inside the prison. "Thank you, my friend."

Artor grunted. Grey studied his heavy features a moment. Stone-like eyes stared forward and his mouth remained an impassive slit. When he backed away, she looked at Callis.

"He can't talk, can he?"

"No. His face no longer moves. I had no idea if he'd show up today."

They turned to survey the inside of the prison. Grey shivered at the high walls that seemed to draw closer at the top where they met the arched ceiling. Darkness rushed over her, and the wall of floodwater echoed in her memory. She shook her head to banish the sound of descending waves.

"Do you hear that?" Callis whispered.

Maybe it wasn't her imagination. "Water?"

"Yes."

Grey struggled for breath as her surroundings pressed in. They stood on a walkway a short distance from another door, this one metal painted a dull cream color. Tiny squares of courtyard lay on either side of the walkway, hemmed in by the soaring walls of the building.

"Are you ready?" Callis took a step toward the inner door, and Grey's gaze followed, taking in a series of black marks tracing its perimeter. The design tickled Grey's memory, but she couldn't stop to study it. Callis waited, his mismatched eyes on her.

She joined him, gripping the cane before her body with both hands. For a moment they stood on the threshold of Harrowstone. Grey focused, not on the door Callis was about to kick through, but on the modified porcie. Blaise trusted him. Blaise had saved him. But Callis's loyalty lay with the woman suffering in the depths of this prison. He'd been willing to trade Grey for Seree. No doubt he still was.

The thud of Callis's foot against the wood snapped her to attention. Apprehension skimmed her flesh, raising the fine hairs. Something worse than metal men waited beyond this door.

Thud.

Thud.

Callis angled the tock half of his body against the door and heaved. A crack spread through the wood. One final kick split the door in half. They pushed the panels aside and stepped onto a ledge in a cavernous room.

Grey sucked in a breath and flattened herself against the wall. Inches from her feet, the floor disappeared. A pit of darkness lay below and humidity choked the atmosphere.

Across the chasm, on a platform, crouched the strangest tock Grey had seen yet. He had a bulbous black body and eight tentacle arms, each stretching to a thick chain positioned over the abyss. He faced away from the ledge where Grey and Callis stood. Just as Grey became aware of a faint ticking sound, the platform beneath the tock shifted a notch to the right. One of the creature's pincher-like claws grasped a chain and began to tug. The chink of metal blended with the faint rushing water, the ticking, and another sound.

Grey swallowed as her brain sifted through the noise. As the chain ground through the pulley, the final sound grew more distinct. Screams lifted from the pit below.

Blaise tumbled through the air over an open field beyond the factory district. He pressed the button for his wing release and blew out a pent-up breath when they extended. The second free fall and jolt of the day wrenched his injured arm, but the sight on the road jarred him through and through.

Redcoats trailed the airship. Pops from their muskets rang out and puffs of smoke wafted through the air as they ran toward the Weatherton estate.

He circled back to the Clang. Gagnon had righted the vessel, but her speed had decreased. Dark smoke poured out of a hole in one of the boilers. Blaise swore. One of the tin soldiers had gotten off a lucky shot.

He flew as close as he dared. The smell of tainted water clogged his nose, and steam coated his skin, gluing his clothes to his body. If they could strike the hub and get out before the engine lost too much pressure, they might crash in Cog Valley instead of this field.

With no way to repair the leak, Blaise turned his attention to the soldiers. More and more red-coated men poured out of the factory district. Hatches opened along the Clang's belly and long muzzles poked out, but the airship crew would only be effective at close range and then only for a short while.

The nearest soldier halted and aimed his musket at the airship. Blaise swooped toward him, arm extended. He curled his fingers around the trigger bar in his palm and squeezed. The bullet fled the chamber, the report knocking his arm back. The shot ripped a hole through the soldier's chest. The tin man dropped his musket and stood, arms levering up and down. His shaggy black hat swung from side to side as he thrashed.

Another soldier raced by his malfunctioning comrade and took aim at Blaise.

The shot whizzed through the air on his left. Blaise dodged to the right, but a wave of panic drenched him. He craned his head over his aching shoulder. No holes in his wing—they both still beat a steady pace. He fell back and directed his gauntlet gun at the soldier, aiming through the haze of growing smoke. The shot missed.

Shouts of "Mad Tock" went up along the stretch of road, and a wall of soldiers advanced from the factory district. Blaise fell back, flying higher than the range of the musket rifles.

Weatherton's estate lay ahead to the right of the road bordering the factory district. Surrounded by green pastures and clusters of trees, the three-story house with massive colonnades sat at the end of a long pathway. But the object of their mission lay at the far corner of the plantation. The Clang made for a gigantic purification locus designed in the shape of a water drop.

The Shelf curved around the far border of the Weatherton property. Beneath the soil, tock diggers tunneled toward the pipeline feeding the hydro hub. If their plan succeeded, the water would bypass Weatherton's hub altogether and flow through a secret channel into Gagnon's new locus.

And they were there simply for target practice, or to send a message to Blueboy and the ruling porcies. High in the air, Blaise watched as two clockwork horses pulled a cannon down the road. The platoon line ate up the ground between the city and Weatherton's property. Shots cracked through the air. Blaise frowned as the blasts came in short succession. He scanned the ground for the source and spotted a group of soldiers around a tripod-mounted mini cannon. The soldiers loaded multiple rounds and fired, sending a stream of shells into the air. As he watched, the whole operation picked up, moved forward several yards, and positioned for another volley.

Blaise swung down to the hatch at the bow.

"Cannons," he called to Melc, who peered at him through the raised window. "You've got to move faster."

"We're losing altitude," Melc yelled. "Draw 'em off."

Blaise cursed and rounded the far side of the ship. He hovered near the stern for a moment. Myver moved in a mechanical blur just inside the portal. Below, an army assembled in the field. The huge cannon rolled off the road, the horses cutting through the field and gaining on the Clang. But the men operating the smaller cannon were almost directly beneath the ship's hull.

After a few quick pulls to stoke the cinderite in his pack, Blaise dove. The pistons in his wings whined under the force of his dive. Arm extended, Blaise aimed the gauntlet gun at the mini cannon and fired. The sound of consecutive fire reached him just before his bullet hit its mark. The cannon exploded as Blaise lurched in the air. He dipped to the right and threw his arm out for balance. Stuck in a jolting wheel pattern, Blaise turned his head in time to see his right wing crumple.

The screams drew nearer. Grey couldn't look away from the black abyss. She reached a hand out and found Callis's arm.

"What is it?" she whispered.

The modified porcie shook beside her. "The prisoners."

Emptiness seeped into Grey's heart. They'd expected to fight a few remaining guards. Callis was armed with a glass gun and magnetic bullets and her cane concealed a heavy awl in the handle, but what good could their weapons do against this mysterious machine?

The circular platform across the empty space clicked another notch to the right. As if triggered by the movement, the tock reversed the chain he'd been pulling. The screaming faded. Another hand took up the lifting action on a different chain. More screams lifted from the pit, growing louder with each second.

A few more ticks of the dais and Grey and Callis would be in the creature's line of sight. Grey trembled as if one of the great claws closed on her. She forced her eyes to the man next to her.

"What do we do?"

Callis studied the rectangular perimeter of the room. "I think this ledge runs all the way to the platform. I'm going to try to get closer. Maybe I can figure out how the beast operates."

"What is it?" Grey hissed.

Callis stared at the strange tock. "The jailer. A horror from the cinderite warrens, I expect."

She forced her next words past a stone in her throat. "Where do you think Seree is?"

The modified porcie's eyes followed the chain now clanking through a pulley. "Down there. We'll have to get him to haul her up."

"How?"

"I don't know." Despair dragged at his voice. Back flattened to the wall, Callis inched a few steps from the door.

"What should I do?" Grey whispered after him.

He turned to look at her. His mechanical eye glowed pale blue in the darkness. "Distract him."

A tick echoed through the chamber. The chains clunked, raising and lowering according to the tock creature's pattern. Screams mingled with the distant rush of water below.

Her back to the wall, Grey faced the next shift of the platform. It came all too soon. The jailer's black head lifted and swung toward her. Grey shuddered under the gaze of the face across the chamber. Not a tock face, but a porcelain face. A smooth forehead began just under a crown of moving parts. Black eyes contrasted with the stark white of the cheekbones and nose.

The jailer spoke in a high-pitched whine. "Who are you?"

She couldn't tell across the distance, but she didn't think the lips moved. Another click brought the platform around so that the jailer faced her directly. Grey's knees turned to sponges. She opened her mouth.

The mechanized buzz continued. "State your name immediately."

Straightening her shoulders, Grey yanked off her hat and pulled the scarf from her lower face. She took as bold a step forward as the ledge would allow. "I am Lady Grey, the new mistress of Curio City."

The dais jolted another notch, but the jailer's face realigned to keep Grey in sight. "Made you a lady, did he? Poor Fantine. Still, she didn't end up here, so one can't pity her too much."

A wheezing sound drifted from the still lips as the jailor laughed.

Another tick angled the creature's body toward the left of the chamber. Grey kept her gaze on the smooth, white face, but in the corner of her eye Callis crept along the ledge. If the tentacled tock's face aligned with its body, Callis would be visible.

Grey plunged into her lie. "Yes, Benedict bestowed great kindness on Fantine. She lives in the second-most-elegant house in the city."

The jailer's neck craned toward Grey as the platform moved. The pattern of the chains never stopped. "But wait. My little tin men told me you ran away. They bring me all the news. They told me Lord Blueboy was in a rage."

"I didn't run. I was kidnapped."

The chain in the creature's claw rattled back a foot before it tightened its grip. "Oh, really? Do tell me the tale. I love a good story, Lady Grey."

Callis darted closer to the back of the hollow room as the jailer's head swiveled to keep Grey in sight. She ignored the sweat breaking out on her forehead and palms and attempted a storytelling voice.

"I was sleeping in my room when the strangest creature burst through my window. They call him the Mad Tock. I've since learned I'm not the first to be kidnapped by him." She went on, spinning an elaborate tale. The jailer's white face elevated above the squat body on a long, articulated neck, swiveling to remain intent on her.

"After I escaped and returned to Benedict, we learned that one of the rebels had been brought here. We have questions for her, if you'll kindly bring up the prisoner. I'm told her name is Seree."

Grey let her eyes fall to the dark pit for one moment. A scuffling sound echoed through the chamber. She whipped her gaze to Callis, immediately wincing at her mistake. The jailer's head pivoted to the rear of the room where Callis clung to the ledge with his hands, his feet dangling toward the chasm below.

The creature let out a screech heavy with the grinding of machinery. Grey's legs locked. How could she distract it? How could she help Callis? But the jailer didn't go for the modified porcie. Instead the head zipped across the gaping floor toward Grey.

"Look out," Callis shouted.

The head whizzed to a stop inches from Grey. She swallowed a scream. Moving gears showed between the molded lips of a porcelain mask and above the crown of the forehead. Flat black eyes stared into hers.

Scrapes and oaths carried from across the room, but Grey could only gape at the creature before her.

"Traitor." Two antennae-like arms descended from the jailer's head with pinchers open.

Grey stumbled back, tripping over the remains of the door. The pinchers closed on her waist and her feet left the ground. She screamed as she sailed over the dark chasm.

"You dishonor the name of Lord Blueboy and you bring me lies and false stories." The whir of gears behind the mask merged with the ticking and clank of chains grating in Grey's ears.

Pain stole her breath. She squirmed and pushed on the metal claws cutting into her waist. Callis yelled taunts from his position. He must've climbed back onto the ledge. But the jailer paid him no heed. The pinchers dug deeper.

Then the grip released. Grey's limbs splayed as she plunged through the darkness.

Blaise scanned the sky for the airship. The Clang coasted about four yards from where he spun and dipped at the mercy of his damaged wing. Musket fire whizzed through the air around him, and the boom of the large cannon cracked the atmosphere.

Gritting his teeth, he reached behind his back for his wing. Pain lanced his shoulder joint, but he yanked the wing out, gripping the framework with wind-whipped fingers.

He made for the Clang, forcing his left wing to beat. If he reached the open stern, the propulsion of his pack and a well-aimed dive would land him in the ship.

Black smoke poured from the first boiler, trailing the airship, which plowed on toward the teardrop hub. So much for Gagnon's ballistic orbs—an airship collision would bring this locus down.

Too late to change his course. Blaise thrashed his way closer to the deck. Every time he dipped into the Clang's slipstream, the current shoved him backward. Sweat and steam coated his body only to evaporate in the chill air. With a yell, he beat his wing as hard as he could, rising above the airstream and surging the final distance to the stern. He let go of his left wing and pushed the button to retract the right, bent at the waist, and dove.

The deck zoomed by. Blaise flailed, his left hand catching a grip. A cry escaped his lips as the weight of his body wrenched his shoulder. He hung from the grid at the bottom of the opening, his feet treading air.

Metal fingers gripped his wrist. Blaise groaned as he was hauled upward, the edge of the grid scraping him chest to waistline.

Myver got his hands under Blaise's arms and tugged him onto the floor. The tock gaped at Blaise's chest.

"Sir, you're leaking, er, that is to say . . . are you deanimating, sir?"

Fire burned in Blaise's shoulder joint, but the long, bleeding gashes on his chest that drew Myver's concern were shallow. He pushed himself into a sitting position, head spinning with pain and the unfamiliar sensation of a stable floor after the buffeting of the wind.

"I'm fine, Myver. Mostly animated, thanks to you."

The tock offered his hand to help Blaise stand. "Glad to hear it. I saw you take out that ugly little cannon. Splendid, sir!"

"Little good it does us now." Blaise got to his feet and cradled his left arm with his right.

Myver stood, arms dangling at his sides, eyes fixed on Blaise's face. Frantic noise from the bow of the ship swirled around them. Blaise's head cleared.

The cinderite. The bin behind the tock was empty.

"We're out of fuel?"

Myver nodded.

A shout rang out from the quarterdeck.

"Brace for impact!"

Whit stumbled, a patch of floor whizzed toward his face. An exclamation sounded from a long tunnel behind him.

"Stupid potion head," a voice above him said. Someone dragged him up and hauled him toward a flight of stairs.

"Come on, City Boy."

Whit followed; his feet floated up the steps. He couldn't feel ground beneath him. But that was fine. Everything was fine. He had what he needed. No stripes clawed at his back, and no monster gnawed at his empty insides.

"Run," the other boy told him.

Whit ran.

The street ahead lay open and bare, inviting him to sprint for miles. His legs pumped. Faster. Faster. Were his feet touching the ground?

Ahead, the dark-haired boy looked over his shoulder and dove for an alley. Whit followed, coming to a stop against a wall where the boy—he knew him, didn't he?—waited.

Between gulps of air, the kid questioned him.

"How bad is it, man?"

"How bad is what?" Whit heard his own voice answer.

"How bad are you rolling?"

The conversation made no sense so Whit turned to go. Something pulled at his memory and he stopped, half-turning back to the boy. How did they know each other? The answer waited just beneath the surface. But going there meant pain. He didn't want pain, though it was already there. He winced. Fingers dug into his shoulder. The boy jerked him.

"Whit?"

"Yes?"

"Whit, we've got to move." The boy's face shoved into Whit's. He couldn't tell if the kid whispered or shouted. "We've got to get back to the meeting place. You're not safe out here like this."

Why argue? They hugged the backs of buildings and skulked through alleys. The other boy kept looking over his shoulder. Whit looked too. Every time he turned around his eyes flew to the watchtower looming behind them. When he looked ahead once again he felt the shadow of the tower falling on him, no matter where they were. His feet no longer glided but snapped to the pavement beneath him as though magnetized.

Cold seeped into Whit's awareness. He jammed his hands in his pockets. Maverick—the name plunked back into his brain—pointed to the back of a building across the street.

"If I bring you in there, you gotta be solid, okay, man? They're not gonna be happy with me for showing up dragging your tanked head."

Whit nodded. The empty street beckoned. He could run home if he wanted. Run so far he wouldn't feel the tower at his back. He scrubbed a hand over his eyes and focused on Maverick.

"You got it together?" Maverick gritted the words out between his teeth.

"Yeah. I'm good." It was true. The strange, numb energy faded. Whit recognized Marina's brother, and reality hammered his senses.

After double checking their surroundings, Maverick stepped off the shaded sidewalk and out into the open road. Whit followed. The watchtower summoned with an invisible hook in the back of his skull. Whit ignored the pull and concentrated on Maverick's skinny back.

No awning or trees shielded the rear door of the one-story building. Maverick knocked three times in quick succession, then once. He shifted from one foot to the other and scanned up and down the street behind them.

The door swung open, and Maverick snagged Whit's sleeve and stepped inside, yanking Whit behind him. Inside, the light from the gas fixtures pushed on Whit's eyeballs. He blinked while voices cursed and questioned Maverick.

Marina slid up next to him, and Whit shook his head. His thoughts still struggled to line up in order.

"Where am I?" He thought he whispered it to Marina, but across the room a man in a delivery uniform answered.

"Nowhere."

Maverick was talking fast. Whit heard "potion," "Cagey," and "totally tanked."

"I didn't have a choice," Maverick said to the occupants of the room. "If I let him go off like that, he'd end up in a facility and likely spill it all to the Council."

"So this was your plan?" a woman screeched at Maverick. "Bring him here so he can expose us all?"

Whit zeroed in on the speaker and started to defend Maverick until the woman in the next seat over caught his eye. He'd seen her before. She perched on the edge of her chair, her rounded shoulders slumped forward. She looked at Whit, recognition widening her eyes.

The other ration dispensary worker from the Foothills Quarter. What was she doing here? The woman shifted in her seat and winced. Realization hollowed Whit's gut. She'd been striped, recently.

Marina and Maverick were pulling on Whit's arms. They led him through the gathering of twenty or so people and out to the front of the building.

"What's going on?" Whit looked from Marina to her brother and back to Marina.

"Shh, Ration Boy. We're taking you home."

Once they stepped out under the awning at the front of the building, Marina and Maverick darted to the edge of the protective shadow, eyeing the road and buildings around them. After a couple of checks, Maverick motioned for Whit and Marina to follow. Out in the street he placed himself between his sister and Whit, despite Marina's disguise. They walked, heads down, for a couple of blocks before the train station came into view.

"I can take the train back," Whit said.

"We have no idea how strong this mix is," Marina said around her brother.

Maverick sighed. "I didn't think he'd do that, Whit. I mean, there's always a chance with a dealer, but we've bought from Cagey before. I thought that'd count for something."

"You shoulda taken him to the mamas, Mav. Why you gotta show off, you stupid potion head?"

Maverick didn't answer her.

Weight dragged at Whit's limbs, and the sweat on his back made his shirt stick to his stripes. Home and his bed called, but even more, he wanted to feel the absence of fear Cagey's potion allowed. Why had it only lasted a few short minutes? Whit balled his hands into fists. That wasn't right. But it had only been a swallow of potion. What would it feel like to take more? The next time he'd know what was going on, and he could control his thoughts better.

"Here's the truck," Maverick said, pointing to a tall black vehicle parked at the end of an alley between two buildings. It looked like an older version of the trucks that carried vegetables from the farms in the east.

After a quick perimeter check, the three of them slipped down the dirt track. Maverick and Marina set to work readying the vehicle. Whit shadowed them as Maverick explained the workings of the steam engine. When the fuel tank was fully pressurized, the truck whirred with motion not unlike a train gathering momentum. They piled in, and Whit dropped to the floor between the two seats in the cab. Marina pointed out gauges, explaining air pressure and temperature. When the truck rolled forward, he craned his neck but couldn't see much out of the windshield. Marina pushed his head down.

"Look, if we're caught, that's it, okay? Don't do anything to attract attention."

Whit folded his arms around his knees and scowled at a lock of Marina's hair that had escaped her bowler and blew in the breeze from the open window. "So what was going on back there?" He hooked a thumb in the direction of the meeting place.

Marina exchanged a glance with Maverick.

"Fine." Whit dug his fingers into the wool of his trousers. "Don't tell me anything. I risk my life for you, but you two don't owe me a thing."

"You're a grumpy potion head, you know that?" Marina fired back.

They bumped along in silence for a while before she spoke again.

"We're planning to steal potion from a dispensary in the Foothills Quarter."

Maverick swore.

Marina shrugged. "He's right. He did risk his life to bring us potion, and he nearly got caught. And then *you* got him high on Cagey's poison."

"I want in," Whit said before he thought about the words.

"Of course you do." Maverick took a sharp turn and Whit grabbed the back of the seat to keep from sliding across the floor.

"Wait a minute." His brain caught up with Marina's words. "Foothills Quarter? That's where I live. And what's going to happen to the people who don't get their ration that day?"

"Oh, so now it matters, huh?" She shot him a look. "Relax, we're not planning to let everyone in your quarter suffer. Eleatha's our inside woman. She worked at the dispensary. She says that on any given day there are rations left over after everyone picks theirs up in the morning because deaths, arrests, and runaways haven't been entered into the records. The extra rations end up going back to the Council tower."

"Eleatha? I've seen her at the dispensary. Why did she get striped?"

Marina studied her hands. "For giving away one of those extra rations. I guess she convinced them it was a mistake, but she lost her position."

"Won't they know she's in on it? They'll execute her for ration dealing."

"Not if she comes with us."

"She's willing to become a refugee?"

"Why not?" Marina tugged her frock coat tight over the loose shirt she wore. "Her husband is dead and her son is grown and works in the agro domes. She says she's got nothing to lose."

Whit didn't respond. He did have something to lose. A lot to lose. The cab of the truck seemed to shrink in on him. What was he doing? In less than two weeks, he'd broken the law, been striped, broken the law again, gotten involved with refugees, nearly been caught, bought potion from a dealer, and now he was contemplating robbing a dispensary. All because of Grey. Because he'd known her as long as he could remember. Because her father treated him like a son. What would Steinar Haward think of Whit's actions, if he were still alive?

"Chug boat ahead." Maverick's voice sliced through the hum of the truck's engine.

Whit's heartbeat jumped. "What do we do?"

Maverick reached beneath his seat and pulled out a packet bound in oilskin. He jerked his head toward the rear of the vehicle. "You and Marina crawl into the back. With any luck they'll believe I'm on my way back from a delivery in my dad's truck." He flashed a document with licensing information in front of Whit's face.

"Come on." Marina uncurled from her seat, gesturing for Whit to retreat down the narrow aisle between two empty shelving units.

He shuffled into the back of the truck. Instead of two more shelves he found empty space near the door and gray, padded blankets.

"Hide," Maverick called from the front.

Whit sat with his back to the metal frame of the unit and pressed his body against the side of the truck. His shoes bumped the closed rear door. Marina snatched one of the blankets, but instead of retreating to the other side of the truck, she squeezed in with Whit.

She fit her little body between his legs, pressing her spine into his chest. Then she covered them both with the blanket.

Her hat went missing in the process and a tumble of hair fell down her back.

"What are you doing?" he whispered.

"Does it really matter?" Her hiss had the edge of fear. "If they catch us, that's it. If they catch me . . . I'm not registered. Technically, I don't exist. They can do whatever they want with me. Drain my blood right into a chug boat tank."

Her tremble traveled through him, kicking his heartbeat into overdrive. Remnants of the tainted potion fired in his veins. His muscles flexed. He wanted to kill every deputy in Mercury City. So what if it was a trick of Cagey's concoction? He wrapped his arms around Marina, pulling her tight against his chest. Her hair caught his stubble as he lowered his chin to the crown of her head.

"They're not going to find us," he murmured as Maverick slowed the truck.

She whimpered and Whit dropped his face into her shoulder, planting a kiss on the ridge between her neck and arm. She was right—they had no chance for mercy if they were caught. If he was going to get striped for indecent contact again, then he bleedin' well wanted that contact to mean something. He brought his knees up around her, protecting her with as much of his body as he could.

The engine sputtered as the truck slowed. The deputies must've flagged Maverick down. Whit's heart sank.

"Name?" a voice demanded.

Marina tensed.

"This is my dad's truck." Maverick avoided the question. The shuffle of paper suggested he held the license document up for inspection.

Silence followed. Whit cringed. No doubt one of the deputies entered the name into a device on his arm.

"Says here Angelo Rosa is missing."

Marina sucked in a gasp.

"That's right. He took off, left us to fend for ourselves."

"And *your* name?" Suspicion spiked the deputy's tone.

"Garren Rosa."

A pause.

"Get out of the truck."

Marina breathed a silent scream. Whit crushed her into his chest. "Shh," he murmured in her ear.

Another deputy's voice mingled with the sound of Maverick opening the truck door.

"What's the fuss, Trager?"

A rustle of paper, then the first deputy's tone. "Boy says this is his father's truck, but records say the man is missing. Gave me a phony name."

The second deputy raised his voice. "What's your name, son?"

Maverick's feet scuffled on the ground. "Garren Rosa."

"Age?"

"Sixteen."

"Why are you lying to us, boy?" the second deputy asked. "I reckon you ain't reached your Stripe."

Trager's voice dropped an octave. Whit strained to hear. "Are you unregistered?"

Marina gave a squeak, and Whit clamped his hand over her mouth.

The deputy's tone returned to normal. "Ah, that's it, ain't it? Let's go, refugee."

Marina thrashed in Whit's hold.

Maverick's voice quaked. "To a facility?"

"Nope. Unregistereds go straight to the tower."

The sound of footsteps sent Marina into a frenzy. She rocked in Whit's arms. He threw a leg over hers and locked her in place. "We can't help if we're taken," he said into her ear.

"I'll send a message to the station about the truck." The second deputy's voice diminished as he walked away.

The thrum of the deputies' vessel bellowed into the afternoon. Whit shifted, relaxing his hold on Marina. She flailed, beating at her knees and rocking. No sound escaped her lips for a few moments until a wracking sob filled the back of the truck.

Whit grabbed for her hands, curling his fingers around her fists. "Shh, shh." What could he tell her? "Shh, sweetheart, shh," was all that came.

Finally she turned and curled into him, burying her face in his chest. He would've held her forever, but . . . "We've got to go before another chug boat gets here."

He pried her away. Black waves of hair covered her face, except for her mouth, which was stuck in a grimace.

"We've got to go," he said again.

When she didn't respond, he untangled himself from her slender body and crawled toward the cab. Crouching on the truck floor, he craned his neck to see over the low doors then lifted his head higher to look out the windshield. A few horses and carts moved along the side street, their drivers too intent on avoiding the deputies to bother with the idling delivery truck. Whit slid into the seat. Another patrol might arrive at any second, leaving them one chance to get away. A thrill snaked up his arms as his fingers curled around the wooden wheel. He checked the temperature, air, and steam pressure the way Maverick had shown him, then applied his foot to a pump in the floor to pressurize the fuel tank.

The afternoon shadows lengthened, the threat of curfew advancing with them.

Movement from the back of the truck caught his attention. Marina scooted by him and sat in the other seat. Her hair was pushed under her hat again and red rimmed her eyes, but her features looked stony.

"We gotta go," Whit said above the hiss of the engine.

She nodded.

He eased a lever forward and the truck shuddered into motion. The wood and metal beast around him lurched and drifted. Whit jerked the steering wheel, and the truck barely missed clipping a wagon that crossed in his path. He had to do better than this. He wasn't riding in a train, separate from the locomotion around him. This vehicle was connected to him, an extension of his limbs, his will, like the hydraulic mining suits. He bent his concentration to the operation of hands, feet, engine, and wheels. The truck picked up speed.

He made a wide left turn that sent pedestrians scuttling for safety as the truck narrowly missed the sidewalk. Carriages, wagons, and automobiles bustled along Flamel Avenue. Whit's pulse skittered as the other vehicles converged and horns blared.

"Where can we go?" Whit thought out loud. He jerked his fingers through his sweat-dampened hair.

A bit of Marina's forceful pitch returned to her voice. "I have to get to Tonio. If both Mav and I don't come home, he'll panic."

"But I've got to make the ration run tomorrow. You don't understand. My mother—" He couldn't finish. Marina didn't need to know his mother shared her potion with him—that she had for years without his knowledge. She'd wasted before his eyes, and he'd been too selfish to see it. He clenched his teeth, waiting for the flush of shame to leave his cheeks. When he glanced Marina's way again, she wore a blank expression.

"You won't make it before curfew. You should stay in town tonight."

Her hands made fists on her knees. "I have to get back to Tonio. I won't have him thinking both his brother and sister are gone. He's only twelve!"

Whit plunged across traffic and careened onto another side street, checking for chug boats in the lane and dusters amongst the hurrying citizens. Eyes flicked in their direction. Heads turned. They were attracting attention. "We have to find somewhere to hide. Soon. Is there a way to get a message to Tonio?"

She didn't reply.

"Marina, is there a way to reach him?"

"No."

He smacked the heel of his hand on the steering wheel. The truck swerved, and he gripped the wheel with both hands again. Couldn't she see he was trying to help? Every minute brought them closer to curfew and getting caught with a stolen truck. With a refugee by his side and a dealer-supplied bottle in his pocket, he might as well type his own sentence into one of the deputies' devices. The image of a gauntlet writer crystallized. He turned to Marina.

"What about the Chemist device I saw you hide on Saturday? Does it have any power left?"

Marina's tea-and-milk complexion blanched. "So you did see it?"

"Yeah."

"When I found it in Burge's pack, I knew we were moving forward with the dispensary robbery. With gauntlets we could coordinate with each other. Maybe even send false information to the station. But I hoped you didn't spot it."

"Why?"

"Why do you think, Whit? The only way to get a device like that is to take it off a deputy. It's not like that's easy. I told you Burge was loco. When I saw the gauntlet, I thought . . . I thought maybe he'd killed a deputy and taken it."

Whit's throat tightened. "Where is it now?"

"I hid it in our cabin."

"So we *can* get a message to Tonio."

Marina went full-on shrill. "Sure thing, Whit. All we need is another gauntlet. You up for bumping off a potion head to get one?"

"We don't have to kill a deputy to get one of their devices. All we'll need is a rock to smash a window."

CHAPTER

The air whooshed from Grey's lungs on impact. Her mouth opened, but no sound escaped despite the wracking pain. Any second water would close over her head.

A suffocating moment passed. And another.

She wasn't drowning. At least not yet. Beneath her a metal structure bruised every point of contact with her body. But it had broken her fall.

She managed a shaky gulp of air, eyes straining into the inky blackness. Somewhere out in the dark, water flowed. Movement from under the metal surface made the hairs on her neck stand on end. Something brushed her ribs.

The structure beneath her lurched down. Grey scrabbled for a handhold, her fingers closing around a wet metal bar. She was on top of one of the cages.

"Hello? Who's down there?"

Another heave jostled the cage. Moans drifted between the bars. The stench of contaminated water intensified as another jolt brought them closer to the unseen surge below.

"Who are you?" a weak voice said.

"My name is Grey. Who are you?"

"Lilan," the voice answered before another jerk brought them lower. A splash sounded from directly beneath at the same time screams lifted from across the chamber.

"We're going under," Lilan said.

Grey felt around the bars below then pushed up onto her knees. She stretched her arm as far as she could to the right and encountered empty space. The chain moved again, the clinking sound coming from in front of her. Grey crawled forward as groans mingled with the lap of water. Her hands closed around a slick metal link, and she pulled herself to a stand. Pain flared from her arm, knee, and hip, but her bones were intact.

The next lurch plunged the cage beneath the black surface. Water covered her feet and splashed up her boots. Her long coat dragged in the current. Clinging to the chain, Grey shrugged out of the garment and dropped it into the water. Her teeth chattered, but at least she wouldn't be pulled under by the weight of the wet coat. She'd move more easily in her breeches and blouse anyway.

Seconds went by with screams, moans, and splashes marking the progress of the suspended cages. From high above, faint voices floated. If Callis incapacitated the jailer with his magnetic gun, she and Seree would be stuck down here. He had to convince the creature to haul them up.

After a failed attempt to climb the slippery chain, Grey returned to her position, arms and legs wrapped around the woven links. A commotion sounded above just as the top of the cage cleared the surface of the underground water. Grey tensed, her senses probing the darkness.

Voices drifted down. Hurried commands overlapped a frantic argument. An odd stillness overtook her. Something was different. She whipped her head from side to side, searching the darkness. The ticking had stopped. The cage she stood upon swung upward, rising through the abyss with steady speed.

"Lilan, is there a porcie named Seree in there with you?"

The name was whispered through the enclosure, but no one responded.

Light from the upper chamber drew nearer, and the buzz of voices grew louder. The cage ground to a halt suspended over the abyss. Callis stood on the dais, his glass gun aimed at the jailer's rounded body. He threw Grey a glance, then his eyes moved to the inhabitants of the cell. Grey looked down.

The jumble of misshapen faces and distorted limbs beneath her feet sent a wave of shock throbbing through her bones. Out of nowhere, her Defender mark spiked, sending granite-hard strength flooding from her torso outward. She bent, the crazy notion of tearing the bars off the top of the cage swirling through her brain.

A voice stopped her.

"Why, there you are, Mistress Grey."

She straightened, a name pushing past her teeth. "Benedict."

He stood on the ledge. Beyond him in the outer chamber, soldiers waited, no doubt raised by the guard who'd escaped. Blue eyes hooded by black lashes narrowed at Grey. "You'll address me as Lord Blueboy."

A cackle from the jailer sent a shiver up her back, but didn't penetrate the layer of stone covering her insides like armor made of courage. She brushed the hair out of her face and planted her feet on the top of the cage.

"We've come for the prisoner, Seree."

"Have you now? You and"—he shifted his gaze to Callis—"the Mad Tock?"

Grey didn't answer.

"How fortunate to find my missing prize and the culprits behind the terrorist attack all here in one place." His lips curved in a smile then fell into a hard mold. "Jailer, deliver Mistress Grey and the Mad Tock to my soldiers."

"Wait."

Benedict had turned toward the door, but Grey's shout drew him up. He shifted back. "Yes?"

"Release Seree and Cal—the Mad Tock. I'll go with you."

"You're mad too if you think I'll let this creature escape. He's confessed. He and the tavern owner are insurgents." He raised hands that glowed white in the darkness and gestured to the prison. "When I'm done with them, they'll long for the comforts of the Dulaig's layer."

"Question them if you want but give me their punishment." The words flowed from a space deep within Grey, sounding strange in her own voice. She locked eyes with Benedict.

"Very well." He turned his back. "Jailer, release the prisoner Seree as well. We'll see just how many charges Mistress Grey will answer for."

The crash shook the Clang from bow to stern. Blaise tumbled against the wall as equipment and debris dislodged from the ceiling. Myver staggered under the airship parts raining down, his arms out as if he could catch the detritus.

Creaks and groans rose from the hull as the ship gnashed its way into the hydro hub. A massive rushing sound drowned out shouts from the quarterdeck.

Staggering to his feet, Blaise turned to see a spout of black water surge through the ship. The mid-ship tocks were up to their waists in swirling water. Blaise stared. *Water?* Myver stood frozen in the stern. The tock made a sound between a scream and a chime just before the swell reached him. With his right hand Blaise grabbed a pipe on the wall, stretching his left arm toward Myver, but he was gone. Flood water poured through the hull, rushing over the open stern in a torrential waterfall. The tide dragged at Blaise's legs, the water level rising by the second.

The sound of cracking glass rose over the gush. The tubes running from the water tank up through the Clang's metal ceiling creaked. Trapped by the water pressure, a tock body squirmed against the tube that carried gas to the balloon above—Gagnon.

Blaise reached for a metal seam two feet from him, wincing as the force of the water strained the grip of his injured arm. He hauled himself forward as the flow carried tocks and bits of the Clang's inner workings past him and out of the stern opening. A zing in his ear sent alarm pumping though his veins. Bullets! The flood hadn't washed away all of the soldiers.

With a loud chink, the crack in the glass snaked upward. Blaise found another handhold and heaved himself one step closer to the pinned captain. Water pushed against his chest. The weight of his steam pack lugged his shoulders and torso back into the surge. He struggled another step. And another.

Bullets ricocheted off the metal walls, tearing into pipes and plopping in the water like jumping metal fish. Gagnon's head was jammed against the glass, his face angled in Blaise's direction. The gears in the tock's face were still, but his eyes focused on Blaise.

Curling his right arm around a protruding bar, Blaise planted his feet on the grid five feet below the water's surface and extended his left hand to Gagnon. The tock watched the rescue attempt, immobilized either by the current or the corrosion spreading through his workings.

Blaise shifted, gripped the bar with his hand, and leaned farther into the flood. His fingers touched Gagnon's limp arm as it trailed in the current. Finally, he was able to grip the tock's wrist.

A pop set Blaise's ears ringing. The tube at Gagnon's back shattered, sending glass shards slicing through the air and water. Sparks glanced off the tock's body as a bullet lodged in Gagnon's chest cavity. Before Blaise could react to the injury, flames whooshed upward in the remaining portion of the glass tube. The heat singed Blaise's skin for a split second before Gagnon's weight yanked his hold on the bar loose. The water sucked them down ship and over the edge of the stern.

Black water filled Blaise's vision as he tumbled toward the ground, still gripping Gagnon's dead weight.

Hands shackled and waterlogged boots squelching, Grey marched between Callis and Seree. The woman next to her barely resembled a porcie. From the wet hair clinging to her cracked face to the frayed hem of her skirt, she was the color of ashen mud. Only her amber eyes retained the startling beauty of the porcelain people. They lifted from the street to stare at Grey.

"Who—?" A gurgle broke off the question and Seree bent, retching sludge-like water into the street. The soldiers surrounding them sidestepped the mess, their eyes fixed ahead. Seree stumbled on.

Led by Blueboy in a low horseless carriage, the procession moved first through the bleak streets surrounding Harrowstone, then into a quiet neighborhood with tall, narrow houses. The clang of the soldiers' feet jarred Grey's memory. She'd landed here almost two weeks ago, the night Haimon sent her to Curio. She studied her surroundings as best she could from her place in the convoy, but no hints of a way out presented themselves. If Blaise thought the lock in the glass forest was their best hope, then that's where they'd start. That is, if she managed to pull off her plan and escape before Benedict imprisoned her—or worse.

On her left, Callis whispered, "We won't abandon you to the Dulaig's prison, Grey. Blaise will think of something."

His words underscored her growing dread. What had she done? The smirk Benedict gave her in the prison confirmed Blaise's assessment of the ruler's intentions. Her body was no longer hers, those glittering blue eyes had declared. He thought he owned her just as he owned his estate and Fantine. And he would bring her as low as the tormented woman at Grey's side.

Sensation flickered behind Grey's Defender mark. A shell of stone crept outward, lining her body with an internal shield. She lifted her chin. He would not find her as soft and pliable as he expected. All she needed was the right opportunity—an unguarded moment—and she would break Benedict's rule and break free from his grasp. She and Blaise would be on their way home.

The noise of the procession brought porcies out from their homes. They pointed and a few called insults. But as the convoy moved into the grand neighborhood bordering Benedict's estate, the jeering subsided.

Seree stumbled, going down to one knee in the street. Callis darted to her side, and the soldiers around the prisoners halted, their attention on the two huddled figures.

Shouting carried over the heads of the tin men. Grey craned her neck to see ahead. Two soldiers, identical to the rest, sprinted from an adjoining street. They bypassed their comrades and made for Benedict's carriage, disappearing from view as they gained the head of the line.

In a few moments the parade was moving again, but whispers carried through the ranks of soldiers. They turned their flat metal faces to the east. Grey followed their gazes. A black column of smoke rose on the horizon, billowing over the city like a monster made of fog.

A soldier on her left muttered, "Explosion."

She clutched her chest where a hole opened in her heart, sucking the Defender strength out of her. The Clang had crashed.

Blaise.

No, he wouldn't have been on the ship. He was supposed to fly outside, running interference while the airship targeted the hydro hub.

A hard tip jabbed into her back.

"Move," a voice droned.

She jerked away from the gun muzzle. Every one of the soldiers carried a weapon. Did Blaise stand a chance against so many?

Grey put one heavy foot in front of the other. The mark on her belly grew cold, but she trained her eyes on the pillar of smoke, willing the Defender connection to tell her Blaise was alive.

Blaise slammed into the surface of the water, jarring every bone before the unwavering blackness sucked him under. Noxious liquid flooded his mouth, nose, and eyes. He thrashed, Gagnon's weight hauling him down, down.

The ground shook and a massive burst of light illuminated the water. Black particles like waterborne dust filled his vision, rushing past him on random currents.

He managed to get his feet under him, and at last his head broke the surface. Standing, he discovered the floodwater only reached his chest, though the swirling currents tugged at his limbs and threatened to sweep his feet from beneath him. All around, chunks of metal plopped into the water and ash drifted down to float on the sludge. The Clang had exploded. Blaise coughed and dragged Gagnon's head above the waves, though the tock didn't need to breathe so much as visit Blaise's lab for repairs—if anything remained of the lab after Blueboy's raid.

Another blast jolted him, followed by another and another. Blaise waded away from the hydro hub as smaller explosions pounded his ears and sent debris raining down on top of him.

Once he escaped the metal storm, he turned back. Smoke billowed from the tattered fabric of the hydrogen balloon. The hull of the Clang, what was left of it, was wedged into the bottom portion of the demolished hydro hub. The two twisted-together metal structures resembled a giant cradle or feeding trough.

Water rushed over the ground below the purification locus and out onto the field, sweeping away soldiers and mechanical horses. But the swell flowed away from the road, which followed an embankment. Soldiers lined the barrier, muskets aimed at the few tock crew members still functioning after the crash. Blaise stopped, eyes on the gun muzzles nearest him.

He could run for the far side of the field. The soldiers wouldn't follow him into the tainted water, but at this range, with a hundred weapons trained on him, he wouldn't make it two feet.

Gagnon's weight anchored him in place. Blaise glanced down. He held the captain with one arm. His left hand hung at his side. He flexed his fingers and wrist, but when he tried to raise the arm, the agony set a ring of black mist around his vision.

Shouts penetrated the pain-laced fog and snapped Blaise back to the present. Following the soldiers' new focus, he squinted, then staggered in the water and shook his head. What sort of creatures—?

Half a dozen pairs of huge, articulated legs attached to round metal baskets slogged through the water toward the hydro hub and the Clang's floundering crew. Porcies and tocks rode high above the sludge in the swaying, open-air carriers. As the first conveyance neared, an impeccably dressed porcie leaned out, scanning the scene. A tock behind him operated the vehicle.

At a gesture from the porcie, the tock turned the pair of mechanical legs toward the row of soldiers. The contraption sloshed to a position in between Blaise and the firing squad.

A clear, deep voice rang out. "Who is in charge of this company?"

One of the red-coated men stepped forward. "That would be me, Sir Weatherton. I'm the captain."

The tock piloted Weatherton's walking carriage toward the speaker.

"Perhaps you can tell me, Captain, why a hunk of burning metal is lodged in my hydro hub."

The captain stood rigid. "We believe this to be another anarchist attack by the Valor Society." The man pointed to where Blaise sagged over Gagnon's body, fighting to focus his attention on the conversation while keeping himself and Gagnon upright.

"That is the Mad Tock right there, with a member of the crew. If you'll step aside, a bullet should slow him down considerably."

Ames Weatherton cast a hard eye over his shoulder at the Clang then returned his gaze to the soldiers. "You'll not be shooting anything else today, thank you very much. My men and I will retrieve the radicals from the water and lock them in my cellar."

"But, sir, they must be transported to Harrowstone at once—"

"This is my estate. I have the right to question the rebels and exact my own punishment. When I'm done with them, I'll hand them over to you."

The captain sputtered. "Lord Blueboy will demand to be present at their interrogation, and will want to be the first to question these captives. I'm sure we can make arrangements for you to be present at Harrowstone when—"

Weatherton held up a gloved hand. "Captain, if you want the prisoners, come and get them."

With that, the pair of legs swung around and tromped straight for Blaise. From the corner of his eye, he saw the other conveyances plodding through the water toward the malfunctioning tock crew.

Blaise staggered a step backward as the walking carriage towered over him. His right arm gave out, and he caught Gagnon's body with his knee. Weatherton's distinguished face appeared over the basket edge.

"Are you indeed the Mad Tock?"

Blaise's fingers closed on the sinking Gagnon's jacket. He nodded and panted. "Mad Tock, at your service."

"Well, well." Weatherton motioned to the tock behind him. A long pole appeared over the side of the basket, and a cord with a hook on the end descended toward Blaise. Weatherton's black eyes watched the process.

The hook neared and Blaise ducked, but the cord followed, the hook snapping at him like the claws of a beast. It snagged a strap on his harness and lifted him from the water. He tried to keep his grip on Gagnon, but his strength gave out. With a splash, the captain's body tumbled back beneath the murky surface.

"Don't worry about him," Weatherton said as Blaise lurched into the craft. "We'll fish him out too."

The tock disengaged the hook by means of controls at the base of the long pole then went after Gagnon with the apparatus. Blaise cradled his arm while studying the immaculate porcie who leaned against a control panel at the front of the carriage.

"Have a seat." Weatherton nodded to a cushioned bench curving around the back portion of the basket. "I have a number of questions for you."

The gates of Blueboy's estate clanked shut behind Grey. Callis and Seree huddled nearby. The porcie woman looked like she'd crumple to the ground if not for Callis's support. A platoon of soldiers flanked them as Benedict's steam-powered carriage growled to a stop between the prisoners and the courtyard. He didn't wait for his driver to come around and open the low door, but angled his tall frame out of the seat. His black hair and the dark blue of his suit set his pale face in stark relief. Grey shivered, as his frozen expression recalled the tock jailer's porcelain mask.

He walked straight toward her, and she struggled to pull up her Defender guard. Where was it when she needed it most? Fear frayed the edges of her heart. In the east, the smoke from Weatherton's estate had mingled with the ever-present Curio fog. Grey brushed a fleck on her arm and stifled a cry. Ash.

"Welcome back, Grey." Benedict hovered over her, the cold beauty of his features highlighting her own peril. His lids lowered so that he peered at her through those long black lashes she'd once found so beautiful. The gesture banished the soldiers, servant tocks, and her fellow prisoners. It was just her and Benedict. Just as it had been in the jeweled grove. Grey fought the urge to cross her arms over her body. Instead she thrust her chin toward him.

Could she go through with this? And if Blaise were gone—her throat spasmed—if Blaise were gone, what good would the key do her? She might search the glass forest for a hundred years and never find the tree with the lock.

Benedict turned as his butler came up behind him. Lord Blueboy murmured something too low for Grey to understand, then he shifted his attention back to her. He spoke with command in his tone.

"Drakon, see that Mistress Grey is cleaned up. If she tries to escape, if she causes you any trouble at all"—his gaze shifted briefly to Callis and Seree—"start with their fingers."

A surge of stone flared in Grey's gut. "I told you I'd cooperate. I'll tell you everything you want to know. No need to punish them."

Benedict leaned closer, his voice low in her ear. Hot steam coated her cheek where his lips brushed her skin. "Oh, I'll hold you to your promise, and if you don't cooperate *fully*, well, I've become quite good at devising punishments for my tocks and porcies. I have no doubt I can come up with something exquisite for you."

He stepped away, and Drakon took hold of Grey's elbow. The butler pulled her around the fountain in the circular drive and up the shallow steps toward the double front doors. Behind them, soldiers escorted Callis and Seree.

Grey met Callis's eyes as he and Seree were led toward the back of the house. Mismatched shades of blue darkened with worry. She thought his lips formed "Blaise." Or maybe her heart formed the name. She shook her head. Even if he'd made it, the Clang was down, the mission failed. The crew would surely be captured. It was up to her to take the lead now, and that would require a dangerous game with Benedict. Perhaps, if she gave him selected snippets of information and offered a compelling argument, she could negotiate freedom for her and Blaise and better conditions for Cog Valley.

Drakon propelled Grey to the elevator, where steam sifted up from the crack in the floor, gluing Grey's shirt and breeches to her body. She wrinkled her nose as the odor of untreated water clogged her nostrils. Black stains covered her clothes and skin, and her hair hung in smelly clumps around her face.

She stepped into the elevator at Drakon's prompting and turned as the butler pressed the button for the second floor. After meeting Artor and Gagnon's rough crew, Drakon looked like a toy. She clenched her hands as the elevator shuddered upward. She could knock this smooth-faced tock to the floor and make a run for it, but what could she, a lone outlaw, do in an unfamiliar city?

Flat eyes noted her perusal, and as if he guessed her thoughts, Drakon spoke in a bored voice. "Once we've broken their fingers off, we'll move to their faces. Ears, noses, eyes. I daresay neither has any beauty left to lose, but it will hurt, I assure you."

Grey sank against the wall. She had to think clearly. Her plan depended on getting close enough to Benedict to obtain the key, either by diplomacy or stealth, but her skin crawled with the memory of his hot breath. Though the porcies produced no odor, the prison stench clinging to Grey's body seemed like the residue of his nearness. She clamped down on the bile rising in her throat. Maybe after seeing her drenched and filthy, Benedict's fascination with her appearance would fade, leaving only his desire for power to contend with.

When they reached the second floor, Drakon led her to the east gallery. Grey's pulse picked up. Fantine? Fantine would help her, surely. Blueboy's mistress might've only had a passing affection for Grey, but the beautiful porcie didn't want to see her position flouted. If Grey could somehow alert

Fantine, maybe the porcelain woman would be an ally, if only to be rid of a perceived rival.

Grey's eyes flew to Fantine's door as soon as they crossed into the pink and burgundy gallery. She stomped her feet, but the plush carpet swallowed the noise. Drakon didn't even turn around.

The butler led her toward a room at the end of the wide hallway. Grey had visited it before, of course. No doubt warm water already flowed into the tub behind the door. As they drew closer, a tock appeared from one of the servants' staircases.

Grey blinked away sudden tears. "Nettie!"

The little maid gave her a small smile, but bowed her head and preceded Drakon into the washroom.

Grey didn't need persuading when Drakon gestured that she should enter the room. Nettie would help her. She could even take the maid with her when all this was over.

She tried to entreat the tock woman through the steam filling the chamber. But Nettie waited by the large tub with its padded edges and waterproof cushions, her eyes on the floor.

Never mind. Once Drakon was gone, her friend would be all concern and support. She rushed toward the tub as the door behind her closed. Nettie looked up and Grey opened her mouth to speak, but another voice—Drakon's voice—cut her off.

"Proceed with her bath."

Grey whirled to see the butler blocking the door, his dull eyes fixed on her. A tendril of fear snaked around her spine.

Now that they'd reached the Foothills Quarter, Whit's slick palms slipped on the steering wheel. He searched his head for a remnant of the drugged potion. When he found none of the bottled courage, he searched for an argument to give Marina.

"You know, it's only one night. You can take the hunter's train up first thing tomorrow. It's a matter of hours before you can see Tonio and let him know you're all right."

Marina stared out the windshield. "I have to tell him Maverick's gone. I have to tell him we're alone now."

Whit reached for her arm. She didn't move when he touched her sleeve. "You're not alone. I'll help you, I promise."

"And how long before they take you?"

"Well, it could be a little longer if we don't break into the store right now."

"I have to tell Tonio . . ." Her dead voice ended his attempt at reason.

"All right, all right. It's just . . . there's this Chemist who's been hanging around in our quarter. He's connected with Steinar's family somehow. I get the feeling he's watching me."

Marina said nothing.

Whit pulled the delivery truck behind a grocer's on Colfax then swiveled in his seat to study her profile. The pointy little chin stabbed forward. Her tears were gone, but she was white as gauze. She'd lost her twin, the person she knew better than anyone. A gash opened in Whit's heart. Grey's absence ached. Beneath the ache was the sense of loss his father had left behind and his anger over his mother's sacrifice. Marina had lost too much as well. So what if she couldn't see beyond the simple task of talking to her little brother? What if there wasn't anything beyond that conversation? Last conversations happened every day.

"All right," he said. "Let's go."

She met his gaze then, her eyes wide and dazed, and nodded.

They climbed out of the truck and crossed the gravel lot behind the grocer's to the connecting alley running behind the Colfax storefronts. The sun sank dangerously close to the mountains looming over Foothills Quarter. Shadows bled across the dirt beneath their feet.

After a brief search, Whit hefted a chunk of broken cement. His fingers curled around the rough surface, pressing in until his palm stung. The pain was nothing. Nothing compared to an exsanguinator striping his back. Would he experience it anew for the girl next to him? In the truck when he'd held her, he'd been almost willing. Now his brain screamed, "No." But his feet continued down the path. Perhaps he did still have Cagey's potion running through his veins. Or maybe he was just stupid.

He stopped at the back door of Haward's Mercantile and peered through the beveled glass. Nothing moved inside. He checked the alley for onlookers then hoisted the rock and lobbed it through the pane. The shatter of glass carried through the quiet. Marina jumped and scanned the alley.

"Clear," she muttered.

He snaked his hand through the opening and felt around for the knob inside. His stomach soured. Why hadn't he thought—the lock probably required a key like the front door. He gnawed his lip. There! A bolt. He slid it over and tried the outside handle.

The door swung open, and he and Marina ducked into the darkened back room. The sleeve of her frock coat brushed against his arm. In the silence the whisper of the broadcloth against the tweed of his jacket sounded like a chug boat engine.

Whit dragged a hand over his forehead and stepped around a small table placed in the middle of the back room. Marina followed but caught her thigh on the corner of the table.

"Ouch." She kicked the leg then swore when the table didn't move.

"Shh." Whit motioned for her to follow.

They crept into the front of the store. Gray-green light filtered through the front windows, giving the ravaged contents of the shop the look of a bleak landscape.

"What happened here?" Marina picked through the debris.

"I don't know. Steinar's father, Olan, owned this store. Now he . . . he's dead."

Marina squinted at the Chemist placard hanging in the door. "What did he do?"

"I'll explain later." Whit pointed to the side of the store where Olan had repaired Chemist devices. A lump formed in his throat as he stepped over a toppled stool, the one Grey's grandfather had always sat on while working. He swallowed and began sifting through the piles left behind by whoever searched the place.

Would they have left a gauntlet writer on the premises after the Hawards' rebellion? Whit dragged his hand through his hair. Of course they wouldn't.

"Here." Marina's whisper brought his head up.

"You found something?" He squatted down next to her.

"Maybe." She dug through a pile of gadgets. Without the green glow of Chemia, they looked like ordinary objects—a lantern, a compass, even a camera with a strange reddish-black substance coating the bellows.

This had been a fool's errand from the beginning. Even if they found a gauntlet, without Chemia, how could they operate it?

"Here!" Marina uncovered a slender wooden case with leather straps dangling from beneath it. She stuffed the gauntlet writer inside her coat.

"Let's go." He straightened to find the light had dimmed in the few minutes they'd spent in Haward's.

They sneaked by the ransacked cabinets. Olan's books were strewn over surfaces and spilled onto the floor. What had the deputies been looking for here?

In the back room, Whit eyed the hole he'd smashed in the door. At the sound of voices carrying down the alley sweat broke out, adhering his shirt to his scarred back. He flung a hand up to signal Marina. She stumbled back, colliding with the center table again before moving to the side of the room.

Whit drew back against the wall, eyes on the floor. What would the passersby see if they looked through the window? Faint light washed the bare floorboards and touched the edge of the rug beneath the table.

He stared at the square of carpet. In the back of his brain, two thoughts struggled to intercept one another. The table was small and so was the rug beneath it. So why didn't the furnishings budge when Marina stumbled into them?

The voices drew closer. An oil-slick tone twisted around the other speaker's gravelly words. Ice slid through Whit's stomach.

"Chemist," he hissed to Marina.

Her eyes bulged and her chest heaved up and down.

Following his hunch, Whit darted forward and lifted the table up. The rug came with it, as did a section of the floor, the boards creaking up on hidden hinges. Marina gasped and rushed to his side, dropping to her knees to peer into the hole. She turned her gaze on Whit.

"What's down there?"

"I don't know." The Hawards had more than their share of secrets.

Marina's eyes darted to the broken door. "What do you say we find out?"

She lowered herself down and Whit followed. A flight of wooden stairs disappeared into the darkness below. He stopped after a few steps and pulled the trapdoor down by a rope attached to the underside. Just before the light disappeared, he spied a latch attached to the ceiling at the hatch's seam. He slid the hook in place and turned into complete darkness.

An exclamation carried from the alley. They'd discovered the break-in. Whit froze, blinking in the heavy blackness. Could the magic of a Chemist's monocle reach through the floorboards to read his thoughts?

Whit focused on the darkness in the hidden cellar as footsteps sounded overhead.

If only he'd warned Marina . . .

Darkness.

What were the men above doing?

Blackness.

The voices carried to his position. He couldn't keep them out. ". . . likely simple vandalism or theft," the gravelly voice said.

Whit's head snapped up. That was Olan's assistant, Haimon.

Adante's voice cut in. "Who would risk a striping for the rubbish in this store? No, this is no random misdeed.

Haimon, if they've escaped . . . if you've fouled this up again, I'll banish you to one of the tower vaults."

Footfalls creaked almost directly overhead. Dust sifted down from the floor above to coat Whit's face, but he remained rigid.

"She got in by accident," Haimon said. "The lock on the outside will accept any blood it's given, but mere happenstance cannot get them out. The system is far too intricate for that."

The groan of weight on wood filtered through the trapdoor. Was Haimon sitting on the table? Whit's heartbeat pounded in his chest. The man had to know about the secret cellar. He'd seen Haimon disappear into the back room often enough.

The Chemist's light footsteps moved away. Adante probably searched the store. After seconds that cramped Whit's neck and turned his heartbeat to lead, the conversation above continued.

Adante called from the other room. "No signs the enchantment has been altered."

The table creaked. "See, she's gone. Your Chemia has held for one hundred years. They're not getting out of that cabinet anytime soon."

Whit tried to focus on the blackness, but his brain buzzed with the overheard discussion. Enchantment? She? *She* had to be Grey. He knew it in the place that ached for her. But one hundred years? Would he never see her again?

Ears ringing with the rhythm of his own pulse, Whit followed the tread from the front room back to where Haimon waited. The store assistant hadn't moved from the table. He was guarding the trapdoor.

"Stay here." Adante's slippery voice held a bite. "I'm due to report to the Council tonight. I have extra agents in the Foothills Quarter, but I can only divert resources so long without an explanation."

"What's there to worry about? You have Steinar in the tower, Olan is ossified in his living room, and Grey is banished." Haimon's voice lowered, taking on an almost threatening tone. "No one but me knows."

"That isn't true."

"The others have as much to lose as you do."

Steps moved toward the back door. "Just stay here, Haimon. If Blaise and Grey get out of that case together, I will see you skinned."

Whit's heartbeat slammed with the bang of the back door. Silence followed, lulling him out of panic. He craned his neck, searching for Marina in the darkness at the bottom of the stairs, but movement above his head immobilized him.

The sound of wood squeaking signaled Haimon's attempt to access the trapdoor. The latch rattled but held.

"Grey?" Haimon's whisper came from the seam as though the man pressed his mouth to the floor. "Grey, is that you?"

Whit pressed his lips between his teeth. Haimon had only just finished telling Adante there was no way Grey could escape. Why was he expecting her to be in the cellar of Haward's Mercantile?

After a few seconds, Haimon spoke through the floorboards again. "Whoever you are, you're better off pleading your case to me than Adante."

Whit kept silent, but a voice in his head agreed with the man.

"You don't want to be here tomorrow when he returns," Haimon said. "Come on, who's down there?"

A noise at the bottom of the stairs told him Marina waited. Their only chance to get out and escape punishment was with Haimon. The Chemist would show no mercy.

He lifted his head toward the door. "It's Whit."

"Whit? Grey's friend? What are you doing down there?"

A muffled oath floated from the dark cellar.

"It's a long story," Whit said.

"Open the door. You have nothing to fear from me."

Scuffling from below told him Marina had probably fled into whatever chamber lay below the store. He unhooked the latch and pushed on the trapdoor. It lifted from his hands, and Haimon's face appeared in the dim light.

Whit started to climb, but Haimon put a hand out.

"Stay there. I'll come down. You've missed curfew, so we'll need a plan to get you home."

The glow from Haimon's lantern flooded the staircase as Whit made his way down to the room below. Haimon followed, pausing at the bottom of the stairs to light a fixture on the wall. Greenish-white illumination spread across the cellar. No, not a cellar.

Whit blinked as what first appeared to be clutter took shape as mechanical contraptions, various instruments, and glass beakers filled with what looked like potions of differing colors. Long counters supported the collection of laboratory equipment. An odd, padded chair with an attached footrest that appeared to lever up and down occupied the center of the room. Beyond it, Marina huddled against the far wall, her eyes whizzing about the space.

"Dealers?" she asked Whit, before zeroing in on Haimon.

"No, the Hawards aren't dealers. The Hawards are . . ." Who exactly were the people he'd lived next door to his whole life? He leveled a stare at Haimon.

The man with the scars crisscrossing his face drifted to stand before a curtained-off area below the stairs. He studied the two of them with iron-colored eyes.

"Who is this?"

"A friend. A refugee from the outpost."

Haimon lifted gray eyebrows. "Making friends with the mountain folk now? One striping wasn't enough for you, Whit?"

Heat built in Whit's chest. He stepped toward the wiry man. "Steinar was arrested because of me. Olan is dead and Grey is . . . gone because of me. I had to do something."

A flicker of annoyance passed over Haimon's face. "None of this happened because of you, boy. This mess between the Amintores and the Hawards began long before you were born."

Whit shrugged off the declaration. "Someone had to carry on Steinar's work."

Haimon eyed Marina, who hunkered in the back of the room like a cornered rabbit.

"So what are you two doing here? You'll find better supplies at a dispensary, if that's what you need."

"We needed a communication device. Marina's twin brother was taken today." He cleared his throat. "She needs to tell her little brother, but she can't get back to the camp tonight. They had one of the deputies' gauntlet writers up there."

"Ah, so in addition to ration running—I assume that's what you've undertaken at the outpost—you thought you'd add theft and destruction of property to your Stripe Report?"

Whit threw up his hands. "What does it matter to you?"

"Breaking the law matters to all of us."

"So you are going to turn us in." Whit backed toward Marina, though he couldn't protect her. He saw no way out but the stairs.

"No, I'm going to help you."

Whit stopped inching backward. "Why?"

Haimon lifted his hands, displaying his myriad stripes. "Do I look like someone who plays by the rules?"

Whit couldn't look away from the device Haimon held, a small metal cylinder with a scalpel point. An urge to vomit mixed with the tug of unconsciousness. The whir of the machine Haimon had switched on muffled all rational thought.

"Sit down, Whit," Haimon commanded.

He clutched for the surface of a table, missed, and staggered.

"I'm not going to stripe you, Whit. Now sit down before you keel over."

He stumbled into the padded chair and covered his face with his hands. When he could look up again, the heat of shame stung his cheeks. But Marina watched Haimon's preparations with the same blank expression she'd worn in the truck.

"Almost ready." Haimon adjusted the tube running from the syringe to the box containing a swishing bellows.

"I don't understand. Why do you have—?" He pointed to the contrivance.

"An exsanguinator? It makes all of this"—Haimon's eyes traveled around the lab—"a bit more convenient." With that he plunged the lancet into a vein in his arm. The bellows pumped, and blood flowed out of Haimon's arm, then through one of the rubber tubes attached to the instrument and into a glass vial. The whole process took seconds. Haimon pulled the needle from his flesh and pressed a bandage to the wound.

"Is that how you got all your scars? I thought you'd broken the law. A lot."

Haimon's lips twisted into a rueful smile. "My scars are not from our research." He switched off the machine and removed the rubber tube from the vial on the counter. Then he detached the hose from the bellows apparatus and placed it in a basin.

When Haimon poured the tube of his own blood into a beaker of green potion, a bubble of unease expanded in Whit's gut. Just who was this man who'd worked alongside Grey's grandfather? Not a hint of the Chemist coloring showed in Haimon's features. In fact, no hint of color what-soever marked the thin, gray man. Whit opened his mouth to probe further, but Haimon spoke, his back to the room.

"Bring me the gauntlet writer you stole."

Marina pushed up from a narrow faded sofa positioned against one wall. An untouched biscuit slid from her knee to the floor. She hadn't spoken since Haimon raided a stash of food in one of the cabinets and divvied it up between them. She pulled the writing device from her coat without a word of apology and handed it to Haimon.

He gave her a sideways glance. "You memorized the position of the magnetic dials on the other device?"

She nodded.

"Clever girl."

Whit left his chair and stepped closer to the counter. A pungent scent, a mixture of rust and a sulfur smell he associated with the gold mills in the Northern Quarter, invaded his nose. Haimon dipped a dropper into the noxious green mixture and filled it. He thumbed open a compartment on the gauntlet writer and inserted the potion into the device.

The dull platen turned a vibrant green and a glow outlined the letter keys. Haimon handed the gauntlet sleeve back to Marina. "Adjust these dials to match those on the other writer. If the one your brother has still has a bit of potion in the workings, it might pick up your message."

Marina snatched the gauntlet writer and scurried back to the sofa, where she huddled over the device, punching letters with one finger.

Whit kept his voice low. "What do you know about unregistered prisoners? What will they do to Marina's brother?"

Haimon turned back to his potions. "They'll take him to the Chemist tower. All unregistereds are checked for Defender characteristics."

"Defenders? Aren't they all dead?"

Haimon squinted at Whit. "Your history books are wrong. Oh, the Defender Cleanse happened, and the Chemists would like you to think they're all gone. But a few remain, still walking among us. And the Chemist fear more will arise."

Whit shook his head. "Weren't they giants? How could they go unnoticed?"

"Not giants, although most tend to be large of stature. Here in the Foothills Quarter, they might be called Outsiders."

"But the Defenders came from the Old Country. They were immune to the First Disease. All the Outsiders who come to Mercury fall prey to common ailments and seek the Chemists' potions." Marina's family had, and though the illegal ration they purchased saved them from influenza, they still succumbed to potion dependence.

Haimon turned to Whit. "Defenders are a mutation, just like Chemists."

"I don't understand. The Chemists claim to be a superior race. How could they be a mutation?"

"Again, your history books are wrong. The First Disease and the actions of an alchemy coven created the Chemists as you know them now, as well as the potion dependence. The Defenders arose out of necessity. Nature counterbalances itself, but there are always those who seek dominion, not balance."

Whit's gaze landed on the black curtain hanging beneath the staircase, concealing even more of Haimon and the Hawards' secrets. He didn't look away from the heavy cloth when he asked his next question. "What really happened a hundred years ago?"

"Oh, it goes farther than a hundred years. Almost three hundred, in fact. In the seventeenth century, a remote hospice in the Alps harbored a coven of alchemists who fled persecution in their own country. But within the ranks of the foreigners, who called themselves Regians, bitter conflict raged. While some of the alchemists sought knowledge for the betterment of humankind, others delved for unnatural secrets: ill-gotten wealth, power, and eternal life. They teetered on the edge of a great schism when Olan Harvardsson arrived and became the spark that ignited the growing feud."

"Olan Havard—"

"You know him as Olan Haward, Grey's grandfather. He did indeed carry what we now refer to as the First Disease, a plague that had swept all of Italy and claimed Olan's parents. But Olan survived with the help of the noble alchemist Balthasar and a miraculous secret even Balthasar didn't know.

"Alas, Balthasar's brother-in-law, Adamarin, was already twisted by his desire for power. He was convinced Balthasar possessed alchemic knowledge he refused to share. When Adamarin saw that Balthasar's family lived while Adamarin's own son neared death, he went mad. He took Balthasar's life, using his blood in an elixir that changed all who drank it—the alchemist clan, the servants, and the monastic brotherhood within the hospice. The alchemists gained the terrible power of Chemia, and the others, though cured of the lung ailment, were left unable to digest food.

"Olan, now the defender and guardian of an ancient wellspring, rushed to share this miraculous curative with those suffering, but it was too late. The evil of Adamarin's blood magic could only be counterbalanced with an equally horrible solution—a potion made of Olan's blood. Olan gave his lifeblood and continued to give it until his ossification. And that is the truth of the Defender justice system."

Whit leaned against the counter to keep from staggering. "But the subjugation. The whipping boy practices."

"A symbolic system from our early days as a colony in the New World, meant to keep Chemist blood greed in check."

Whit's head swam. The daydreams of history class returned and he pictured evil giants battling Chemists for dominance in a war that claimed the lives of innocent, potion-dependent citizens. His instructor at the Council Boys' School had said the bloodshed only ended when the Chemists wiped out every last Defender. His head snapped up. "There were more, not just Olan but Steinar and"—he cleared his throat—"Grey. Grey is one too, isn't she?"

Iron eyes studied Whit, as if testing his trustworthiness. For a moment he let his cloak of anger and shame slip away, and he was again the boy who'd grown up with Grey Haward. Whatever else she might be, she was first his friend. He put the depth of his connection with the Haward family in his voice. "I would never betray her."

Haimon nodded. "Grey is special. Her father is a Defender, son of Olan and Valera, two Defenders. Her mother is descended from the potion-dependent servants of the hospice, who have passed down the starvation trait generation to generation. Both Grey and her brother were given potion as a precaution. But Olan believed their Defender blood could overcome the starvation trait. He believed it when Banner gave his potion away and was arrested, and he believed it when Grey stood between you and the deputies. If he was right, a potion made of Grey's blood could be the key to the cure we've sought."

Whit shaded his eyes, but in the darkness of his cupped hand he saw the Hawards' faces and the world he knew—Chemia and rations—through a blood-red veil. This sick system of blood magic and blood dependence must end, but at what cost to Grey? "Where is she?" He dropped his hand. "Where is Grey? Adante said something about the cabinet."

Haimon retrieved the lantern he'd hung on a hook and motioned for Whit to follow. At the black curtain, he paused. "Adante made a prison for the one Defender whose existence must remain hidden from the Chemist Council. Blaise Amintore is the foundation upon which a treaty was built between the Defenders and the Chemists. The Defenders willingly surrendered in exchange for Council Head Jorn Amintore's promise to end further blood experimentation. Olan and Steinar were allowed to continue their work in service to Mercury's citizens because they alone know who and what Blaise is." A bitter smile snagged Haimon's lips. "My own existence was the convenient means of Blaise's imprisonment. But when the Chemia didn't kill me, Adante made me into a warden of sorts."

Haimon pulled the curtain aside, revealing a crude hole in the wall beneath the stairs. Whit ducked through the opening after his guide. A low-ceilinged cavern with a dirt floor opened before them.

Whit squinted at the glass wall dividing the room. "What is that?" He walked closer, hand out to examine the strange rectangular pillar.

"I wouldn't touch it." Haimon shuffled up next to him. "We don't know what makes it grow, and, well, the bigger it is, the more chance they have of getting lost in there."

The walking carriage dipped and swayed, and Blaise's stomach echoed the motion. His shoulder burned, the pain eclipsing all other thought. He worked at the harness of his steam pack with his right hand. It felt wrong to surrender his precious wings, even if they were damaged, but the weight on his shoulder forced his decision.

Ames Weatherton turned his attention from the wreckage outside his conveyance to Blaise. Speaking at a normal volume, the wealthy porcie's voice lost some of its harshness.

"I take it you are damaged?" He leaned closer. Bits of ash mingled with his black hair. "Ah, your flying apparatus detaches."

Blaise shrugged out of the harness and shifted his steam pack to the floor. No reason to put this off any longer. The porcie's keen eyes already scrutinized him. Blaise shoved his goggles up on top of his head and unclasped his mouthpiece, leaving the metal grid to dangle off his face.

Weatherton's obsidian eyes sparked. For a moment he said nothing, then he took a seat on the other end of the bench so they faced each other. "You are like Lord Blueboy's new masterpiece, the supple porcelain. I met the fascinating Miss Grey at a sip last week."

Blaise controlled the curl of his lip. "Grey and I are not pieces to be collected."

Weatherton either didn't hear or chose to ignore the warning in Blaise's voice.

"We were not permitted to touch her beyond a clasp of the hand, but from the way Blueboy handled her I could tell—"

Blaise lunged, snatching the porcie's gloved hand with his good arm and throwing all his weight against Weatherton's wrist. Any second he'd hear the crack of breaking porcelain.

Metal fingers closed around his arms, yanking him off Weatherton and pinning his hands behind his back. Pain seared his shoulder.

"Here now." Weatherton righted himself and glared. "What was that about?"

Blaise swore. "I told you, Grey is not a piece of art. She's not a toy to be handled. She's . . . she's . . ." *Mine.* He bit back the word. He'd be just as bad as these foolish creatures if he made a claim on Grey, if he lied to her about who he really was and what he'd done. If he kissed her and touched her, letting her believe he'd only done good here in Curio.

He thrashed against the vise grip of Weatherton's serving tock.

"Let him go, Brahman."

The tock released him, and Blaise stood in the walking carriage, staring at the aristocratic porcie whose hydro hub he'd attacked. Weatherton straightened his clothes. Eyes on his cuffs, he said to Blaise, "Do sit down so that we may carry on."

Blaise considered the odds of jumping from the walking carriage, landing without further injury, and escaping. They weren't good. He sat down.

As the carriage rocked into motion, Weatherton eyed the crumpled body of Gagnon resting under the control console. He chuckled under his breath.

"The leader of the Valor Society, is he?"

Blaise said nothing.

Weatherton's gaze snapped to his face. "Is that what you believe?"

Again, Blaise kept silent.

The porcie man leaned back in his seat, surveying his fleet of walking carriages and the soldiers picking their way from the road up the long drive to his estate. Their conveyance was in the lead. The tock in control seemed to be heading for an outbuilding near the sprawling mansion.

"I can assure you he's not."

"What?" Blaise focused on Weatherton.

"I can assure you this tock is not the leader of the Valor Society."

Blaise slid a glance at his immobile friend. Callis would've told him if Gagnon was the rebel leader. The tock was a skilled inventor and a believer in equal rights to purified water, but Gagnon's gearish face and gravelly voice lacked a leader's charisma. Did Callis know who led the secret society? Had his friend hidden the truth from him? Blaise met Weatherton's eyes.

"Then who is?"

The porcie smiled, revealing a row of large, straight teeth. "I am, of course."

In the absence of her Defender protection, in the absence of any protection whatsoever save a few bubbles and a cloud of steam, Grey retreated to a place within herself she hadn't known existed. She locked out everything—dread, humiliation, her determination to get home, even the warmth of Blaise's face.

She let Nettie scrub her head to toe and wash her matted hair, watching the sponge glide against her skin as though she watched a sculptor dab at clay. If Nettie yanked the tangles in her hair, if the water was too hot or her bruises tender, she didn't feel it.

Drakon never moved an inch from his post. His gaze never wavered. His expression never changed.

When the bath was over, Nettie rubbed a creamy polish into Grey's skin. The tart, chemical smell made her eyes water and every surface sting as though bitten by winter wind. She looked down, expecting to see red patches, but her body gleamed, her skin almost as radiant as a porcie's.

Nettie slipped a gown of ice-blue lace over Grey's head. The numbness cracked and tears throbbed behind her eyes. She clenched the fabric in her hand.

"I'd rather be naked than wear this, Nettie."

The tock maid stilled in the act of wrapping a sheer blue robe around Grey's shoulders. Her scolding was gentle. "Oh, no, Miss Grey. You look lovely in this color."

"It's *his* color."

Drakon shifted at Grey's tone.

Nettie drew the robe closed over the plunging neckline and tightened her metal fingers around the fabric. Her voice whirred low. "Oh, Miss, just be good. Just be obedient and he won't hurt you."

Grey clasped her hand around Nettie's wrist where the outline of a water compartment in her metal skin spoke of Benedict's abuse. "That's not true. You know that's not true."

"Enough!"

Nettie jumped back at Drakon's command.

"Is she ready?"

Grey searched the tock woman's face for any sign of aid, a tiny clue that hinted she was an ally. Nettie's soft brown eyes studied the floor. She didn't answer Drakon, and when the butler marched to Grey and clenched her upper arm, Nettie shuffled aside.

Out in the gallery, a door clicked shut. Grey bored a hole into Fantine's door with her eyes, willing the porcie to open up and confront what was going on beneath her own roof.

When they reached the door of the gallery, Grey could hold it in no longer. "Fantine!"

A metal hand lashed her face. The blow stung her lips and sent the pink and wine room spinning into a chamber of flesh and blood.

Drakon propelled her into the outer gallery and back to the elevator, where he punched the button for the third story. Grey's stomach plummeted as the elevator surged to Benedict's private floor. She'd never been to this part of the house. Maybe she'd look for the first window and throw herself from it. Out of nowhere, the memory of flying with Blaise overtook her. She closed her eyes and let it soak through her. When the elevator stopped, she took a deep breath and tripped over the threshold before Drakon could pull her arm out of its socket.

A black marble floor shot through with azure veins gleamed beneath her feet. No rugs or carpets softened the unforgiving surface. Tall windows in the center of the cavernous room let in what little remained of the daylight. Grey consumed the view to the east. The column of smoke had diminished, but thick clouds lay over the city, muting the lights of homes and establishments. Was Blaise out there somewhere? She strained to see a dark shape flying over the city. Nothing.

Drakon hauled her away from the towering windows, past groupings of dark furniture, a full-length mirror in a silver frame, and arrangements of blue roses with stems so dark green they were almost black.

Grey surveyed the apartment. Half a dozen doors led off from the main room. The one he dragged her toward surely wasn't the exit. Maybe the door by the mirror led to freedom. Or the one on the left that she suspected led to the tower stairs. Another door, tucked in an alcove near a wooden cabinet, might be the way out. Yes, the cabinet probably held a water station, and the plain panel next to it was likely a servants' access. If she managed to get away, she'd try that door or the tower.

Drakon opened an ornate door and shoved Grey inside, following her and closing the door behind him. The bedchamber echoed the deep blue and black of the outer rooms. Silver curtains filtered ghostly light over sleek furniture and the patterned rug beneath her feet. Grey started for a grouping of two chairs and a small table by the window, but Drakon's grip stopped her.

"You're to be restrained, Mistress."

A cold stone sank in Grey's gut, but she held her head high. "That's not necessary. I came willingly. I told Lord Blueboy I would give him the answers he seeks."

"And you've proven yourself a liar before." His hold on her wrist tightened and he yanked her toward a bed with blue-black furnishings and wicked spiked posts at each corner.

Grey's heartbeat sped, sending waves of panic crashing through her body. She dug in her heels. "No. No, no, no."

The butler's metal fingers pinched her wrists tighter than the manacles she'd worn earlier. "I will leave here and go directly to your friends if you don't cooperate, Miss Grey," he said.

She forced herself to breathe. She'd agreed to take Callis and Seree's punishment, but this wasn't their punishment. This was Blueboy's curiosity and cruelty. This was *her* punishment for refusing him. For daring to flout his power.

"Drakon, take me back to Harrowstone, to the Dulaig. I'll serve the sentence there for my friends. Please. I will cooperate, but not like this." She pulled against his grasp.

The butler picked her up. Had she really thought he looked like a toy earlier? He deposited her over his shoulder and carried her to the bed. Grey kicked and beat against his back, but the hands holding her never lost their unnatural grip.

A moment after her back hit the mattress, an iron knee lodged in her ribcage. Grey gasped for air.

Drakon produced a coil of rope and tied it around her left wrist, then secured the other end to the corner post. Grey flailed despite the metal limb jabbed into her chest. Drakon tied her right hand up then bound her legs together. The moment he stood back, she thrashed with all her strength, screaming and panting with the effort.

The butler's face returned to the blank expression he'd worn as Nettie bathed her. He backed toward the door.

"I'll tell my master you're ready."

Evening stretched over Weatherton's estate, sped by the dark clouds of smoke in the air. Blaise blinked when the walking carriage tottered into the well-lit barn. Brahman piloted the contraption into an empty bay and flipped a few levers. A portion of the basket wall slid away and a ladder descended toward the floor.

Weatherton grinned and swung himself down with a porcie's natural grace, but none of the caution.

Blaise sat, his head a muddle of pain and confusion. They'd attacked the hydro hub of the leader of the Valor Society? It couldn't be a coincidence, and yet the porcie appeared every bit the aristocrat despite his fondness for odd transportation.

"Are you coming, Mad Tock?" Weatherton called from the bay entrance.

Another walking carriage trekked in, heading for the next open bay. Steam horses shifted in their stalls, swinging their gently puffing heads to watch the action.

"I say, if we're going to conceal you before Blueboy's men arrive, we'd better be about it."

Brahman was already lowering Gagnon to the ground with his pole-winch system. Blaise scooted toward the ladder, dragging his steam pack with his right hand. He halted, preparing to jump rather than navigate the ladder without the use of either hand.

Weatherton peered up, "Brahman, bring the Mad Tock's flying device, and be quick. Leave the rebels in one of the bays if you must. Once I head off Captain Crimson Croaker, we'll get them all below."

Blaise scrambled down the ladder and followed Ames Weatherton deep into the recesses of the barn. The porcie glanced back at him, black gem eyes twinkling.

"I'm afraid you'll have to manage another climb, if you can." He stepped into an unused stall. No, not unused. A mechanical pony with a barrel belly and a large key planted in her forehead clambered to her feet as Weatherton stepped to the middle of the stall. She made a friendly sort of clicking sound and shuffled to the side.

"You should hear the noise she makes when a stranger comes back here. Oh, don't worry, she won't mind you with me here, will you, Hillary?"

The pony's yellow eyes rolled in Blaise's direction, but she offered him the same clicking sound.

Weatherton paced to the back wall, where a collection of tack hung from hooks and nails. He slid his hand beneath a bridle and a faint droning sound sifted through the floorboards.

Blaise eyed the spot where Hillary had rested a moment ago. A section of boards dropped inward, leaving a rectangular opening in the ground.

"You'll find a lighting mechanism on the wall to your right. Hurry now." Weatherton waved a hand toward the dark cavern.

What choice did he have? It was either attempt to slip past Weatherton, out of the barn and away from a small army—all with a useless left arm and no wings—or trust the man who claimed to head the Valor Society.

He lowered himself into the opening, finding rungs with his feet. Wrapping his right arm around the side of the ladder, he continued his blind journey. The hatch above his head closed, plunging him into total darkness.

Bit by bit, he made his way down until his foot landed not on another rung but solid ground. He turned, right hand stretched out. Stumbling sideways, he connected with a wall and ran his hand over the surface. His fingers landed on a switch, and a second later flickering light flooded the area.

Blaise blinked. He stood in a long hallway with white walls and white tiles beneath his feet. If his guess was correct, the tunnel led in the direction of Weatherton's house, probably connecting the barn to the mansion. Doors led off from the passage. Blaise opened the first and found a store room. Jugs of what he guessed to be water filled a floor-to-ceiling shelf occupying an entire wall. So the household wouldn't suffer without their hydro hub, at least for a few days.

Another door led to a dormitory room with neatly made bunks, and another opened onto a private chamber with a bed, dresser, and wardrobe. Blaise continued to explore, poking his head into a room stocked with oil, cleaning brushes, and other tock necessities. Just over halfway down the hall, he opened a door on his right and paused. Light from the passageway leaked into the room but failed to reach the far corners. Whirs, bubbles, and muted ticks combined into a pleasant rhythm. Blaise located another switch just inside the door and flipped it.

His jaw dropped. A spacious laboratory spread out before him in well-ordered segments. He recognized some of the equipment—tubes, slender pipes, gears, and tools for repairing tocks and porcies. But Weatherton's modifications surpassed Blaise and Callis's repairs. Molds for hands and legs, ears and fingers hung in brackets on the wall. Blaise shivered as he walked farther. Completed clay-colored body parts lay in straw-lined crates.

Moving on, he discovered intricate tock designs, from internal mechanisms to tiny, lifelike creatures that skittered around the countertop when Blaise wound them. He touched the back of a round creation with six little legs and a beady head. When it didn't move, he picked it up, turned it over, and wound it. The legs wiggled, and the thing flipped itself over on his palm. Machinery mimicking sentience. That's all it was.

He tapped the creature's back again. A current zinged from his fingertip into the beast's shell. He dropped it on the counter and crammed his hand in his pocket.

He didn't want that power. He squashed the surge of energy so different from his Defender state. He'd never needed it to fix porcies or tocks. Once he replaced their broken parts with working substitutes, the new devices integrated with the magic already in place. Callis could see out of his mechanical eye and feel with his metal hand just as any other tock absorbed sensation with their strange metal skin. That was enough for Blaise.

"I still don't know how it all works."

Blaise whirled at the sound of Weatherton's voice.

The tall porcie strode through the lab, running gloved fingers over counters and tapping devices as though greeting friends in a crowded room.

"I don't either," Blaise said. But the power flickered inside him, like a flame waiting for him to fan it into a fire.

Weatherton came to a stop near Blaise and tugged at the fingers of his gloves. "That wasn't the answer I'd hoped for."

A chill crawled down Blaise's spine. He planted his feet and searched for a weapon, but the porcie man merely drew off his gloves and set them on a table. He stood eyeing Blaise for a moment then stepped closer, hands extended, palms downward.

As the cuffs of Weatherton's riding coat slipped up, fine lines appeared on the pale skin of his right wrist and left forearm. Blaise leaned in. They weren't ordinary porcelain cracks repaired by a glueman. They were seams.

"Two separate accidents." Weatherton lifted his right hand and turned it. The seam ran around his entire wrist. "This was the first. Carriage accident. When I was able to repair myself, I thought there was hope." His voice grew husky, and he dropped his gaze to his hands, studying them as though he'd never seen them.

"Come."

The command startled Blaise, but he followed his host to the back of the lab. Another door led into a midsized chamber decorated in rich yellow and gold. It was as if he'd stepped into one of the bedrooms in a grand house. Blaise took in the paintings, flowers, and even a sipping cabinet in the corner, but Weatherton crossed the room to stand by the bed.

When Blaise turned, a knot formed in his stomach. Beyond Weatherton's figure, a shape lay on the bed. He forced his feet to take a few steps closer, but his eyes darted, landing anywhere but on the form Weatherton studied.

The porcie twisted to nail Blaise with his dark gaze. "I'd like you to meet my wife."

Sheer will propelled Blaise to Weatherton's side. He slid his eyes to the shape on the bed and clamped his lips shut. A de-animated porcelain face stared up at the ceiling.

"Clara was shattered," Weatherton said. He traced a finger over the lifeless cheek. "I remade her just as I remade my hand, but she won't re-animate."

Silence gathered in the room. Goosebumps pinched Blaise's arms and he backed away.

"I know of your work, Mad Tock. I've seen modifications you've made. If you know the secret to life, please share it with me."

Somewhere deep inside Blaise the magic sparked, but he doused the flame and turned to leave the room.

Grey yanked at the cords around her wrists until the skin beneath them burned. She fell back, choking on panic. Being tied up was not in the plan. She'd counted on tricking Benedict into believing she was willing to come to a civilized arrangement. She'd counted on having the awl from her cane concealed in her clothing in case negotiations grew heated. She could've done some damage with the little weapon.

As she tugged at her bonds again, sweat ran from her temples and tears stung her eyes. Her heartbeat dashed and blood pounded in her ears. She had to get calm. If she passed out, she didn't have a chance. She needed to talk her way out of this.

Grey forced her eyes closed, though it went against every instinct. She hauled in one breath after another until her breathing stabilized. Maybe she could access her Defender state. Though to this point the granite sensation seemed to come and go of its own free will, she focused on the memory of strength gliding beneath her skin, willing her core to harden to no effect.

She recalled the night she first felt the Defender state, the night Whit was taken, but the memory of his face and the faces of her family hitched her breath. A sob threatened. She worked her way back to a tenuous calm.

Without prompting, her heart reached for Blaise, pulling the memory of him close. She felt his arms circle her. Smelled his scent, sawdust and machinery and sweat. Experienced the touch of another human, but not just any human, a Defender like her. Strong, built for justice, built to resist tyranny. She held the moment close, willing her mark to leap to life and dance with their connection.

A scraping sound banished the phantom Blaise. Grey went cold. Her extremities numbed as sensation curled inward, forming a tight ball in her lower torso. She struggled for shallow breaths.

"Ah, this is not how I wanted it."

Grey turned her head toward the door. Night had fallen, and the shadows swallowed all but Benedict's pale face and hands. He glided forward, pausing to slip out of his jacket and toss it over a chair. The dark material of his shirt gaped and a twinkle of glass glimmered against his chest.

Grey concentrated on her mission and willed her voice to sound composed. "It's not how I wanted it either."

He stepped to the bed and gazed down, his sapphire eyes fixed on hers. "Then let's try it another way, shall we?"

A shard of hope pricked inside. She held perfectly still as Benedict sat on the edge of the bed.

He drew one long finger over the tender skin of her bruised jawbone. "Drakon will answer for the mark he left on my prize." He secured her chin between his thumb and forefinger, turning her head left and right.

Grey suppressed a shudder. His skin was warm, almost hot. No chance of him cooling before he got what he wanted from her.

"I still find you beautiful, Grey." He released her chin and traced her lips with a searing fingertip. "Do you understand? You are more fascinating than any painting I've ever seen, more exquisite than any porcie I've ever known."

Grey strained to follow his movements as his fingers glided over her neck and dipped into the hollows of her collarbone. The panic welled inside her again and a whimper escaped.

She jumped when he sat back, her whole body rigid in dread. But he didn't attack her. Instead he flattened one hand on the bedspread and leaned away, scanning the darkened room. The languid pose gave an air of intimacy, almost friendship.

"Let's try another approach." Benedict sounded thoughtful. He looked at her again, perfect features arranged in a mask of cool benevolence. "You answer my questions and I'll untie you."

Grey nodded. Fear and hope stabbed her heart.

His full mouth pulled into a smirk. "I beg you not to run. Surely you understand my position. If you were to make a second attempt at escape, even my consuming fascination with your design wouldn't keep me from exacting a complete punishment.

"Now." He pushed out of his casual pose and moved his hand to her knee. His fingers slid the length of her leg and stopped at the rope around her ankles. "I know the mangled porcie in my scullery isn't the Mad Tock. I've had reports of an attack on the Weatherton estate. The Mad Tock was seen there before his flying contrivance crashed."

Grey gasped. The smoke on the horizon had written the rebels' fate across the sky. Was Blaise trapped? Burning? Dead?

"Ah, this news affects you. Good. Then tell me, who is the Mad Tock?"

"I don't know, really."

Benedict's hand shifted from the ropes to her calf. His fingers pressed into her skin, harder and harder, digging toward her bone.

Grey winced and her words tumbled out. "I met him for the first time the day of the flood."

The vise grip on her leg eased.

"What does he hope to accomplish with these attacks?"

Scenes from Cog Valley flashed in Grey's head. "They want access to purified water. That's all. The porcies and tocks in the valley, they're all sick."

Benedict's dark brows scrunched. "What good would pure water do them? They're disfigured, broken. They're never going to rejoin society."

"They're people," Grey said.

Benedict's handsome features twisted in confusion. "People? What does that mean?"

"It means they matter, even if they're not *Beauty's Best*." She spat the words at him.

Blue jewel eyes snapped to her face. "That's Valor Society rhetoric. Who told you that?"

"No one."

Quicker than she'd ever seen a porcie move, Benedict straddled her, pinning her to the bed with stone-hard legs. His mouth stiffened, losing all semblance of civility.

"Who told you that, Grey?"

Pain lanced up her sides. "No one had to tell me that. I can see it with my own eyes."

"Is the Mad Tock behind the valor talk? Did he start the movement?"

"I don't think so."

"Why does he steal Curio's citizens?"

"I don't . . . He doesn't . . ." Grey struggled beneath Benedict's body.

He shifted, bringing his face close to hers. His knees and arms formed bars around her torso. "What does he want with the tocks' keys?"

Grey's eyes instinctively darted to Benedict's chest. His shirt hung from his shoulders, allowing the chain he wore to swing freely between them. A glass key about the size of Grey's pinky dangled inches from her face.

She averted her gaze, though a moment too late.

A slow smile tugged his molded lips. "Ah, it's *my* key he's after. Then his object is to overthrow me."

Grey's thoughts swam. "But you're a porcie. You don't need a key."

He made a disgusted sound. "No, I don't need it to operate like a common tock. This key is mine to guard. It was given to me by the gray one. The one like you."

Haimon had given Benedict the key. Then Haimon must've known the way out all along. Why didn't he tell her to take Benedict's key? Why were his final words to her, "Find him and bring him back"? He had to have meant Blaise, a Defender strong enough to free her father. But Blaise was probably dead, and though the key dangled in front of her face, she could no more wrap her fingers around it than she could send Benedict flying across the room with the power of her mind.

A shift in the atmosphere drew the tiny hairs on Grey's neck and arms to attention. Benedict still hung above her, but his expression had changed. Hooded eyes followed the curve of her neck. His lips parted a moment before he lowered his head.

Grey held in a scream when Benedict's mouth touched her neck. Pain seared her as boiling steam escaped his lips, leaving raw patches on the delicate skin over her jugular. She squeezed her eyes shut, but tears leaked out and trailed into her hair.

Heat and horror locked her in a cage worse than Harrowstone's cells.

His exploration traveled along the neckline of her gown. Hands bracing her back, he pressed his ear to her chest. Grey choked on raw terror. Shadows edged her vision and violent tremors wracked through her locked muscles.

"Such a different sound, this *thump-thump, thump-thump.*" He shifted, looking up at her with questions in his vivid blue eyes. "And this is what makes you strong, warm, unbreakable?"

I'm not unbreakable. This time she didn't say it aloud. He rose up to his knees, reaching behind with one hand to the rope around her ankles. A lazy smile etched his face.

"Answer the question, and I'll untie your legs." His fingers already worked at the knot.

Grey shuddered. Maybe she didn't want him to untie her legs. She squeezed her thighs together, her mind full of steam and pain and violation. But with her legs free maybe she could manage a kick.

Benedict's hand paused. Ice seeped into his tone. "What makes you and the caretaker different? Where does your power come from?"

"Blood." The word slipped out before she could think. Energy skittered over the mark on her belly.

"I remember." Benedict pulled a section of the rope free, his fingers working while he watched Grey. "You told me about your blood during our conversation in the jewel grove." He paused, a distant expression snagging his features. "And Fantine mentioned something about warm red water on your palm."

The rope slipped off her legs and Benedict crawled back up her body, eyes raking over her skin. "Show me."

"My hand." Grey looked up at her roped wrist. "Untie my hand, and I'll show you my blood."

A low laugh sent steam curling through her hair. His breath scalded her ear. "I think not."

"Ask me more questions then."

"Maybe I'll find my own answers." His weight settled on her hips.

"Cut me." Grey's chest heaved. The words had come out of her lips completely without permission.

He veered back to meet her gaze.

"Cut you?"

"Like a crack, only different."

"Why would I crack my new masterpiece?"

The glimmer of an idea took hold. "Because I'll heal. Go on, look at the palm of my hand."

Benedict rolled off of her and stood. Grey gulped in air as he bent over her secured hand.

"See the pinkish lines? When I came here I had scratches. Cuts. They're gone now."

"The glueman came. He repaired you."

"My skin repaired itself."

His eyes snapped to her face, his features wide with shock. "Then you are indeed unbreakable."

Grey squeezed her eyes shut. Once he saw her blood flow, she would appear damaged. No longer a masterpiece. When she didn't heal immediately, maybe his fascination would fade. It was a gamble, but she'd take it.

"Get something sharp and drag it over my skin."

He examined her wrist, drawing the edge of his finger-nail over her flesh. The action recalled a similar scene. Fine lines on metallic skin flashed in Grey's memory—the tock maid Benedict drank from.

She whipped her eyes to his face and caught the moment his expression changed, the moment he remembered the same scene in the grand hallway or countless others like it.

Darkness gathered deep behind Grey's Defender mark, crawling through her body until it landed in her soul. She tried to look away, but her mind played a scene—a sequence of events that began with Benedict's mouth on her wrist and ended with her drained, scorched inside, and lifeless.

Blaise sucked in a breath when he stepped out of the cham-ber into Weatherton's laboratory. Surrounded by clockwork, equipment, and the accoutrements of steam power, he focused on the otherness of it all. Machinery and parts didn't tug on the buried energy like the sight of Clara Weatherton's de-animated form. A step sounded behind him. Weatherton shut the door to the bedroom.

"So you cannot help her?"

Blaise didn't face him. "I wish I could."

The porcie was silent a moment. "Then you've never repaired one such as her?"

He stuffed back a vision of Callis's fragmented head and torso and said, "No."

After another stretch of silence, Weatherton's boots clipped against the tiled floor. Blaise tensed. Would the porcie hand him over now that he knew Blaise had no answers for him?

A hand rested on his left shoulder. "Let me have a look at the damage," Weatherton said.

Blaise turned. "You don't understand. You can't glue me back together or replace my gears. I don't work that way."

The society leader paused in his search through drawers and cabinets. He glanced about the room before his gaze landed on Blaise. "I didn't get this far without exploring every mechanism, every principle, every mystery I could. Perhaps helping you will get me closer to the answers I seek for Clara."

Fingers of guilt closed around Blaise's heart, but he sat on the stool Weatherton rolled under one of the green-white tubes of light running the length of the lab ceiling.

"Let's see it then." Weatherton pointed to his shoulder.

Blaise shrugged out of his shirt, wincing. Discoloration spread over his skin from his encounter with the soldiers at the warehouse, but the pain was a hundred times worse.

Weatherton circled him, his black eyes keen. First he prodded Blaise's right shoulder, his firm fingers following the shapes of bones. Then he shifted his focus to the left shoulder. Blaise grit his teeth as the porcie probed his injured joint.

"This shoulder has a different shape." Weatherton pointed to Blaise's upper arm. The bone beneath his skin looked square instead of rounded like the surface of his right shoulder.

"It's dislocated."

Weatherton's brows lifted.

Blaise gave him a brief description of the human skeletal system. The porcie stared at Blaise's bare torso as if trying to see through his skin.

"How fortunate your skin is so pliant. We never would've seen the internal damage had you porcelain skin."

"Oh, I don't need to see it to know it's there." Sweat beaded on Blaise's forehead. Without the distraction of battle or Weatherton's lifeless wife, the pain beat at his senses.

Weatherton went back to his probing, this time digging his fingers into Blaise's right shoulder joint.

"I think I could—"

Footsteps in the hall interrupted his words. Brahman appeared in the doorway.

Weatherton took a sharp step forward. "Is there a problem?"

"You mean in addition to the burning airship, the flood, and Lord Blueboy's army?"

"I assume you've not sought me out to make jokes, Brahman."

"Indeed not, sir. The army is camped on the road, awaiting your *release* of the prisoners. We've relocated the ship's crew to the dormitory. They await your attention."

"And?"

"Our network has learned of an attempted break at Harrowstone."

Blaise straightened, the pain shifting to the back of his mind. Weatherton caught the movement and shot him a questioning glance before returning his attention to the serving tock.

"A prison break? That is valorous! It seems we have more than one group desiring change in our stuffy city." Weatherton glanced back at Blaise. "Friends of yours?"

Was there any point in denying it? Blaise nodded.

Weatherton addressed Brahman again. "Was the break successful?"

"I'm told one prisoner was removed from Harrowstone, but she and two other individuals were marched to Blueboy's estate in a procession of soldiers led by Blueboy himself. Rumors are spreading that Lord Blueboy will use this incident and these captives to send a message."

The stool clattered as Blaise jumped to his feet. "I have to go."

Weatherton turned to him. "You won't get far like that. I think I can help if you'll let me try." He motioned for Blaise to sit again.

"You don't understand." Blaise's hands shook, though not with pain. "Blueboy wants Grey. He wants . . . I have to get there before he hurts her."

Weatherton's eyes narrowed. "Brahman," he called over his shoulder, "get the Mad Tock's flying apparatus and bring it here immediately."

The tock dashed off.

Blaise started toward the door, but Weatherton planted porcelain fingers on his chest.

"Wait one moment. I can help you. I *will* help you despite the damage you and your friends have caused. I'll risk exposure before I'm ready because I sense we believe in the same thing, and, of course, because it's the valorous thing to do. But"—the porcie's eyes locked on Blaise—"if I do this, you must promise to tell me everything you know about reanimation. I know there's more to it than water coursing through a jitter pump."

The spark of that hideous knowledge leapt in Blaise's core. Entertaining it even for a moment meant admitting what he really was. But Weatherton didn't know of Defenders and

Chemists. He didn't know about blood and magic. And if Blaise could reach Grey in time . . . Images of Blueboy touching her, hurting her, nearly sent him tearing for the door. He grabbed the base of his skull where pain and torment threatened to explode, then he dropped his hand and met Weatherton's stare.

"I'll help you."

"Good. Now sit down. I think I can maneuver these bones of yours back into proper place."

Benedict studied her bound wrist a second longer, then his gaze traveled to her face. Blue fire burned beneath coal lashes. His lips parted as though he were thirsty.

He turned his back and moved into the shadows. Grey braced her feet and pushed herself toward the headboard, pulling against the ropes with all her strength. She craned her neck, trying to reach the cords on her wrist with her teeth. The bed creaked with her efforts.

Benedict's voice carried from across the room. "If I knew you wouldn't run, I'd untie you."

"I won't run."

His low laugh dragged her heart into her stomach. "Yes, you will."

He stood at a waist-high bureau set against the far wall, his hands busy with an arrangement of deep blue roses. When he faced her again, his fingers curved around something she couldn't see.

He sauntered back toward her, and Grey drew her knees up, compacting her body into as little space as possible.

"This game we're playing, Grey, I'm indulging it. I'm enjoying it."

He sat on the bed and circled her ankle with his heated fingers. For a moment, the veins in her foot distracted him. He traced the blue lines, then the cold eyes met hers again. "But you must understand, having you is the next step. You are like the gray one. The gray one put me in power." His hand slid beneath his shirt, snagging the key and holding it out. Grey couldn't keep her eyes from the little glass prize.

Benedict continued. "The gray one is the only being I know of, besides the Designer, who has more power than I. Though unlike you, he seems more accustomed to using it." He stroked her leg from knee to ankle. "When I possess the same power, I can challenge him. Get answers. Perhaps . . . perhaps even leave Curio City without fear of breaking, without fear of losing the beauty that keeps me in power here."

He lowered his lips to her knee. Keeping his gaze on her face, he murmured against her skin. "You're my key, Grey. Much more useful than the trinket around my neck."

She winced as steam burns bloomed wherever his breath touched.

"If you cooperate, I'll forgive your treason. I'll pardon your conspirators' deeds. I'll make you my mistress, and you'll have more power in Curio City than any other save myself. I won't hurt you."

Tears tracked down Grey's cheek. Her voice shook. "You *are* hurting me."

"I know, beautiful one." He glanced to her ropes. "It's a necessary step. You're too strong. You need a few cracks to hide. A reason to duck your head in my presence."

Blood drained from Grey's face. Deep inside a voice screamed for help, for strength, for Blaise. She neared an edge, a cliff that echoed with hopelessness. But there was a place beneath the pain and the terror that Benedict could not reach—a part of her that no one could touch or take.

She pulled courage from that secret well, lifted her chin, and stared into Benedict's ice-blue eyes. She put every ounce of remaining strength into her voice.

"I will never duck my head for you."

His pale face went still. Then he moved, so quickly Grey was still processing the motion after Benedict straightened. He stood by the bed now, his hand clenched. Something warm seeped down Grey's wrist.

The skin on the heel of her left hand gaped and blood trickled from the wound. Grey waited for the pain. As she'd known would happen, Benedict dipped his head toward the little river of blood. She braced herself for the burn of his breath, the tug of lips on her slashed skin, the torment of teeth locked around her wrist. No sensation registered.

He leaned away, blood on his lips and frenzy in his eyes. As if from a great distance, Grey watched his dark head bend over her hand once again. The scene belonged in a nightmare. Someone should do something for the girl tied to the bed. Someone should pull the monster off of her. Someone should smash his face into the bedpost.

A hard knot formed behind Grey's navel. It pushed outward, forcing her body to uncurl. Her Defender state spread, so much stronger than fear-rigid muscles, so much stronger than porcelain skin. Granite crawled from her mark, skimming beneath her skin to encase her legs, her feet, her arms, her hands.

Yes, someone should do something for the girl tied to the bed.

A whispered word escaped Grey's lips. "Unbreakable."

Grey wrenched her arm away from the post. The crack of wood echoed through the room. Benedict made a wet, startled sound, but Grey palmed his face and thrust with all the inescapable force of a mountain. He flew backward.

Snapping the rope around her other hand, she vaulted from the bed.

Benedict was on his feet already, his face as inhuman as the Dulaig's. He approached, hands poised to grab her.

"Don't make me call Drakon."

The threat bounced off Grey. He didn't want the tock butler in here any more than she did. Her eyes slid toward the door.

"You'll never get out of my house even if you manage to get by me."

The tall windows she'd glimpsed in the room outside appeared in her mind's eye. She stepped sideways, angling herself toward the door. "Maybe I can fly."

Benedict matched her steps, placing himself between her and the way out. "Your friends went down, Grey. They fell out of the sky. There's no one there to catch you."

She faltered at the thought of Blaise, broken amongst the wreckage of the Clang. Benedict used her moment of distraction to move closer. She shrank back, eyes darting between the door and the porcie ruler. Her hip connected with a narrow table pushed against the wall, and she stretched her right hand the length of the marble surface, pulling her body along as though the table offered some hope of security.

Blood still stained Benedict's lower lip and teeth. His eyes traveled from her dripping left hand to the broken bedpost.

"You tricked me. The moment your blood flowed, you grew stronger."

It was true even if it made no sense. Chin raised, Grey inched toward the door.

Benedict's eyes glowed in the darkness. "It seems you shared that strength with me."

He lunged for her. Grey shifted but he slammed into her side, his arms locking around her like the limbs of a statue.

No pain radiated from the contact, but the force of his grip held her prisoner. She pushed, flexing her muscles against his power. She would not go back to that bed. She would not go back to that terror.

A cloud of red steam billowed before her eyes. The heat took a moment to register. Droplets of moisture clung to her face and hair. Her blood. He breathed out steam laced with her blood.

Grey's stomach turned, her senses lost in a wave of revulsion even as Benedict shoved her up and backward onto the marble top of the table. Her spine and head collided with the wall, the crash reverberating through the room. Noises sounded from the hallway outside. Drakon? Guards?

She braced her arms against Benedict's shoulders and pushed. Slick with her own leaking blood, her left hand slid across the material of his shirt. The haze of bloody steam hung between their faces, tinting the black shadows red. It smelled of rust and wet clay. He wedged himself between her knees, but she dug into his porcelain midsection with her granite-lined legs.

The sound of a scuffle penetrated the heavy door on Grey's right. A scream carried through.

Benedict's head turned and he uttered an oath. His grip on her lessened a fraction as the door of the room burst open. Dark figures, outlined in the light from outside, tumbled into the room. Slipping her right hand inside Benedict's shirt, Grey closed her fingers around the glass key. Then she pulled her leg up and planted her foot in his stomach.

She kicked with all her might, and the pressure of his body caging hers vanished. He stumbled backward, eyes wide and mouth agape before he connected with the bedpost and went down.

A crack rent the air, underscored by screams and the whirring of mechanical voices and limbs.

Key in hand, Grey slipped off the table and ran toward the door and the muddle of silhouettes. She'd crash through them if she had to.

The red mist cleared and Fantine's face materialized in her vision. Behind the porcie woman, Nettie struggled in the iron grip of Drakon. Grey hurtled into the tock butler, scrabbling at his face and hands.

They'd come for her. Fantine and Nettie had come for her. A measure of her Defender strength faded as tears pulsed behind her eyeballs. She thrust the emotion to the back of her mind and kicked at Drakon's shin. The butler held fast to Nettie.

Fantine shrieked, her voice shrill as a boiling kettle in Grey's ears.

"Come on," Grey yelled to the porcie woman.

But Fantine's hysterical screams still echoed through Benedict's lair. Grey tugged on her arm, dodging Nettie's form to land kicks to the butler. The porcelain woman refused to move.

Nettie went limp in Drakon's arms. Grey searched the tock maid's frame. What had he done to her? But Drakon stood with mouth slack, his arms supporting Nettie but no longer imprisoning her. Fantine's screams fell into sobs as all three of the newcomers stared into the room behind Grey.

She wanted to push past the little group and run for one of the escape routes she'd spotted earlier, but a scraping sound, punctuated by low moans and Fantine's whimpers, drew her attention. She inched her head around until she faced the room.

Benedict hunched by the bed, shoulders bent and dark head drooping. Grey's eyes followed the curve of his body inward to where he supported his left wrist with his right hand. Her gut jolted.

Red-tainted water trickled from the jagged edge of Benedict's arm. A white hand lay on the floor just beyond the spiked bedpost.

The porcie ruler lifted his head. The frost-blue eyes landed not on Grey's face but on Fantine.

"You."

Fantine trembled and took a step backward.

Holding his shattered arm up so that the gush of fluid slowed, Benedict pushed out of his crouch and straightened into a stand.

"I'll see you sent to Dulaig for this, Fantine. But not before I make some changes to your appearance myself."

Fantine clamped her hand over the fabric of her high collar. Holding her throat, she tried to retreat through the doorway. Her shoulder knocked into Grey's as she backed into Nettie and Drakon, but the stunned butler wouldn't budge. He blocked her path.

Benedict's face twisted, his eyes stabbing at Fantine. When he launched across the room, instinct moved Grey's body. No thought fired in her brain other than the image of Fantine behind a shield. She slid in front of the porcie woman and raised her arms, crossed at the wrists, before her own body.

The sharp edge of Benedict's smashed arm drove into Grey's left wrist. A snap jarred her body. The sensation of stone beneath her skin retreated, crawling upward from her wrist. Agony enveloped her, licking like flames, like searing steam.

Grey fell backward, tumbling into hard, jutting limbs, porcelain and tock body parts. The haze was back, but this time depthless black rimmed her vision.

Metal fingers closed around her upper arm and yanked her into the light of the hall. Grey stumbled, pain and darkness pulling her toward the ground. She put her arms out to catch herself.

Her right hand curled around the key. Her left hand dangled in her field of vision, blood and bone and tendons exposed, attached to her wrist only by a thin strip of skin.

Then the black swallowed her whole.

Whit eased his upper body off the floor. His muscles cramped and a couple of his scars twinged, but he kept his lips sealed.

Marina lay curled up in a ball on the couch a foot away. With her face to the back of the sofa and her hair almost taking up more space than the rest of her body, she looked younger than her sixteen years. But if those eyes opened and turned on him, he'd see far too much misery for such a short lifetime.

He scooted away and rose. When his vision adjusted, he picked his way around counters and machines. He paused at the stairs and looked back at Marina's form. Her voice had broken whenever she'd said Maverick's name, but then her face would fall back into a mask.

Whit had talked to her for hours, seated on the floor with his back against the lumpy sofa cushion and his knees drawn up. He'd made promises, planned rescue attempts, said the stupidest things to her in an effort to shrink her loss. Maybe she'd faked sleep to get him to shut up. Who could blame her?

But as he rambled, one thing became clear to him. He needed an edge. Something that just might make his plans possible. Something that drowned out the pain long enough for him to act.

Whit jammed his fingers through his hair, pushing it away from his face. He dragged his eyes from Marina's huddled figure and made his way up the staircase toward the trapdoor. All was silent above, but Haimon guarded the empty store. No doubt he expected Whit and Marina to emerge in time for the morning ration run.

An internal clock told Whit the hour was early. As he unlocked the latch and lifted the trapdoor with its attached disguise of rug and table, only the faint glow of a streetlight cut through the darkness.

He climbed out of the opening in the floor and lowered the trapdoor, waiting until the last minute to let go of the planks. The section of wood drifted into place with an almost imperceptible sucking sound. Whit crouched and waited. Chills and surges of heat traversed his spine.

When the rush of blood in his eardrums quieted, he detected the sound of even breathing. Haimon must be sleeping in the front of the store. He hoped the man's slumber was deep.

Whit straightened but didn't take a step, caught between slipping out the back door to disappear into the early morning, darting back to the safety of the underground lab, and carrying out the plan he'd hatched while staring at the bones of Marina's spinal column beneath her shirt.

There wasn't a choice. Not really.

He'd rather live on the fringes than spend another day following Council rules.

Whit crept toward the main section of Haward's Mercantile. Grey's face, Olan's face, Steinar's face, even his mother's face, rose before him, their expressions grim. He pushed them all aside and located the sleeping Haimon. The man lay on the floor, head cushioned on his arm and one hand pressed to the enchanted glass case.

Goosebumps tugged at Whit's skin, and he turned away from the awful thing, picturing Gray trapped in the bizarrely expanding cabinet like a magician's assistant in a gruesome sideshow act. No matter what Haimon said about the inside, it looked too much like a glass coffin to make Whit think of anything other than a death sentence.

He edged his way behind the display case on the opposite side of the room from where Haimon slumbered. The place had been wrecked, objects overturned, scattered, the contents of cabinets and shelves dumped, but whoever did the damage had a goal other than theft. Valuable equipment and antique pieces remained strewn over the floor and countertops.

With one more look at the immobile shape of Haimon, Whit went to work. He shoved a few pieces of jewelry into one pocket and a few smaller Chemist devices in the other. His hand lingered on the cash register, but he passed on. He didn't know how to open the drawer, and if he did, the ringing sound it made would wake Haimon.

When his pockets were full, he turned toward the little back room. He wasn't really stealing from the Hawards. The Council had closed this shop when Steinar was arrested and Olan turned to stone. The merchandise would sit, gathering dust, for who knew how long. He might as well put it to good use.

As he skulked by the prone form of Haimon and into the back room, a shadow moved near the door, raising the hair on Whit's neck. He froze.

An outline separated from the wall and stepped into the jagged segment of light falling through the broken window.

Marina.

Whit crossed the floor and leaned down, keeping his voice a whisper. "What are you doing?"

"What are *you* doing?"

"Shh." He held one finger up toward her lips then crooked it toward the front room. "Haimon."

Her pale eyes lost all hint of color in the darkness, and the pupils stood out against gray rings. She fixed him with a depthless stare.

"He's going to help us. Why are you leaving?"

Heat flushed his cheeks. He hoped she couldn't see in the darkness. "I'm done with this, Marina. I'm done living here, working in the mine, waiting in ration lines."

Her wide mouth formed an O, but then a flash lit her eyes. "You don't know what you're saying. You don't know how lucky you are to have your name on a ration list, to know there will be a bottle of potion for you every day."

Her voice rose as she spoke. Whit scanned the opening between the rooms, but no movement indicated Haimon had woken. He faced Marina again and cupped her shoulders with his hands. *She* had no idea what it was like to live without the freedom of a simple touch like this. For a moment, he just stared into her eyes.

"I can get potion. You and the refugees need my help, and I'm not going to continue down here in the quarters now that I know what you face every day."

"Please, Whit." She stepped closer, placing her hands on his sides. "Play by the rules, like Steinar. He was careful."

"He was different," Whit hissed. Steinar hadn't needed any potion. Day after day, he delivered all of his ration to the outpost. But it wasn't enough. It would never be enough.

"You're different." Marina's voice was so quiet he almost didn't hear the words.

"What?"

"You're different. *And* stupid. Everyone else spends their life avoiding punishment, but you're about to go find it, aren't you?"

He clenched his teeth against a growl. After a moment, he trusted himself to speak. "Let me do what needs to be done."

"Let me go with you."

"No."

"Why?" Her high-pitched voice, muted though it was, lent a childish tone to the word. It was frustrating and cute and enticing all at once.

He pulled her into him, dipping his head low to cover her lips with his. A squeak escaped her throat, but then she was all fire and motion. He couldn't keep up, couldn't catch his breath as Marina's mouth joined with his, moving like some ravenous animal's.

She pulled away too soon, and yet he gasped for breath as though he'd been underwater.

"You're stupid," she whispered again, then she tucked her wild head into his chest.

He'd lost too much time. Rosy light skimmed the snow-covered peaks behind him. Every time Whit looked back, the glow had spread farther down the mountainside. He shoved his hands deeper into his pockets, fingers closing around the jewelry and odds and ends he'd taken from Haward's.

They hadn't parked the truck far, so why did his steps drag? Why did it feel like hooks sank into his shoulders, hauling him back toward the shop?

He put Marina's face—her lips—out of his mind and went to work starting the truck. After what felt like ages, it fired up. He rumbled through the business center of the Foothills Quarter and past a few sleepy neighborhoods to the road circling the quarters like a great wagon wheel. Alternating tremors of excitement and alarm slammed through his system. Driving over the empty dirt road in a stolen vehicle felt like kissing Marina in the yard of the morality hall with a dozen Chemists looking on. He hunched low over the steering wheel and squinted into the rising sun. Far off in the plains, other delivery trucks would be heading into the city, bearing produce from the greenhouses.

He needed to complete this errand, make it back in time to pick up his ration—the last authorized ration he'd ever receive—then drive the truck to the outpost with Marina before his absence at the mine was noted. His mother could honestly say she didn't know where he was. It was better that way. He'd visit her, check in, and she would never again pour potion from her own bottle into his.

As Whit exited the boundary road into the southern quarter, he ran a finger beneath his collar. The wide streets and sprawling buildings of the southern communities left him exposed. The watchtower rose in the distance, marking the end of Mercury City limits, though Chemist influence extended far into the wilderness surrounding the metropolis, maybe even as far as the West Coast.

He had the urge to drive straight for that dark pillar jutting up into the sky. What would he find? A gate? A wall? Surely a swarm of deputies, most of them potion heads who bought their supply from the southern dealers. But what lay beyond the final outpost of Chemist civilization?

A smile tugged Whit's lips, but he shook the daydream off and pulled the truck behind a deserted factory and left it. When he reached the main streets of the Southern Quarter on foot, people had begun trickling from doors. At first he only saw a few: Women with ratty hair and faded red clothes. Bony men who shuffled along with determined faces.

No one looked at Whit. He kept his hands in his pockets, lowered his head, and tried to recall the way Maverick had taken him yesterday. He remembered a few landmarks from their trip to Cagey's, but it didn't help that everything after their arrival was a blur.

A line formed outside a dispensary as workers unloaded crates of ration from a black truck at the side of the building. Whit crossed to the other side of the street but kept an eye on the operation. Only two deputies oversaw the procedure, with no chug boat patrols in sight. Perhaps robbing a ration delivery in one of the outlying communities wasn't such an impossible feat. With enough backup, you could subdue the deputies and be off with the contents of the truck before the Chemists heard a whisper of it in their central tower.

He put thoughts of the raid aside. There'd be enough time to join that cause after he proved himself a part of Marina's world.

The crumbling boarding house ahead looked familiar, and Whit checked for unwanted eyes before he jogged to the entrance. Residents filed out of the glass doors, exchanging no greetings.

Whit waited until a woman wearing a red shawl over a dressing gown exited the building then he stepped inside. The smell choked him—garbage and human waste. His eyes stung, but he shuffled down the stairs and followed the hall to the door marked 3.

He rapped on the door and waited. And waited.

A tread behind the door sent a jolt of apprehension through him. He glanced to each end of the hall just before the door of number 3 opened.

Cagey stood in a greasy suit, a smile stretching his scarred and saggy skin.

"Back so soon?"

Whit gulped as the three little words slid inside him, planting doubt. He squared his shoulders.

"I have a proposition for you."

The man leaned out of his door, surveying the hallway much as Whit had. Satisfied, he motioned Whit inside.

Again a force repelled him from Cagey's quarters, but Whit stepped into the room. The sagging couch drew his eye, and Maverick appeared in his memory as real as if he still slouched in the seat.

Cagey lifted one slender arc of an eyebrow. "I didn't expect to see you here—well, not till you gave the twins the slip, anyway."

"Maverick was taken." Whit cut right to it. "Yesterday, on our way back."

Cagey clucked. "I'm sorry to hear that. I am."

Whit brushed off the useless words. "I want to take his place."

Silence.

With effort, Whit forced his eyes off their circuit round the room and onto the wrinkled face.

"And what is it you imagine Maverick did for me?"

"I know he bought ration from you. You were one of their suppliers."

"And how do you suppose Maverick managed to pay me?"

"I can pay." Whit clutched the stash in his pocket.

"Sure you can pay *now*. A good boy like you probably has a stash hidden in his room. But what about tomorrow? Next week? What about when your back is shredded and you're afraid to look out your window much less come down here for a visit?" Cagey moved toward the passage leading to the back of his chambers. "Go home, boy. This isn't the life you want."

Whit fished a handful of jewelry out of his pocket and held it in front of him. Cagey caught the movement and stopped, his head turned so that he faced the wall but spoke to Whit.

"Ah, now we come to it. Cagey's mix got to you." He pivoted back, a grin stretched over his face. "You don't care about the refugees. You're not looking to be a supplier to the poor, suffering mountain folk."

His tone brought bile to Whit's throat.

The dealer's beady eyes flicked to the contents of Whit's hand. "Oh, I'll sell to you, my boy, but I'll be needing more than that if you want the same arrangement Maverick had."

Whit fumbled in his other pocket. How much did a couple bottles of Cagey's mix cost? "I can get more."

"No, no, no. Trust me, you can't get enough." Cagey moistened his lips and stepped closer. His voice dropped a level. "But if you want to play hero and maybe get tanked on the side, then there is something you can trade for my potion."

Whit's mouth went dry as paper. He could only lift his eyebrow in a silent question.

"Maverick sold for me. A day's work and he went home, pockets clinking with potion bottles. Simple enough."

Cagey leaned back, giving Whit a long look. "All right, I'll give you a chance. Now, let's see what's in those pockets of yours."

Whit cursed all the way back to the Foothills Quarter. The satchel of rations tucked beneath the truck seat did nothing to lift his mood.

He didn't want to sell potion for Cagey. He wanted his own supply. He wanted the connections Maverick had. And he wanted the numbness that erased the events of the last two weeks, and his life up until then.

Another delivery truck approached, horn blaring. Whit jerked the wheel, swerving too far to the right. The tires bumped along the gravel at the side of the road. He forced his attention back to the road. More vehicles were out now, ration trucks with the purple Chemist logo and delivery wagons coming up from the greenhouses. Though the increased traffic made his truck less conspicuous, he shrank from the window whenever another driver looked over.

This was his life now. Running, hiding. Dealing ration.

He turned into the Foothills Quarter and took a route to Colfax, intending to pull into the alley behind Haward's and park the truck. A thrum vibrated in his chest and throat. His heartbeat exploded. He peered out the window, his head whipping this way and that in the cab. Then he froze.

The chug boat churned overhead. Whit's mouth went dry. The deputy vessel swooped down in front of the truck. Green steam clouded his windshield and swirled into the cab.

Whit coughed. His eyes watered with a mixture of noxious fumes and dread.

But the craft didn't swivel to accost him, and instead floated forward. Whit gulped a breath, his grip tight on the steering wheel.

Why were they creeping down Colfax as though they didn't want to be seen?

He scanned the street. Where were the business owners coming to open their shops? Static from the chug boat engine leaked through the cab windows and zinged over his skin. The patrol vehicle drifted toward the corner, deputies braced against the craft's low sides and clutching their clotters in ready positions.

Whit examined the street ahead, zeroing in on Haward's Mercantile. As long as Marina was inside, she was probably safe.

He cranked the wheel, easing the truck onto a gravel path that connected Colfax with the alley behind the storefronts. When the door of Haward's swung open, he cranked the brake. The tires spun out and the contents of the cab flew forward, papers scattering and empty biscuit tins rolling beneath his feet. Even the canvas bag with potion bottles stored in individual pockets slid out from beneath the seat. Whit ignored the mess, his eyes on the two figures standing in front of Olan's store.

One of them, Haimon, eyed Whit's truck stalled in the middle of the turn. The other, the rangy Chemist, Adante, stared in the direction of the stealthy chug boat.

Haimon pulled his hand from his pocket and signaled Whit to continue on to the alley.

"She's still inside," Whit breathed. He shook so hard his vision blurred.

He got the truck moving again and pulled it behind the storefronts. After shoving the satchel back beneath the seat, he swung out of the cab. Shouts and the hum of chug boats carried from the street beyond. A hollow feeling in his gut told him the commotion came from Reinbar, but he pounded up the alley toward the Haward's back door. He slid to a stop, his throat prickling as he grabbed the knob. He wiped his palms on his trousers and stole into the quiet shop.

After he checked the front portion of the store and made sure Haimon and Adante no longer stood on the sidewalk just outside the front door, he eased the trapdoor open.

"Marina?"

No answer.

He ducked down the stairs. Daylight crept into the secret cellar. Maybe she'd fallen asleep waiting for him to return.

He dashed around the corner. "Marina?"

She wasn't on the couch or in the alcove under the stairs.

"No. No. No." He dug his fingers into his hair.

The prickle in his throat spread to his chest, joining with the knot in his stomach. His nerves fired hot. The dispensary raid, today?

He dashed back up the stairs, his footsteps too loud on the wooden steps. It didn't matter. In the shop above, he paced, jerking toward the front door, then the back.

"Think. Think."

He couldn't. He flung the front door wide and took off down the sidewalk. Haimon and the Chemist were nowhere in sight, and the noise from one street over had died down. Whit's steps, ringing against the concrete, echoed in the quiet.

He rounded the corner and skidded to a halt. Citizens stood like petrified tree trunks, dark, gnarled, frozen. Two black chug boats formed a V in the street, and figures in dusters moved between them while others went in and out of the dispensary. Whit's brain took in the whole scene, although he couldn't look away from the strip of pavement before the ration facility. Bodies lay in a line on the street, stretched out in orderly horror. They were stunned. That was all. They'd been stunned.

He studied the shapes. He didn't want to see, but he couldn't close his lids. There at the end, a mass of dark hair. The morning breeze picked at the strands, whipping them about the small, still form of Marina.

Whit clutched at his chest. He couldn't breathe. Not Marina. First he'd lost Grey, and now Marina? How could he live on the fringes without her? Selling illegal ration, stealing from stores like Haward's. He'd end up with more secrets than Haimon. A crazy husk of a man hoping for a miracle out of a dusty curio cabinet.

A shadow fell on the sidewalk before Whit. Two black, pointed shoes appeared in his narrow vision. He looked up into Adante's angular face. Poison-green eyes flashed into his.

Wind slipped around Blaise in buffeting streams, slowing his progress. Each beat of his patched wings strained his relocated joint but no longer sent agony coursing through him. He grit his teeth not in pain but in desperation to reach Grey.

He'd outdistanced Weatherton's troop of walking carriages, each concealing a handful of Valor Society tocks. Weatherton planned to engage Lord Blueboy in an extended debate about what to do with the crew of the Clang while Blaise rescued Grey, Callis, and Seree. If the diversion failed, Weatherton was prepared to fight, but he and his followers didn't stand a chance.

Weatherton's steady gaze haunted Blaise. After the porcie had maneuvered his shoulder back into place and done a hasty patch job on his steam pack, he'd drawn Blaise aside. Tocks rushed about them, preparing for the mission, but Weatherton rested his hand on Blaise's good shoulder.

"Keep your promise. If not to me, then to Clara."

Blaise had agreed.

Now, with all of downtown Curio City buzzing with the day's events, soldiers swarming the streets, and Blueboy's mansion as locked down as Harrowstone, the chances of any of them making it back to Weatherton's plantation seemed remote.

Blaise circled Blueboy's estate, giving the busy courtyard and stables a wide berth. The gardens at the back of the house lay quiet under the night sky, tinged brown due to the smoke from Gagnon's demolished airship hanging low over the city. Blaise kept to the acrid clouds as long as he could. When he heard the thuds of Weatherton's carriages marching up the street to Blueboy's gate, he dropped altitude and surveyed the rear of the house. Two soldiers were positioned at the back door, but they didn't see him swoop to land on the high roof.

With the slate tiles beneath his feet and the ground far below, he might as well be standing on top of a fortress. Where was Grey in the enormous house? Where were Callis and Seree?

He trotted along the apex of the roof toward the east wing. With his left shoulder bound to his body by strips of canvas, he struggled to maintain balance. His foot slipped, and he nearly tumbled down the roof before righting himself again. He reached the edge and peered down at the little balcony outside Grey's room. No light shone through the thin curtains.

His gut clenched. The mark on his skin pulsed a warning just as a new sound carried above the bustle in the courtyard. Screaming.

He ran back to the center of the roof, but growing noise from the front gate drowned out what had surely been porcie screeches. Weatherton's arrival had thrown the ranks into upheaval. Shouting rang in the courtyard. Taking advantage of the distraction, Blaise crept to the front edge of the roof.

Tall windows stretching nearly the height of a story marked the very center of the mansion. Benedict's quarters, no doubt.

Light seeped through the panes, but Blaise couldn't see anything else from his position. Below, Weatherton made a fuss of climbing down from his carriage and arguing with the commanding officers. Soldiers ringed the six other carriages loitering in the courtyard.

Blaise hunkered down, the knuckles of his right fist tapping an impatient beat on the roof. Where was that tin can of a butler? He got to his feet and made a round on the rooftop, checking over the sides. A door at the base of the tower opened and two tocks slipped out. The shorter of the two wore a butler's distinctive tailcoat.

Flattening himself on the slate, Blaise hung his head over the eave to hear their conversation. He picked out the words *glueman* and *leaking* before the taller tock turned and loped toward the back wall. He didn't break stride for a moment but stretched on expandable legs until he vaulted over the brick barrier. His head disappeared as he sank out of sight.

A runner sent for the glueman in the middle of the night. A porcie was damaged. It didn't matter how, for now Weatherton's distraction would fail.

When the butler closed the door once again, Blaise glided down to the side yard. The plainness of the entrance marked it as a servants' access. If he were lucky, whatever accident required the glueman's presence had everyone's attention focused elsewhere.

His Defender mark burned and stone spread beneath his skin. The reaction took less than a second and left Blaise reeling from the intensity. He folded his wings in and wrenched the door open. The hinges creaked and the door swung free of the frame. So much for stealth. He clenched his fist, trying to rein in the Defender strength before his noise raised the whole household.

But no tocks waited in the tower to capture him.

Rounded walls closed in on him, and a tight staircase twisted upward into darkness. Another door on his left led to the ground floor, but instinct tugged him to the steps. His wings clattered against the iron frame of the coiled stairway, but he couldn't stop long enough to shrug out of the steam pack harness. His mark tugged him higher and higher, and he ricocheted off the narrow tower walls and spiraling metal.

At the top of the staircase, Blaise pressed his ear to a low door. High-pitched steam whimpers drifted to his hiding place along with mechanical speech and clattering footsteps. He strained to pick up Grey's husky tone. Nothing betrayed her presence, but his mark sucked his torso forward. Before he could comprehend his actions, he'd pulled the sling off his left arm and dropped it to the floor. He yanked the door open and stepped onto the top floor of Lord Blueboy's mansion.

A few servants bustled in and out of a door in the middle of the cavernous chamber, carrying steaming pitchers, brooms, and other cleaning supplies. Between the backs of two male tocks, Blaise glimpsed Fantine huddled on a couch, both hands clutched to her throat. Her mouth opened and a faint wail escaped, although her eyes darted around the room, never landing or focusing.

A tock with a mop moved in front of the open bedroom, his attention on the floor he cleaned. Blaise followed his action as he lifted the mop and prepared to plunge it in a bucket. Dark-pink water dripped from the gray fibers. Blood.

His eyes were everywhere, tearing up the elegant apartment. Where was she?

And then he saw.

In an alcove on the opposite side of the floor, a tock maid hunched over a still form. As he watched, the maid pulled away, revealing a prone figure with a tangle of blonde hair. The tock reached to the floor, never taking her gaze away from the head cradled in her lap. She snagged a pitcher and brought it to Grey's lips. The water ran down Grey's cheeks and chin, but the maid kept pouring.

Blaise forged past the tocks guarding Blueboy's mistress, pushing his goggles up and yanking his mouth grid off as he went. Drakon emerged from the open door and buzzed an exclamation, but Blaise planted one hand on the butler's chest and shoved him aside.

A red stain beneath Grey's body stole the air from his lungs. The maid poured more water over her still mouth as his mind took in snippets of the scene. The pieces wouldn't come into focus.

Two big tocks in uniforms flanked him, but he walked forward, eyes moving over Grey's form.

Her arm lay in a pool of blood. Her hand . . .

He covered his mouth.

Crashing to his knees next to Grey's body, he searched for something to stop the bleeding. She wore only a flimsy blue gown. He tugged at his shirt but the straps of his harness interfered.

"We have to stop the blood." He barely recognized his voice.

He tore his eyes from the wound and looked at the maid's face.

"We have to stop the blood," he said again.

She tilted the water pitcher again, but Blaise gripped her arm.

"That won't help. I need . . ." His voice cracked. What did he need? "I need a scarf or a cravat. I need cloth to wrap around her . . . her arm. I need—"

But the maid was moving. She slid from beneath Grey, pulled off her blood-soaked apron, and ripped one of the strings off. She handed it to Blaise then whipped her cap off and handed it to him as well.

He tied the apron string around Grey's upper arm, but the blood drenched the maid's cap in seconds.

"I need something more." Blaise looked around, but a voice lashed through his concentration.

"So you're the Mad Tock."

Ice replaced the granite beneath Blaise's skin. He met the maid's gaze, grabbed a fistful of her skirt, and held it to Grey's stump. "Stop the blood," he said.

He rose and whirled to face Benedict.

The porcie leaned on his butler, a steaming cup in one hand and . . . Blaise met the cold blue stare.

"She took your hand so you had to take hers?"

A faint smile etched Benedict's features. "Only seems fair, doesn't it?"

"I will grind you into sand." Blaise lunged.

The tocks at his sides grabbed him, and he tore away only to collide with a solid object. Drakon. The butler's metal frame registered in Blaise's mind, but his Defender sense blocked all sensation save strength. He wrestled the tock to the wall, maneuvering one hand to the side of the automaton's face. With a snap, the butler's head hung at a broken angle.

Blueboy had retreated to the door of his chamber. Blaise dashed across the floor, ice in his veins and rock in his fists. Benedict went down beneath him, and the sound of porcelain meeting marble echoed through the apartment.

Metal hands clawed at Blaise. He shook them off but more snagged his limbs, lifting him off the ruler of Curio City. The tock servants hauled him backward, locking his arms behind his back. From her couch, Fantine shrieked as Benedict struggled to rise.

Blaise flexed against the tocks securing him. He could send them flying, he knew it. The Defender state engulfed him.

The door of the lift ratcheted open, and a knot of redcoats jumped out. One of the soldiers rushed to hoist Benedict off the floor, though the tock nearly dropped the ruler when he got a good look. Dark cracks snaked all over Benedict's face, neck, and collarbones, but he stood, throwing back his shoulders. He lowered his lids, leaving an arrogant slice of blue still visible.

Blaise didn't let the porcie speak. Freeing his hands, he pushed the tocks away and held them at arm's length as he stared down Benedict.

"The only way I walk out of here without leaving you a pile of dust is if you give me Grey *now* and release Callis and Seree."

Blueboy's lip curled. "My estate is surrounded by soldiers. You can't fight them all off."

"No. But I can smash you to pieces before they take me."

Blaise stepped forward. The tock hands grasping him felt like sticks snagging in his clothing and breaking off as he passed.

Benedict's eyes widened. He held his one remaining hand up.

Blaise paused, brows raised.

Blueboy jerked his chin toward Grey. "Take her."

"And my friends?"

Benedict raised his voice, sliding his gaze to a group of stunned soldiers. "Release the other prisoners."

Blaise put every threat he needed into one look aimed at the porcie's cruel eyes. He turned on his heel and raced to Grey.

The maid had done her best, folding Grey's arm in layers of torn petticoat. She whimpered in her soft tock tone when Blaise lifted Grey.

"Thank you." He crushed Grey's limp body to his chest.

She was as cold as a porcie on the operating table.

The mark on Blaise's stomach fluttered then cooled.

She strained against the white-hot bond on her wrist. The rope cut into her flesh. Terror coursed through her veins.

The pain woke her. She screamed. All went black.

The rope wouldn't give. It was agony to fight against it, but she had to. She had to get away. She gathered her strength, loosing a wail meant to be a battle cry. A feeble whimper trickled to her ears. She tried again.

The pain stole her breath. She gasped and choked.

"Shh," a voice whispered near her head. "Shh, Grey. You're safe."

She drifted off, a pleasant warmth around her navel siphoning the worst of her pain.

Grey opened her eyes and focused on a dark shape near her head. Black cords of hair stretched over a white surface as though they'd reached for her and fallen short. She followed the thick, copper-woven twists to their source. The hair partially obscured his face, sallow beneath the natural tan.

Black lashes fanned over sunken cheeks and faint stubble crusted his jawline.

"Blaise."

She started at the croak of her own voice. He didn't move. He was so pale.

She tried to lift her hand to touch him but pain lashed her wrist. *The ropes. Benedict!*

"Blaise. Blaise." Panic edged her raspy words.

His lids opened and deep umber eyes locked on her. "Shh, you're safe," he murmured. The lashes lowered, hiding those liquid irises. Without their anchoring light, she sank into confusion.

"Blaise, please."

This time his pupils sharpened.

"You're awake."

A sob clenched her throat. "I . . . Benedict, he . . . Untie the ropes. It hurts."

Moisture gathered along his eyelids. He shifted, a wince clamping his features. His warm hand cradled her cheek.

"I know it hurts. It'll get better. Your Defender blood will help you heal."

Something cold crept into a corner of Grey's heart. "Why won't you untie me? My wrist hurts."

He dragged himself closer, rising up to press a kiss on her cheek. "Shh, Grey. You're safe. I promise."

Tears spilled out of her eyes. The cold grew, gnawing at her insides. "Blaise?"

He collapsed beside her, rolling onto his back so their shoulders pressed against each other. With his warm body flush against hers, the fear receded. His fingers traced from the crook of her elbow down. She held her breath as pain seared her wrist. Then the sensation changed. He pressed her palm, but it felt like her hand remained in a Defender state. A layer of stone muted his touch.

His fingers glided between hers. She flinched as he lifted their clasped hands and her wrist throbbed with the movement. A white bandage wrapped his arm at the elbow.

"Hold on to me," he said before their twined fingers came into view.

She clutched his hand.

Their laced-together fingers hovered before her eyes, white and brown so tangled that none of the digits seemed to belong to her. Her wrist burned and she rotated her arm. She choked and cried out. A white glove of porcelain skin covered her hand. Fine metalwork, like lace, extended from beneath the seam of the glove and clamped into the skin of her forearm.

The cold in her chest cracked and ached.

"My hand."

"We gave you a new one."

"A new one? You mean—?"

He pressed his cheek into the pillow, eyes skimming her face. "We couldn't save yours."

"Who is we?"

"Weatherton and me."

The name sounded familiar, but Grey couldn't attach meaning to it. "Who?"

"Never mind. You'll meet him soon enough." Blaise dropped their hands between them as though holding their two arms up took too much strength. Grey tested her new hand. She could wiggle her fingers and detect Blaise's fingers notched into her own. When she concentrated, the warmth of his touch transferred through the smooth porcelain skin. But how?

She rolled her head into Blaise's shoulder, but he didn't respond to the movement.

"Blaise?"

He jolted and then shivered. "Yes?"

"Where are we?"

"Weather'slab." His words ran together.

"What happened?"

"Too much," he murmured.

She glanced down. A soft white gown covered her upper body, and a blanket lay over her torso and legs. Blaise's legs stretched all the way to the end of the bedspread. His bare feet poked up out of dark pant legs. His left hand lay on the bare ridges of his stomach, and a brace of some sort strapped his upper arm to his chest.

Grey's eyes swept to his face. His dark lashes were lowered again. The strong features looked vulnerable under the unusual pallor. A line of faint green edged his full lower lip. She fought an urge to shake him awake.

"What is it?" she breathed, scanning his body for other injuries. Splotches of purple bruising spread from the crook of his arm, livid against the white of the bandage. "What are you not telling me?"

He didn't respond. His chest rose and fell in shallow breaths.

"Blaise, you're scaring me."

The dark eyes drifted open, and a ghost of a smile played over his lips. "Shh. Safe now."

"What's wrong with you?" Grey yelled, clamping his right forearm with her new fingers.

He winced. A twinge of pain flared in Grey's right arm. She shook back the gown's sleeve and found a matching bandage clamping her elbow.

"What happened?"

The door opened then. Grey started as a porcie man with dark hair stepped inside, but he wasn't someone she recognized. He strode over, the green-white light reflecting off his shiny locks.

Grey pushed up into a sitting position. "You're Weatherton, right? What happened to Blaise?"

The tall porcie sat on a chair and glanced around the bare bedroom before he returned his gaze to Grey.

"The truth is, I'm not sure. Were he a porcie, I'd say he was de-animating. We tried giving him water and, I believe you call it 'food.' Items from our paintings? But nothing helps."

"What did you give him?" Grey demanded. "It has to be a picture of food—real food—or we can't eat it. Flowers and candlesticks won't do."

The porcie offered a sad smile. "He told us what to bring him. It didn't help."

"But why? Why is he like this?"

Weatherton leaned forward, resting his elbows on his knees. He studied Blaise, his gaze lingering on the bruises. "He said you'd lost too much blood. He showed me how to connect the wires."

"The wires?"

Weatherton scowled at Grey's bandaged arm. "The tubing. What did he call it? Veins. Yes, he had me connect your veins to draw the blood out of him and into you."

Grey's head swam with the nightmare of what Weatherton described. No, surely such a thing could not, *should not*, be done.

"I'm sorry," Weatherton was saying. "I've never done anything like it. He insisted we continue even when I could tell it was draining him. I believed him when he said he would recover."

Grey turned away from Weatherton. She ached to bury her face in Blaise's neck and feel his arms clench her close, but she stayed still, looking down at him.

"And my hand?" she finally asked.

"I've done some experimenting of my own. I had the materials. He guided me through the process while his blood flowed into you. Thankfully, I was able to finish when he lost animation."

A tear dripped off Grey's chin. She swiped at it with her left hand and felt silky smooth skin over her jawline. "How is it that I can still feel with this, this modification?"

"Why wouldn't you be able to feel, my dear?" Weatherton lifted his own hands, revealing patched-together porcelain.

She gave up her futile questioning and slid her new hand underneath the covers. At least for now she didn't have to look at the alteration that came at such a high price.

"Do you know how to help him?" Weatherton's voice, a mixture of command and sharp curiosity, snapped Grey to attention.

"I need to take him home. I don't think the food here can replenish his blood. He needs real food."

"I will help."

"We will help." The musical words came from the hallway.

A woman in a long yellow dressing gown stood in the doorway. The light from the hall gave her brown hair a halo of red-gold. She didn't look anything like Fantine, but for a moment Grey saw Blueboy's mistress studying her with cautious friendliness.

A smile transformed Weatherton's severe features. He stood and turned, holding his arm out for the woman.

"My wife, Clara. The Mad Tock—Blaise—walked into her room while we readied you for the procedure. He came out leading Clara. She . . . I've been trying to bring her back for a long time."

Clara's brows crumpled as she took in Blaise's still form. "Is he the Designer?"

"No . . . Well, I don't think so." Grey frowned. Blaise was trapped here, imprisoned. Who would design their own prison?

"Then how did he bring me back?" Clara's voice sifted through the quiet room.

"I don't know."

The bandage on Blaise's arm caught Grey's eye. Red mist tainted her memory and the smell of wet rust invaded her nostrils. She shook off the recollection of Benedict's steam breath mixed with her blood and thrust the blankets off her lap. When she swung her legs to the floor, the room spun. She pressed her hands into the mattress, her stomach heaving. A crackle of foreign energy skittered through her veins then hid itself somewhere inside her body. Grey shivered and Clara rushed over with a robe.

"We'll have sustenance brought." Weatherton moved toward the door. "Now that we know what to look for, the house is fully stocked."

Grey accepted the robe Clara offered and pushed to her feet.

"Thank you for all you've done, but I have to get Blaise home." She couldn't put into words the ache that overtook her when she looked at his tall form motionless on the bed.

"Then I suspect you'll need this." Weatherton turned back and extended his hand.

Grey raised her palm and accepted the object. "The glass key."

"You had it in your hand—your right hand—when Blaise brought you here."

It weighed more than she expected. The finger-length blade had a cylindrical shape, and when she held it up to the light, it appeared hollow. Three symbols were etched into the crystal—a closed fist, an open hand with fingers splayed and stretching upwards, and a hand forming a cup as though begging for water. Something Haimon had said played in the back of her mind.

She brushed her hand over the carving. "Do you know what these symbols mean?"

Weatherton shook his head. "I've never seen anything like it."

She let her eyes return to Blaise's face. "Maybe he'll recognize them. He knows where the door is. When he wakes up—"

"I'm afraid our situation is even more complicated." Weatherton backed toward the door, Clara's hand in his. "We're at a standoff with Blueboy's army. Under siege, as it were. Which would be a welcome diversion if not for the urgency of your needs."

Grey tried to read his expression. "I'm not sure—"

"The revolution is upon us." The porcie's eyes gleamed. "Getting you away from my estate will take a little creativity."

I 've made a few modifications." Ames Weatherton circled the workbench, eyeing the steam pack. "The wings are larger, able to support more weight. And I tinkered with the internal mechanism. The cinderite will heat more quickly, which will get these pistons pumping faster."

Grey ran her hands over the spine of one long wing and Blaise's dazzling smile popped into her mind. The thought of him pale and lifeless twisted her insides, and the need to get him back to the human world sent Defender armor shooting through her limbs. Under the desperation and determination, something else sparked. It reminded her of summer storms building over the mountains. Whenever the electric energy surged, she had the instinct to seek cover. But how could she hide from something inside of her?

Callis strode into the lab and Seree marched in behind him. Weatherton had restored the dark-haired rebel porcie to full animation. Her amber eyes flashed in her cracklined face. She stood on the other side of Callis, hands locked behind her back and gaze shifting about the room—anywhere but in Grey's direction.

Weatherton fiddled with the new harness straps then hoisted the pack and walked behind Grey, holding it up to her back as he muttered about lift and propulsion.

Callis's porcie lips lifted in a smile. "We have another Mad Tock on our hands."

Grey looked down at her borrowed clothing. The cap-sleeved blouse, little more than a chemise, would allow the belts and buckles of the flight harness to fit snugly. A waist cincher secured baggy breeches that must've once belonged to a short tock. Her trouser cuffs grazed a pair of Clara's old ankle boots now fitted with navigation fins, thanks to Weatherton. A set of goggles hung from her neck.

Worry doused any tendrils of excitement over flying again. "Callis, did Blaise ever show you the tree with the lock in the Glass Forest?"

The modified porcie's smile faded. "I never accompanied him on his trips to the forest. Whatever he found in there, he never shared it with me."

Grey accepted this news with a jerk of her chin. "How soon can we be off?"

Weatherton had the flying device back on the workbench and a tool in hand. "The pack is ready." He tested the bellow cord. "Yes, the pack is ready. But we've devised a plan to get you away from the city before you have to use it."

Callis stepped closer. "The soldiers are on the lookout for the Mad Tock. The moment you're spotted, they'll pursue. With Blaise . . . Well, he'll not be much help in his current condition."

Seree made a noise like a gear rattled in her throat.

Heat—and a sting like the snap of electricity—flared in Grey's cheeks. Could she help it that Blaise's blood ran through her veins now? She thought her heart would explode with the truth of it. "I'll get him back home." She forced the words through a tightening throat. "He'll get better there." Provided they didn't step right into Adante's hands.

What hope did they have of saving her father when she was returning with an almost dead warrior? But she was a Defender too. Grey shoved that thought—and the gravity of the situation back home—out of her mind and faced the next step of their plan.

"How are you going to get Blaise and me out with the army ticking away on the front lawn?"

"Gagnon's hydro hub." Callis's smile returned.

"The thing with all the arms? I thought it distributed water in the Cog Valley."

"It does. But who's to say it can't distribute a couple of fugitives too?"

"We need to be at the far edge of my property in exactly one hour," Weatherton said.

"We're going over the Shelf then?" Grey scrambled to fit the pieces together.

"Seree and I will see you safely across Cog Valley," Callis said. "If we're followed, perhaps we can stall Blueboy's men while you and Blaise fly."

Grey frowned at both porcies. "The two of you against countless soldiers?"

Callis lowered his voice. "It was just you and me against the Dulaig."

Grey humphed. "And look how *that* turned out."

"My point exactly," Seree's voice cut in.

"Then why risk it?" Grey turned to the porcie rebel. "If Blaise and I fly out of here, we'll draw all the attention. It's just our necks on the line."

Weatherton cleared his throat. "That wouldn't be very brave, my dear."

Grey massaged her forehead. "Being brave for bravery's sake isn't much better than being beautiful for beauty's sake."

Three voices chorused, "What?"

"Oh, never mind." Grey let her hands smack against her thighs, ignoring the flash of pain in her wrist. "Weatherton, show me how I'm going to fly this thing with Blaise unconscious."

Brahman led the way, holding a lantern out into the darkness of the tunnel ahead. Weatherton and Callis followed, a litter stretched between them supporting Blaise. Occasionally he came around, but his periods of consciousness were growing fewer and farther between. Grey and Seree brought up the rear of the little band.

Orange glow from the tock servant's lantern cast wavering shadows on the walls but ended a smidge beyond Grey's boots. She kept her eyes on the path, always a step behind the light.

"He must love you." Seree's whisper sent a shiver over Grey's skin.

She clutched the key hanging from her throat and trudged a few steps before finding words for an answer. "We just met, really."

"But you're the same. You have the same skin, same heat, same blood." The porcie woman struggled with the last, unfamiliar word.

Grey held her porcelain hand up. The lantern light turned the smooth skin translucent, revealing the vague outline of gears and clockwork inside. She was one of the modified now. "We're not the same everywhere."

"Do you love him?"

Grey flinched in the darkness. The words "I need him" sprang to her lips, but she swallowed them. Seree wouldn't understand. Grey didn't quite understand. But her Defender mark pulsed. It dragged her feet forward so that she tripped over stones and ridges in the dirt. Like two magnets attracting one another, the pull of her mark consumed her senses when Blaise was near. Was that love, or something even stronger? She measured it against her affection for Whit and found that while she still loved her friend, her heart beat and her blood danced in time with a warrior's drum.

The silence in the tunnel pressed on Grey, or was it the force of Seree's unanswered question?

"I'll keep him alive, Seree. I promise."

"Couldn't you just give some of his blood back?"

"I don't know. I guess if we can't get out, I'll ask Weatherton to try."

The tension ebbing from the porcie woman at Grey's side eased. "All right," she said after a moment. "I suppose I needed to hear that you would do for him what he did for you."

"I would." Tears pricked in Grey's eyes, blurring the quivering edge of the moving light.

They came out on a ledge set in the sheer face of the Shelf, which overlooked the crowded Cog Valley below. To the right, the land sank, making the stacks and tock buildings appear to slip toward the mouth of Lower. In the distance, across the wide maze of junk towers, a gradual slope led out of the valley to a stretch of green on the horizon.

Gagnon's huge hydro hub stood with arms distended in all directions like some metal organ with pipes for veins. Grey's eyes widened as several of the arms whirred into motion, planting themselves down on the ground. The bulbous sphere moved toward them, the arms rising and lowering depending on the available space beneath the machine. The hydro hub picked its way through the stacks, heading straight for the ledge where Grey and her friends waited.

Weatherton laughed. "Magnificent."

Callis spoke from behind him. "It's coming to take your water, I'm afraid."

The Valor Society leader lowered his end of the stretcher and stepped to the edge. Grey followed and saw a second ledge just under them and to the right a bit. Tocks bustled around a massive capped-off pipe. As the hub neared, they took up positions, ready to oversee the transfer of water into the movable purification locus.

"You'll need to jump," Weatherton shouted over the noise of the approaching hub.

Grey turned. Callis swung Blaise up from the litter, then Seree slid the poles out from the canvas and folded the material. She clutched it to her chest and nodded to Grey.

The hub creaked and shuddered to a stop beneath them and mechanical shouts blended with the clank of the mechanism. A roar shook the ground as water thundered into the locus.

"Ready?" Callis's mismatched eyes locked with Grey's before the modified porcie jumped with Blaise in his arms. Seree leapt after him.

Grey let her mark do the work. With a salute to Weatherton, she let go of the conscious restraint she'd placed on her bond with Blaise. Her feet sprinted toward the ledge, and she sailed over, landing in a light crouch, poised over Blaise. Callis toppled backward on the metal walkway circling the bulb-shaped hub, but a net of fine-woven chains stopped him from plummeting to the stacks below.

Blaise moaned and his eyes opened. Grey leaned over to explain their position, but his lashes fluttered and closed again. If she let him rest now, maybe he'd have strength for her questions later.

Grey stood, finding Seree around the curve of the hub. The porcie woman watched as the tocks shut off the water supply and disengaged the locus. With a jolt, the apparatus shoved away from the cliff face and crawled to the left. Appendages rose and lowered, tiptoeing through the intricate network of passages between the heaps. They moved in a semi-circle, stopping for the humming locus to dispense clean water into small vessels on stilts.

With one hand resting on the rounded metal surface for balance, Grey alternately studied the Shelf for signs of soldiers and squinted ahead at the line of green in the distance.

She checked her harness for the fifth or sixth time but didn't test the wings in the confined quarters of the narrow walkway.

Blaise still lay at her feet where Callis had arranged him. In the light of the Curio morning, his swarthy complexion bore a hint of green. She bent and checked his pulse, probing his neck and wrists until she found the faint *thump-thump*.

Such a different sound—this thump-thump, thump-thump.

Grey shut out Benedict's voice in her head and brushed a kiss on Blaise's still lips. She clasped his hand in hers and leaned closer.

"Hold on to me. We'll be out soon."

The hub traveled on, either following a preprogramed route or—Grey tensed at the thought—choosing the optimal path. But, no, Gagnon built the massive machine she perched on. It was no more alive than the toys in her grandfather's shop. Well, the toys not in this particular curio cabinet.

The hub changed orientation with each move, providing a rotating view of the valley, the diminishing Shelf to the north, and the nearing line of green countryside to the south. Callis appeared from around the curve, and Grey stood, bringing her thoughts back to the next step of their escape.

A light wind lifted the modified porcie's blond hair, blowing it about his reconstructed face. Grey studied the seam that began at his left temple and traveled over the bridge of his nose across his cheek and down below his ear. Questions filled her brain. Did his scars still hurt? How had Blaise known how to fix him? She flexed her own modified hand. How had Blaise fixed her?

Callis pointed toward the countryside. "My best guess is the tree you're looking for lies in the forest to the south. Blaise loved flying over the farmland and spent more time there than anywhere else."

Grey nodded and joined Callis in a constant sideways shuffle that allowed them to keep the southern horizon in view. Ahead and to the right, the stacks dwindled into odd mounds just before the landscape slanted up to climb out of the valley.

"How long has it been since we've seen a village or one of the water collection units?" Grey asked.

Callis's eyes narrowed on the strange mounds. "There wouldn't be many out here."

"Why?"

He pointed to the heaps but didn't answer her question.

Seree moved around to stand with them. "I think you'd better get ready. The hub will only be parallel with the valley's southern edge for a short while."

Grey pulled the bellow cord to heat the cinderite as Seree unfolded the canvas and withdrew a set of prepared ropes from the satchel she carried. The porcie woman set to work threading the ropes through holes in the material. Callis knelt by Blaise and laid his hand on the copper-laced strands of hair. Grey turned away, but an ache crept to her throat.

Seree hauled the sling to Grey's feet and attached the ends of the ropes to the steam pack harness. At close range, Seree's cracks formed a delicate pattern set into sharp relief by her dark hair and tawny eyes. The effect was captivating.

Her swift tug to the ropes yanked Grey into a hunched position.

"That should hold." Seree squatted to arrange the canvas and called over her shoulder. "Bring him."

Callis hoisted Blaise and carried him to the sling.

Doubt scooped a hole in Grey's stomach. She'd never operated the pack. She had no idea where she was going or if Blaise would survive the journey.

Callis and Seree stooped, their heads close together, their hands tucking and smoothing Blaise into the canvas cocoon. Seree pressed her lips to Blaise's then stepped back. Her voice broke.

"We need more time. I can't say good-bye this way."

Callis's mechanical arm encircled her shoulders. "This is the time we have, Seree."

"Will you come back?" She met Grey's eyes.

"I don't know."

The hub lurched, starting its curve to the west.

"Go." Callis jerked his head toward the countryside.

Grey released the wings. They were heavier than she'd anticipated and folded out with a low whooshing sound. The force pulled her back, and her feet left the catwalk around the hub. High-powered streams of heated water coursed through the intricate piping system, setting pistons churning. Grey sailed upward, kicking her heels together to engage the fins on her boots. She jolted midair. The straps of the harness dug into her back and underarms.

Below, the sling lifted off the platform. Callis and Seree guided Blaise's unmoving form up past the chain net and handrail. The wings beat, great gusts of air pushing Grey into the sky. The fins on her boots caught the draft, pulling her legs up behind her.

For a moment, she hovered above Gagnon's moving locus, her eyes lingering on Callis and Seree's upturned faces. Then the huge hub pitched into motion, lumbering away to deliver water to the exiles of Cog Valley. Grey lifted a hand in farewell to the rebel porcies. They raised their hands as well, walking along the dais to keep Grey in sight.

When she turned and flew toward the valley incline, the wind whipped her hair off her face and snatched the tears from her eyes.

With the hub retreating, silence descended on Grey, broken only by the beat of her wings and the faint rush of water and steam in the pack. She left the stacks behind and soared over the farthest section of Cog Valley. Blaise swung a few feet below her, his body folded in the sling. His stillness made her Defender mark clench.

Soon the uneven mounds slipped beneath her. Grey blinked. A face? She'd seen a face. She peered around Blaise's form. Another.

Her throat closed.

Tock faces.

She drew in a sharp breath. The burial slopes continued like foothills leading to the edge of Cog Valley.

Grey shifted her feet left, right, up, down. She pulled on the bellow cord. She had to get away from the hundreds of tock bodies sliding silently underneath her.

The twisted metal gave way to dirt. Grey angled her shoulders up and gave a flutter kick. They glided along the slant of the valley, higher and higher. The first patch of green on the hillside was like ointment on a cut. Grey sped up, shooting over the edge of the basin and out above fields of green stretching for miles.

She flew straight, as Callis had suggested, putting distance between them and Curio City. The blurring ground matched her heartbeat, the speed of her thoughts.

Home.

Home with Blaise.

Please let him live.

Toward glass, then finally the store, her grandfather. Her father.

Away from soldiers and people made of porcelain and clockwork.

Away from Benedict.

She looked down. The sides of the sling revealed Blaise's face; the dark features and full lower lip looked calm.

Away with Blaise, a Defender from another century. The one meant to stand in her father's place.

Grey dropped, flailing until she regained control. She was taking him back so he'd live. And if he did, would she ask him to go up against the Chemists? Take her father's punishment—her punishment—in some archaic substitution ritual?

"No." The wind stole the word.

She screamed it to the speeding meadows.

She dipped again. She was losing altitude as Blaise's weight drew her down. She rolled her shoulders, but the pressure on her back only increased. A few minutes' rest would ease her mind and the pain in her joints.

A patch of red appeared on the horizon, taking shape as she neared: a barn amongst endless fields. Grey made for it, her decline steep. She rubbed her boots together, bringing the fins in. Her legs dropped beneath her, slowing her speed and pressing her into Blaise's still form.

The gaping barn door and the ground whizzed toward her. In a moment it was over. She crouched, feet on the ground and arms braced around Blaise. Her wings still flapped behind her.

Blaise groaned, and Grey lowered him to the ground, collapsing on top of him. The wings made a canopy over them, and she closed her eyes, burying herself in the peaceful darkness.

"Grey?"

She rested her head on something firm, some part of Blaise—his shoulder or his chest maybe—but didn't open her eyes.

"I can't do it." Fabric muffled her words.

"Where are we?"

"A barn somewhere."

He didn't speak again. Was she cutting off his airflow? Grey pulled herself away from him and sat back, folding the wings in. The barn was empty except for the two of them huddled just inside the door. No scents remained to indicate the structure had ever been used to house clockwork animals or store cotton crops.

Grey tucked her knees beneath her chin, careful to keep her legs clear of the ropes attached to her harness. Blaise's gaze flicked around the enclosure. His eyes looked too big for their sockets and his cheeks sank inward.

He rolled his head toward Grey. "What's happening?"

"I'm trying to get you back home. You gave me too much of your blood." Grey held her modified hand up in explanation.

A half smile tugged his green-lined lips. "Oh, right. It's beautiful work. Weatherton's a genius."

She shrugged off the comment. "Blaise, I need to tell you something."

His dark brows furrowed. "I need to tell you something too."

She held her right palm up. "Just let me talk, okay? I came here because my father was arrested for something I did. I think Haimon sent me here to bring you back so you could stand in my father's place. Is that something Defenders did for each other? Never mind, you don't have to answer. I can't do this."

He lay still; only his eyes moved, his gaze dragging over her face. "You can't get home?"

She hugged her knees. "I don't know if we can get home. I don't know where to go, but that's not what I meant. I can't ask you to take his place. I need to do it, but I don't know how to be a Defender. I can't make the strength come when I need it. I can't face Adante. I'm afraid."

Blaise stretched his hand over the dirt, his fingers straining toward her boot. Grey scooted forward and cupped his hand in hers.

He spoke in labored sentences. "First, the tree. From the air the southern border of the forest is a straight line. Fly above the very center of the line. Keep going until you see the white tree. You have the key?"

She slipped it over her head and held it up. "Do you know what the symbols mean?"

"I saw them when I first brought you to Weatherton." His eyes sharpened on the glass surface. "Fist for Defender, open hand for Chemist, cupped hand for one who receives, the potion-dependent."

"Then it does come from our world." She turned the key about, examining it from different angles. "Why do you think it's hollow?"

He shook his head, sweat beading at his temples. His answer didn't fit her question. "All those keys. How could I have thought it'd be one of their keys?"

When he closed his eyes, Grey sprang forward, laying her hand on his forehead. He roused and met her gaze.

"Second thing you need to know is"—he drew one long finger along her jaw—"your Defender state will always come when you need it, but the quickest way to summon it is through your sense of justice. I lost that in here. In a land of brittle creatures, I was afraid of my own strength."

He shifted his head, locking his eyes on the beams of the ceiling. "The third thing you need to know is who I really am. The glass tree will show you that better than I can."

CHAPTER

Grey yanked the bellow cord and forced her shoulders back, straining to keep altitude. Below, smooth branches stretched their colorless fingers up as if they would pluck Blaise from his sling. As far as she could tell, he was unconscious again. Their talk in the barn had ended with his eyes closed and her shaking him a little too hard.

She scanned the forest, her shadow the only break in the endless stretch of clear trunks and leaves. Fog, thicker than in the city, pressed on her from above, robbing her surroundings of all color. The moisture mingled with the sweat on her skin, gluing her hair to her forehead. She scratched at the metalwork securing her porcelain hand to her arm. An urge to tear the new appendage off and send it clattering into the forest below shuddered through her.

How long before she spotted the white tree and what waited there? The only certainty she had was that the boy dangling below her hid more secrets than the Chemist tower.

A layer of mist drifted away and a white silhouette flashed amongst the colorless trees. She aimed for the pale shape, folding her hands to her sides and pointing her toes. Wet air parted before her as she drove toward the white tree.

The milky branches reached higher than the transparent limbs around them. As she neared, a clearing came into view. The black forest floor swallowed more light, making it appear she was descending into a bottomless pit. Grey's senses rebelled, but she disengaged the fins on her boots and swung her legs down to lower into the dell.

Cold twigs snatched at her clothes and hair, and ripples of clinking glass followed her descent. A few translucent leaves dropped to the ground as Grey landed. The earth sprang beneath her feet like moldy black velvet.

Blaise lay as still as the roots breaking through the forest floor even when Grey touched his cheek. She untied the ropes of the sling from the steam pack harness but left Blaise tucked in the folds of canvas as she went to explore.

Still air robbed the place of time like the clear trees stole all color. Grey drew in a breath, and the action seemed foreign in this monochromatic world. The white tree towered at the edge of the clearing across from her. She made her way over the spongy soil, goose bumps tracking up her arms.

Midway up the trunk, a rectangle of frosted glass stood out against the glossy pattern of the bark. There was no knob or handle, only a keyhole set in the center of the rectangle.

Grey smiled. "I found it, Blaise. We're here."

She turned to head back to Blaise, but a fleck of color caught her eye, a rusty brown hue that lodged in her brain. She scanned the trees closest to her then dropped her gaze to the forest floor. Shadows populated the wood, but Grey locked onto the source of the color. She stepped around the white trunk into the dense line of glass trees and walked only a few steps. There at her feet lay a mound of discarded keys.

The tangled mass of metal stuck in her thoughts, refusing to fall into place. She stared at the pile, and the keys morphed into fingers of rusted copper, bronze, tarnished silver, iron, and gold. Fingers and faces. Motionless tock bodies, piled at the edge of Cog Valley.

Grey covered her mouth with both hands and backed away from the heap of tock bones. How many lives lay here on the forest floor? And how had . . . ? But she knew.

She stumbled across the clearing to Blaise and fell on her knees next to him. His long twists of hair writhed across the canvas as she shook his shoulders.

"Blaise, wake up." Her voice carried in the stillness.

"Grey."

She forced her fingers to unlock from his sleeves and sat back, pressing her fists to her temples. "The keys. I saw the keys."

His liquid eyes didn't waver from hers. "Then you know. You know what I am. You know where the legend of the Mad Tock comes from."

"How could you do that?"

"In the beginning, all I wanted was to escape. I didn't want to believe that the porcies and tocks were alive, like us."

"Why didn't you take their keys back when you found out they wouldn't unlock the door?"

He winced. "I tried. But by the time I stopped stealing keys and started trying to repair the damage I'd done, they'd scavenged the de-animated tocks for parts and dragged what was left to the edge of Cog Valley."

Grey slumped to sit on the ground. "I saw."

"I'm sorry." His voice thickened. "You don't know how sorry. I tried to do penance, tried to help them, but I can't take back what I did all those years ago."

Grey stared at her porcelain fingers, moving them in a pattern against her leg as though she played the piano. Words of judgment formed in her thoughts, but she kept them inside.

"I won't blame you if you leave me here," he said.

Her chin jerked up. "But I need you."

"You never needed me. You're a better Defender than I could ever be."

Grey studied his face. "But you're more than a Defender, aren't you? My hand? Clara?"

He pressed his pale lips together and gestured toward her throat. "Give me the key."

She pulled it off her neck and held it for a moment. The object of Blaise's hundred-year search rested in her palm. She could run over, jam it in the lock, and be gone, leaving him to either die or continue his exile. She ran one porcelain finger over the etchings in the glass. Who was to say she wouldn't have stolen the tocks' keys? Who was to say she wouldn't have done worse to get back to her family?

Blaise watched her, a question in his dark eyes.

Grey dropped the key into his palm.

He gripped it between his hands and twisted. The two pieces separated and Blaise held them up for her inspection.

"Look, it's not broken." He held the hollow piece in one hand and the intricately designed bow in the other.

"But, why—?"

"You never needed me," Blaise repeated. "All you need is my blood."

Grey gaped at Blaise then at the key. "I don't understand."

"I'm guessing Steinar married an ordinary citizen. Your mother?"

"Yes."

Blaise tapped the symbol of a cupped hand on the hollow shaft. "And your father is a Defender." He touched the etching of a fist. "So was my father." His finger rested on the figure of the open hand. "My mother was a Chemist."

"But Chemists only marry other Chemists—"

"And Defenders only marry other Defenders, or at least that's the way it was before the Chemists exterminated the

400

Defenders. That's why this combination"—he stroked the symbols from top to bottom—"isn't exactly common."

Electricity zinged through Grey's veins. "I have it now, don't I, because I have your blood in me."

He nodded. "Magic in your veins."

The phrase burrowed deep into Grey's mind, transforming out of Blaise's voice and into her grandfather's and finally into her own. She muttered the chant Granddad had spoken in his shop what seemed like years ago.

"Love is magic in our veins. Love the hand of the punisher stays. Love heals what justice flays. Love defends and mercy reigns."

Blaise smiled. "The old Defender Codes. So your father has taught you something of your heritage."

"My grandfather. He said it when I brushed my hand over the curio cabinet in his store. He checked my palm for blood and then he said those words."

"Blood is the way in and blood is the way out." He handed her the two pieces of the key.

A tiny glass knife was attached to the bow of the key. When the two parts were together, the hollow shaft hid the sharp edge.

"You're free to go, Grey." Blaise's tone fell and her name came out in a whisper.

She curled her palm around the key and met his eyes. "You're going with me."

"I saw the way you looked at me, after you found the keys. You were right to judge me. If I can't fix what I did, then I should pay for the lives I took with my own."

Grey shook her head. "You have paid. Callis. Seree. All the tocks and porcies you fixed. Me. You're dying because of what you sacrificed for me."

"No, I can't run from what I did."

Grey closed her porcelain fingers around the bow of the key and drove the glass knife into the flesh of her other palm. Dark blood welled up and she pressed the tube part of the key to the wound. Her blood flowed into the vial, filling it in seconds. When she'd staunched her bleeding and twisted the two parts of the key back together, she held it up for Blaise to see.

The blood key glowed ruby red against the colorless backdrop of the clearing. Grey looked from the key to Blaise.

"We'll come back here. Together."

His eyes met hers, the deep brown outer ring soft and searching. He jerked his chin down once.

Scrambling to her feet, Grey eyed the distance between Blaise and the tree. She grasped the corners of the sling and lugged it across the velvet earth. When she got him to the base of the white tree, his lids fluttered.

"Not yet. Stay with me a little longer. I'm not sure how this is going to work."

He forced his eyes open, but his lashes drifted down as though weighted. She knelt but couldn't keep her hand on him and reach the keyhole at the same time. Would the tree trunk open like a door? Would she be sucked through like she was when she entered Curio? That scenario seemed more likely.

While she struggled to position Blaise, the pile of rusted keys drew her gaze again and again. The sight picked at her brain, crawling into dark places and festering. It was wrong and ugly. A visible testament to something broken inside Blaise.

She let her eyes rest on Blaise's face once again. He'd lost consciousness despite her quiet urging. The mark on her stomach pulsed as though reaching for him. The strange surge of his Chemist blood skimmed beneath the surface of her skin, mingling with her Defender strength to form a liquid shell, like a second skin beneath her own.

Even if she got him home, he might not make it. He'd lost so much blood. Given it to her. She let her eyes travel to the hoard of keys once more. If Blaise died, she would come back and see every key returned to the tock he'd taken it from. If it meant staying in Curio, if it meant facing Benedict and his soldiers, so be it. She'd see it done.

Strength flared from her gut outward, flashing through her limbs like a potent mix of thunder and lightning. She stooped, lifted Blaise in her arms, and propped him against the white tree trunk.

With her body pressed close to his, Grey thrust the blood key into the lock and turned it.

Whit stood where Adante ordered him to, in the back corner of Haward's Mercantile, surrounded by the remains of Grey's grandfather's store.

How much had his thoughts given away to the Chemist? He tried to remember what crashed through his head when he saw Marina lying on the pavement, stunned. But all he could see was her still body and the strands of her hair blowing in the wind. He thought his chest would crack in two.

The Chemist stood over Haimon like a black crane challenging a heron. Whit heard his own name in Adante's slick tone.

"Whitland's thoughts indicate otherwise, Haimon. Why did he picture you hunched over the case and attach hope—pathetic hope—to that image? It seems you're counting on a different outcome than you've led me to believe."

Haimon looked up into the Chemist's eyes, his own scarred face expressionless. "That emotion belonged to the boy, as you well know. You can't connect my feelings and actions to his thoughts."

"No, but I can see you in his mind just as he sees you."

"It proves nothing."

"And the blow that leveled me the night Grey disappeared? That wasn't just the power fluctuation of a budding Defender, was it? Grey had nothing to do with rendering me unconscious. It was you!"

Misery swallowed their argument. Whit's stomach clenched, giving the pain in his heart competition over which would kill him first. The bottles of Cagey's mix stashed in the truck lingered at the back of his mind. His errand cost him Marina, but if he could swallow one potion, the pain would vanish. Maybe he'd find a way to get her back.

The thought twisted into his soul until the image from the street killed it. They'd loaded her into a chug boat and, since she was unregistered, she'd be taken straight to the tower. He'd never see her again.

A pulse like the energy of an electrical storm pushed Whit backward. His spine cracked into the shelf behind him. The wooden edge tore a couple of his stripes open. He couldn't stop his fall. His legs buckled and he slid to the floor.

Haimon's face appeared over the display case, Adante hovering behind.

Whit opened his mouth to speak, but bright light poured into the store. He squinted and shielded his eyes. Adante yelled something, and the sound of hurried footsteps amid clutter carried to Whit's crumpled position.

"Holy Defender," Haimon breathed.

Whit dropped his hand from his eyes and felt them widen despite the remaining glow.

Grey stood in the opposite corner, holding up a sagging form with long, tangled hair. She wore a strange white glove on one hand and an odd contraption on her back. Were those folded-up wings?

Adante appeared, standing before Grey and blocking Whit's view. Haimon dashed around the corner of the split counter.

Whit's fingers found the edge of the display case nearest him. He dragged himself up in time to see Grey falter. She tried to step away from the Chemist, but between the body in her arms and the bulky pack, she stumbled.

Adante reached out and took hold of the lifeless form, supporting him so that he didn't drop to the floor.

"No," Grey screamed, her arms clutching the body. She glared around the lolling dark head. The words she spoke took Whit back to the night the deputies caught them in the alley.

"Take me. Take me. Not him."

Green eyes drove into Grey's. Adante kept his hands on Blaise despite Grey's efforts to retreat.

The Chemist's quiet voice somehow filled the room. "Haimon, you assured me this would not happen."

From behind Adante's tall form, Haimon spoke. "You broke the treaty long before you turned Olan Haward to stone. The stripings. Luring people to Mercury with the promise of a better life only to enslave them. Did you think his forbearance would last forever? Did you think his death wouldn't be avenged?"

"How was I to know he was that close?" Adante spat out.

"The Chemist reign is over. I knew when Grey came running out of the night that Olan had sent her for Blaise. This is your mess, Adante."

"Then it's up to me to clean it up, starting with the traitors in this room." He tugged on Blaise's inert frame.

Grey refused to relinquish her burden. "I won't let you take him. I will take my father's place. Not Blaise."

A strange smile quirked the green-tinted face. "Do I have your word?"

"No, Grey!" Haimon yelled.

Grey tilted her chin, energy and strength coursing through her. "I'll pay for the crime I committed, and I'll pay for any crimes you've accused my father of."

A fever light flickered in Adante's eyes. He reached for Blaise again. "Don't worry. I won't hurt him." Bending, he put his shoulder into Blaise's chest, guiding his weight from Grey's arms into his.

"Haimon, help me," Adante said.

Grey pocketed the key in her hand and followed their movements as Adante and Haimon lifted Blaise onto the long display case. She opened her mouth to object. He'd probably rather be on the floor than stretched out on another glass cabinet. Movement in the opposite corner caught her eye.

"Whit!"

He leaned on a cabinet across the room. His face was pale, his cheeks hollow. But he managed a half smile. "Grey, been taking shortcuts through curio cases?"

Tears stung her eyes. She ached to hug him despite Adante's presence. It didn't matter anymore. She didn't operate by the rules of Mercury City, or the belief system of Curio for that matter. She straightened her shoulders and started across the room, but Adante halted her steps. With monocle raised the Chemist moved in front of her, all the force of his mind intrusion hitting her in a venomous wave.

Whether it was her Defender blood or the traces of Blaise's Chemia flicking through her veins, Grey's hybrid strength somehow blocked the attack. He recoiled but didn't back down. Instead tendrils of exploration darted at her from all sides like fingers of smoke.

"So you've come into your Defender state." Adante's face twisted into a disgusted expression. He jerked his chin toward Blaise's still form. "No doubt he filled your head with valor and ancient codes of sacrifice."

Grey struggled to pull her thoughts together. She knew little of the Defender lore other than snippets from school history, Blaise's hints, and her own overwhelming drive to protect.

Adante must've picked up on her confusion. "Do you even know how this works?" He gestured between them. "You're so willing to accept Steinar's sentence, you haven't even bothered to ask what it is."

"All I need to know is that he's still alive."

The Chemist dipped his head once.

"Then I'll take his place in battle as he meant to take mine. *I* gave my ration to Whit that night, not my father. And I didn't sell it to him, by the way. I *gave* it to him, which is not ration dealing."

Adante swooped closer. "One ration a day for each registered citizen. *That* is the law. You broke it and your father broke it."

Grey pushed her face into his. "Your laws need amending."

He chuckled. "And one family of Defenders, or should I say one Defender and his cocky daughter, are going to change that?"

Grey's eyes darted to Blaise.

"Oh, he's not going to be any help. The minute this is over, I'll hide him away again. No more deals with Defenders. No more trusting worthless guardians." The poison-green eyes slid to Haimon.

Grey brought her chin up. "And if I win?"

The Chemist lifted one black brow, contempt stamped on his features.

"If. I. Win."

"You and your father are free to return to a life of civil obedience."

Grey crossed her arms. "I want Blaise."

"You can't have my worthless cousin, little girl."

Grey's thoughts reeled, but her Defender state kept her expression stony. Blaise was Adante's cousin, half Chemist and half Defender. Was that why he'd been hidden away all these years? What threat did he pose to the Council's rule? She narrowed her eyes at Adante.

"He stays with me or I reveal his identity and his existence to everyone."

"Including the Chemist Council," Haimon added. "Either way, things are going to change. You can be sure Jorn Amintore will hear our demands if we harbor his grandson."

Adante didn't take his eyes from Grey's face. "Haimon, I am going to kill you."

"Go ahead," came the reply. "You don't need me to go into Curio anymore. You can't imagine how tired I am of being bound by my own blood to a cabinet meant to hold knickknacks."

Grey faced down the Chemist. "If I win, you return my father, Blaise stays with me, and—"

"Grey," Whit interrupted. "My friends are in the tower."

"And you release Whit's friends."

Adante spread his hands. "And if I win?"

Grey pressed her lips together. What was he asking of her?

He flickered before her eyes then stood an inch away from her, his breath gliding over her forehead. "If I win, I carry out Steinar's sentence on you, which in this case is death by striping. Do you know how many stripes it takes to kill a Defender?"

408

She willed her lip not to tremble.

He continued. "It depends on how close they are to ossification. Which in the case of a sixteen-year-old who's just come into her Defender state, is not close at all."

Grey swallowed and stepped back. "I accept your terms."

"No weapons," Adante said.

Grey lifted her hands. "I'm unarmed."

He zeroed in on her porcelain hand. "What's this?"

"I lost my hand inside Curio. This is the replacement Blaise designed for me. It doesn't have a clotter hidden in the pinky, in case you're wondering."

He nodded to the tips of the folded wings visible above her shoulders. "And that?"

Grey yanked the straps loose and shucked out of the steam pack harness. When she was free, she stepped out into the open section of her grandfather's store.

"Now what?"

Adante flickered out of his position and appeared before her. "Now this."

Energy slammed into her with the force of a boulder. Grey stumbled backward and toppled into the wreckage of the store. She was up before Adante could move.

Her mark clenched, sending a river of granite flooding through her body. Adante's hands curled at his torso as if he held a large ball, but Grey was ready. She ducked sideways into an aisle. The blast hit the shelf on the far wall, sending books and objects flying.

Grey bent her knees, pulling her body low and backing down the row of merchandise. She ran her hand over the shelf on her right but kept her eyes fixed on the space where she expected Adante to appear at any moment. Her fingers closed around an object, something heavy. Adante stepped around the corner and Grey sent the marble bookend flying at his head. She turned and ran. A crash and a light thud told her she'd missed her mark.

She dropped to her knees and crept toward the front of the store. Green light exploded above her and an empty potion bottle clattered to the floor. She covered her head as heat bore down from above, sending pain sizzling over the skin of her human hand. Grey yelped and jerked her hands down. The heat gathered in her porcelain fingers but didn't burn.

Adante's voice interrupted her discovery. "This is not the way Defenders fight, Grey Haward. Show yourself."

Grey crawled to a huge bookcase and shuffled to the other side before inching up the wall into a stand.

"I won't give you a second chance," Adante called. "Show yourself."

Whit's startled cry cut the air. His voice gave out and a heavy crash echoed to Grey's position. She flung herself toward the door, stepping out into the main aisle.

Adante lurked in the back corner where Whit had stood moments before. His eyes flicked to the floor behind the counter then back to Grey's face.

"What did you do to Whit?" Grey lurched forward.

"I told you, no hiding."

"Whit?" Grey screamed.

Haimon darted from beside Blaise, sliding to a stop before he reached Adante. "He's breathing, Grey. Adante, the Codes state a punishment battle takes place between a Chemist and a Defender. Bystanders are not to be harmed."

The tall Chemist flickered in place. One moment his hand was at his potion belt. The next it stretched toward Haimon, who crumpled to the floor.

Grey's shriek stuck in her throat.

"That's better, isn't it?" Adante moved so fast she only saw his hands after he'd loosed the ball of energy.

The orb slammed into Grey's gut, glowing green on impact. She buckled. Pain radiated from her stomach outward, and for a moment she was frozen. Creaking footsteps brought sweat to her forehead.

Just in time, Grey regained movement and rolled into an aisle as another potion bottle skittered across the floor where she'd lain a second before.

"No hiding," Adante ground out.

But Grey scuttled to the end of the aisle and ducked out of sight. On the floor, she huddled, breathing hard from the direct hit. Her mark glowed blue through her clothing. Grey put her hand over the symbol, the link to her Defender blood, and Blaise's blood. She pushed to her feet, concentrating on the stone beneath her skin. Adante's blasts might steal her breath and light her nerves on fire, but it'd take much more to crack her Defender strength.

She whipped around the corner into the aisle, hands at the ready. She visualized a shield before her body, and to her surprise the hard shell beneath her skin seemed to expand before her.

But Adante was nowhere to be seen. Grey checked each corner. A tall shelf and several barrels formed a barrier in the front corner. Grey held her shield before her and eased toward the blind spot.

"I thought Defenders and Chemists didn't hide from each other, Adante." Grey's taunt rang out in the silence.

No reply came.

She moved toward the center aisle, eyes scanning the far corner and its jumble of tables, shelves, and equipment.

The flash of green irises above a hawkish nose appeared from out of nowhere. Grey couldn't see the rest of him. She tried to lift her hands and extend her shield, but her hands stayed poised before her torso. They wouldn't budge. She couldn't turn her head. She couldn't move at all.

She scanned the room before her. A surface reflected her widened blue eyes. A mirror. Adante stepped around her, brushing her immobile arm as he passed. A hard shudder wracked her body, but not one finger twitched.

Her breathing sped. Was she stone? No, Blaise had said it took many years, many battles, for a Defender to ossify.

Adante whirled to face her, the sweep of his dark hair bringing Blaise to mind. A tingle of electricity shot through her core, but she remained locked in stillness.

"I'd call this battle over, wouldn't you?" He tilted toward her. "Unless you know how to break out of my clotting spell. No?"

Grey closed her eyes on the sharp face and concentrated on her Defender state, but the brush of air across her face brought her lids flying up.

The Chemist studied her from inches away. "What *are* you doing?" He chuckled. "It takes years of training to become a real Defender. That one over there"—he pointed to Blaise—"was whispering in my head and repelling my spells at ten. Fierce as an entire Apache raiding party. He made my life hell till I locked the half-breed up. Doesn't look like it did him any good."

A wall of energy pushed on Grey, or was it her shoving against Adante's spell? She threw all her strength at the barrier holding her immobile. Nothing. Not even a flex in her toes.

"I told you, stop trying to resist. You can't."

Pain exploded inside Grey, following the path her Defender strength took, eating away at the armor. A whimper escaped her clenched teeth.

"I remember the Cleanse, Grey Haward. The Chemists overpowered the Defenders with barely a finger lifted. Why should you be any different? The old system is dead and there will be no reviving it."

Grey's muscles begged for collapse. Instinct told her to crumple into a fetal position, but Adante held her erect as wave after wave of his evil magic tore through her. Where was the strength Blaise promised would come when she needed it? She needed it *now*.

Little by little her shell cracked and withered, leaving her body completely vulnerable to Adante's attacks. All that remained was a trace of something warm just behind her navel, a current of buzzing power. Grey focused on the little spark. It felt like flying and kissing Blaise in the stacks and his hand holding hers. Heat bloomed in her porcelain fingertips.

Adante shifted back ever so slightly, his gaze whisking to Blaise. "Haimon's right. I have a mess to clean up, and a family disgrace to hide. But with the blood in this room, I'll build an invulnerable fortress. None of you will see outside these walls again."

Grey's porcelain palm tingled. With Adante's focus on Blaise, she angled her gaze down to the left. Was her pale hand brighter somehow?

Adante turned back and the pressure driving against every inch of her skin increased. Grey kept her eyes steady on Adante's, but shifted her concentration to her porcie hand. Her fingers moved.

She sent an image to Adante's mind. The Grey in her message fell to her knees before him, begging for her life. Begging for release.

Black brows lifted. "Oh, very good. I guess experience is the best teacher. You've managed to push your thoughts into

413

mine, or perhaps your terror merely leaked out now that I've torn down your little Defender fortifications."

Grey kept the image of herself begging like a shield over her thoughts, but willed the little charge lurking behind her Defender mark into her hand. Electricity skimmed up her torso, into her shoulder, and down her arm. She curled her fingers into a fist.

Adante leaned close again, his voice a purr. "Very well, I suppose I'll start the cleanup with you."

White blurred through the air. Grey's porcelain fingers closed over the Chemist's neck before she realized she'd willed her limb to do so. The enchantment broke, and Adante staggered back, Grey propelling him with the force of her hand.

He clawed at her fingers. "Burns. Burns!"

Grey pinned him to the end of an aisle where two shelves came together back to back. Her hand clenched tighter and tendrils of green smoke drifted from his skin.

He left off scrabbling at his throat and dropped his hands into a loose oval in front of his torso. One jerk of her knee broke his attack position. Grey yanked him off his feet, her hand translucent. Beneath the skin, the clockwork glowed green. She opened her fingers, and Adante flew over Blaise's stretched-out form and crashed into the shelves of books behind the counter. He slid down and Grey rounded the corner, hand poised.

Dark blood trickled from the Chemist's mouth. He looked at her. "Chemia? How?"

Grey slid her eyes to Blaise then back to Adante's blanched face. "It's in his blood. And now it's in mine."

With a swipe of her hand through midair, Adante's eyelids closed. He remained where he'd landed, in a broken heap amid piles of old books.

Grey dashed to Blaise and checked his pulse. A thready *thump-thump, thump-thump.* Such a welcome sound.

She strode to Haimon, and as she crouched to probe his scarred neck, Whit stirred only a few feet away. He sat up.

"Grey?"

"I won," she said over Haimon's limp form.

Whit hauled himself to stand. "Adante. Where is he?"

She gestured to the other side of the room. "He shouldn't wake for a while."

"How? How did you—?"

But Grey couldn't answer. She shook Haimon and slapped his cheek. "Haimon, wake up."

The man groaned and blinked.

"Help me." Desperation choked her voice. "You have to help me with Blaise. He gave me his blood in Curio. It was too much. I didn't know and Weatherton didn't stop in time."

A tear slid off Grey's nose. "Haimon, help me. I don't know how to fix this."

She tugged on his arm, gaze whipping from the wakening man to the unconscious boy.

A scarred hand rested on her human fingers. "Grey, look at me."

"You have to come." A sob broke through Grey's lips.

"Look at me." Haimon pushed up on one elbow.

Grey forced her eyes to Haimon's colorless face. Iron-gray eyes set in a deeply scarred face traveled over her features, assessing.

"Are you looking now?"

She swallowed a sob and nodded.

He lifted himself up to sit against the counter, then he pulled his sleeves up one by one, revealing endless stripes.

"I am like Blaise, half Defender, half Chemist. Or at least I once was. Now, well, now I'm this." He twisted his scarred arms. "Adante made Blaise's prison with my blood and added a drop of ordinary blood to ensure he could never break out. Your grandfather and I found a way. You found that way as well. But, Grey, I lived. Blaise will live as well. We're hard to kill, those of us with melded blood."

"Will he . . . will he—?"

"Be like me?" Haimon shook his head. "I don't know. I was a prisoner, already weakened, when Adante discovered I'd suit his purpose."

Whit came to stand by Grey. His presence filled a hole deep inside, a place not connected to Defenders, Chemists, or magic. He was sunlight and card games, licorice and walking home from school. She breathed in the comfort of him and leaned her shoulder into his arm for a moment. He stiffened, but the tension melted and he leaned back.

"We'll get your friends back, I promise." She shot a glance up at him. He nodded, but a muscle worked in his jaw. A brittle cold lined his blue eyes. But then he turned away to help Haimon stand.

Grey stepped around debris and moved to stand by Blaise. She captured his hands, pulling them off the cold glass and holding them between her own. Warmth spread from her fingers into his.

She dropped her cheek to rest on his chest and closed her eyes. The motion of his breathing carried through her body, hooking her Defender mark and setting it ablaze. The electricity danced over her skin, and when she lifted her head she saw the blue of Blaise's mark glowing through his shirt.

His lids drifted up. Dark, liquid eyes focused on her.

"We did it." She put her porcelain hand over his mark. Heat curled up through her fingertips. "We made it. Welcome home, Mad Tock."

Epilogue

Grey studied the yellowed grass, so dead and hard-packed it barely crunched beneath her feet. If she lifted her head, the grief would escape her mouth in some hideous form. She balled her fists in the pockets of the brown duster she wore over her blouse, knee pants, and tall boots. A hard swallow brought her emotions under control.

Ahead, Father climbed, his broad shoulders still bandaged beneath the layers of clothing. He carried his end of the wooden plank, and its precious burden, with careful strength. Haimon and Whit supported the other end of the board, their tall, lean figures leading the funeral procession up the wind-bitten hill.

At the sound of scrabbling feet, Grey turned and stretched her porcelain hand to steady her mother. "Are you all right?"

Mother's fingers wrapped around Grey's new limb then dropped back to her side. "Trust your father to pick a mountain instead of a hill for this occasion." Her voice broke on the last word, belying her complaint with the depth of her sorrow.

Grey eyed the final two figures in their group, one in crimson and one in pinstripe trousers and a borrowed coat. Josephine Bryacre caught up to them and took the hand

Mother offered. The two women helped each other up the steep path leading to Excelsior Peak, leaving Grey to contend with the mandate of her Defender mark. She planted her feet to keep from running back down the trail.

Blaise looked up and answered the tug between them with increased speed, despite his still weakened condition. He stopped just below her position and gazed up, his dark eyes pulling her in. After a few days of rest and recovery, only the faintest tinge of green remained about his lips and eyelids.

Grey motioned to the charged space between them. "Will it always be this way?"

"You mean will the very sight of you make me wish for wings? I expect so." The wind snatched his now shoulder-length hair, whipping it about the back of his head. No copper wire remained among the black locks to catch the mountain sunlight, and though she was infinitely glad he was free of his prison, part of her missed his tock disguise.

He joined her and nodded to the procession ahead. "Olan once told me about the day he met Valera, your grandmother. He said he could feel her coming when she was still a mile off, and while she lived the connection remained as strong."

Moments passed before Grey trusted her voice. "I hope he's with her now."

Blaise took her hand, winding his fingers through her porcelain ones without hesitation, and together they continued up the path. When they reached the mesa where the others gathered, Haimon and Whit were already guiding their burden to a low plinth erected for this purpose. Father raised the other half, steadying Granddad's stone shoulders.

The scene captured Grey, breaking her defenses. Once she allowed herself to look, she could do nothing but stare at Granddad's hardened features. With raised fists he leaned into the spell Adante had cast, the spell that had turned him into stone. The spell meant for her. His face was locked in determination, his brows narrowed at his opponent. Only his mouth showed a trace of vulnerability. The stone lips were open, not in a scream but in mild shock as if he'd been stung by an insect.

The end of her grandfather's Defender service signaled the beginning of hers. Grey made a fist with her human hand. Her other hand still rested in the grasp of a half Defender, half Chemist boy in blatant defiance of the Council Codes. The blood key hung heavy against her chest, a symbol of hope—a melded and mended solution to an ancient curse.

When Father began his eulogy, Blaise withdrew to the edge of the mesa where the trail connected this secluded spot to the Foothills Quarter. Even after the explanations and apologies, the two men avoided each other. Blaise had spent a hundred years as a bargaining chip, an insurance policy held against a failed treaty, and though his imprisonment was meant to prevent bloodshed, the conditions went against his nature. The growing connection between Blaise and Grey only increased tensions between her father and him.

After Father finished speaking, Grey fell in line behind her mother and took her turn gazing up into her grandfather's hardened eyes. *Thank you.* She didn't know how to command her mind's voice or whether Granddad's spirit remained close enough to hear, but it was enough. His Defender's death meant life for her, and if their hopes proved founded, life for all of Mercury City.

Grey turned to go and the floor of her stomach caved in. Two dark forms crested the hill and strode toward Blaise. Adante, knife-thin and menacing, and an older Chemist who walked with an odd, creaking gait. He wore his dark hair cropped close, and his flat black suit hung off his long bones. His nose and chin bore the same faint dent she saw the first time Blaise removed his mask in Curio.

Haimon and Father moved to stand on either side of Blaise, and Grey rushed to join them. Two pairs of pale-green eyes swept her head to toe, no doubt noting her renegade appearance.

Father leaned in. "Jorn, nice of you to pay your respects to Olan."

The Chemist glanced to Granddad's ossified remains and flinched. "I didn't come to witness Olan's final resting place. I'm here for my kin."

Blaise straightened and flicked a hand toward Adante. "The only kin you have here is the filth you brought with you."

Jorn Amintore's green features rippled with fury. "Be careful, boy. I might rethink my decision to claim you."

Father's hand clenched at his side, a small gesture but one that didn't fail to catch the notice of the two Chemists. He spoke low and steady. "The two of you are no match for the four Defenders here."

"And the four of you are no match for the Council, Steinar."

"I don't see the Council here on this hillside."

Jorn's attention shifted back to his grandson. "If you come with us, your friends will be left in peace. You have my word."

Clouds shifted above, hiding the sun and casting a shadow over Blaise's face. The muted light played with his coloring, highlighting his warm brown skin tone one instant then shifting to pick out the hints of green that lay underneath.

"Your mother still lives." Jorn moved in. "I can make arrangements for you to see her."

Blaise jerked as if slapped but then took a step back, away from Jorn. "My mother hated the Chemia in her veins just as

420

I do. If she lives, I know she would want me to embrace my Defender side."

"He has a home with us as long as he wishes it." Father met Blaise's eyes, a firm promise in his gaze.

"Then you should know, Steinar, that we hold your son in the tower, and the conditions of his imprisonment are not as pleasant as Blaise's."

Grey's heart leapt and Mother's gasp carried into their midst. With a final glare, Jorn turned and started down the trail, Adante following. They'd only gone a short distance before Adante snagged a potion bottle from his belt and dashed it on the rocks at their feet. The two figures vanished in a column of green and red smoke.

Granddad's shop bustled with the cleaning efforts of five people. The twins, who'd been dumped on the Haward doorstep along with Father, moved about the store with a strange confidence, given their short but recent time in the Chemist tower.

Grey didn't quite understand the dynamic between the brother and sister and Whit. The three of them split their time between the mercantile and the hunting outpost. Maverick was surly but sharp, always adding a new angle to the plans Haimon hatched. Whit and Marina spent as much time yelling at each other as they did kissing. Every time Grey rounded a corner and found them tangled together, she would smile and tiptoe away. It was good to see the weight lifted from Whit's shoulders, if only for a few moments.

A similar burden pressed on Grey. The news that Banner lived, along with countless other Defenders in the tower, made their next move tricky. But they were not without allies, not without resources, and not without hope.

"Take these down to the lab." Haimon handed Grey a crate of darkened Council devices. "Blaise'll want them."

Leaving the noise and activity behind, she shuffled to the back room, set the box down a moment, and lifted the table and rug concealing the trapdoor. Her mark zinged the instant her foot met the top stair, and an answering clatter of tools evidenced Blaise's reaction to her nearness.

She lugged the box down to the cellar, averting her eyes from the chair in the center of the room and the bellows and tubing of an exsanguinator lying on a trunk nearby. She'd know the ins and outs of that device soon enough. She let her eyes move to the rumpled blankets nested on the couch against the far wall, where Blaise spent his nights.

Now he sat before tools and device components spread out on the counter before him. He turned to greet her, pushing a clunky pair of magnifying glasses up into his hair. The ghost of his Mad Tock persona remained in the gesture, whispering to Grey of exhilarating flight and the thrill of being pressed against him. He wore charcoal trousers, and his shirt was half buttoned as though he'd lost interest in such a mundane task somewhere mid-chest. Bare feet hooked onto the base of the stool below him.

Warmth stole up her neck and into her cheeks, nearly erasing her errand. "Haimon sent these down." She slid the box onto the counter beside him. "What are you doing with them?"

"Investigating their workings. Learning their secrets." He lifted a small phonograph from the box, and as he did so his shirtsleeve slid back, revealing a fresh bandage in the crook of his elbow.

"How exactly are you doing that?" Grey moved close for a better look.

With his thumb, he slid open a small compartment on the phonograph. Brownish dust filtered out of the slot before he closed it and began turning the crank on the side. Tinny voices drifted from the amplifying horn along with a faint puff of green vapor. Grey's thoughts grew hazy and she shook her head to line them up once again.

"How does Chemia affect its operation?"

Blaise added it to a pile of similar devices and started to scratch his head. When the magnifying glasses interfered, he yanked them from his scalp and added them to the clutter. "My guess is they use it for mass mind suggestion. Perhaps to convey messages to a room of people without their conscious knowledge. The question is, can we use it to our advantage?"

"You're making weapons." She let her hand slide down his shoulder, over the bulge of his biceps to the bandage wrapped around his elbow. "And you're using Chemia to do it."

He lowered his head, refusing to meet her gaze. "Haimon and I are in the unique position of being able to understand our enemy's power. The same evil lurks within us. Well, more so in me than him."

Grey slid between his knees and lifted his face, her thumb pressed to the indentation in his chin. "Your Chemia does not make you evil, Blaise." She released his chin and planted her hands on his shoulders. "When have you ever used it to hurt another? I can see what it costs you to use it now, and it's your reluctance to abuse power that will keep you from the dark path of the Chemists."

Near-black eyes searched hers. "You're wrong." His fingers drifted to her abdomen, splaying over the material of her shirt. The mark on her skin danced beneath his touch. "It's this connection and my efforts to deserve such an honor that will keep my Chemia in check." His hands moved to lock around her hips, and he dropped his forehead to rest against her chest. For a moment his ragged breathing burned through the cotton of her blouse, but then he straightened, twisting back to the counter.

"I want to show you something. Haimon and I have been working on this." He tapped a glass ampule with murky liquid inside.

Grey took a steadying breath and forced her attention to the vial. "What is it?"

He rose from the stool and gently pulled her to his side. His fingers traced the chain on her neck down to the glass key. "May I?" When she nodded he lifted it over her head and twisted the bow from the blade. With the precise movements of a surgeon, he tipped the hollow shaft over the potion, letting a red drop fall.

An instant change widened Grey's eyes. The potion turned a delicate silver and sent up lace-like wisps of vapor. Blaise fastened the key together once again.

"Haimon and Olan were on the right course, but even if they had combined the different types of blood, they lacked the power of Chemia to influence the elements." He swiveled to face her. "Your blood is the key. The Defender trait overcame the potion dependence."

"Just as your Defender blood subdues your Chemia."

He nodded. "This could be the cure. Not a replicated potion, but an end to the dependence."

Grey couldn't help the movement of her eyes. They darted to the chair and the exsanguinator. A shiver shook her to the core.

"I'll be here, Grey. By your side, the whole time." Blaise tilted her chin up. "I won't take too much." He chuckled. "Or give too much this time. Bit by bit, we'll make magic with our veins."

His head angled and she leaned in to meet his lips. Her mark ignited the moment their mouths connected, and judging from the way he crushed her close, his burned white-hot as well. His warm hands left her back long enough to clear tools and devices from the countertop. Then he lifted her to sit on the workspace, breaking away to slip the key back over her head. His lips followed the path of the chain down her collarbone and she buried her fingers in his silky black hair. At the creak of the trapdoor, he groaned into the hollow of her throat, but pulled his head up. Hands braced on either side of her hips, he nipped in for a quick kiss before turning toward the sound of footsteps.

Whit stood with Marina at his side. Grey and Blaise lurked in the doorway between the back room and the front of the shop. Grey's apple cheeks were rosy, her chignon loose, and Blaise had a distracted look that would've earned him a ribbing if they knew each other better. Maverick eyed Whit over the top of Marina's dark head, then they both faced Steinar and Haimon across the waist-high display case.

Steinar set a small, tarnished flask on the surface between them. "Defenders arise when they are needed, and we have need of them now." He nodded to the flask. "The wellspring water my father brought from the Old Country benefits all who drink it, but some it chooses to make into warriors. My father learned to discern common characteristics among those the water chose. Bravery, compassion, loyalty, a certain disregard for personal health and safety."

Marina snorted. "Sounds like you, Whit."

"Yes, it does, doesn't it?" Steinar's tone remained serious. "That's why I've decided to give the remaining drops to Whit, and to you, Marina and Maverick, in hopes that the courage I see in all of you is the sign of mighty Defender hearts."

Whit's lungs stilled. A Defender. He could be like Grey and Steinar? He could be strong as Olan had been, without the help of a dealer's mind-altering potion? He shoved his hands into his trouser pockets to hide their shaking. Marina and Maverick stared at the flask.

"What if it doesn't work? What will happen to us?" Maverick laid a hand on the glass as if he wanted to reach for the water but didn't dare.

"You will be strengthened and restored regardless of whether the water quickens inside you. By itself, it doesn't erase the effects of the Chemia—it must be mixed with Defender blood to mitigate that curse—but all other maladies, it alleviates."

Maverick withdrew his hand and folded his arms over his chest. "Why offer us this curative now?"

"The treaty is broken. The time to overthrow the Chemists has come. With your help we can free our Defender brothers and sisters from the tower, and with Blaise and Haimon's efforts, and Grey's uncommon gift, we can end the suffering around us."

Whit flattened his palms on the glass and leaned in. "I'll do it."

Steinar nodded. "I knew you would."

Marina nudged her shoulder into his side, smiled up at him, then turned to Steinar. "I'm in too."

Maverick's quick eyes made a circuit of the assembled faces then landed on Grey's father. "I trust you, Steinar."

Haimon slid three small glasses onto the countertop as Steinar unscrewed the lid of the flask. Blaise and Grey moved closer as Steinar dropped a mouthful of clear liquid into each glass. Doubt scooped hollows in Whit's chest as he reached for the water. This was the last of the precious wellspring water, and Steinar believed in the three of them enough to bestow it on them.

Let me be worthy.

Whit raised the glass to his lips and tipped it back. Liquid slid down his throat, sweet and pungent, leaving a strange spice on his tongue. He lowered the glass to the counter and stared at it, his focus narrow and inward.

A spark flared just behind his navel. The energy spread outward from his core, singing through his veins and wrapping his muscles with layers of strength. He looked up to see Marina smiling, hands pressed to her midsection and tears spilling down her cheeks. On the other side of her Maverick stared at his hands, clenching and unclenching them, his mouth hanging open.

Grey stepped forward and squeezed his shoulder. "Welcome to the family, Mighty Defenders."

ACKNOWLEDGMENTS

I *couldn't have done it without* . . . An often-repeated but so-necessary phrase. I'll give it my own spin. I would've died alone in a pile of questionable trail mix without my husband, boys, mom, and brother. Kory, Caedmon, Finn, Mom, and Case, you all made this possible. Thank you.

To my sisters in the ink—Brandy Vallance, Carla Laureano, and Cindi Madsen—you have taught me so much about writing, about myself, about bravery, about Henry Cavill. Nearly all of these things have been useful.

There would only be words in a document and in my brain and in indecipherable midnight notes on my iPhone without Jacque Alberta and the Blink team. Thank you for collecting and curating the good words and cutting or curing the bad ones. I'm honored to be in the Blink family.

Kirk DouPonce, your cover art is a gift.

To the mentors and friends who eased the journey with encouragement, prayers, caffeine, margaritas, chocolate, and other magical potions, thank you for valuing my writing, my sanity, and me. Beth Vogt, Mary Agius, Beth Jusino, Lisa Bergren, Beth DeVore, Jeanne Takenaka, Kim Woodhouse, and Karen Ball, you ladies have made the difference.

I am ever enchanted with the notion of grace, with the ideals of love, bravery, and sacrifice. These exist only because of the One who sets eternity in our hearts. To Him I owe the space and beats of my own heart.

Mark of blood and alchemy

In this novella prequel to *Curio*, young Olan flees a devastating plague that took his family, only to be saved by a mysterious group of "magickers" with healing powers. But as he accompanies his rescuers to their alpine enclave, mysteries arise surrounding their potions and powers of alchemy. Especially after Olan notices a deep division forming in the alchemists' ranks.

Olan is thrust into the midst of this dissention after he discovers he is somehow special—chosen as a guardian like the enclave's founder. As he spends time with two of his rescuers—Auriana, a clever and captivating inventor, and Alaric, a brooding young man wrestling with his father's cruel beliefs—Olan realizes he may have the power to direct the course of blood and alchemy.

Introducing readers to the fantastical world of *Curio*, this novella is wrapped in adventure, romance, and intrigue.

Available wherever ebooks are sold

BLINK

BLINK

Want FREE books?
FIRST LOOKS at the best new fiction?
Awesome EXCLUSIVE merchandise?

We want to hear from YOU!

Give us your opinion on titles, covers, and stories.
Join the Blink Street Team today.

Visit http://blinkyabooks.com/street-team to sign up today!

Connect with us

 /BlinkYABooks   /BlinkYABooks

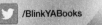 /BlinkYABooks   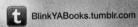 BlinkYABooks.tumblr.com

YOUR NEXT READ IS A BLINK AWAY